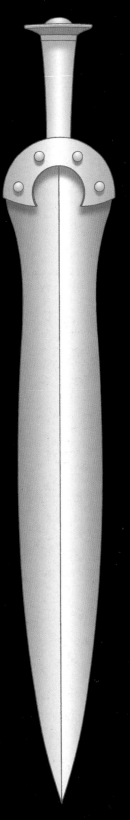

THE SWORD

FIRE

JOSHUA LUNA
Story, Script, Layouts, Letters

JONATHAN LUNA
Story, Illustrations, Book Design

SPECIAL THANKS TO:

Rommel Calderon
Randy Castillo
Dan Dos Santos
Timothy Ingle
Jenn Kao
Marc Lombardi
Victoria Stein
Giancarlo Yerkes

IMAGE COMICS, INC.

Robert Kirkman Chief Operating Officer
Erik Larsen Chief Financial Officer
Todd McFarlane President
Marc Silvestri Chief Executive Officer
Jim Valentino Vice-President
Eric Stephenson Publisher
Todd Martinez Sales & Licensing Coordinator
Betsy Gomez PR & Marketing Coordinator
Branwyn Bigglestone Accounts Manager
Sarah deLaine Administrative Assistant
Tyler Shainline Production Manager
Drew Gill Art Director
Jonathan Chan Production Artist
Monica Howard Production Artist
Vincent Kukua Production Artist
Kevin Yuen Production Artist

www.imagecomics.com
www.lunabrothers.com

THE SWORD, VOL. 1: FIRE
ISBN: 978-1-58240-879-8
Second Printing

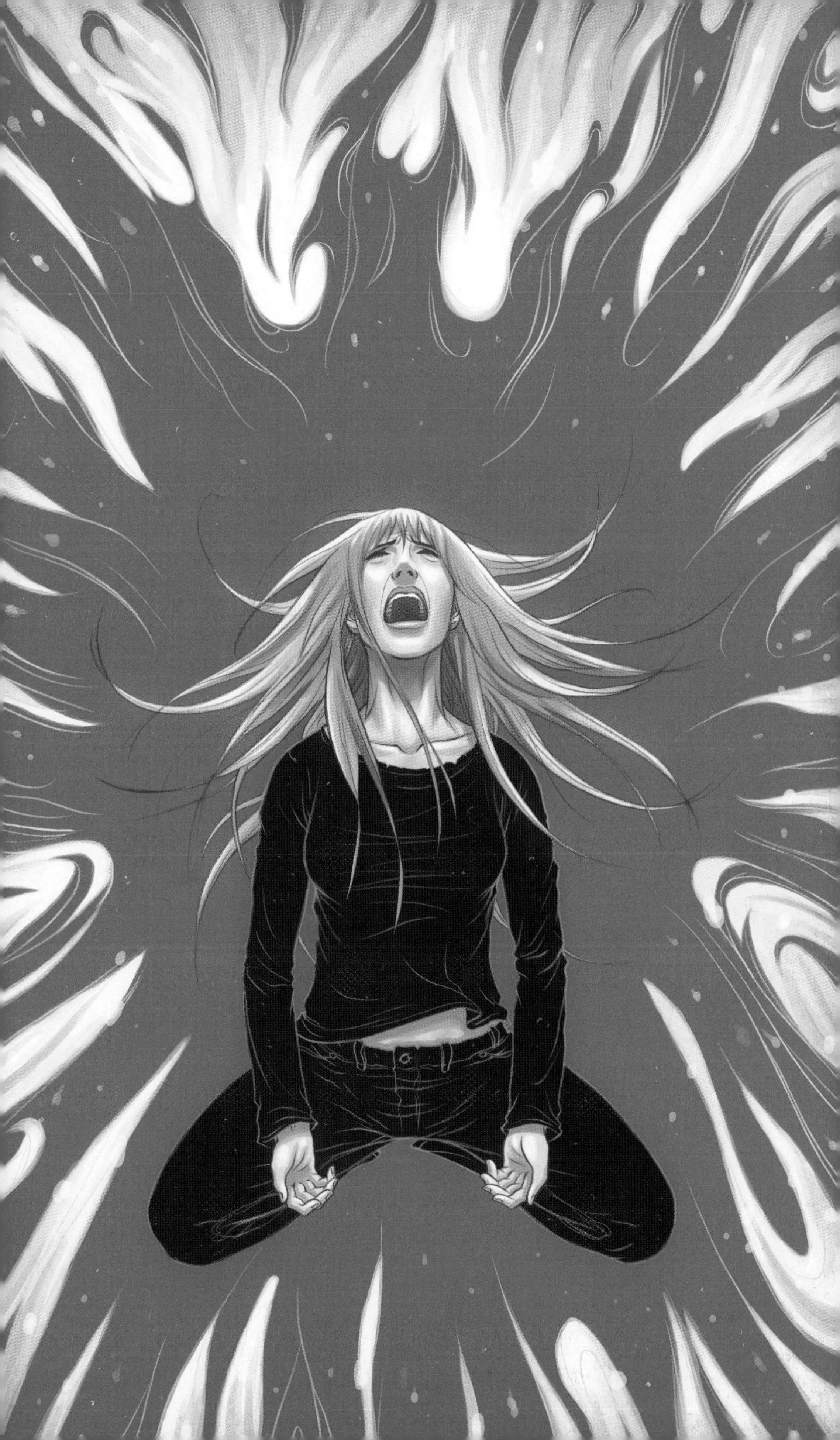

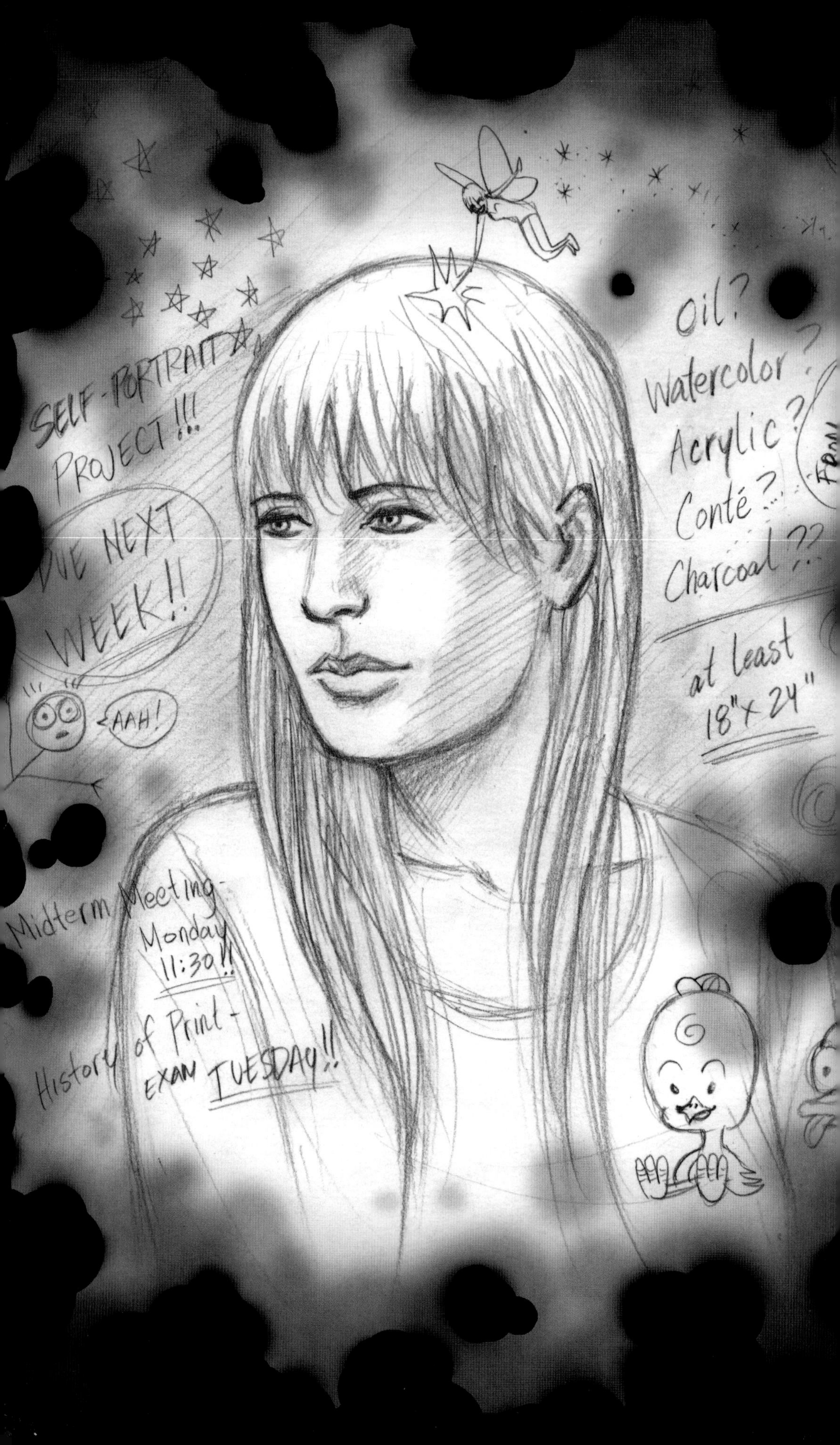
SELF-PORTRAIT PROJECT!!!
DUE NEXT WEEK!!
AAH!
Oil?
Watercolor?
Acrylic?
Conté?...
Charcoal??
at least 18"x24"
Midterm Meeting-
Monday 11:30!!
History of Print-
EXAM TUESDAY!!

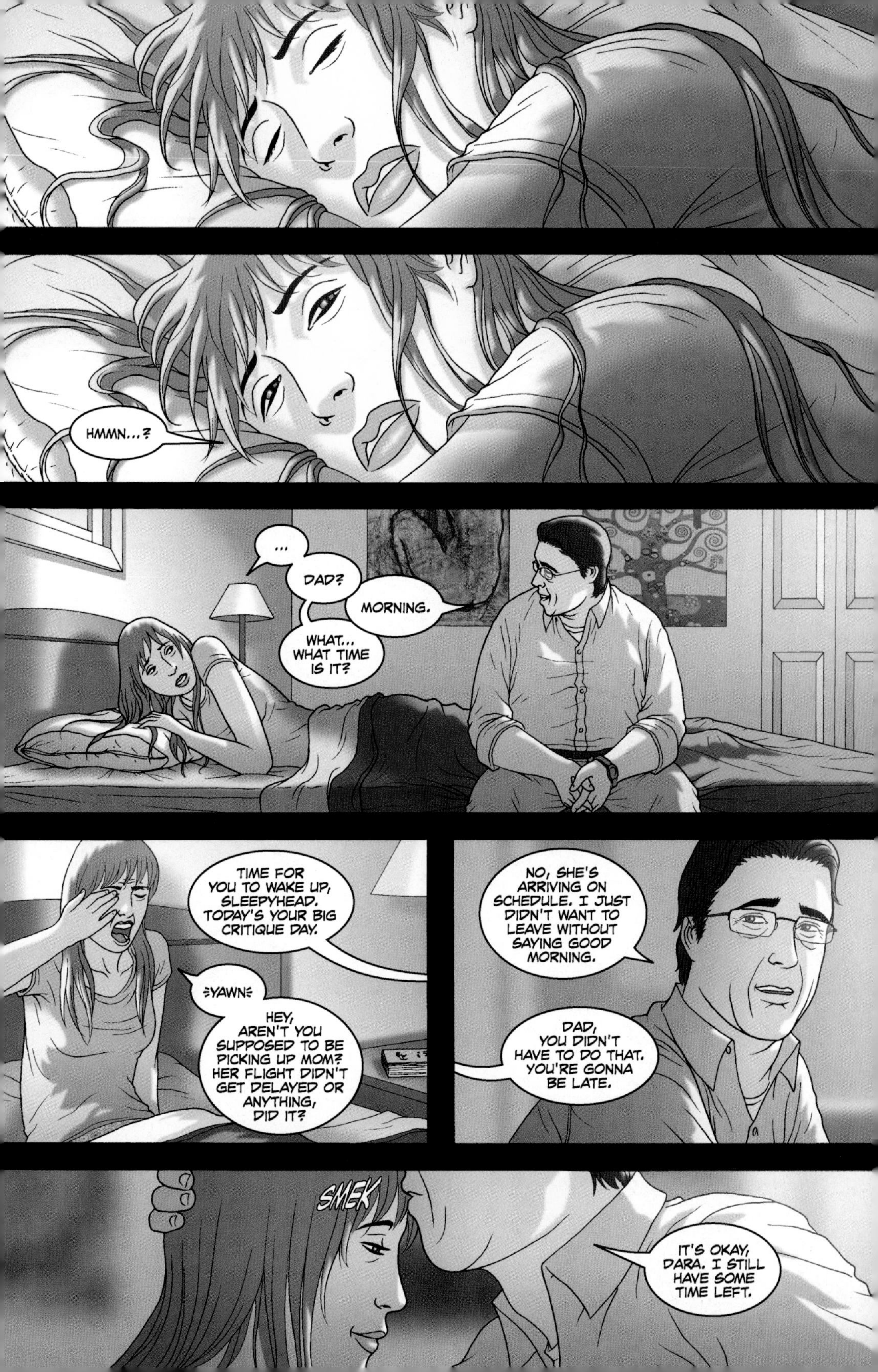
HMMN...?
...
DAD?
MORNING.
WHAT... WHAT TIME IS IT?
TIME FOR YOU TO WAKE UP, SLEEPYHEAD. TODAY'S YOUR BIG CRITIQUE DAY.
≈YAWN≈
HEY, AREN'T YOU SUPPOSED TO BE PICKING UP MOM? HER FLIGHT DIDN'T GET DELAYED OR ANYTHING, DID IT?
NO, SHE'S ARRIVING ON SCHEDULE. I JUST DIDN'T WANT TO LEAVE WITHOUT SAYING GOOD MORNING.
DAD, YOU DIDN'T HAVE TO DO THAT. YOU'RE GONNA BE LATE.
SMEK
IT'S OKAY, DARA. I STILL HAVE SOME TIME LEFT.

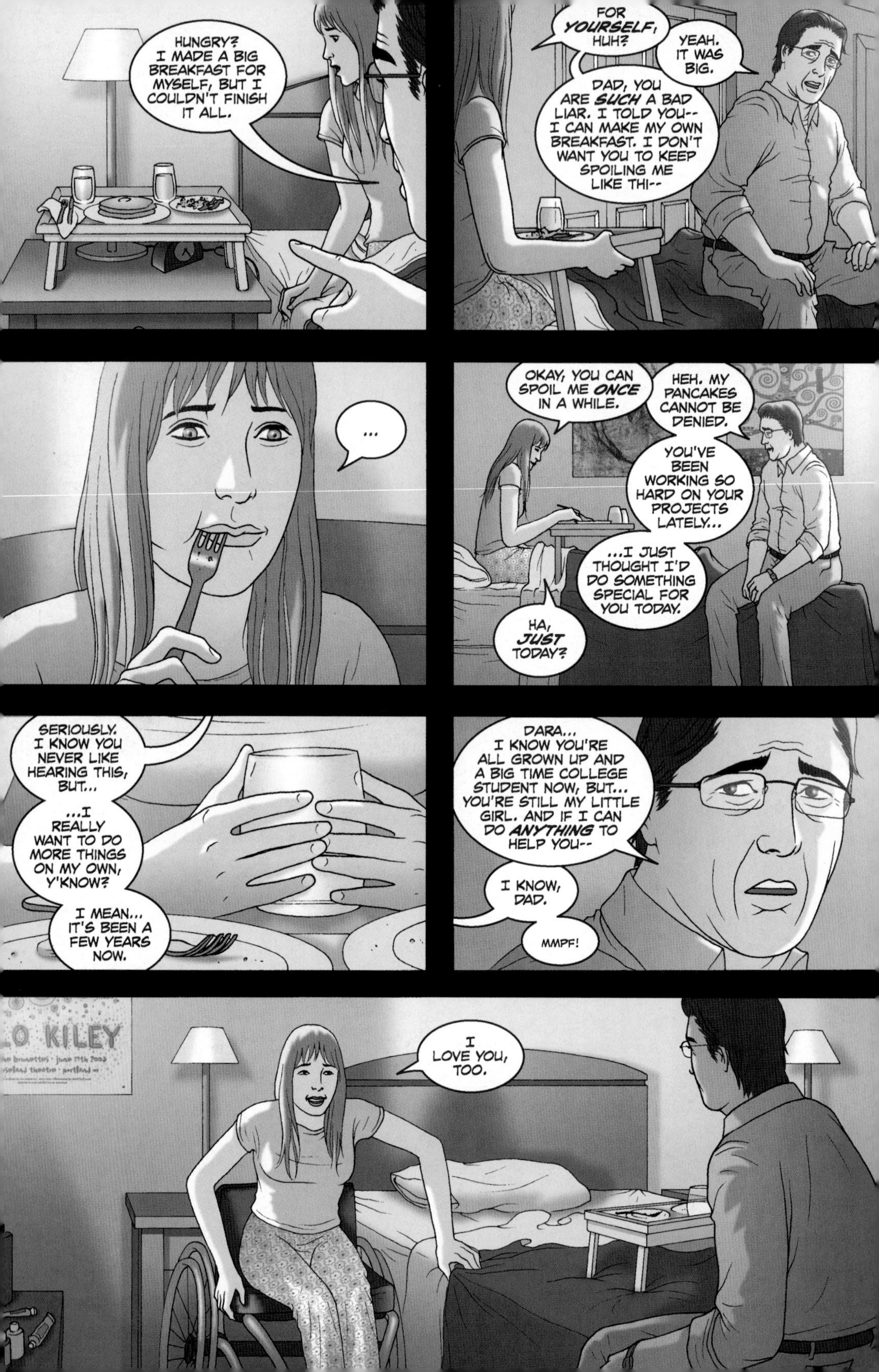
HUNGRY? I MADE A BIG BREAKFAST FOR MYSELF, BUT I COULDN'T FINISH IT ALL.
FOR *YOURSELF*, HUH?
YEAH. IT WAS BIG.
DAD, YOU ARE *SUCH* A BAD LIAR. I TOLD YOU-- I CAN MAKE MY OWN BREAKFAST. I DON'T WANT YOU TO KEEP SPOILING ME LIKE THI--
...
OKAY, YOU CAN SPOIL ME *ONCE* IN A WHILE.
HEH. MY PANCAKES CANNOT BE DENIED.
YOU'VE BEEN WORKING SO HARD ON YOUR PROJECTS LATELY...
...I JUST THOUGHT I'D DO SOMETHING SPECIAL FOR YOU TODAY.
HA, *JUST* TODAY?
SERIOUSLY. I KNOW YOU NEVER LIKE HEARING THIS, BUT...
...I REALLY WANT TO DO MORE THINGS ON MY OWN, Y'KNOW?
I MEAN... IT'S BEEN A FEW YEARS NOW.
DARA... I KNOW YOU'RE ALL GROWN UP AND A BIG TIME COLLEGE STUDENT NOW, BUT... YOU'RE STILL MY LITTLE GIRL. AND IF I CAN DO *ANYTHING* TO HELP YOU--
I KNOW, DAD.
MMPF!
LO KILEY
I LOVE YOU, TOO.

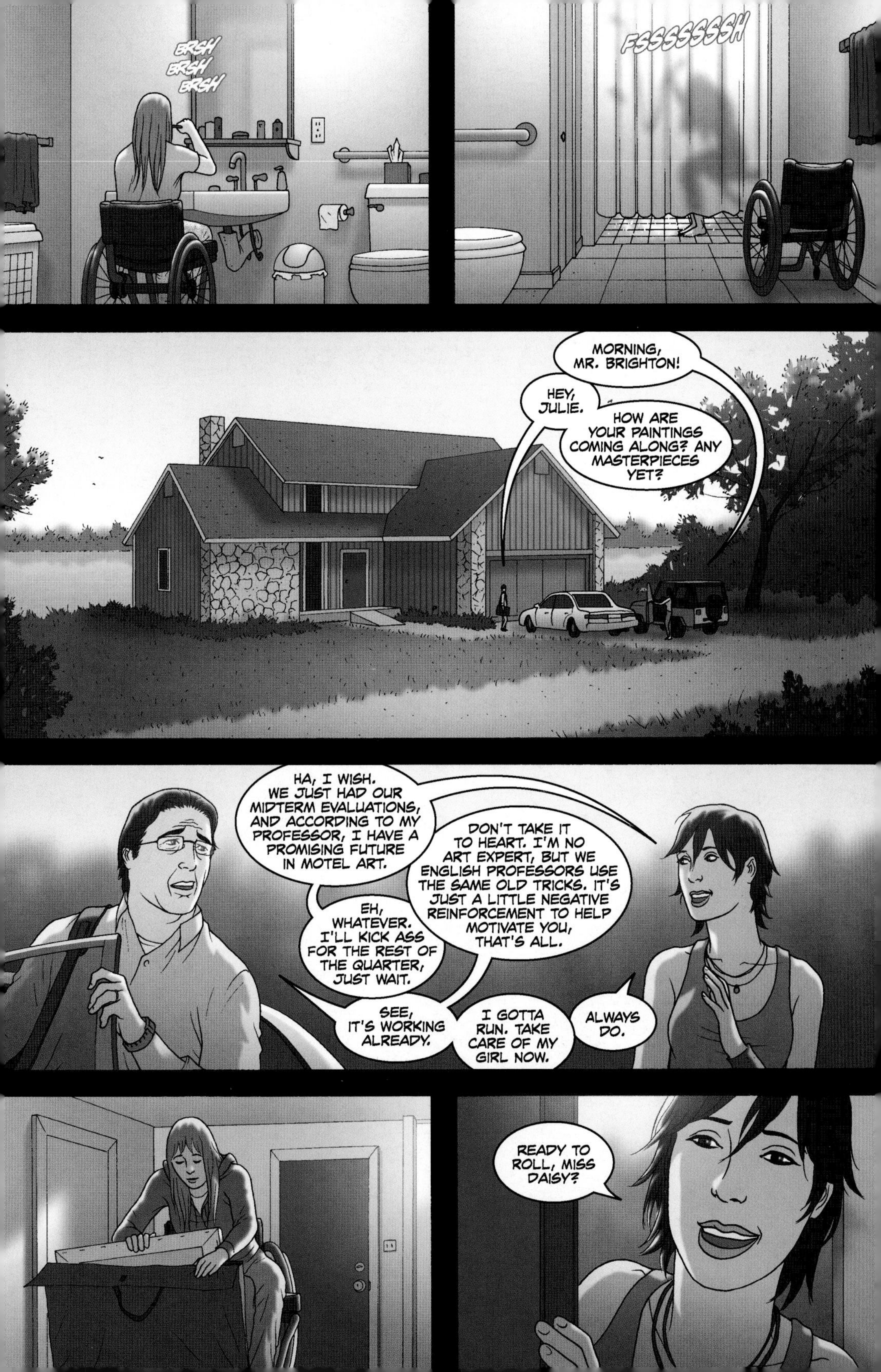

BRSH
BRSH
BRSH
FSSSSSSSH
MORNING, MR. BRIGHTON!
HEY, JULIE.
HOW ARE YOUR PAINTINGS COMING ALONG? ANY MASTERPIECES YET?
HA, I WISH. WE JUST HAD OUR MIDTERM EVALUATIONS, AND ACCORDING TO MY PROFESSOR, I HAVE A PROMISING FUTURE IN MOTEL ART.
DON'T TAKE IT TO HEART. I'M NO ART EXPERT, BUT WE ENGLISH PROFESSORS USE THE SAME OLD TRICKS. IT'S JUST A LITTLE NEGATIVE REINFORCEMENT TO HELP MOTIVATE YOU, THAT'S ALL.
EH, WHATEVER. I'LL KICK ASS FOR THE REST OF THE QUARTER, JUST WAIT.
SEE, IT'S WORKING ALREADY.
I GOTTA RUN. TAKE CARE OF MY GIRL NOW.
ALWAYS DO.
READY TO ROLL, MISS DAISY?

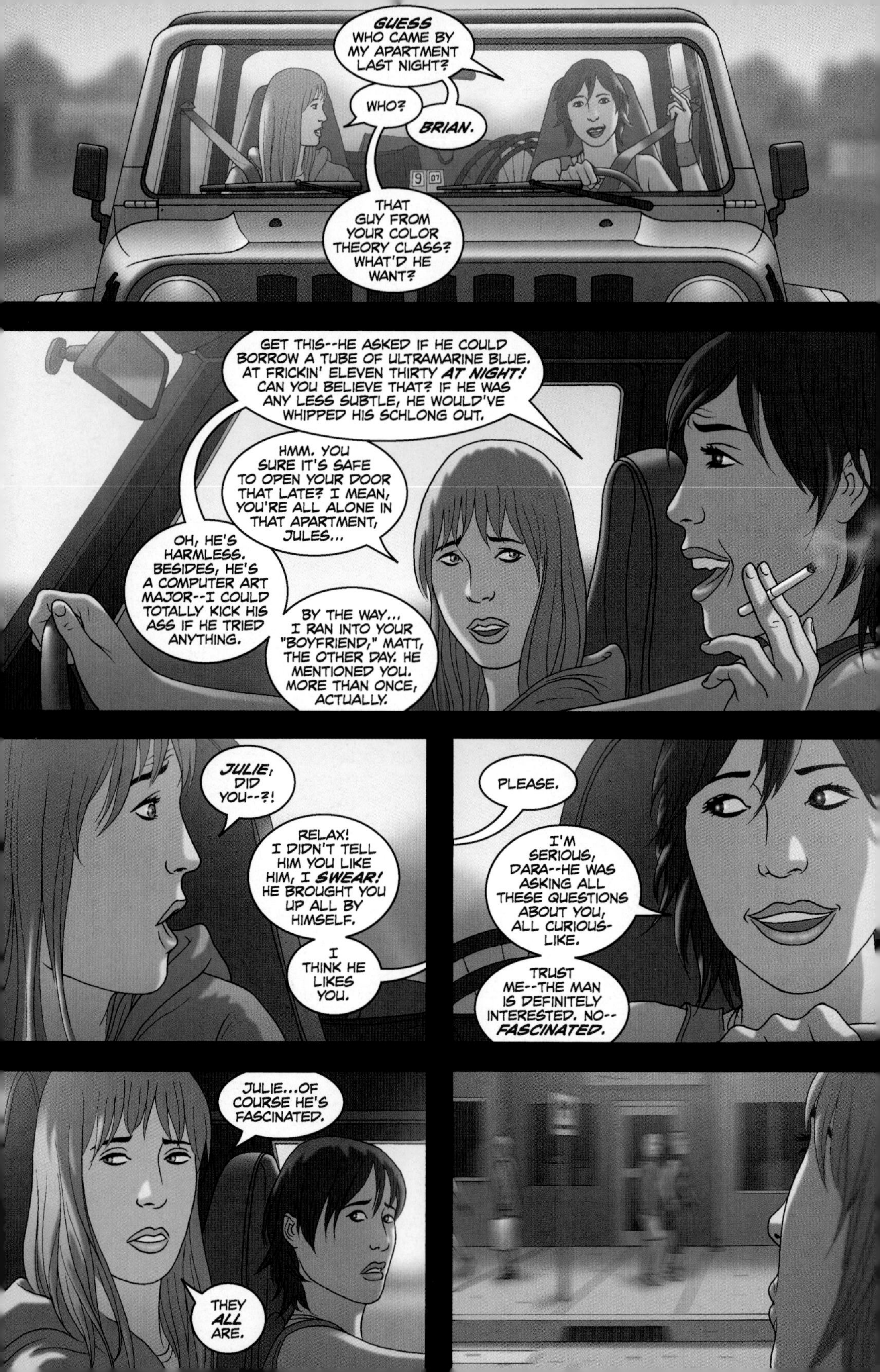

GUESS WHO CAME BY MY APARTMENT LAST NIGHT?
WHO?
BRIAN.
THAT GUY FROM YOUR COLOR THEORY CLASS? WHAT'D HE WANT?
GET THIS--HE ASKED IF HE COULD BORROW A TUBE OF ULTRAMARINE BLUE. AT FRICKIN' ELEVEN THIRTY AT NIGHT! CAN YOU BELIEVE THAT? IF HE WAS ANY LESS SUBTLE, HE WOULD'VE WHIPPED HIS SCHLONG OUT.
HMM. YOU SURE IT'S SAFE TO OPEN YOUR DOOR THAT LATE? I MEAN, YOU'RE ALL ALONE IN THAT APARTMENT, JULES...
OH, HE'S HARMLESS. BESIDES, HE'S A COMPUTER ART MAJOR--I COULD TOTALLY KICK HIS ASS IF HE TRIED ANYTHING.
BY THE WAY... I RAN INTO YOUR "BOYFRIEND," MATT, THE OTHER DAY. HE MENTIONED YOU. MORE THAN ONCE, ACTUALLY.
JULIE, DID YOU--?!
RELAX! I DIDN'T TELL HIM YOU LIKE HIM, I SWEAR! HE BROUGHT YOU UP ALL BY HIMSELF.
I THINK HE LIKES YOU.
PLEASE.
I'M SERIOUS, DARA--HE WAS ASKING ALL THESE QUESTIONS ABOUT YOU, ALL CURIOUS-LIKE.
TRUST ME--THE MAN IS DEFINITELY INTERESTED. NO--FASCINATED.
JULIE...OF COURSE HE'S FASCINATED.
THEY ALL ARE.

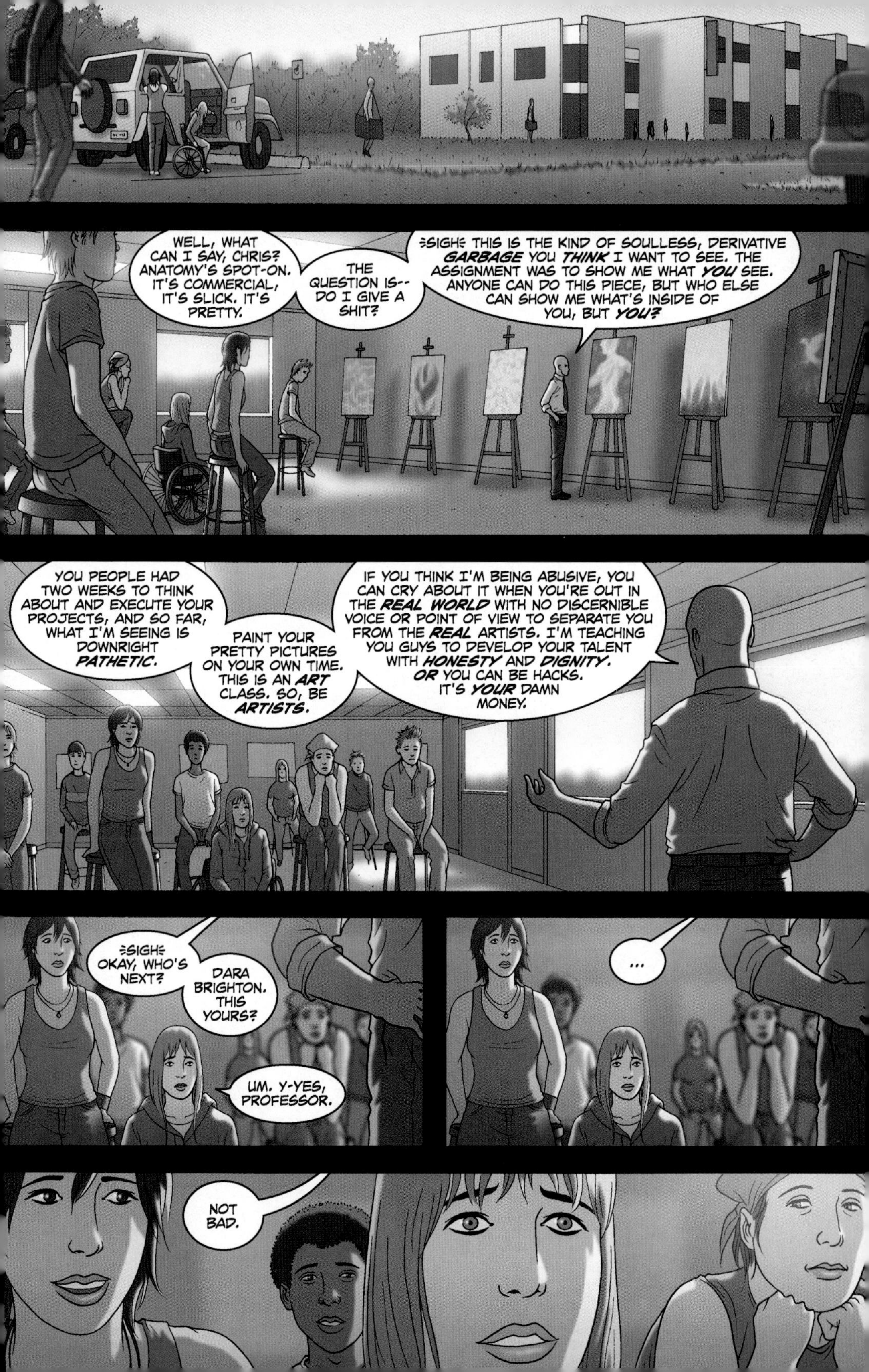
WELL, WHAT CAN I SAY, CHRIS? ANATOMY'S SPOT-ON. IT'S COMMERCIAL, IT'S SLICK. IT'S PRETTY.
THE QUESTION IS-- DO I GIVE A SHIT?
=SIGH= THIS IS THE KIND OF SOULLESS, DERIVATIVE GARBAGE YOU THINK I WANT TO SEE. THE ASSIGNMENT WAS TO SHOW ME WHAT YOU SEE. ANYONE CAN DO THIS PIECE, BUT WHO ELSE CAN SHOW ME WHAT'S INSIDE OF YOU, BUT YOU?
YOU PEOPLE HAD TWO WEEKS TO THINK ABOUT AND EXECUTE YOUR PROJECTS, AND SO FAR, WHAT I'M SEEING IS DOWNRIGHT PATHETIC.
PAINT YOUR PRETTY PICTURES ON YOUR OWN TIME. THIS IS AN ART CLASS. SO, BE ARTISTS.
IF YOU THINK I'M BEING ABUSIVE, YOU CAN CRY ABOUT IT WHEN YOU'RE OUT IN THE REAL WORLD WITH NO DISCERNIBLE VOICE OR POINT OF VIEW TO SEPARATE YOU FROM THE REAL ARTISTS. I'M TEACHING YOU GUYS TO DEVELOP YOUR TALENT WITH HONESTY AND DIGNITY. OR YOU CAN BE HACKS. IT'S YOUR DAMN MONEY.
=SIGH= OKAY, WHO'S NEXT?
DARA BRIGHTON. THIS YOURS?
UM. Y-YES, PROFESSOR.
...
NOT BAD.

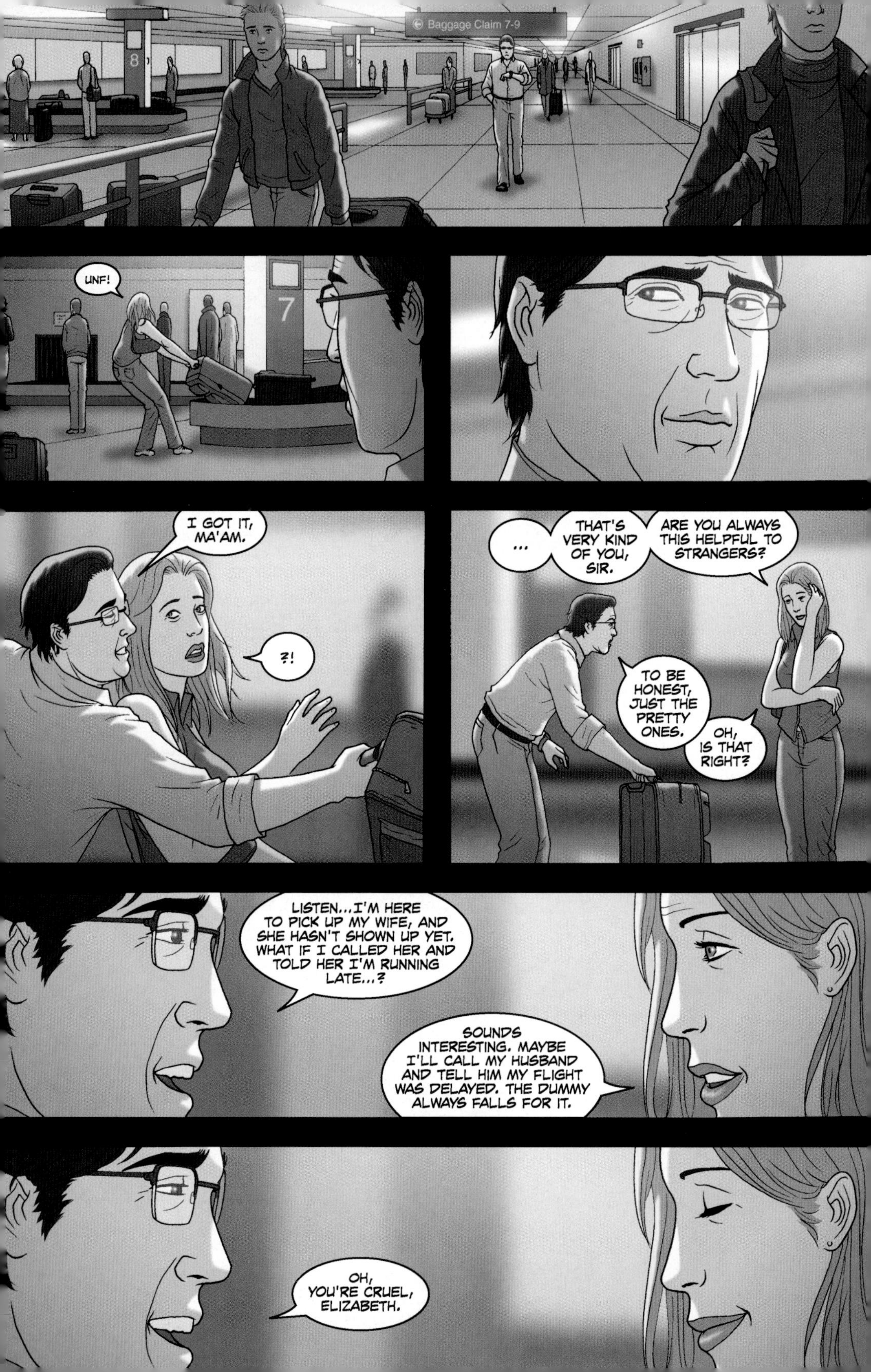
Baggage Claim 7-9
8
9
UNF!
7
I GOT IT, MA'AM.
?!
...
THAT'S VERY KIND OF YOU, SIR.
ARE YOU ALWAYS THIS HELPFUL TO STRANGERS?
TO BE HONEST, JUST THE PRETTY ONES.
OH, IS THAT RIGHT?
LISTEN...I'M HERE TO PICK UP MY WIFE, AND SHE HASN'T SHOWN UP YET. WHAT IF I CALLED HER AND TOLD HER I'M RUNNING LATE...?
SOUNDS INTERESTING. MAYBE I'LL CALL MY HUSBAND AND TELL HIM MY FLIGHT WAS DELAYED. THE DUMMY ALWAYS FALLS FOR IT.
OH, YOU'RE CRUEL, ELIZABETH.

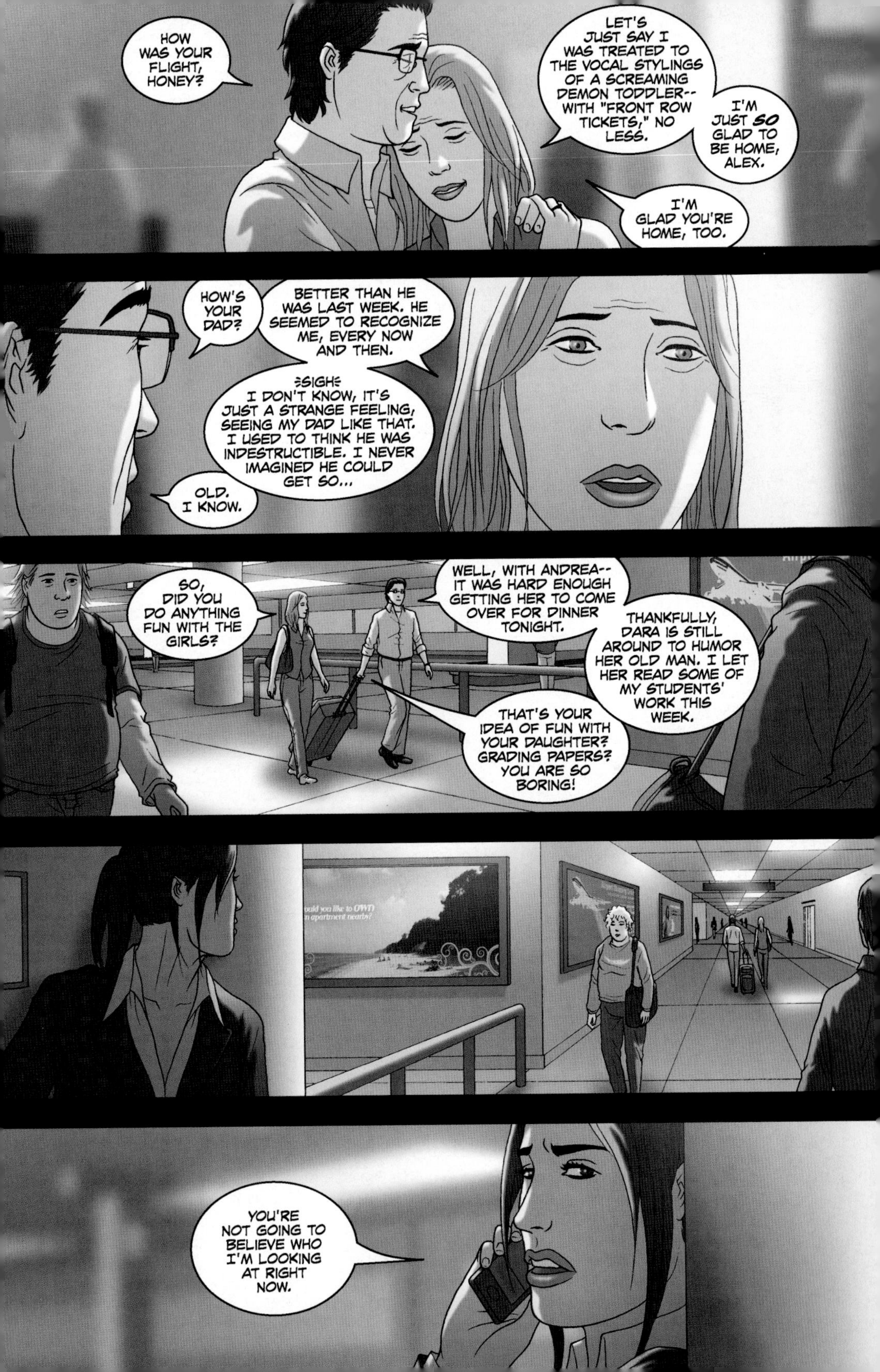
HOW WAS YOUR FLIGHT, HONEY?
LET'S JUST SAY I WAS TREATED TO THE VOCAL STYLINGS OF A SCREAMING DEMON TODDLER--WITH "FRONT ROW TICKETS," NO LESS.
I'M JUST SO GLAD TO BE HOME, ALEX.
I'M GLAD YOU'RE HOME, TOO.
HOW'S YOUR DAD?
BETTER THAN HE WAS LAST WEEK. HE SEEMED TO RECOGNIZE ME, EVERY NOW AND THEN.
SIGH
I DON'T KNOW, IT'S JUST A STRANGE FEELING, SEEING MY DAD LIKE THAT. I USED TO THINK HE WAS INDESTRUCTIBLE. I NEVER IMAGINED HE COULD GET SO...
OLD. I KNOW.
SO, DID YOU DO ANYTHING FUN WITH THE GIRLS?
WELL, WITH ANDREA--IT WAS HARD ENOUGH GETTING HER TO COME OVER FOR DINNER TONIGHT.
THANKFULLY, DARA IS STILL AROUND TO HUMOR HER OLD MAN. I LET HER READ SOME OF MY STUDENTS' WORK THIS WEEK.
THAT'S YOUR IDEA OF FUN WITH YOUR DAUGHTER? GRADING PAPERS? YOU ARE SO BORING!
YOU'RE NOT GOING TO BELIEVE WHO I'M LOOKING AT RIGHT NOW.

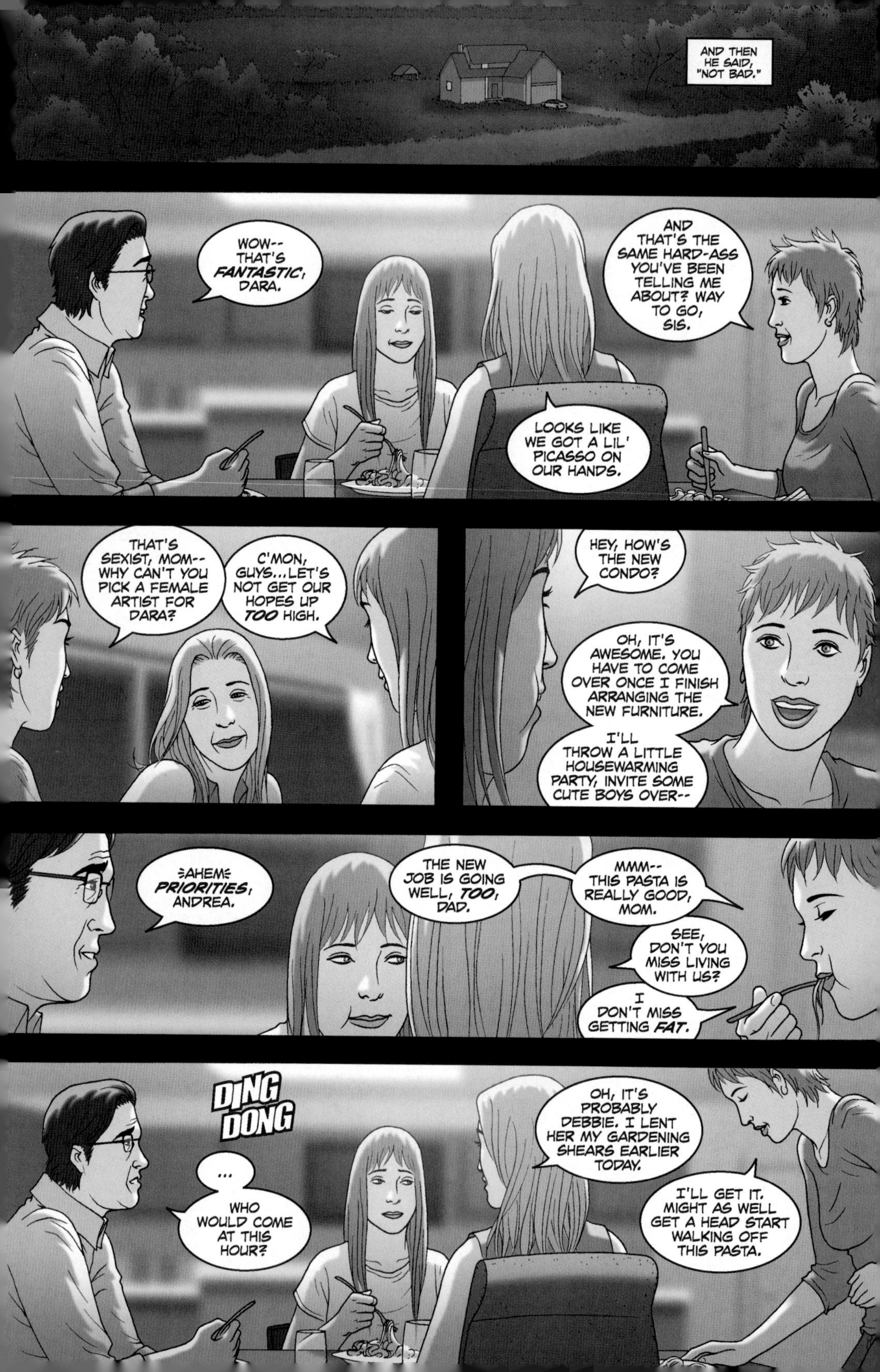
AND THEN HE SAID, "NOT BAD."
WOW--THAT'S FANTASTIC, DARA.
AND THAT'S THE SAME HARD-ASS YOU'VE BEEN TELLING ME ABOUT? WAY TO GO, SIS.
LOOKS LIKE WE GOT A LIL' PICASSO ON OUR HANDS.
THAT'S SEXIST, MOM--WHY CAN'T YOU PICK A FEMALE ARTIST FOR DARA?
C'MON, GUYS...LET'S NOT GET OUR HOPES UP TOO HIGH.
HEY, HOW'S THE NEW CONDO?
OH, IT'S AWESOME. YOU HAVE TO COME OVER ONCE I FINISH ARRANGING THE NEW FURNITURE.
I'LL THROW A LITTLE HOUSEWARMING PARTY, INVITE SOME CUTE BOYS OVER--
AHEM PRIORITIES, ANDREA.
THE NEW JOB IS GOING WELL, TOO, DAD.
MMM--THIS PASTA IS REALLY GOOD, MOM.
SEE, DON'T YOU MISS LIVING WITH US?
I DON'T MISS GETTING FAT.
DING DONG
...
WHO WOULD COME AT THIS HOUR?
OH, IT'S PROBABLY DEBBIE. I LENT HER MY GARDENING SHEARS EARLIER TODAY.
I'LL GET IT. MIGHT AS WELL GET A HEAD START WALKING OFF THIS PASTA.

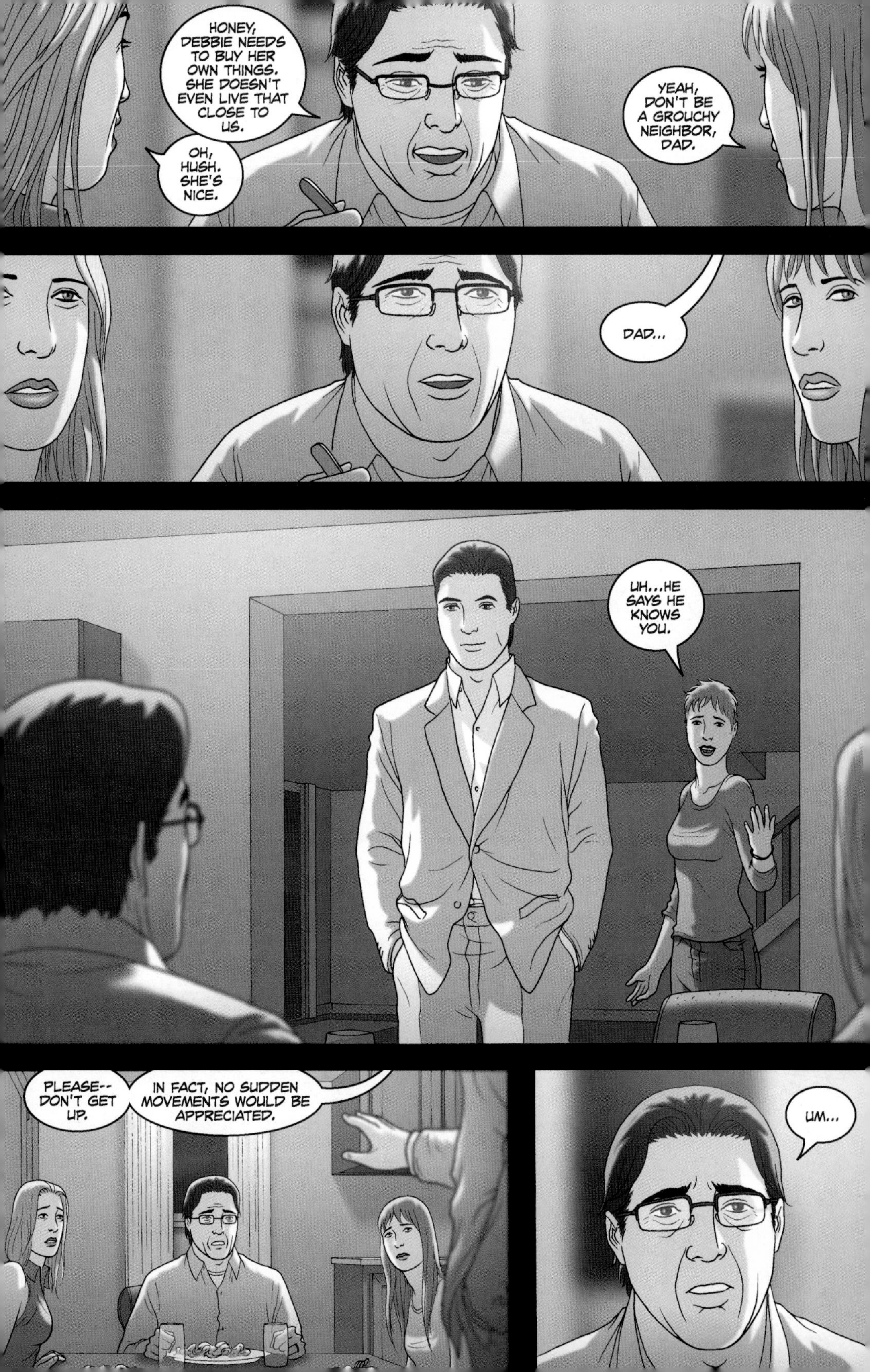
HONEY, DEBBIE NEEDS TO BUY HER OWN THINGS. SHE DOESN'T EVEN LIVE THAT CLOSE TO US.
OH, HUSH. SHE'S NICE.
YEAH, DON'T BE A GROUCHY NEIGHBOR, DAD.
DAD...
UH...HE SAYS HE KNOWS YOU.
PLEASE-- DON'T GET UP.
IN FACT, NO SUDDEN MOVEMENTS WOULD BE APPRECIATED.
UM...

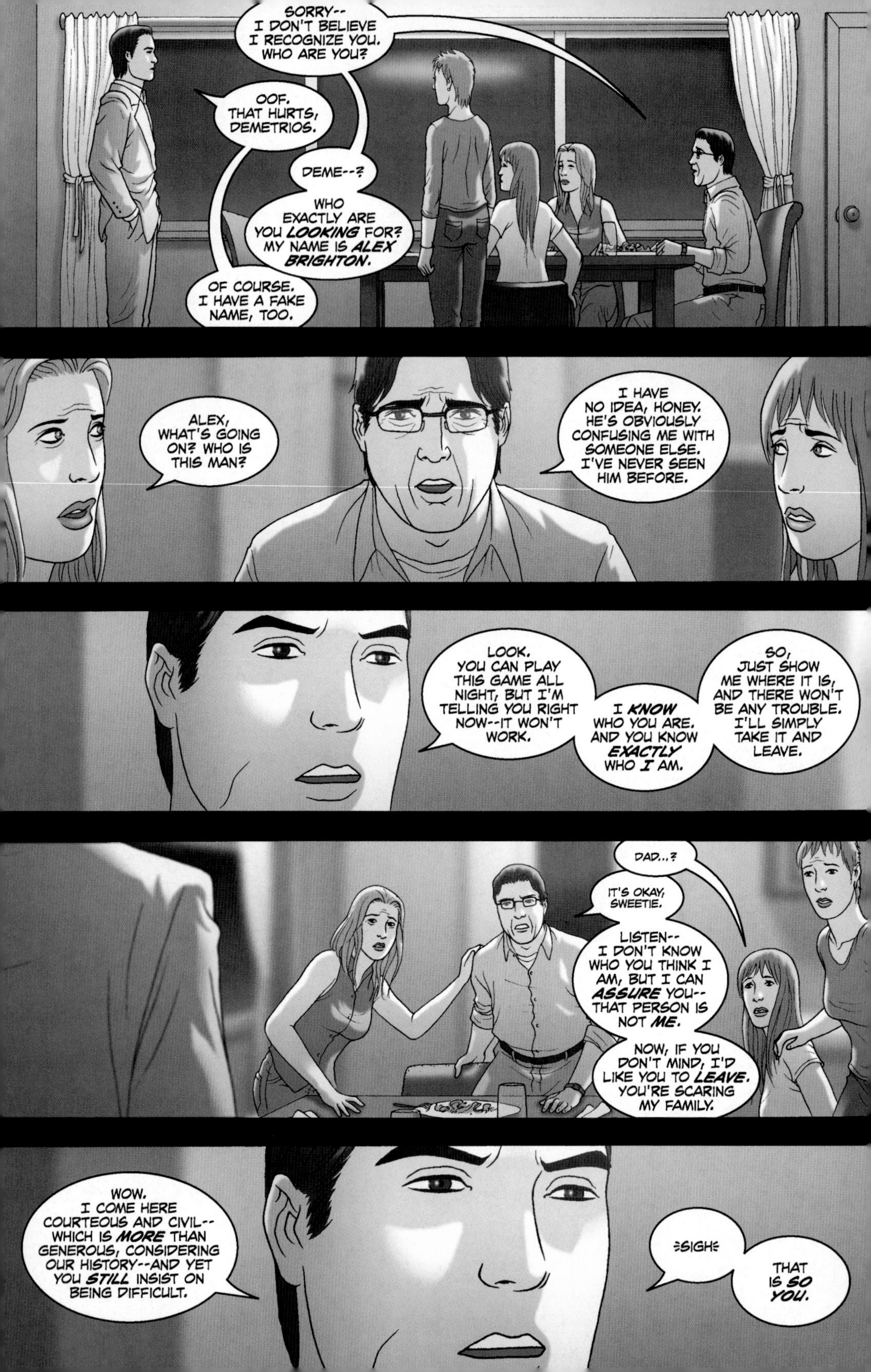
SORRY-- I DON'T BELIEVE I RECOGNIZE YOU. WHO ARE YOU?
OOF. THAT HURTS, DEMETRIOS.
DEME--?
WHO EXACTLY ARE YOU *LOOKING* FOR? MY NAME IS *ALEX BRIGHTON*.
OF COURSE. I HAVE A FAKE NAME, TOO.
ALEX, WHAT'S GOING ON? WHO IS THIS MAN?
I HAVE NO IDEA, HONEY. HE'S OBVIOUSLY CONFUSING ME WITH SOMEONE ELSE. I'VE NEVER SEEN HIM BEFORE.
LOOK. YOU CAN PLAY THIS GAME ALL NIGHT, BUT I'M TELLING YOU RIGHT NOW--IT WON'T WORK.
I *KNOW* WHO YOU ARE. AND YOU KNOW *EXACTLY* WHO *I* AM.
SO, JUST SHOW ME WHERE IT IS, AND THERE WON'T BE ANY TROUBLE. I'LL SIMPLY TAKE IT AND LEAVE.
DAD...?
IT'S OKAY, SWEETIE.
LISTEN-- I DON'T KNOW WHO YOU THINK I AM, BUT I CAN *ASSURE* YOU-- THAT PERSON IS NOT *ME*.
NOW, IF YOU DON'T MIND, I'D LIKE YOU TO *LEAVE*. YOU'RE SCARING MY FAMILY.
WOW. I COME HERE COURTEOUS AND CIVIL-- WHICH IS *MORE* THAN GENEROUS, CONSIDERING OUR HISTORY--AND YET YOU *STILL* INSIST ON BEING DIFFICULT.
=SIGH=
THAT IS *SO YOU*.

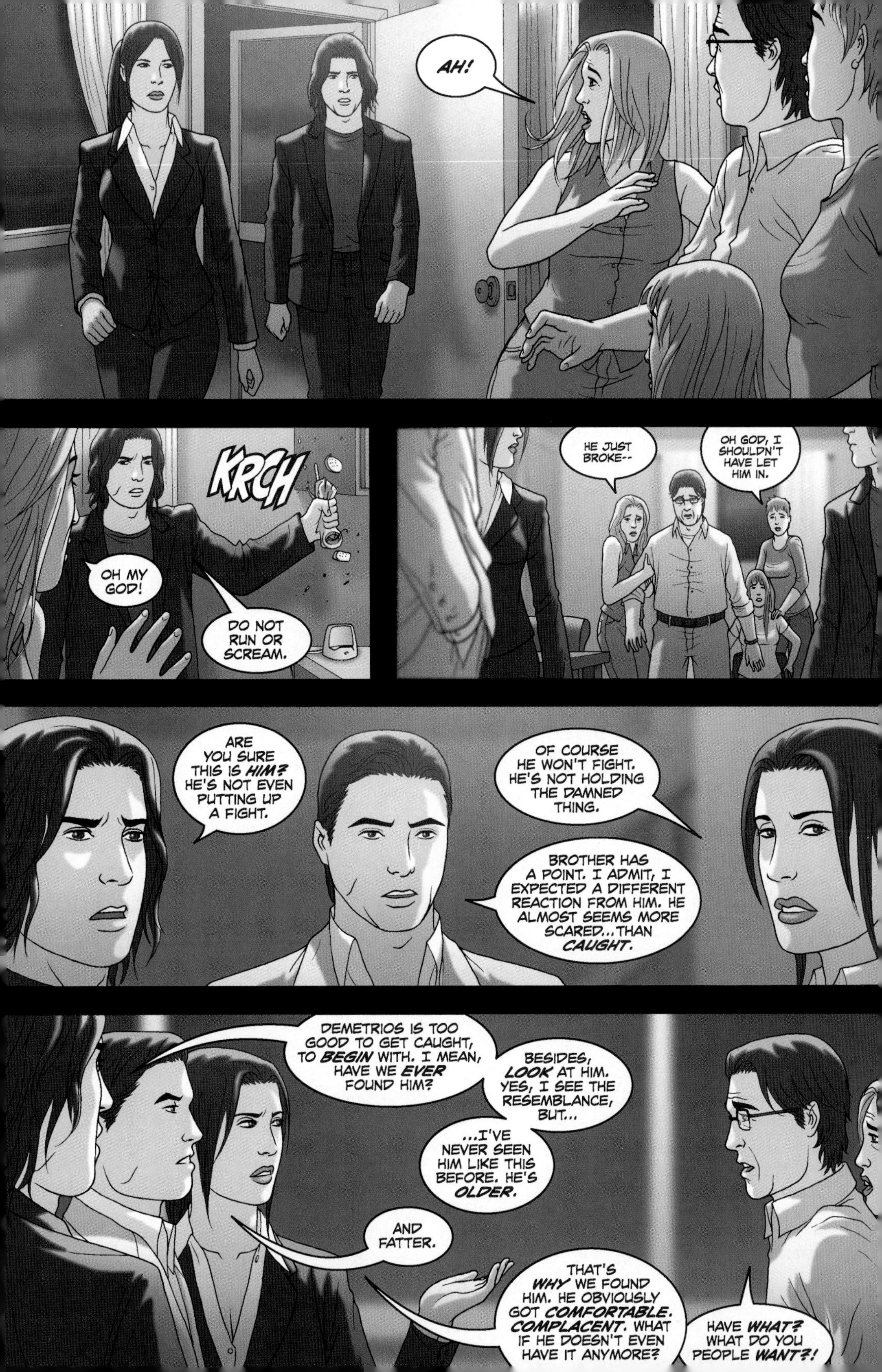
AH!
KRCH
OH MY GOD!
DO NOT RUN OR SCREAM.
HE JUST BROKE--
OH GOD, I SHOULDN'T HAVE LET HIM IN.
ARE YOU SURE THIS IS HIM? HE'S NOT EVEN PUTTING UP A FIGHT.
OF COURSE HE WON'T FIGHT. HE'S NOT HOLDING THE DAMNED THING.
BROTHER HAS A POINT. I ADMIT, I EXPECTED A DIFFERENT REACTION FROM HIM. HE ALMOST SEEMS MORE SCARED...THAN CAUGHT.
DEMETRIOS IS TOO GOOD TO GET CAUGHT, TO BEGIN WITH. I MEAN, HAVE WE EVER FOUND HIM?
BESIDES, LOOK AT HIM. YES, I SEE THE RESEMBLANCE, BUT...
...I'VE NEVER SEEN HIM LIKE THIS BEFORE. HE'S OLDER.
AND FATTER.
THAT'S WHY WE FOUND HIM. HE OBVIOUSLY GOT COMFORTABLE. COMPLACENT. WHAT IF HE DOESN'T EVEN HAVE IT ANYMORE?
HAVE WHAT? WHAT DO YOU PEOPLE WANT?!

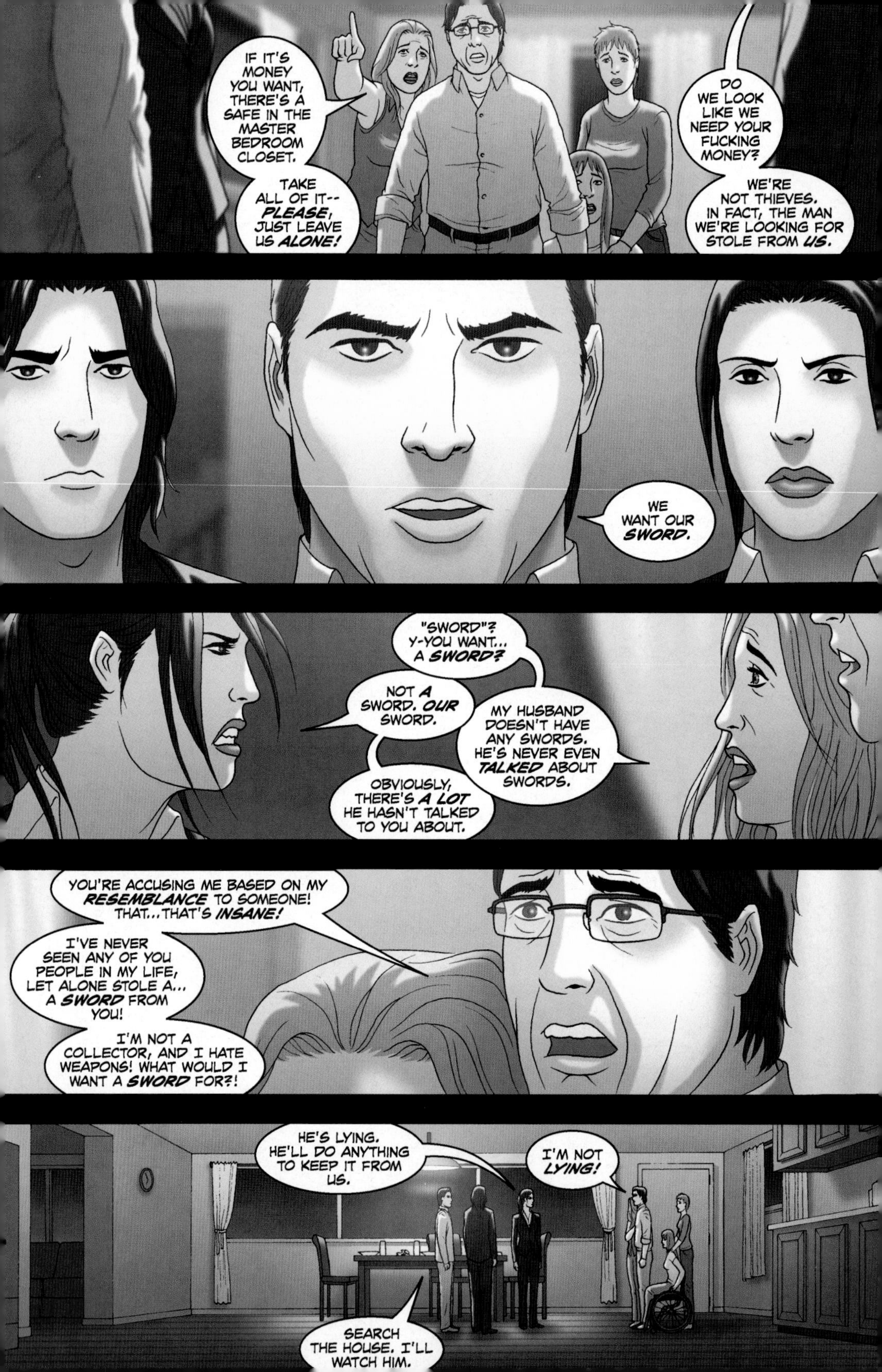
IF IT'S MONEY YOU WANT, THERE'S A SAFE IN THE MASTER BEDROOM CLOSET.
TAKE ALL OF IT-- PLEASE, JUST LEAVE US ALONE!
DO WE LOOK LIKE WE NEED YOUR FUCKING MONEY?
WE'RE NOT THIEVES. IN FACT, THE MAN WE'RE LOOKING FOR STOLE FROM US.
WE WANT OUR SWORD.
"SWORD"? Y-YOU WANT... A SWORD?
NOT A SWORD. OUR SWORD.
MY HUSBAND DOESN'T HAVE ANY SWORDS. HE'S NEVER EVEN TALKED ABOUT SWORDS.
OBVIOUSLY, THERE'S A LOT HE HASN'T TALKED TO YOU ABOUT.
YOU'RE ACCUSING ME BASED ON MY RESEMBLANCE TO SOMEONE! THAT...THAT'S INSANE!
I'VE NEVER SEEN ANY OF YOU PEOPLE IN MY LIFE, LET ALONE STOLE A... A SWORD FROM YOU!
I'M NOT A COLLECTOR, AND I HATE WEAPONS! WHAT WOULD I WANT A SWORD FOR?!
HE'S LYING. HE'LL DO ANYTHING TO KEEP IT FROM US.
I'M NOT LYING!
SEARCH THE HOUSE. I'LL WATCH HIM.

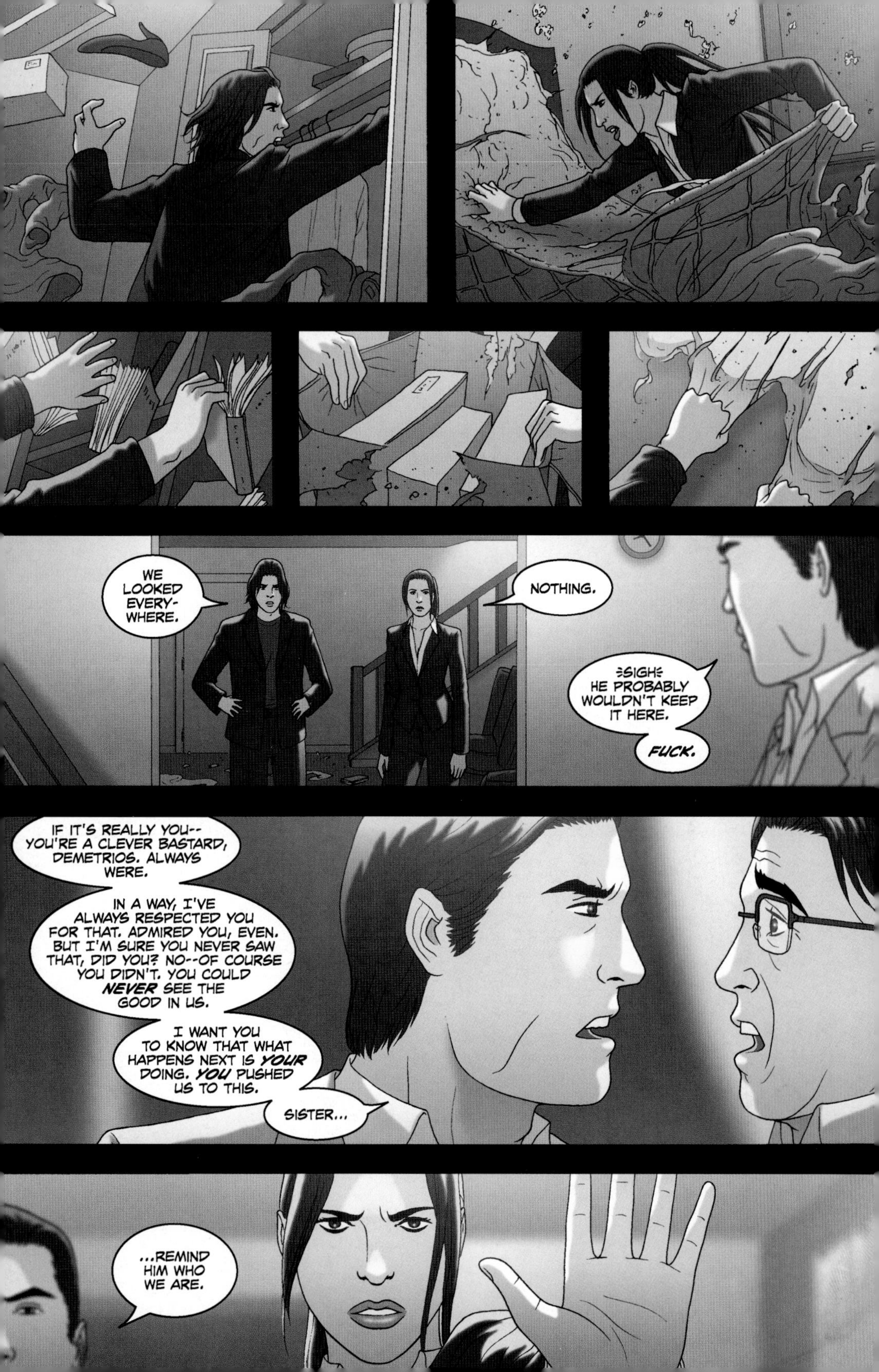
WE LOOKED EVERY-WHERE.
NOTHING.
≡SIGH≡ HE PROBABLY WOULDN'T KEEP IT HERE.
FUCK.
IF IT'S REALLY YOU-- YOU'RE A CLEVER BASTARD, DEMETRIOS. ALWAYS WERE.
IN A WAY, I'VE ALWAYS RESPECTED YOU FOR THAT. ADMIRED YOU, EVEN. BUT I'M SURE YOU NEVER SAW THAT, DID YOU? NO--OF COURSE YOU DIDN'T. YOU COULD NEVER SEE THE GOOD IN US.
I WANT YOU TO KNOW THAT WHAT HAPPENS NEXT IS YOUR DOING. YOU PUSHED US TO THIS.
SISTER...
...REMIND HIM WHO WE ARE.

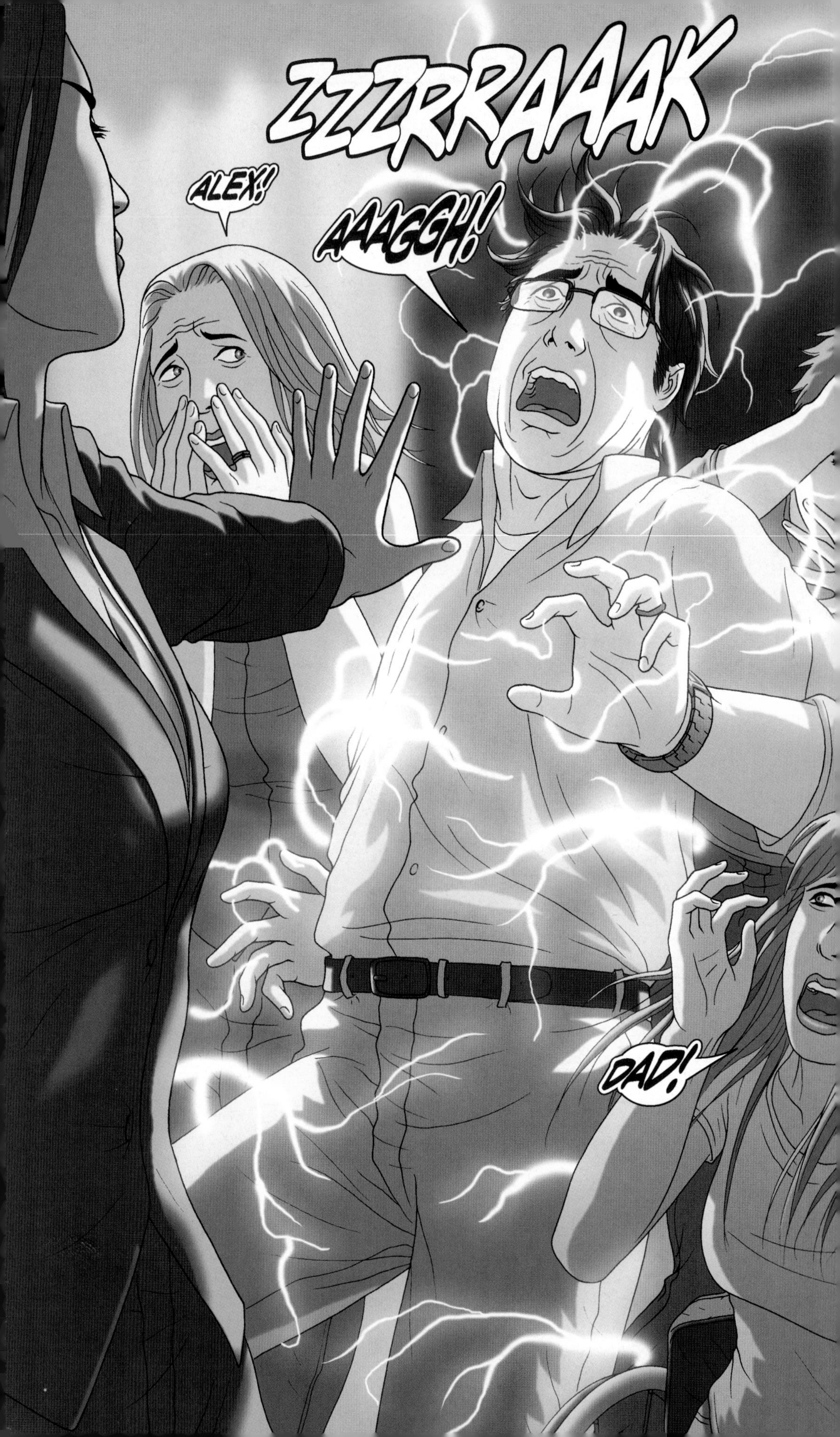
ZZZRRAAAK
ALEX!
AAAGGH!
DAD!

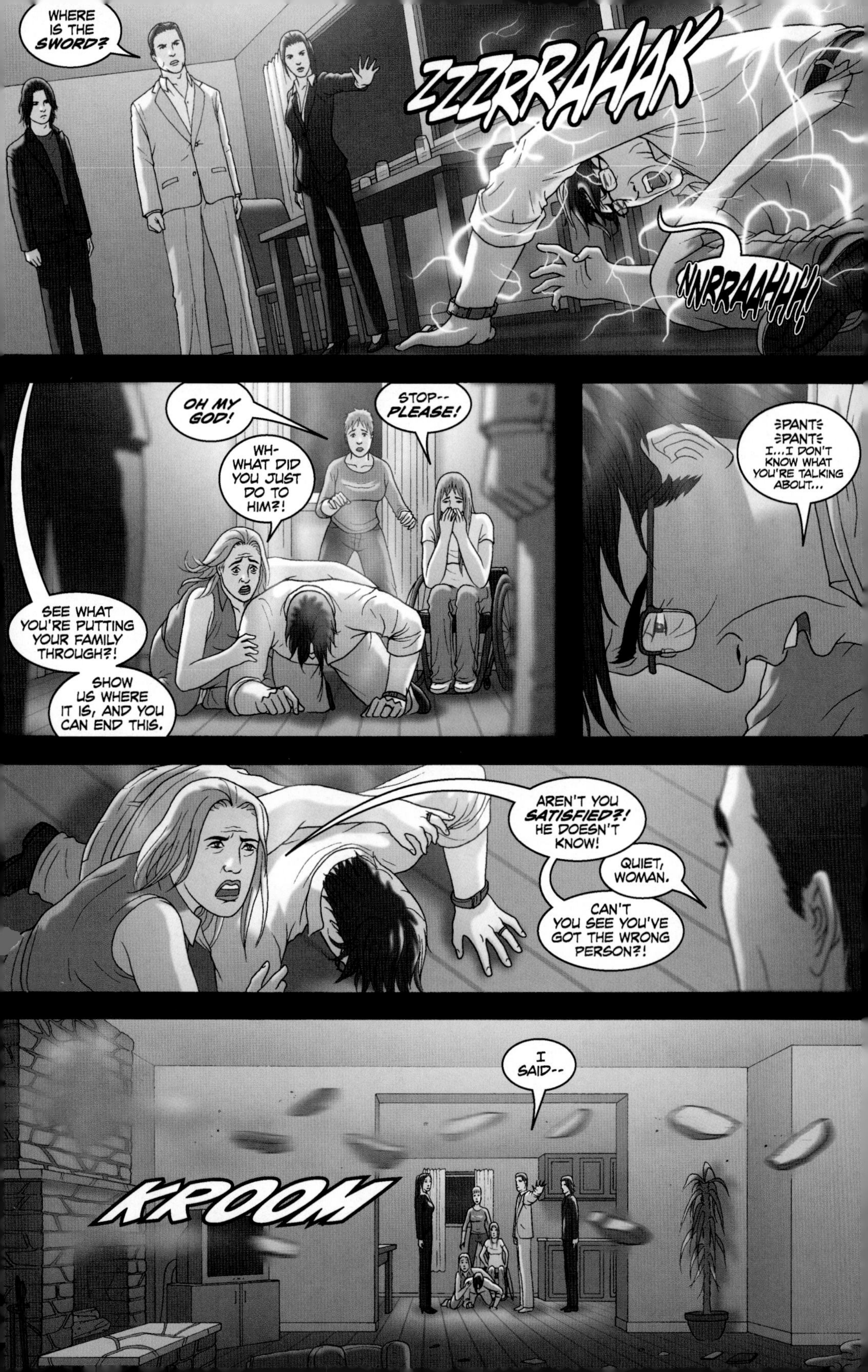
WHERE IS THE SWORD?
ZZZRRAAAK
NNRRAAHHH!
OH MY GOD!
STOP-- PLEASE!
WH- WHAT DID YOU JUST DO TO HIM?!
SEE WHAT YOU'RE PUTTING YOUR FAMILY THROUGH?!
SHOW US WHERE IT IS, AND YOU CAN END THIS.
PANT PANT I... I DON'T KNOW WHAT YOU'RE TALKING ABOUT...
AREN'T YOU SATISFIED?! HE DOESN'T KNOW!
QUIET, WOMAN.
CAN'T YOU SEE YOU'VE GOT THE WRONG PERSON?!
I SAID--
KROOM

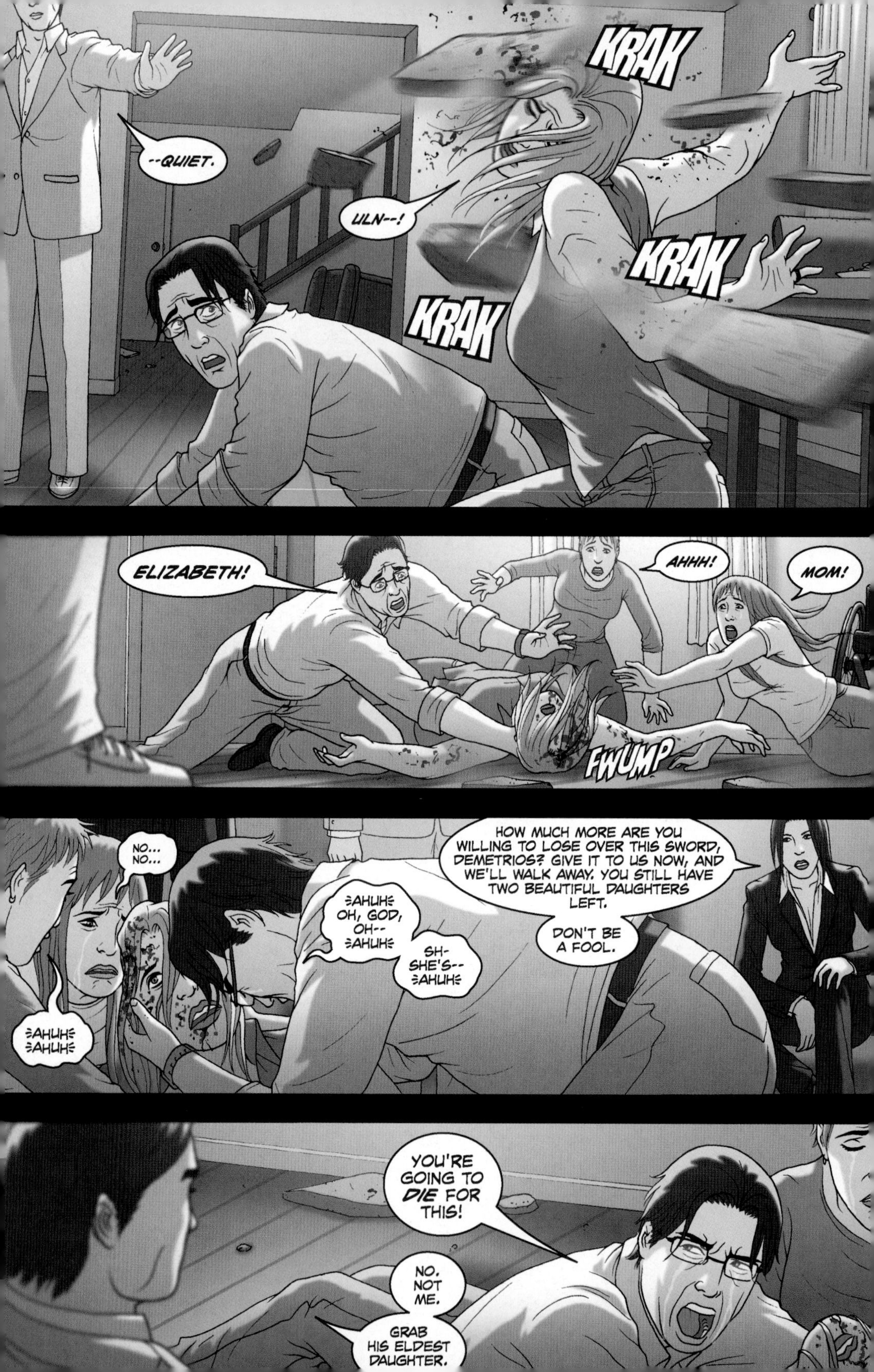
--QUIET.
ULN--!
KRAK
KRAK
KRAK
ELIZABETH!
AHHH!
MOM!
FWUMP
NO...
NO...
HOW MUCH MORE ARE YOU WILLING TO LOSE OVER THIS SWORD, DEMETRIOS? GIVE IT TO US NOW, AND WE'LL WALK AWAY. YOU STILL HAVE TWO BEAUTIFUL DAUGHTERS LEFT.
DON'T BE A FOOL.
AHUH OH, GOD, OH-- AHUH
SH- SHE'S-- AHUH
AHUH AHUH
YOU'RE GOING TO DIE FOR THIS!
NO. NOT ME.
GRAB HIS ELDEST DAUGHTER.

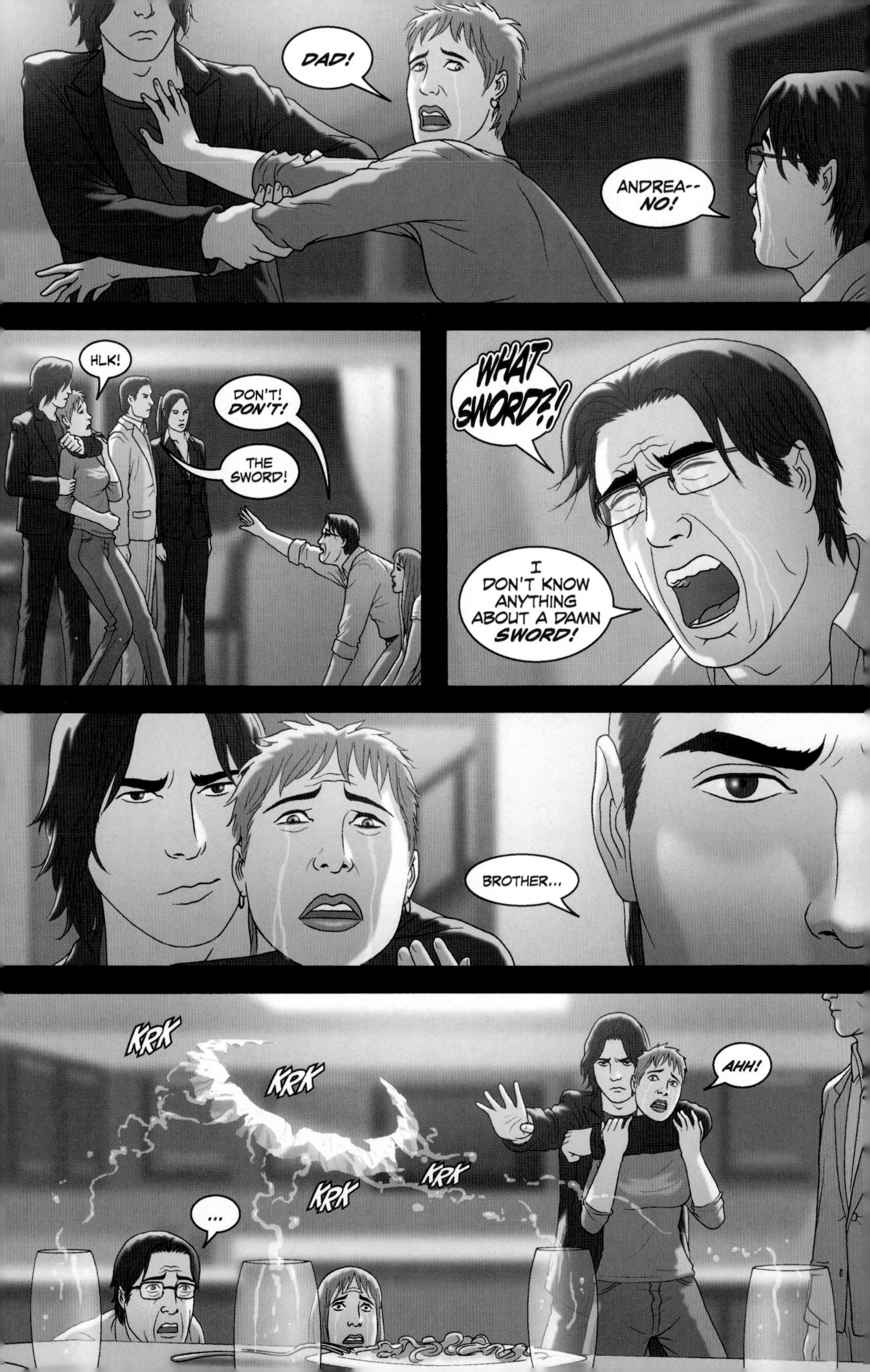
DAD!
ANDREA-- NO!
HLK!
DON'T! DON'T!
THE SWORD!
WHAT SWORD?!
I DON'T KNOW ANYTHING ABOUT A DAMN SWORD!
BROTHER...
KRK
KRK
KRK
KRK
AHH!
...

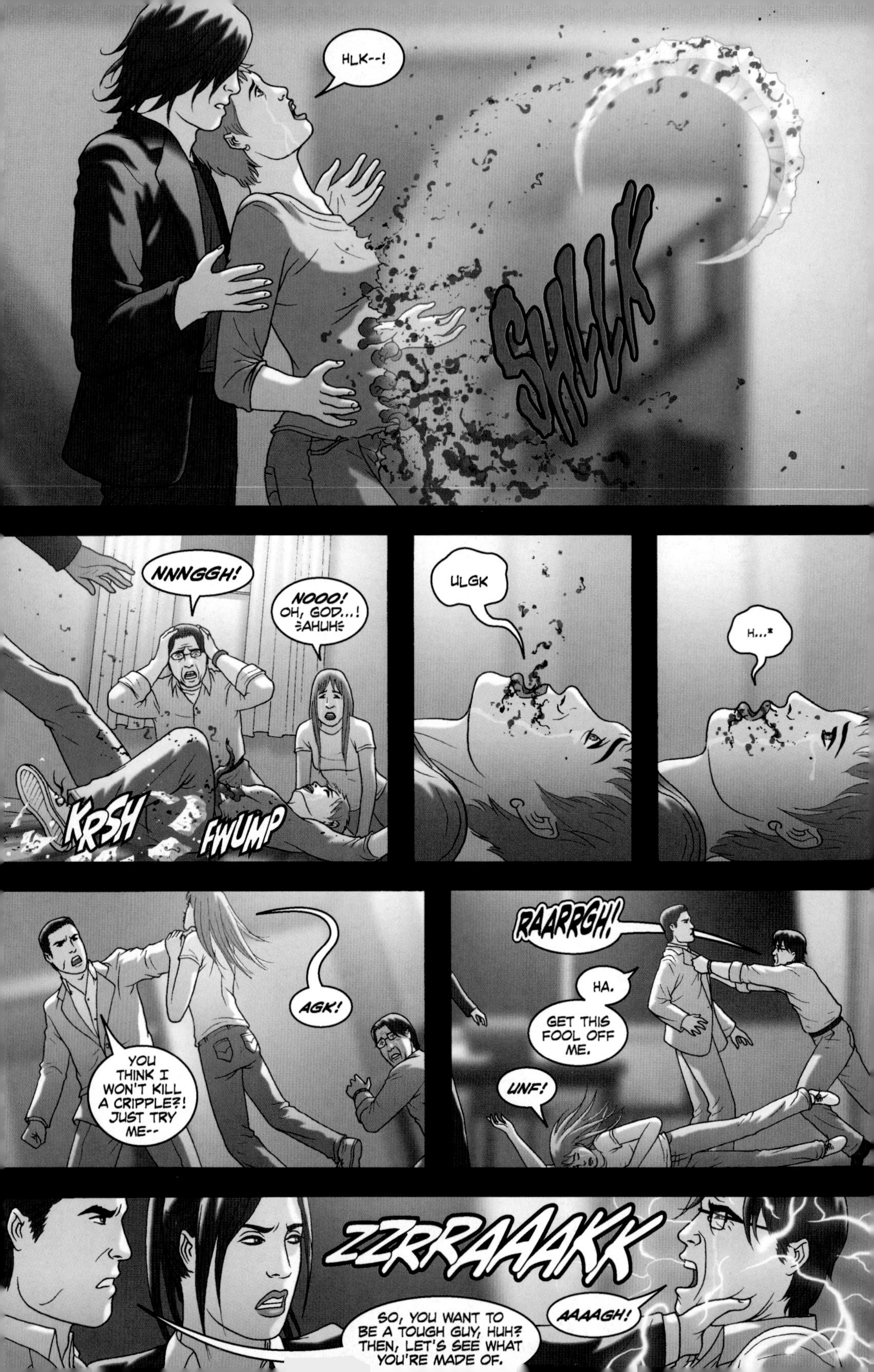
HLK--!
SHLCK
NNNGGH!
NOOO! OH, GOD...! AHUH
KRSH
FWUMP
ULGK
H...*
AGK!
YOU THINK I WON'T KILL A CRIPPLE?! JUST TRY ME--
RAARRGH!
HA.
GET THIS FOOL OFF ME.
UNF!
ZZRRAAAKK
SO, YOU WANT TO BE A TOUGH GUY, HUH? THEN, LET'S SEE WHAT YOU'RE MADE OF.
AAAAGH!

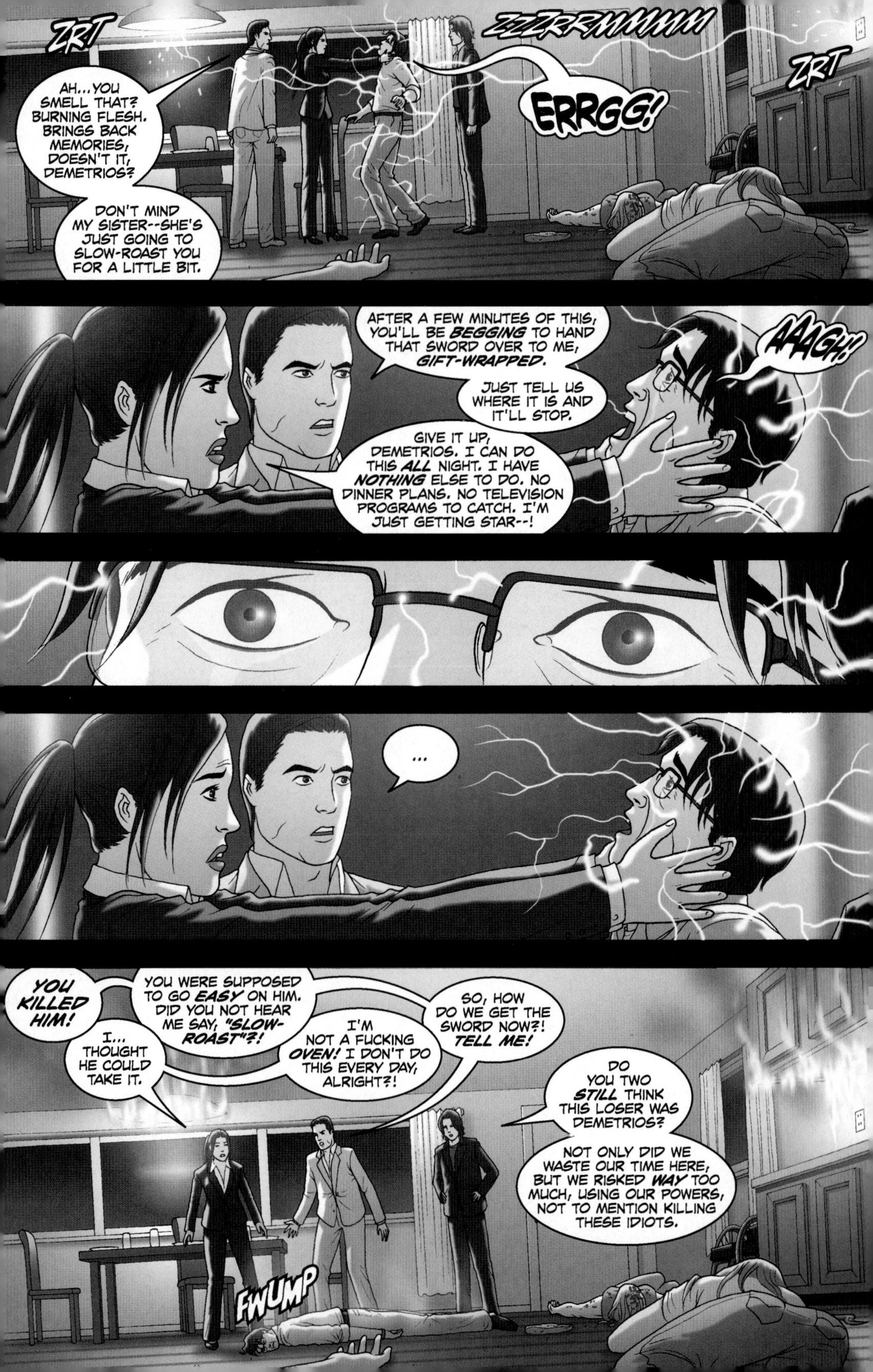
ZRT
ZZZRRRMMMMM
ZRT
AH...YOU SMELL THAT? BURNING FLESH. BRINGS BACK MEMORIES, DOESN'T IT, DEMETRIOS?
DON'T MIND MY SISTER--SHE'S JUST GOING TO SLOW-ROAST YOU FOR A LITTLE BIT.
ERRGG!
AFTER A FEW MINUTES OF THIS, YOU'LL BE BEGGING TO HAND THAT SWORD OVER TO ME, GIFT-WRAPPED.
JUST TELL US WHERE IT IS AND IT'LL STOP.
AAAGH!
GIVE IT UP, DEMETRIOS. I CAN DO THIS ALL NIGHT. I HAVE NOTHING ELSE TO DO. NO DINNER PLANS. NO TELEVISION PROGRAMS TO CATCH. I'M JUST GETTING STAR--!
...
YOU KILLED HIM!
I... THOUGHT HE COULD TAKE IT.
YOU WERE SUPPOSED TO GO EASY ON HIM. DID YOU NOT HEAR ME SAY, "SLOW-ROAST"?!
I'M NOT A FUCKING OVEN! I DON'T DO THIS EVERY DAY, ALRIGHT?!
SO, HOW DO WE GET THE SWORD NOW?! TELL ME!
DO YOU TWO STILL THINK THIS LOSER WAS DEMETRIOS?
NOT ONLY DID WE WASTE OUR TIME HERE, BUT WE RISKED WAY TOO MUCH, USING OUR POWERS, NOT TO MENTION KILLING THESE IDIOTS.
FWUMP

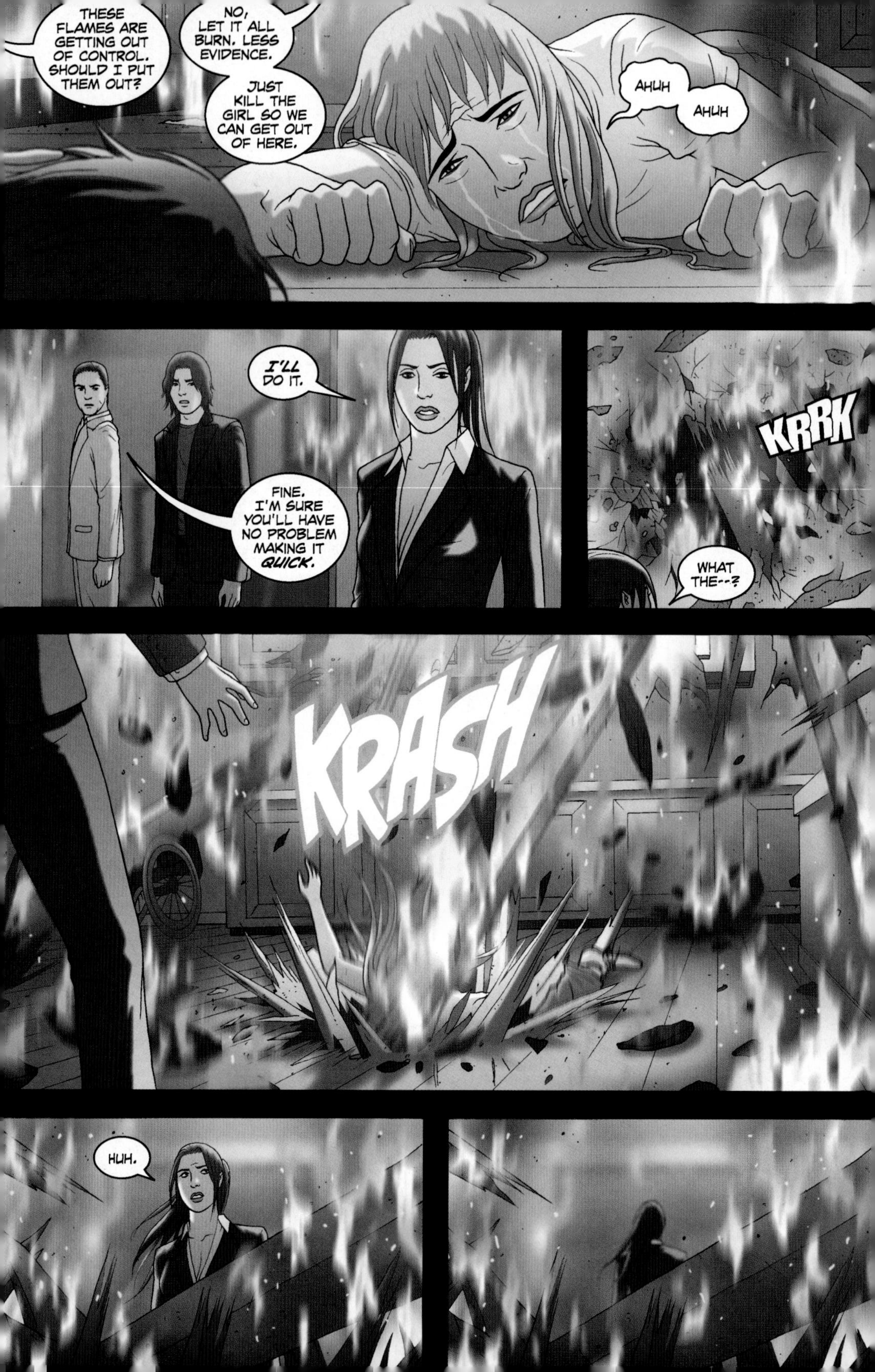
THESE FLAMES ARE GETTING OUT OF CONTROL. SHOULD I PUT THEM OUT?
NO, LET IT ALL BURN. LESS EVIDENCE.
JUST KILL THE GIRL SO WE CAN GET OUT OF HERE.
AHUH
AHUH
I'LL DO IT.
FINE. I'M SURE YOU'LL HAVE NO PROBLEM MAKING IT QUICK.
KRRK
WHAT THE--?
KRASH
HUH.

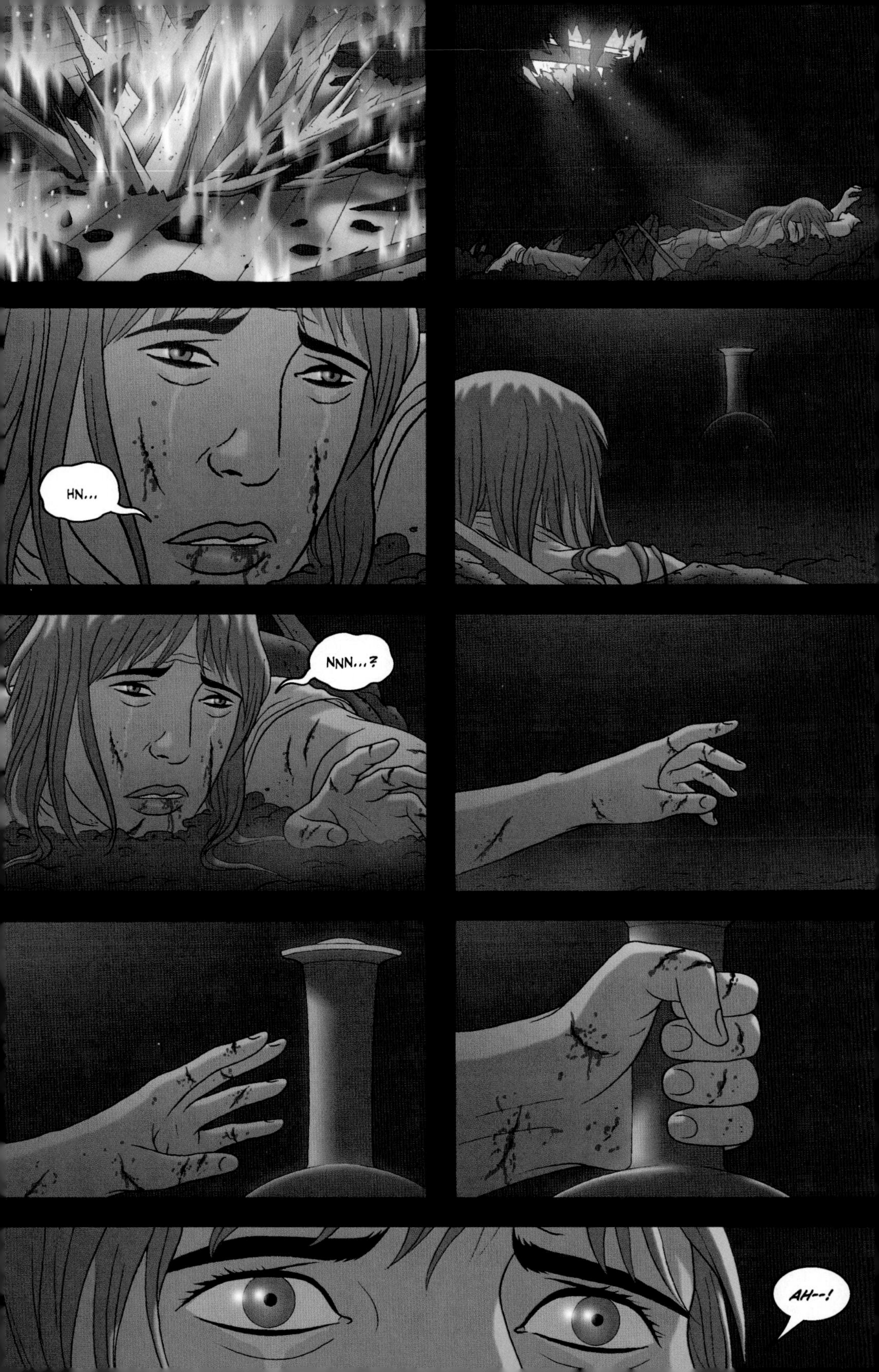
HN...
NNN...?
AH--!

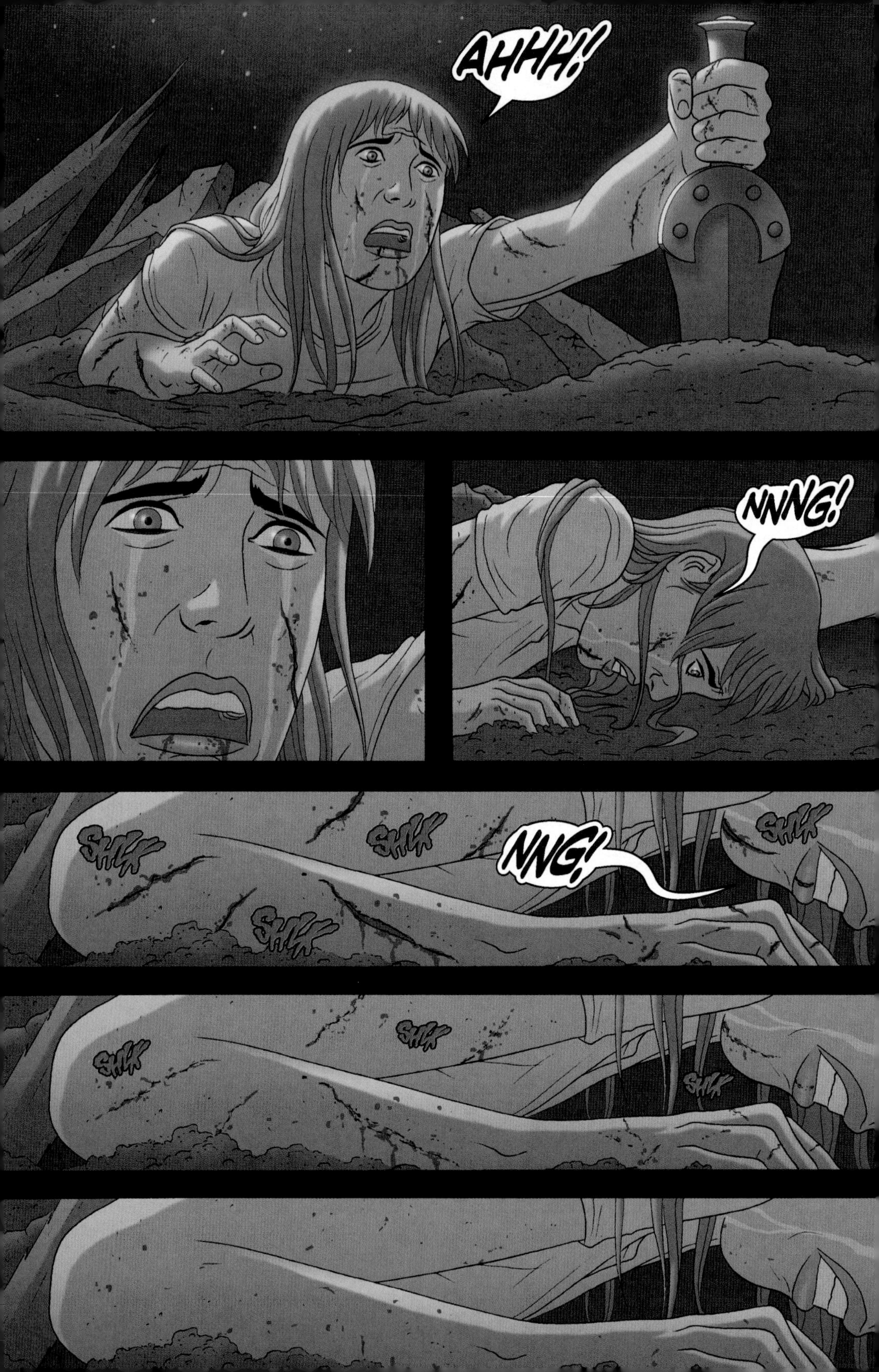
AHHH!
NNNG!
SHLK
SHLK
NNG!
SHLK
SHLK
SHLK
SHLK
SHLK
SHLK

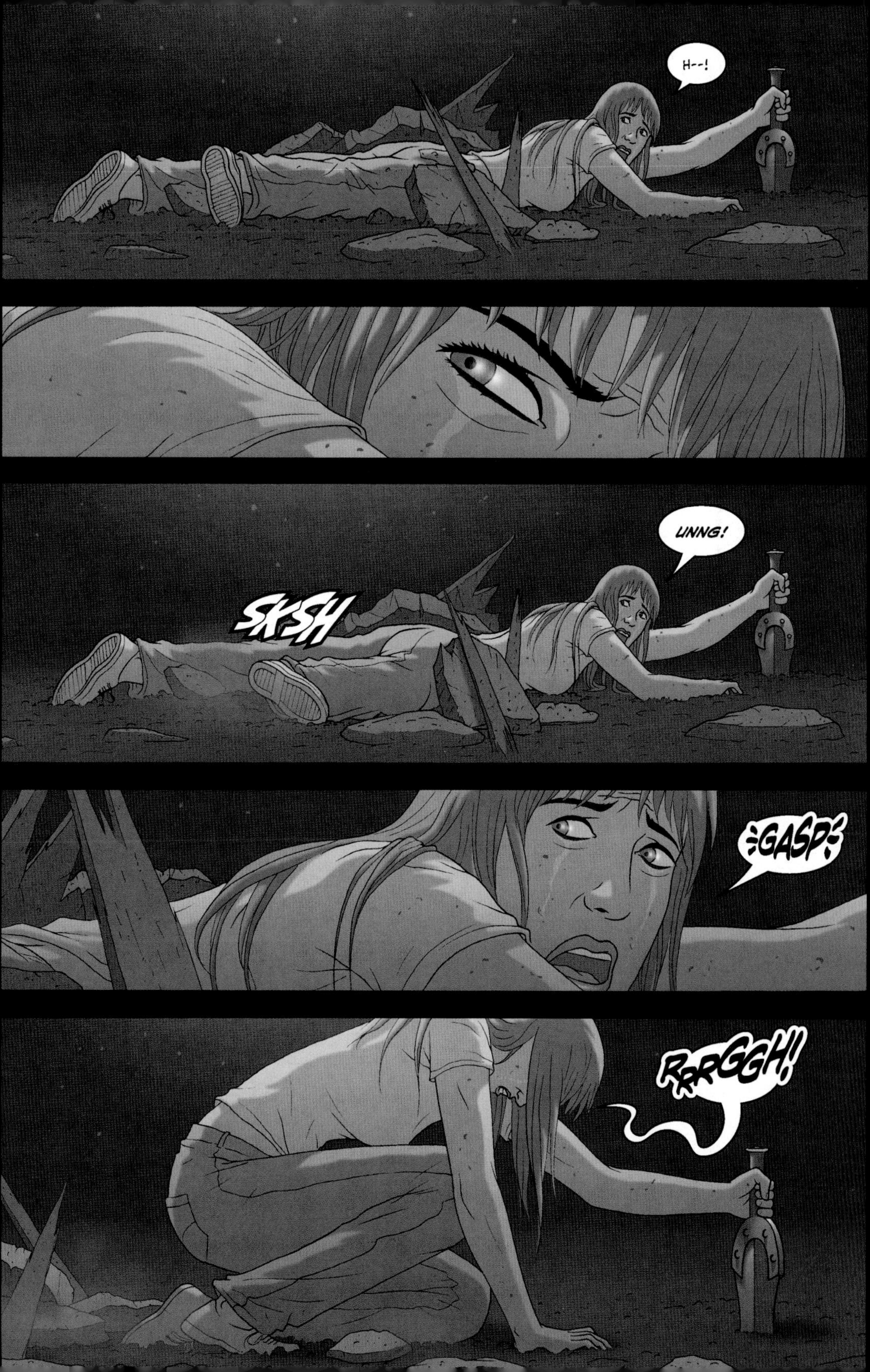

H--!
UNNG!
SKSH
GASP
RRRGGH!

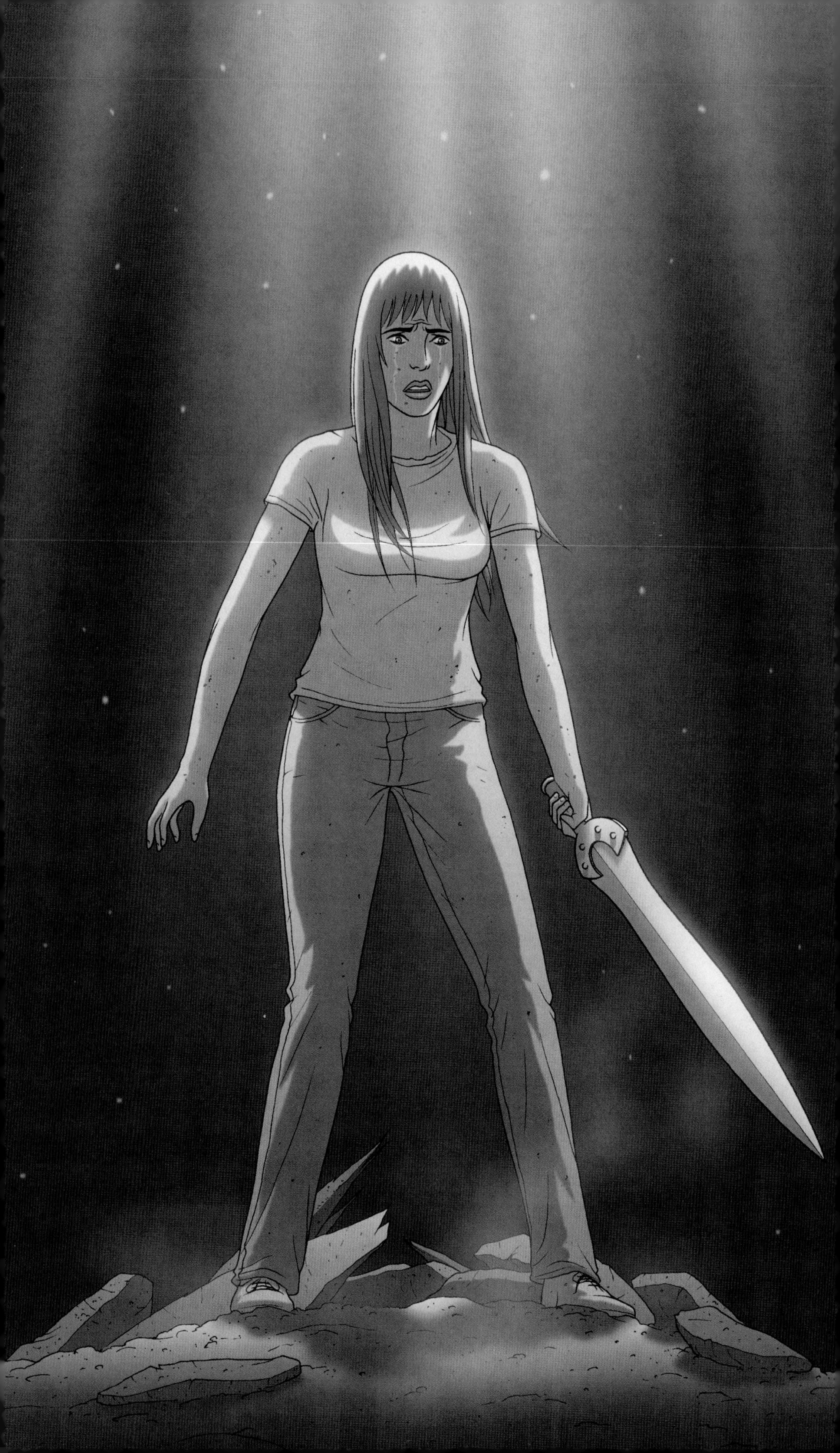

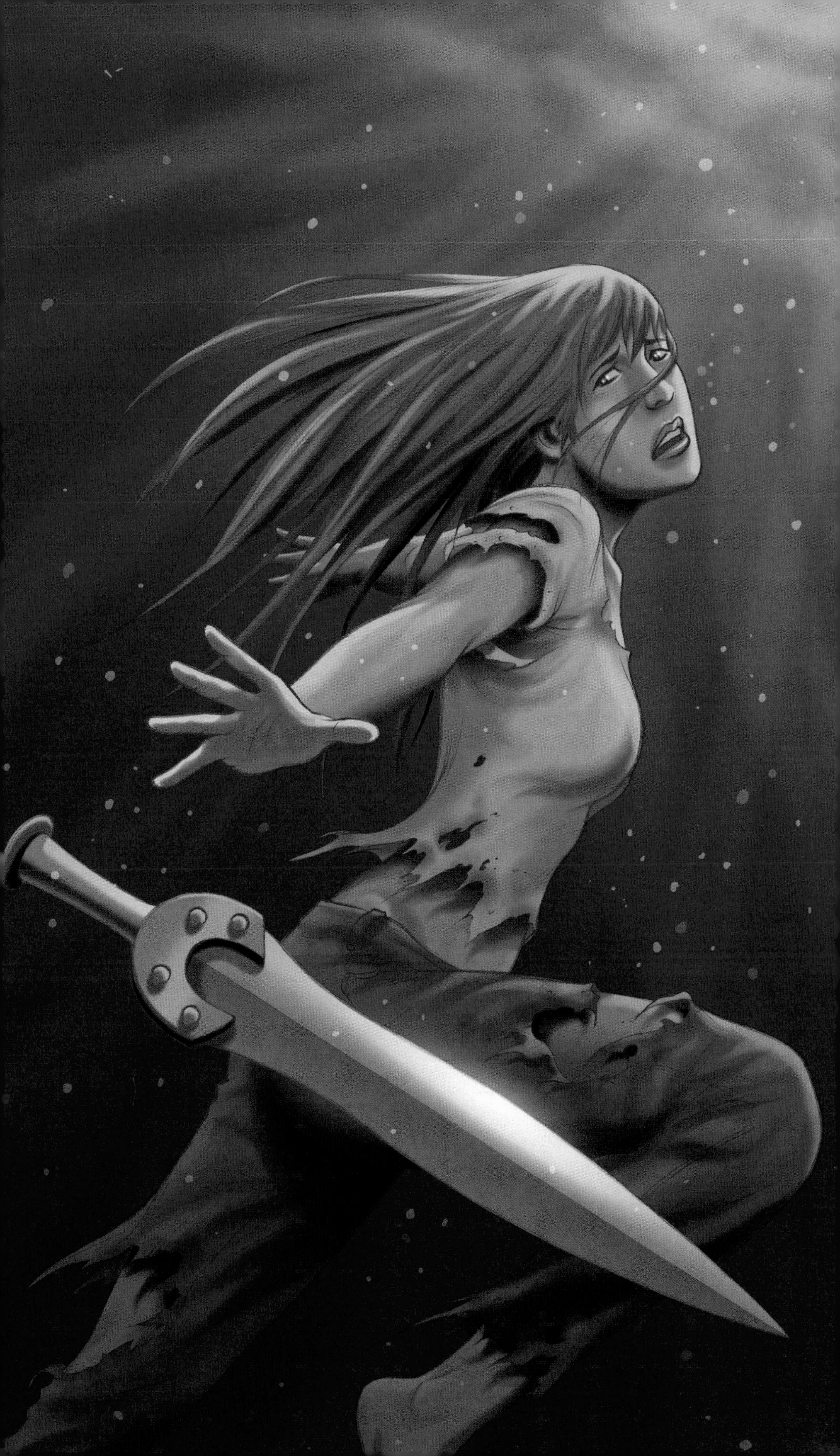

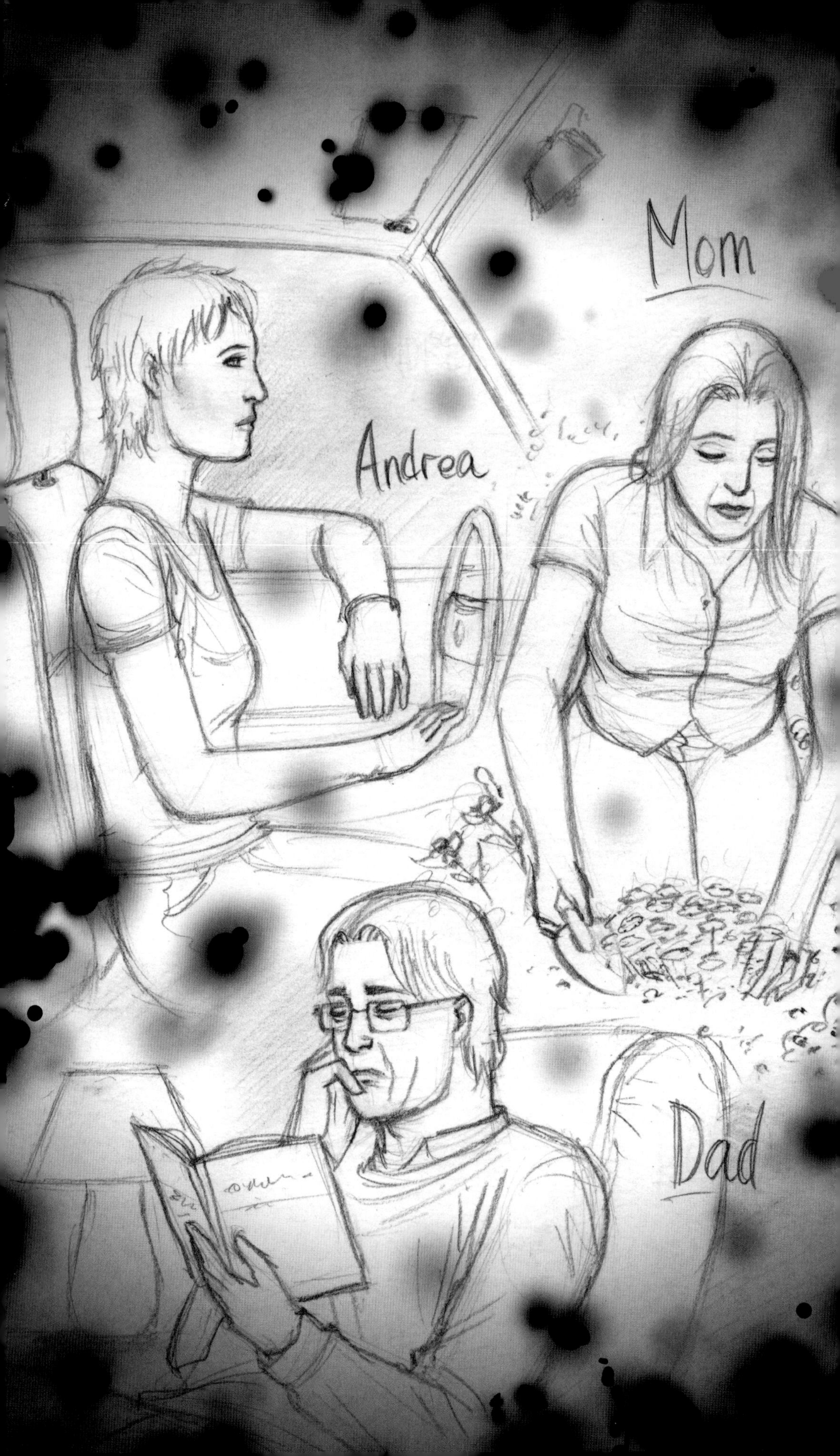
Mom
Andrea
Dad

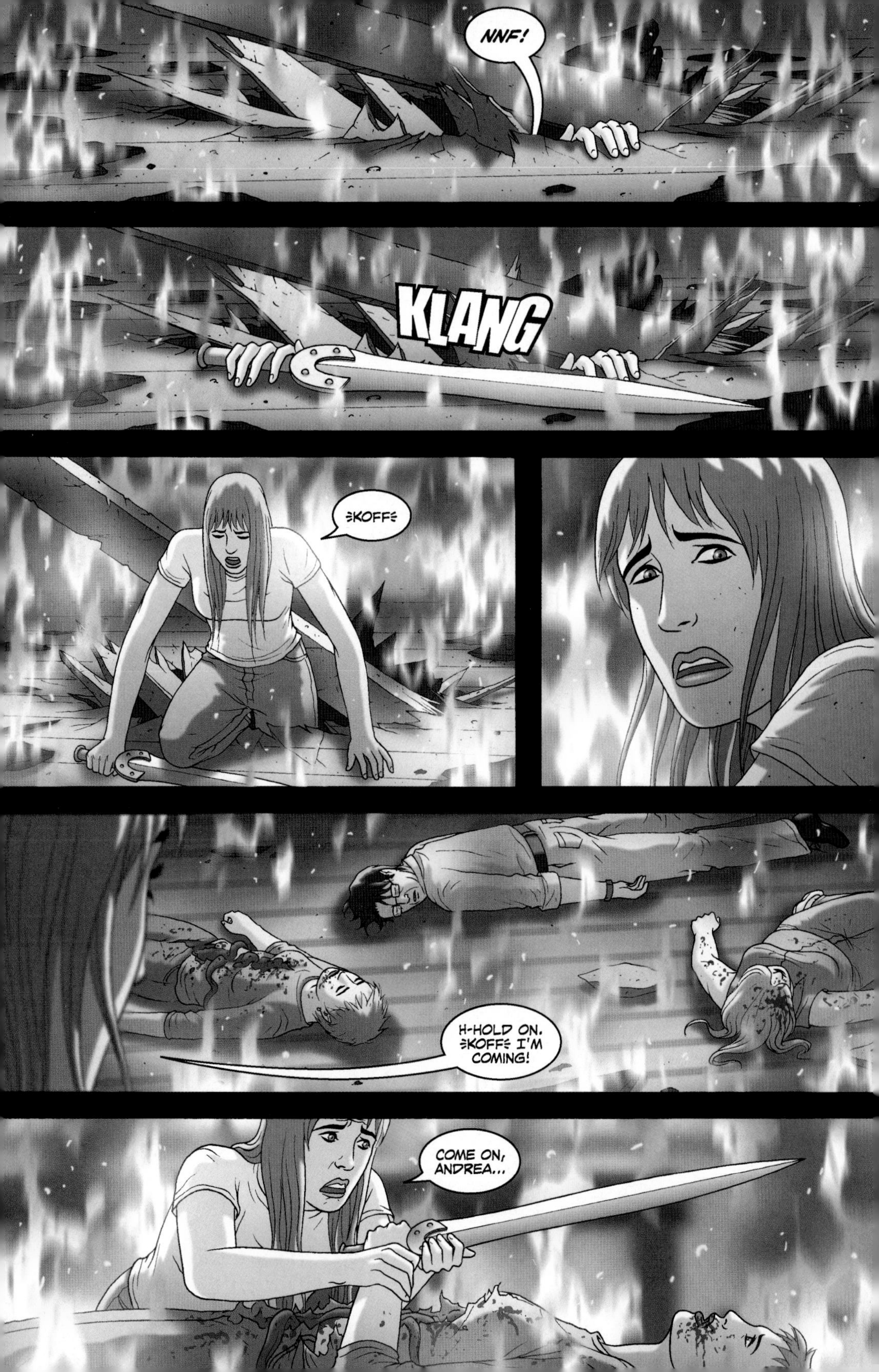
NNF!
KLANG
≶KOFF≶
H-HOLD ON. ≶KOFF≶ I'M COMING!
COME ON, ANDREA...

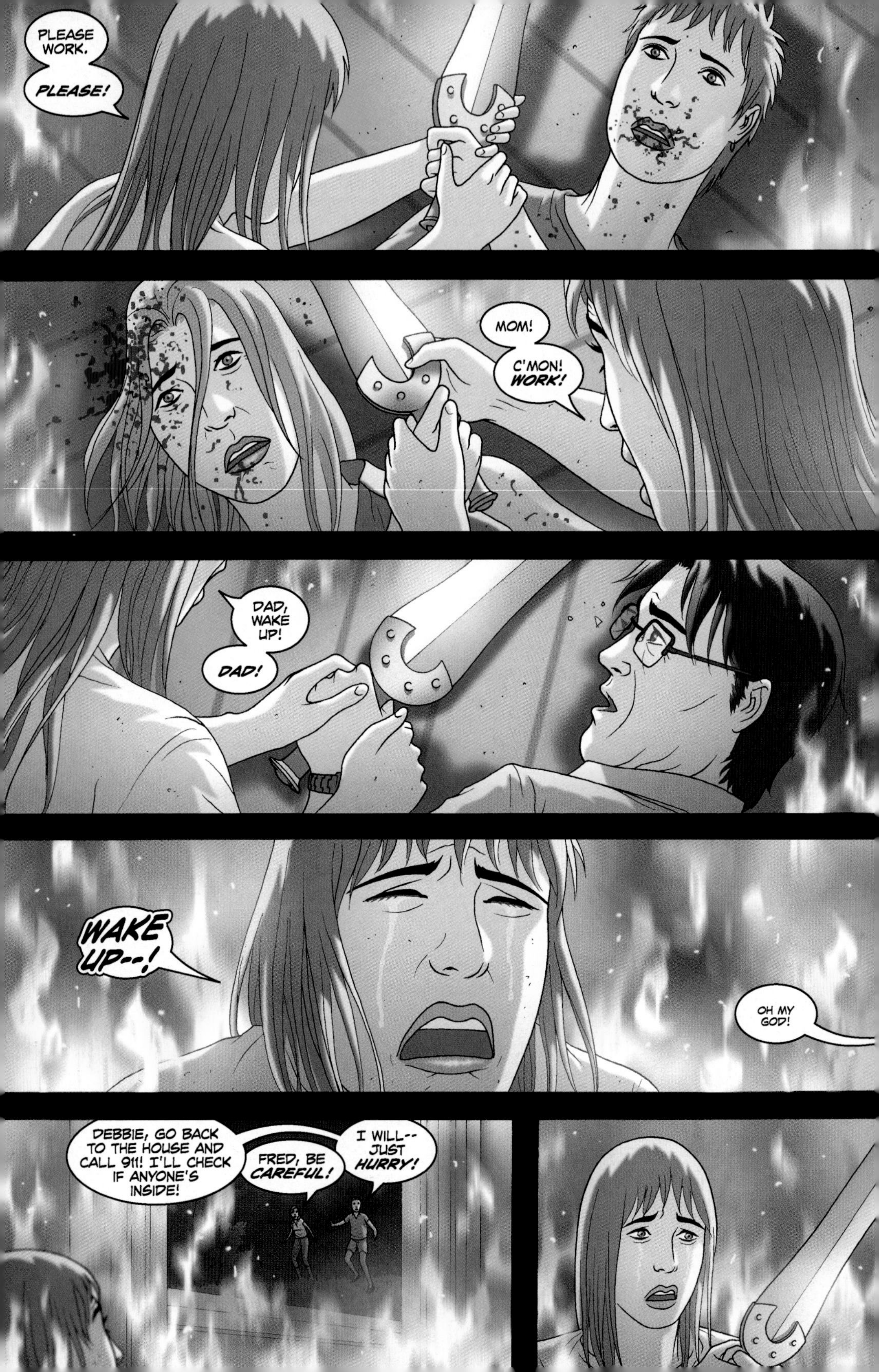
PLEASE WORK.
PLEASE!
MOM!
C'MON! WORK!
DAD, WAKE UP!
DAD!
WAKE UP--!
OH MY GOD!
DEBBIE, GO BACK TO THE HOUSE AND CALL 911! I'LL CHECK IF ANYONE'S INSIDE!
FRED, BE CAREFUL!
I WILL-- JUST HURRY!

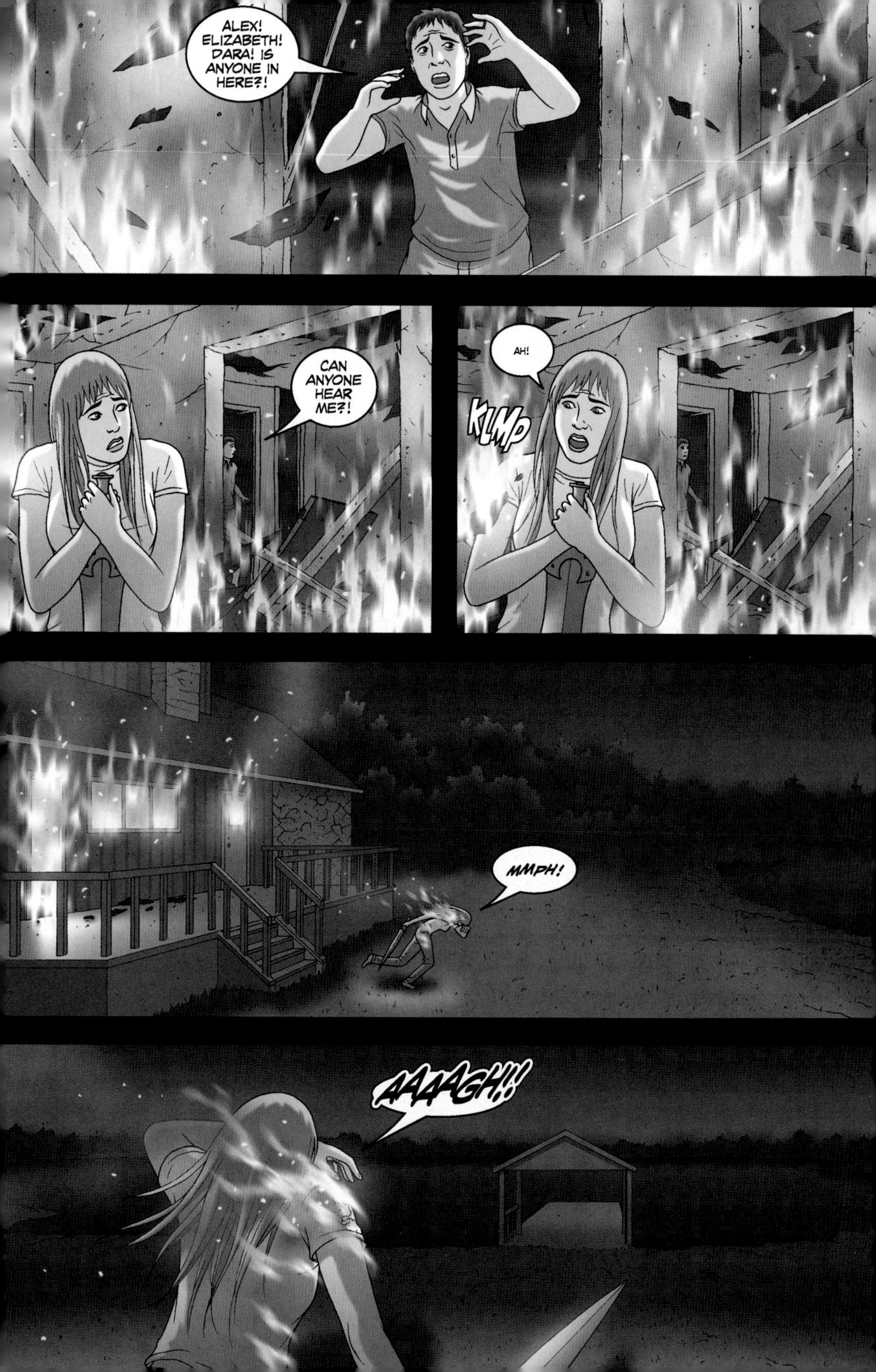
ALEX! ELIZABETH! DARA! IS ANYONE IN HERE?!
CAN ANYONE HEAR ME?!
AH!
KLMP
MMPH!
AAAAGH!!

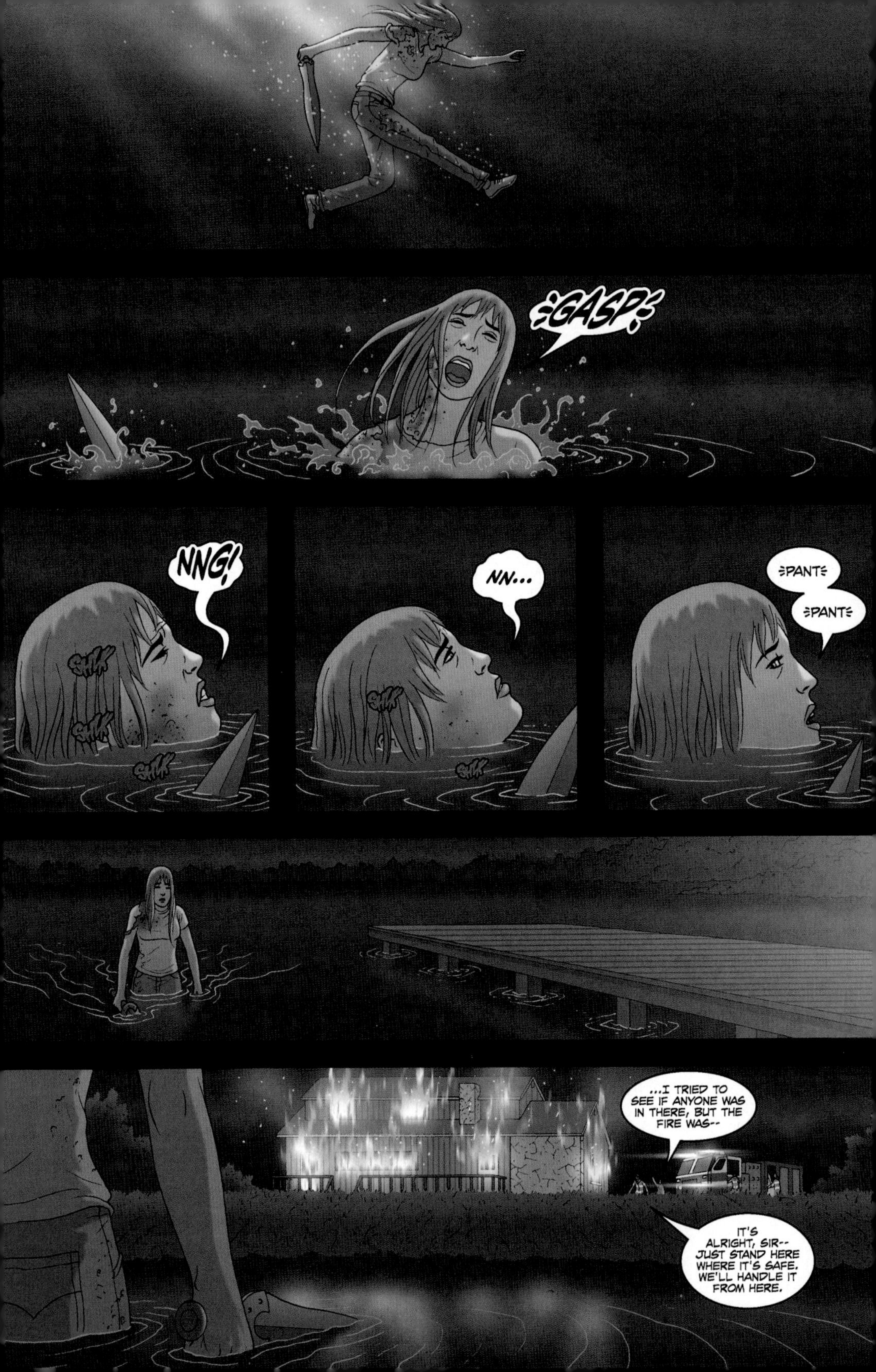
GASP
NNG!
SHNK
SHNK
SHNK
NN...
SHNK
SHNK
PANT
PANT
...I TRIED TO SEE IF ANYONE WAS IN THERE, BUT THE FIRE WAS--
IT'S ALRIGHT, SIR-- JUST STAND HERE WHERE IT'S SAFE. WE'LL HANDLE IT FROM HERE.

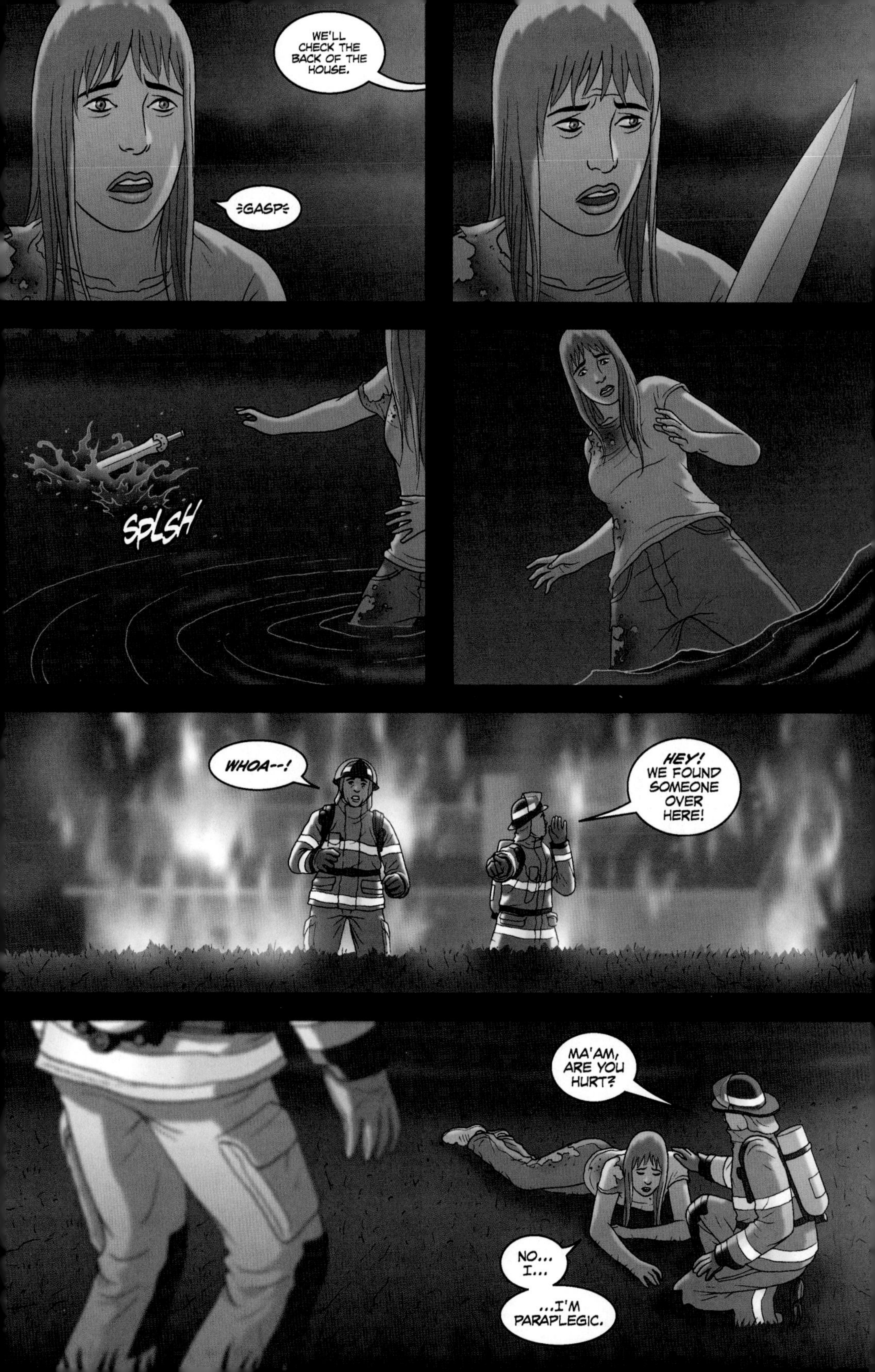
WE'LL CHECK THE BACK OF THE HOUSE.
GASP
SPLSH
WHOA--!
HEY! WE FOUND SOMEONE OVER HERE!
MA'AM, ARE YOU HURT?
NO... I...
...I'M PARAPLEGIC.

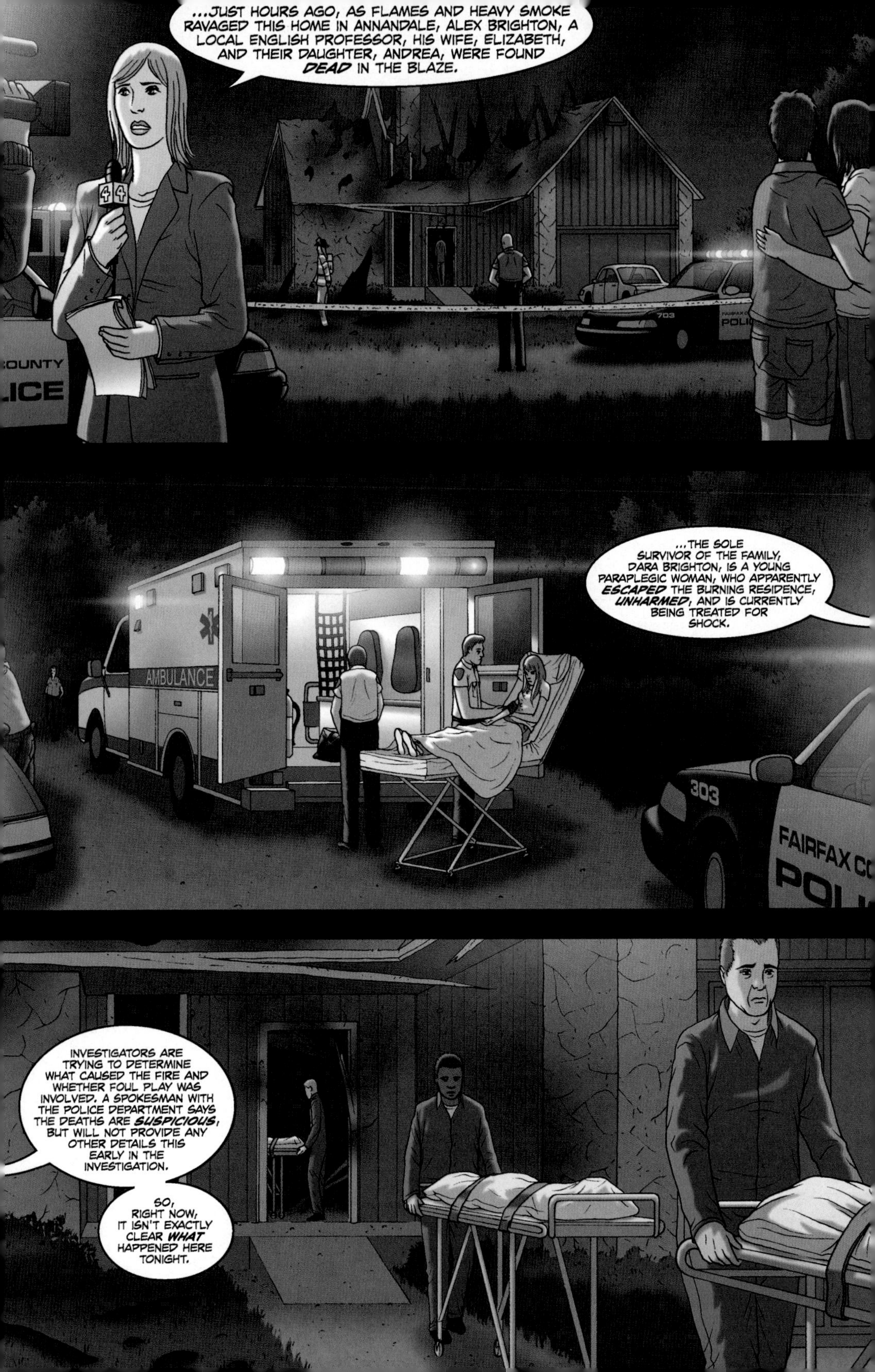
...JUST HOURS AGO, AS FLAMES AND HEAVY SMOKE RAVAGED THIS HOME IN ANNANDALE, ALEX BRIGHTON, A LOCAL ENGLISH PROFESSOR, HIS WIFE, ELIZABETH, AND THEIR DAUGHTER, ANDREA, WERE FOUND *DEAD* IN THE BLAZE.
44
COUNTY
LICE
703
POLIC
...THE SOLE SURVIVOR OF THE FAMILY, DARA BRIGHTON, IS A YOUNG PARAPLEGIC WOMAN, WHO APPARENTLY *ESCAPED* THE BURNING RESIDENCE, *UNHARMED*, AND IS CURRENTLY BEING TREATED FOR SHOCK.
AMBULANCE
303
FAIRFAX CO
POLI
INVESTIGATORS ARE TRYING TO DETERMINE WHAT CAUSED THE FIRE AND WHETHER FOUL PLAY WAS INVOLVED. A SPOKESMAN WITH THE POLICE DEPARTMENT SAYS THE DEATHS ARE *SUSPICIOUS*, BUT WILL NOT PROVIDE ANY OTHER DETAILS THIS EARLY IN THE INVESTIGATION.
SO, RIGHT NOW, IT ISN'T EXACTLY CLEAR *WHAT* HAPPENED HERE TONIGHT.

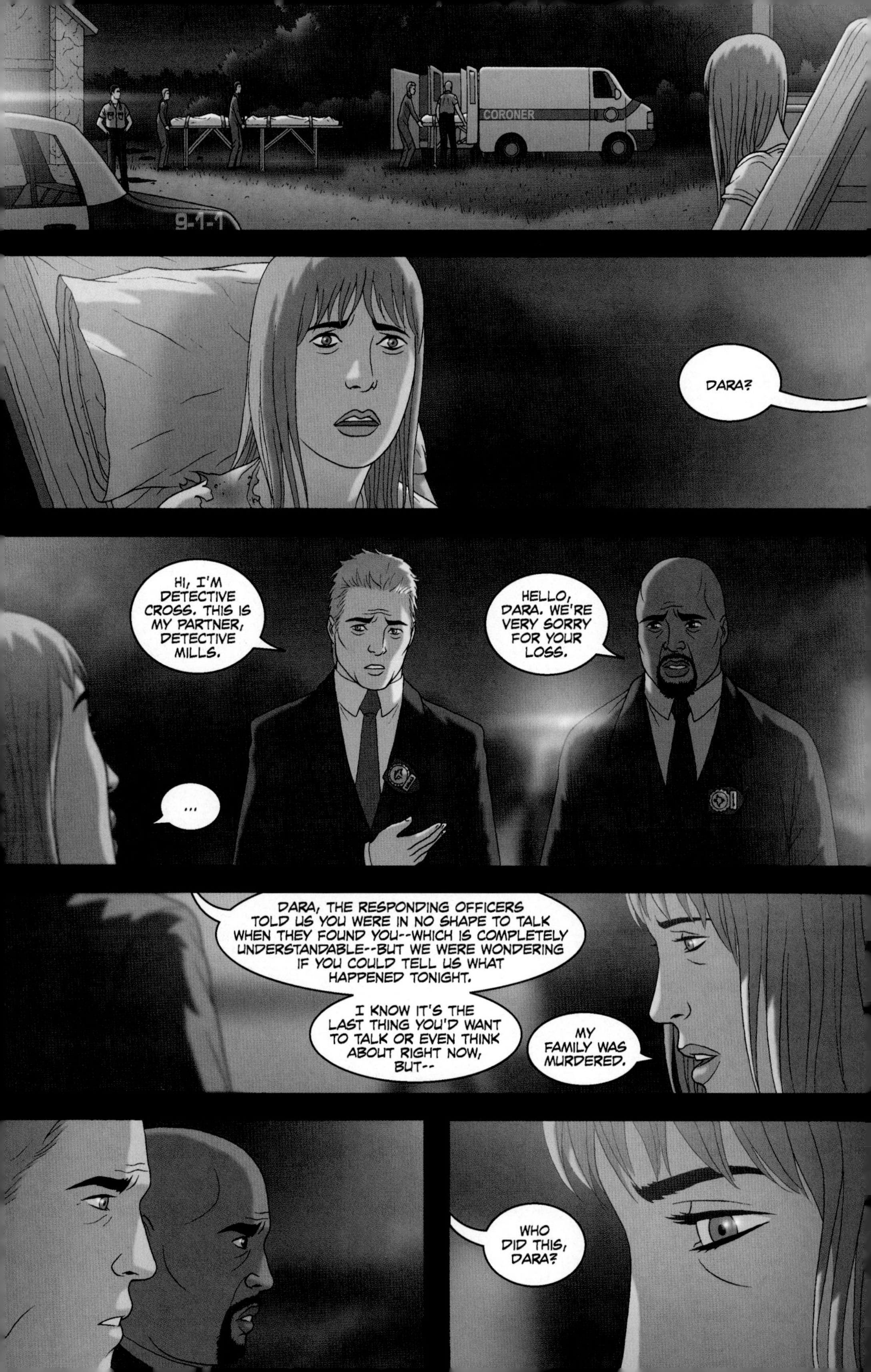
CORONER
9-1-1
DARA?
HI, I'M DETECTIVE CROSS. THIS IS MY PARTNER, DETECTIVE MILLS.
HELLO, DARA. WE'RE VERY SORRY FOR YOUR LOSS.
...
DARA, THE RESPONDING OFFICERS TOLD US YOU WERE IN NO SHAPE TO TALK WHEN THEY FOUND YOU--WHICH IS COMPLETELY UNDERSTANDABLE--BUT WE WERE WONDERING IF YOU COULD TELL US WHAT HAPPENED TONIGHT.
I KNOW IT'S THE LAST THING YOU'D WANT TO TALK OR EVEN THINK ABOUT RIGHT NOW, BUT--
MY FAMILY WAS MURDERED.
WHO DID THIS, DARA?

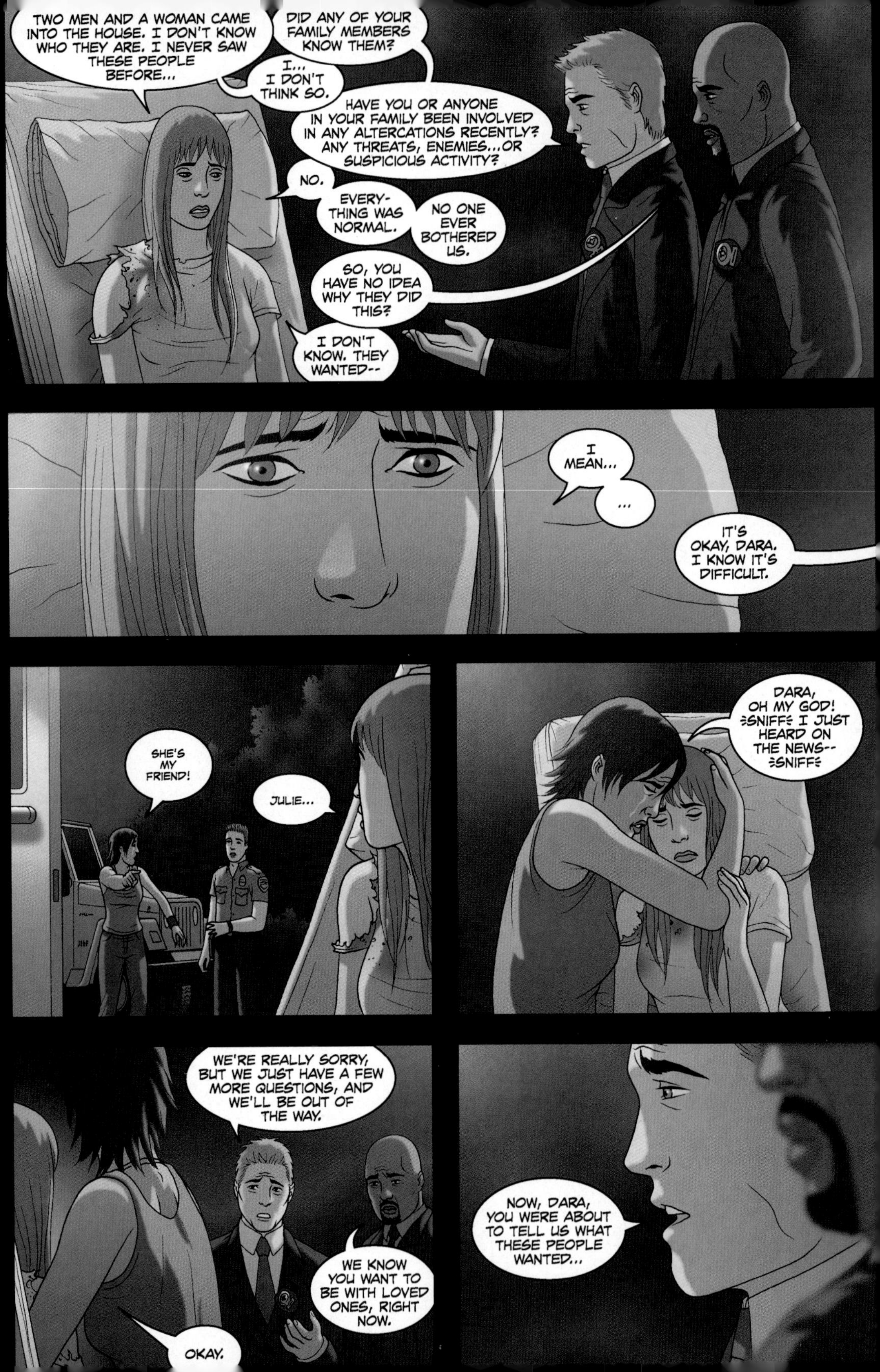
TWO MEN AND A WOMAN CAME INTO THE HOUSE. I DON'T KNOW WHO THEY ARE. I NEVER SAW THESE PEOPLE BEFORE...
DID ANY OF YOUR FAMILY MEMBERS KNOW THEM?
I... I DON'T THINK SO.
HAVE YOU OR ANYONE IN YOUR FAMILY BEEN INVOLVED IN ANY ALTERCATIONS RECENTLY? ANY THREATS, ENEMIES...OR SUSPICIOUS ACTIVITY?
NO.
EVERY-THING WAS NORMAL.
NO ONE EVER BOTHERED US.
SO, YOU HAVE NO IDEA WHY THEY DID THIS?
I DON'T KNOW. THEY WANTED--
I MEAN...
...
IT'S OKAY, DARA. I KNOW IT'S DIFFICULT.
SHE'S MY FRIEND!
JULIE...
DARA, OH MY GOD! =SNIFF= I JUST HEARD ON THE NEWS-- =SNIFF=
WE'RE REALLY SORRY, BUT WE JUST HAVE A FEW MORE QUESTIONS, AND WE'LL BE OUT OF THE WAY.
WE KNOW YOU WANT TO BE WITH LOVED ONES, RIGHT NOW.
OKAY.
NOW, DARA, YOU WERE ABOUT TO TELL US WHAT THESE PEOPLE WANTED...

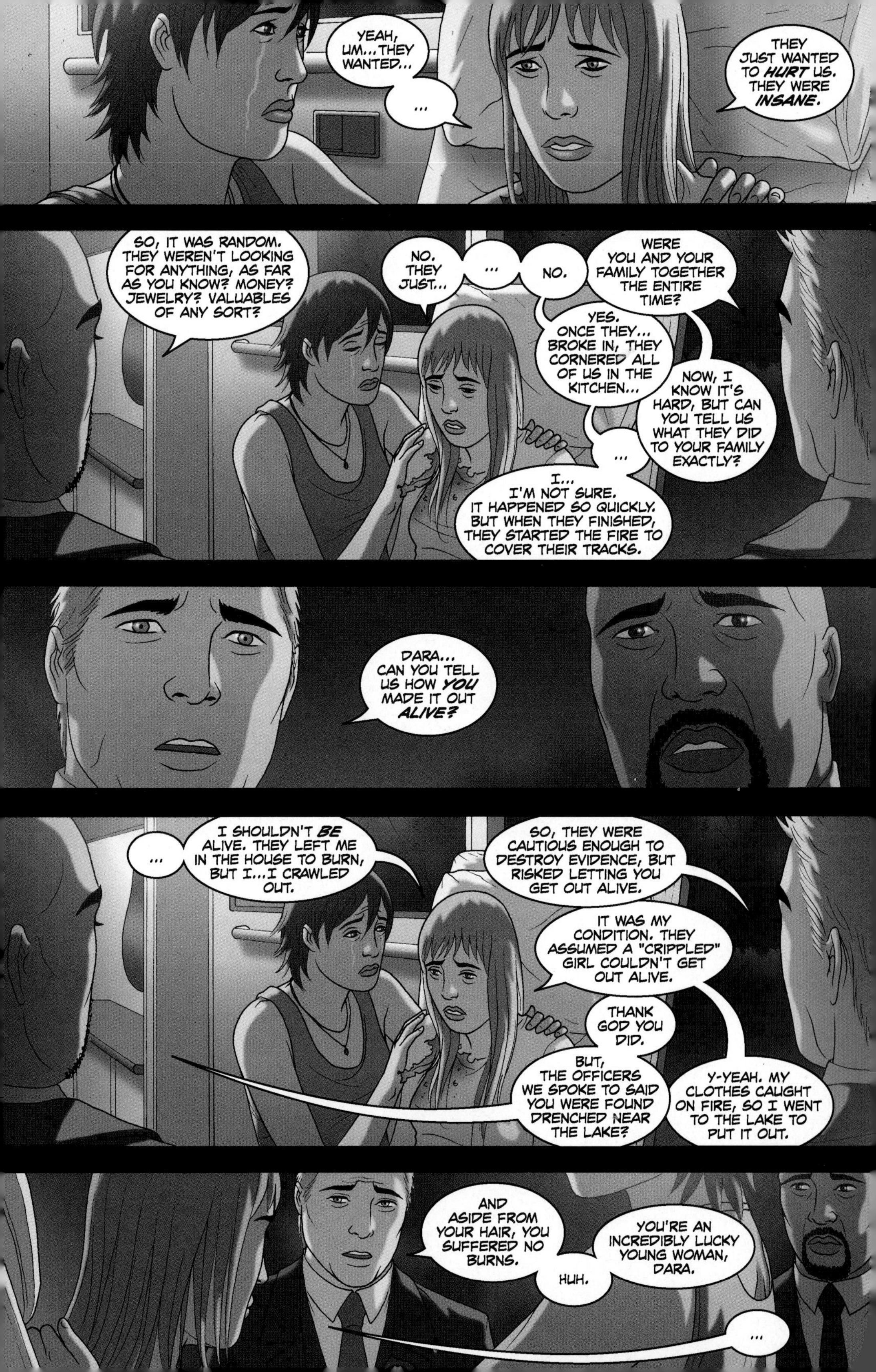
YEAH, UM...THEY WANTED...
...
THEY JUST WANTED TO *HURT* US. THEY WERE *INSANE*.
SO, IT WAS RANDOM. THEY WEREN'T LOOKING FOR ANYTHING, AS FAR AS YOU KNOW? MONEY? JEWELRY? VALUABLES OF ANY SORT?
NO. THEY JUST...
...
NO.
WERE YOU AND YOUR FAMILY TOGETHER THE ENTIRE TIME?
YES. ONCE THEY... BROKE IN, THEY CORNERED ALL OF US IN THE KITCHEN...
NOW, I KNOW IT'S HARD, BUT CAN YOU TELL US WHAT THEY DID TO YOUR FAMILY EXACTLY?
...
I... I'M NOT SURE. IT HAPPENED SO QUICKLY. BUT WHEN THEY FINISHED, THEY STARTED THE FIRE TO COVER THEIR TRACKS.
DARA... CAN YOU TELL US HOW *YOU* MADE IT OUT *ALIVE?*
...
I SHOULDN'T *BE* ALIVE. THEY LEFT ME IN THE HOUSE TO BURN, BUT I...I CRAWLED OUT.
SO, THEY WERE CAUTIOUS ENOUGH TO DESTROY EVIDENCE, BUT RISKED LETTING YOU GET OUT ALIVE.
IT WAS MY CONDITION. THEY ASSUMED A "CRIPPLED" GIRL COULDN'T GET OUT ALIVE.
THANK GOD YOU DID.
BUT, THE OFFICERS WE SPOKE TO SAID YOU WERE FOUND DRENCHED NEAR THE LAKE?
Y-YEAH. MY CLOTHES CAUGHT ON FIRE, SO I WENT TO THE LAKE TO PUT IT OUT.
AND ASIDE FROM YOUR HAIR, YOU SUFFERED NO BURNS.
HUH.
YOU'RE AN INCREDIBLY LUCKY YOUNG WOMAN, DARA.
...

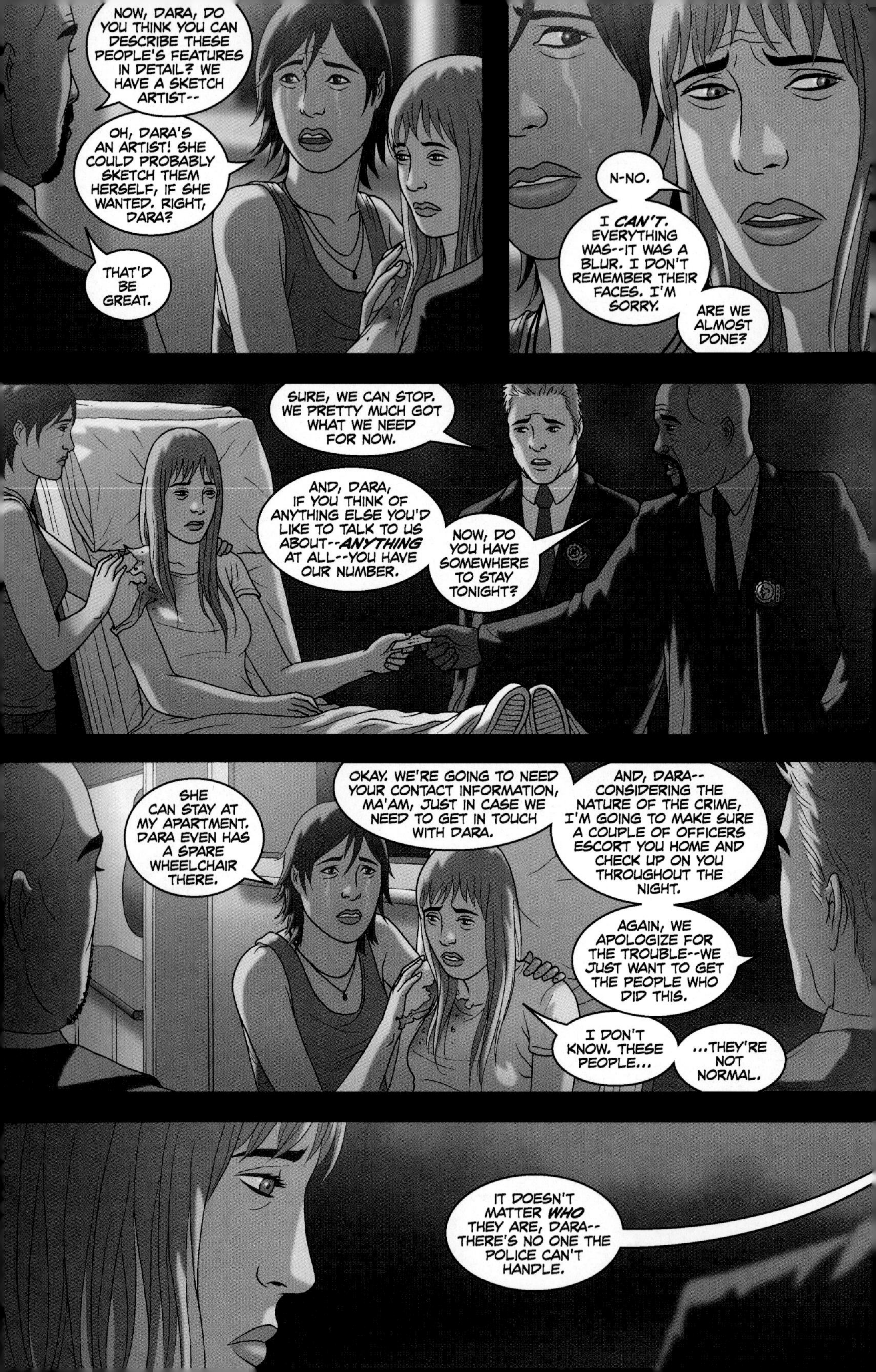
NOW, DARA, DO YOU THINK YOU CAN DESCRIBE THESE PEOPLE'S FEATURES IN DETAIL? WE HAVE A SKETCH ARTIST--
OH, DARA'S AN ARTIST! SHE COULD PROBABLY SKETCH THEM HERSELF, IF SHE WANTED. RIGHT, DARA?
THAT'D BE GREAT.
N-NO.
I *CAN'T*. EVERYTHING WAS--IT WAS A BLUR. I DON'T REMEMBER THEIR FACES. I'M SORRY.
ARE WE ALMOST DONE?
SURE, WE CAN STOP. WE PRETTY MUCH GOT WHAT WE NEED FOR NOW.
AND, DARA, IF YOU THINK OF ANYTHING ELSE YOU'D LIKE TO TALK TO US ABOUT--*ANYTHING* AT ALL--YOU HAVE OUR NUMBER.
NOW, DO YOU HAVE SOMEWHERE TO STAY TONIGHT?
SHE CAN STAY AT MY APARTMENT. DARA EVEN HAS A SPARE WHEELCHAIR THERE.
OKAY. WE'RE GOING TO NEED YOUR CONTACT INFORMATION, MA'AM, JUST IN CASE WE NEED TO GET IN TOUCH WITH DARA.
AND, DARA-- CONSIDERING THE NATURE OF THE CRIME, I'M GOING TO MAKE SURE A COUPLE OF OFFICERS ESCORT YOU HOME AND CHECK UP ON YOU THROUGHOUT THE NIGHT.
AGAIN, WE APOLOGIZE FOR THE TROUBLE--WE JUST WANT TO GET THE PEOPLE WHO DID THIS.
I DON'T KNOW. THESE PEOPLE...
...THEY'RE NOT NORMAL.
IT DOESN'T MATTER *WHO* THEY ARE, DARA-- THERE'S NO ONE THE POLICE CAN'T HANDLE.

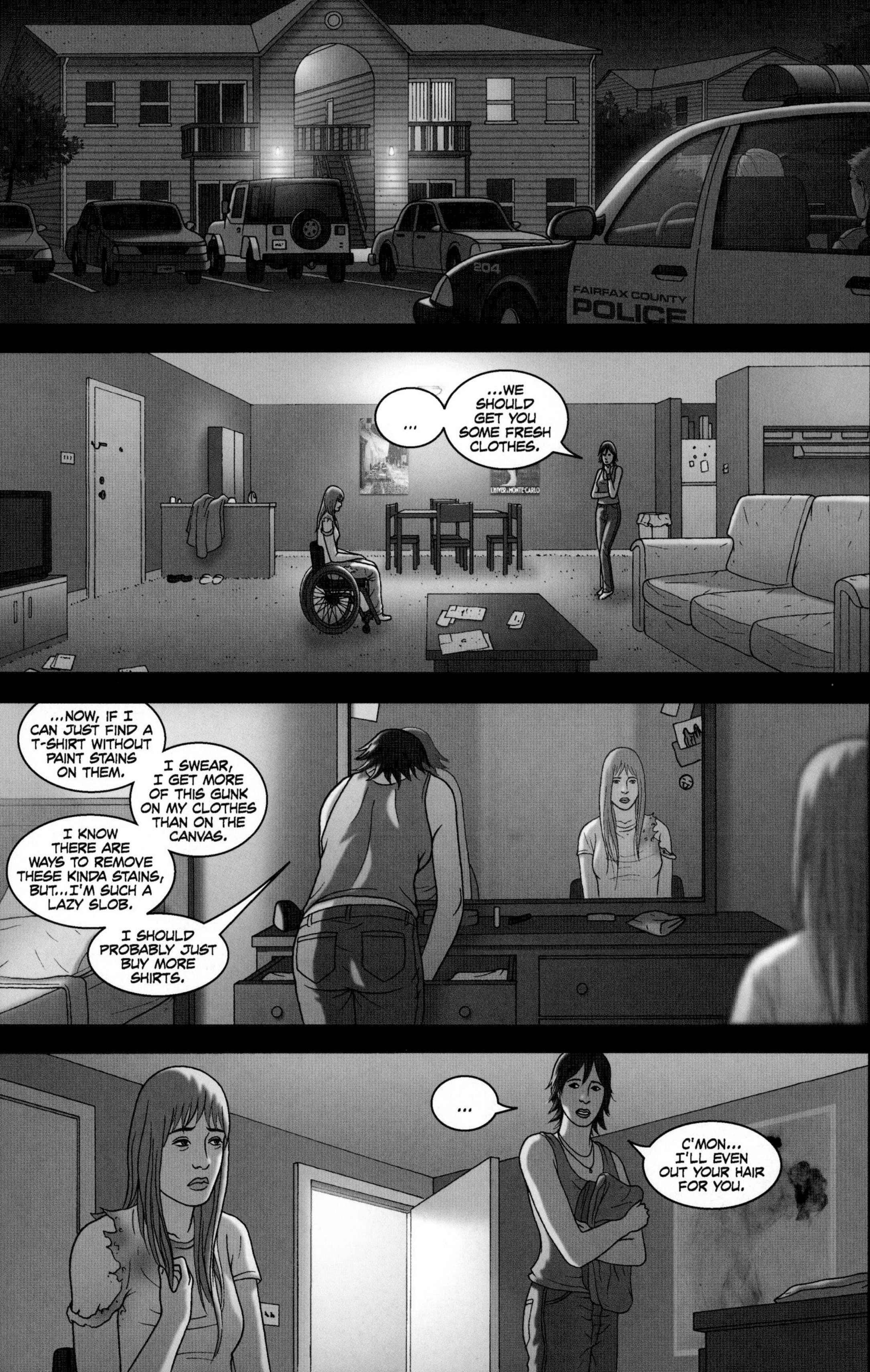
FAIRFAX COUNTY
POLICE
204
...
...WE SHOULD GET YOU SOME FRESH CLOTHES.
...NOW, IF I CAN JUST FIND A T-SHIRT WITHOUT PAINT STAINS ON THEM.
I SWEAR, I GET MORE OF THIS GUNK ON MY CLOTHES THAN ON THE CANVAS.
I KNOW THERE ARE WAYS TO REMOVE THESE KINDA STAINS, BUT...I'M SUCH A LAZY SLOB.
I SHOULD PROBABLY JUST BUY MORE SHIRTS.
...
C'MON... I'LL EVEN OUT YOUR HAIR FOR YOU.

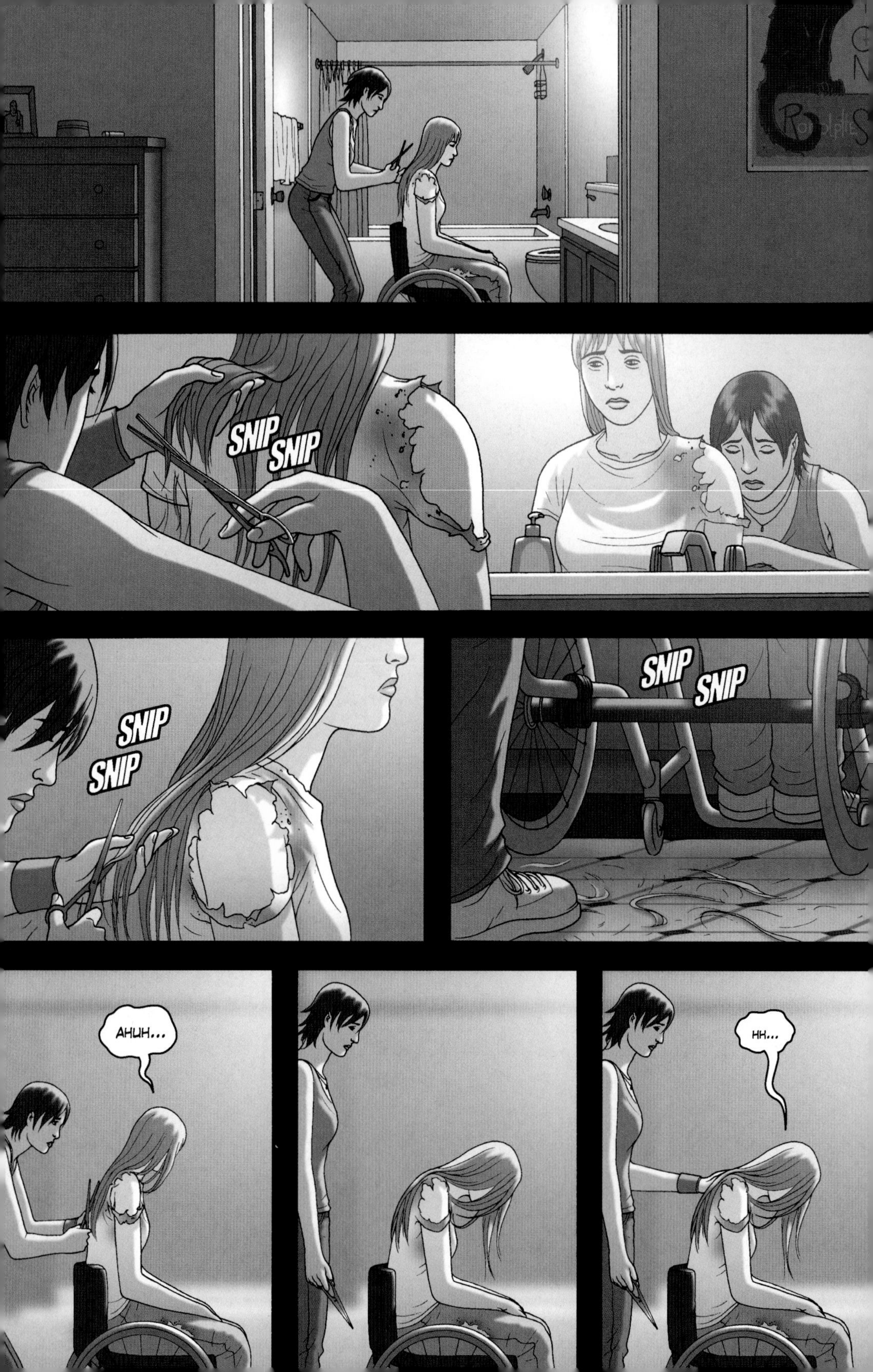
SNIP
SNIP
SNIP
SNIP
SNIP
SNIP
AHUH...
HH...

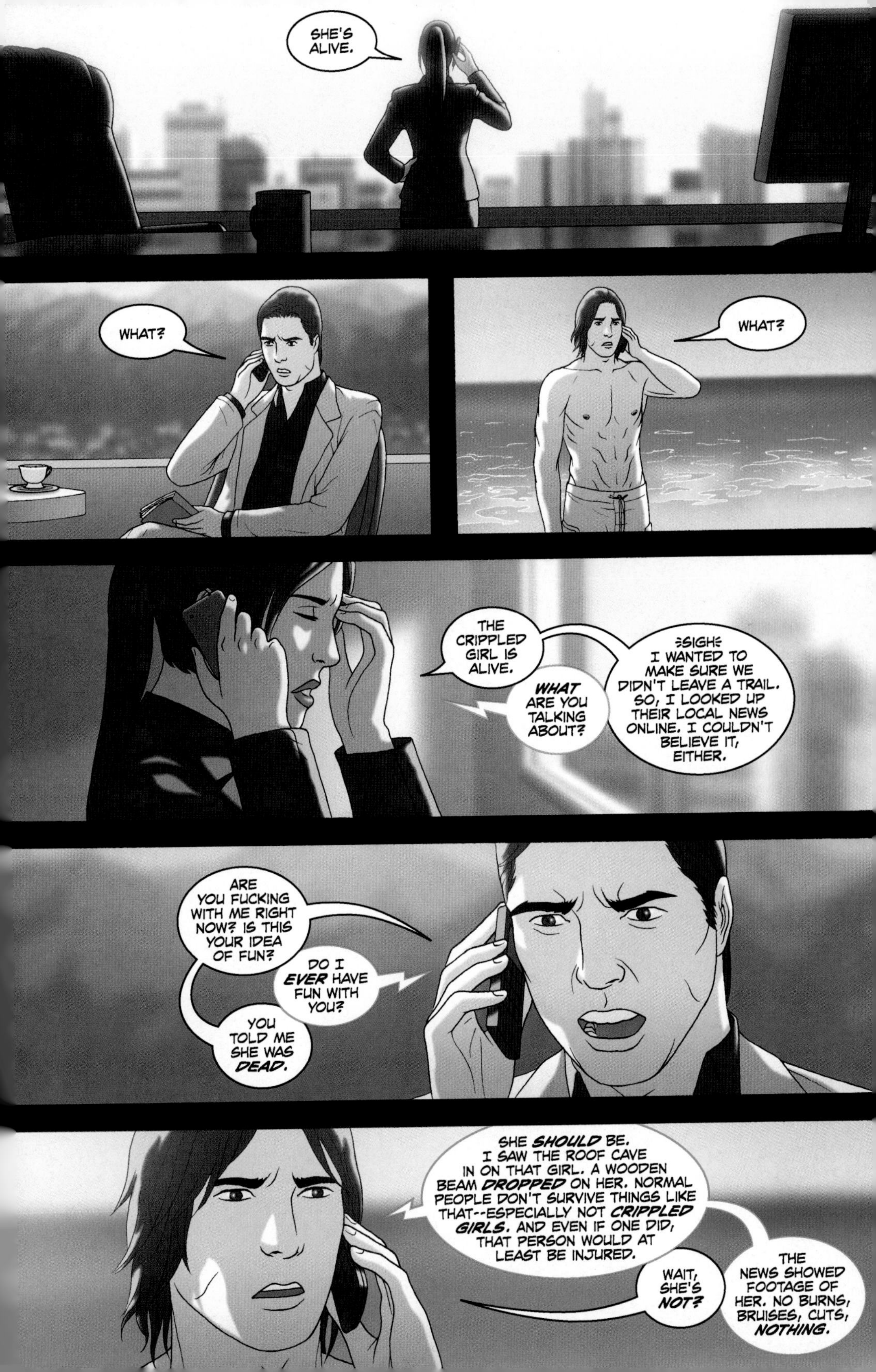
SHE'S ALIVE.
WHAT?
WHAT?
THE CRIPPLED GIRL IS ALIVE.
WHAT ARE YOU TALKING ABOUT?
SIGH
I WANTED TO MAKE SURE WE DIDN'T LEAVE A TRAIL. SO, I LOOKED UP THEIR LOCAL NEWS ONLINE. I COULDN'T BELIEVE IT, EITHER.
ARE YOU FUCKING WITH ME RIGHT NOW? IS THIS YOUR IDEA OF FUN?
DO I EVER HAVE FUN WITH YOU?
YOU TOLD ME SHE WAS DEAD.
SHE SHOULD BE. I SAW THE ROOF CAVE IN ON THAT GIRL. A WOODEN BEAM DROPPED ON HER. NORMAL PEOPLE DON'T SURVIVE THINGS LIKE THAT--ESPECIALLY NOT CRIPPLED GIRLS. AND EVEN IF ONE DID, THAT PERSON WOULD AT LEAST BE INJURED.
WAIT, SHE'S NOT?
THE NEWS SHOWED FOOTAGE OF HER. NO BURNS, BRUISES, CUTS, NOTHING.

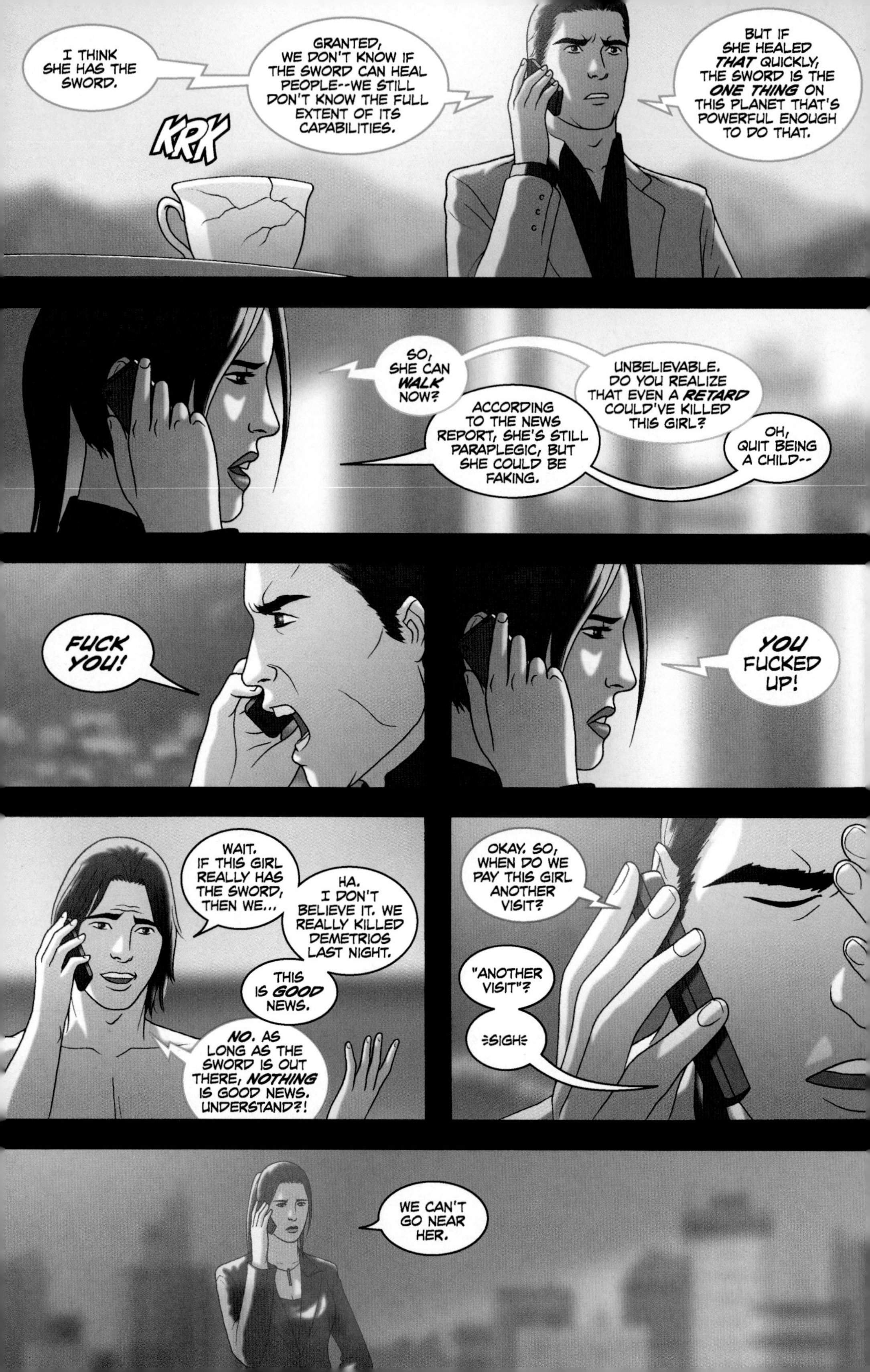
I THINK SHE HAS THE SWORD.
GRANTED, WE DON'T KNOW IF THE SWORD CAN HEAL PEOPLE--WE STILL DON'T KNOW THE FULL EXTENT OF ITS CAPABILITIES.
BUT IF SHE HEALED *THAT* QUICKLY, THE SWORD IS THE *ONE THING* ON THIS PLANET THAT'S POWERFUL ENOUGH TO DO THAT.
KRK
SO, SHE CAN *WALK* NOW?
UNBELIEVABLE. DO YOU REALIZE THAT EVEN A *RETARD* COULD'VE KILLED THIS GIRL?
ACCORDING TO THE NEWS REPORT, SHE'S STILL PARAPLEGIC, BUT SHE COULD BE FAKING.
OH, QUIT BEING A CHILD--
FUCK YOU!
YOU FUCKED UP!
WAIT. IF THIS GIRL REALLY HAS THE SWORD, THEN WE...
HA. I DON'T BELIEVE IT. WE REALLY KILLED DEMETRIOS LAST NIGHT.
THIS IS *GOOD* NEWS.
NO. AS LONG AS THE SWORD IS OUT THERE, *NOTHING* IS GOOD NEWS. UNDERSTAND?!
OKAY. SO, WHEN DO WE PAY THIS GIRL ANOTHER VISIT?
"ANOTHER VISIT"?
SIGH
WE CAN'T GO NEAR HER.

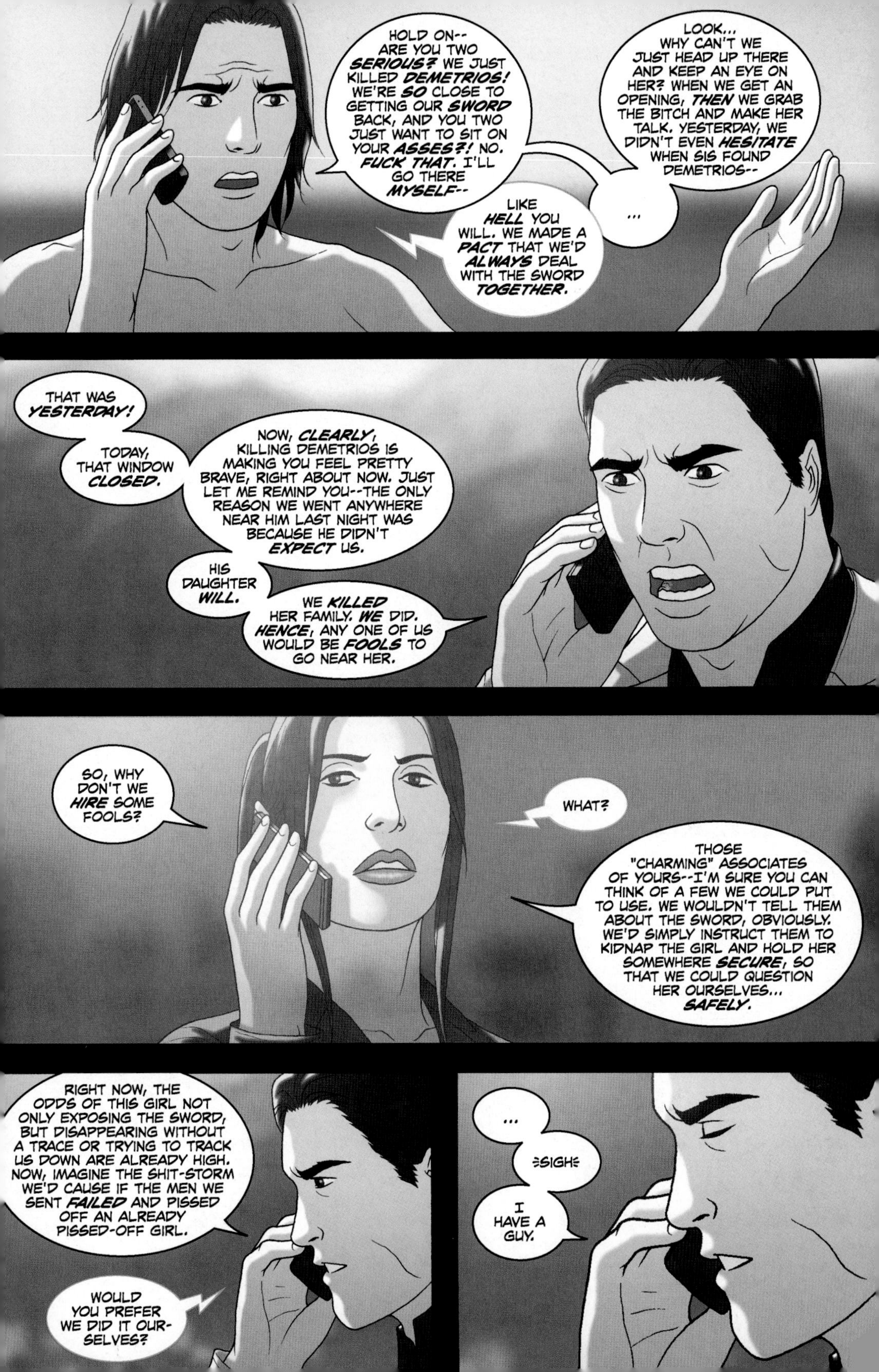
HOLD ON-- ARE YOU TWO SERIOUS? WE JUST KILLED DEMETRIOS! WE'RE SO CLOSE TO GETTING OUR SWORD BACK, AND YOU TWO JUST WANT TO SIT ON YOUR ASSES?! NO. FUCK THAT. I'LL GO THERE MYSELF--
LIKE HELL YOU WILL. WE MADE A PACT THAT WE'D ALWAYS DEAL WITH THE SWORD TOGETHER.
LOOK... WHY CAN'T WE JUST HEAD UP THERE AND KEEP AN EYE ON HER? WHEN WE GET AN OPENING, THEN WE GRAB THE BITCH AND MAKE HER TALK. YESTERDAY, WE DIDN'T EVEN HESITATE WHEN SIS FOUND DEMETRIOS--
...
THAT WAS YESTERDAY!
TODAY, THAT WINDOW CLOSED.
NOW, CLEARLY, KILLING DEMETRIOS IS MAKING YOU FEEL PRETTY BRAVE, RIGHT ABOUT NOW. JUST LET ME REMIND YOU--THE ONLY REASON WE WENT ANYWHERE NEAR HIM LAST NIGHT WAS BECAUSE HE DIDN'T EXPECT US.
HIS DAUGHTER WILL.
WE KILLED HER FAMILY. WE DID. HENCE, ANY ONE OF US WOULD BE FOOLS TO GO NEAR HER.
SO, WHY DON'T WE HIRE SOME FOOLS?
WHAT?
THOSE "CHARMING" ASSOCIATES OF YOURS--I'M SURE YOU CAN THINK OF A FEW WE COULD PUT TO USE. WE WOULDN'T TELL THEM ABOUT THE SWORD, OBVIOUSLY. WE'D SIMPLY INSTRUCT THEM TO KIDNAP THE GIRL AND HOLD HER SOMEWHERE SECURE, SO THAT WE COULD QUESTION HER OURSELVES... SAFELY.
RIGHT NOW, THE ODDS OF THIS GIRL NOT ONLY EXPOSING THE SWORD, BUT DISAPPEARING WITHOUT A TRACE OR TRYING TO TRACK US DOWN ARE ALREADY HIGH. NOW, IMAGINE THE SHIT-STORM WE'D CAUSE IF THE MEN WE SENT FAILED AND PISSED OFF AN ALREADY PISSED-OFF GIRL.
WOULD YOU PREFER WE DID IT OUR-SELVES?
...
=SIGH=
I HAVE A GUY.

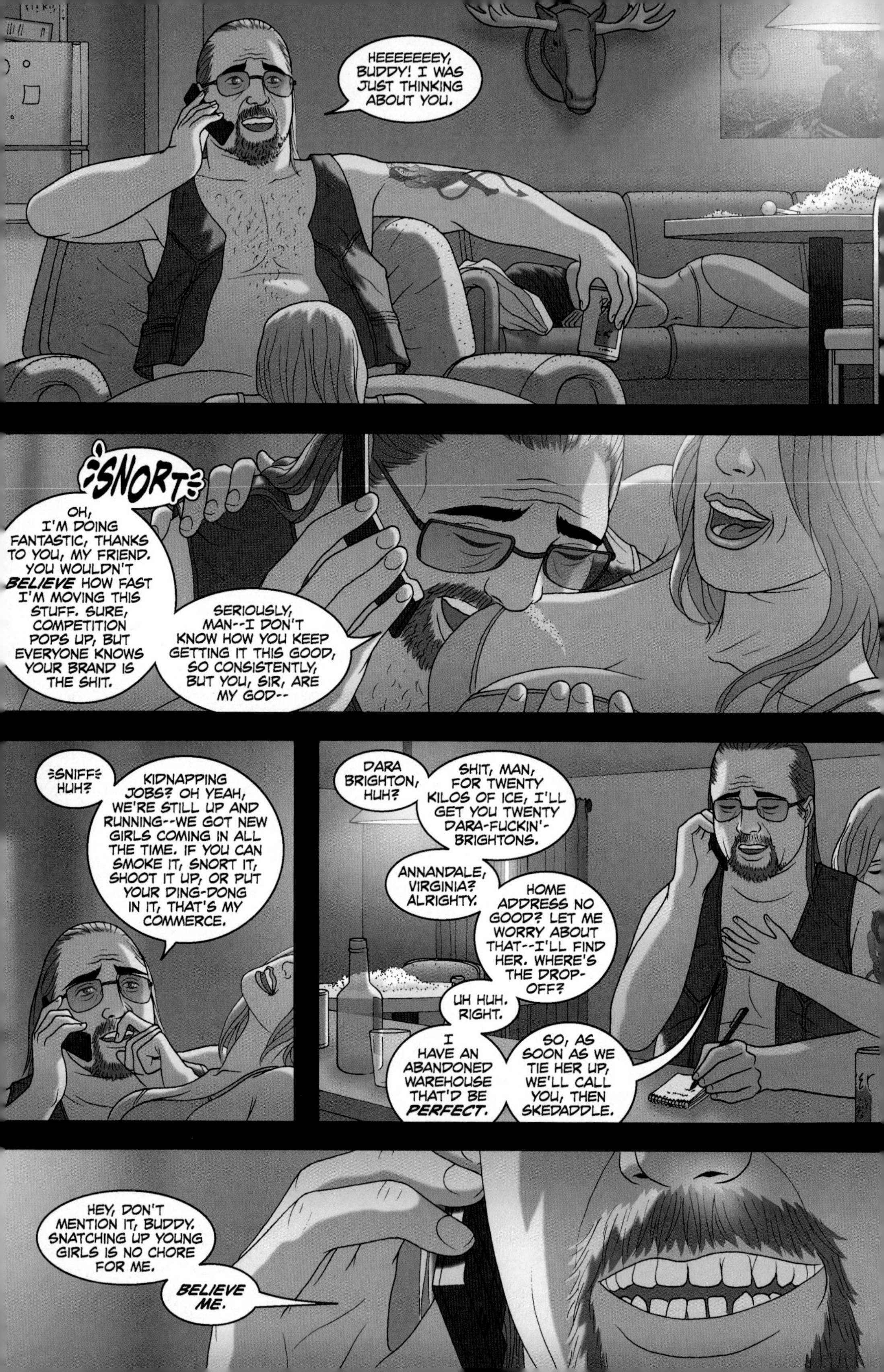
HEEEEEEEY, BUDDY! I WAS JUST THINKING ABOUT YOU.
SNORT
OH, I'M DOING FANTASTIC, THANKS TO YOU, MY FRIEND. YOU WOULDN'T BELIEVE HOW FAST I'M MOVING THIS STUFF. SURE, COMPETITION POPS UP, BUT EVERYONE KNOWS YOUR BRAND IS THE SHIT.
SERIOUSLY, MAN--I DON'T KNOW HOW YOU KEEP GETTING IT THIS GOOD, SO CONSISTENTLY, BUT YOU, SIR, ARE MY GOD--
SNIFF HUH?
KIDNAPPING JOBS? OH YEAH, WE'RE STILL UP AND RUNNING--WE GOT NEW GIRLS COMING IN ALL THE TIME. IF YOU CAN SMOKE IT, SNORT IT, SHOOT IT UP, OR PUT YOUR DING-DONG IN IT, THAT'S MY COMMERCE.
DARA BRIGHTON, HUH?
SHIT, MAN, FOR TWENTY KILOS OF ICE, I'LL GET YOU TWENTY DARA-FUCKIN'-BRIGHTONS.
ANNANDALE, VIRGINIA? ALRIGHTY.
HOME ADDRESS NO GOOD? LET ME WORRY ABOUT THAT--I'LL FIND HER. WHERE'S THE DROP-OFF?
UH HUH. RIGHT.
I HAVE AN ABANDONED WAREHOUSE THAT'D BE PERFECT.
SO, AS SOON AS WE TIE HER UP, WE'LL CALL YOU, THEN SKEDADDLE.
HEY, DON'T MENTION IT, BUDDY. SNATCHING UP YOUNG GIRLS IS NO CHORE FOR ME.
BELIEVE ME.

...IN THE WAKE OF SUCH TRAGEDY, SUCH VIOLENCE, SUCH UTTER SENSELESSNESS, THE HURT AND ANGER WE FEEL IS OVERWHELMING.

BUT LET US NOT DWELL ON THE DARKNESS WHICH TOOK THEM FROM US SO SUDDENLY. INSTEAD, LET US REMEMBER THE LAUGHTER, THE WARMTH-- THE LIVES--WHICH HAVE TOUCHED US ALL SO DEEPLY.

ANDREA, ELIZABETH, AND ALEX BRIGHTON ARE GONE FROM THIS WORLD...

...BUT IN OUR HEARTS AND MINDS, THEY SHALL LIVE ON ETERNALLY.

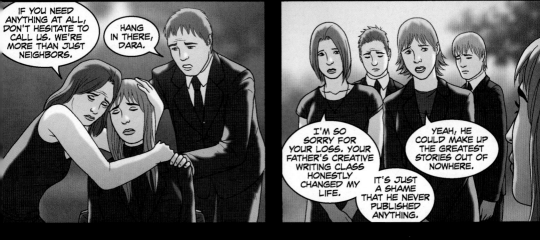

IF YOU NEED ANYTHING AT ALL, DON'T HESITATE TO CALL US. WE'RE MORE THAN JUST NEIGHBORS.

HANG IN THERE, DARA.

I'M SO SORRY FOR YOUR LOSS. YOUR FATHER'S CREATIVE WRITING CLASS HONESTLY CHANGED MY LIFE.

IT'S JUST A SHAME THAT HE NEVER PUBLISHED ANYTHING.

YEAH, HE COULD MAKE UP THE GREATEST STORIES OUT OF NOWHERE.

...

...YEAH...

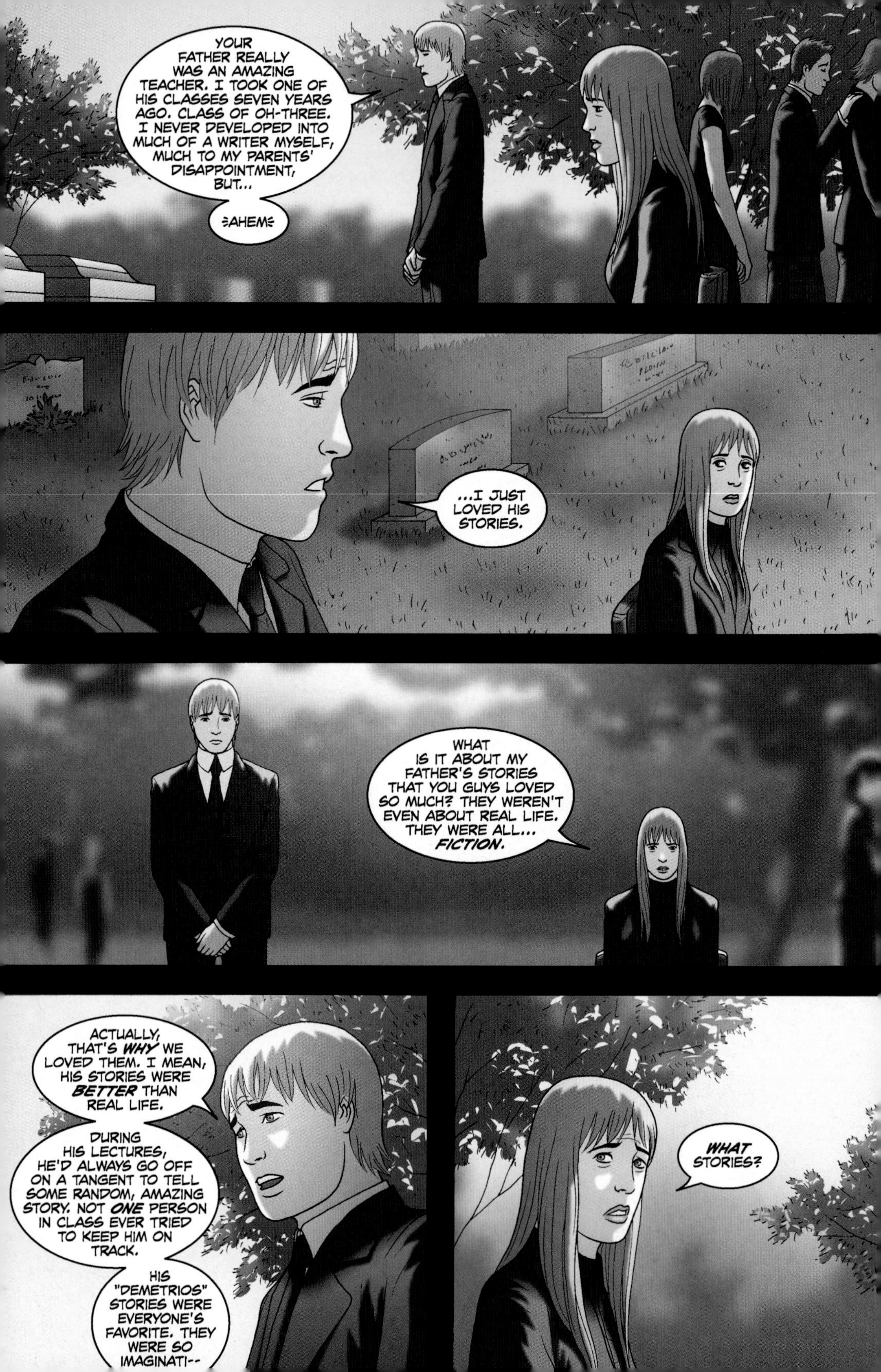
YOUR FATHER REALLY WAS AN AMAZING TEACHER. I TOOK ONE OF HIS CLASSES SEVEN YEARS AGO. CLASS OF OH-THREE. I NEVER DEVELOPED INTO MUCH OF A WRITER MYSELF, MUCH TO MY PARENTS' DISAPPOINTMENT, BUT...
AHEM
...I JUST LOVED HIS STORIES.
WHAT IS IT ABOUT MY FATHER'S STORIES THAT YOU GUYS LOVED SO MUCH? THEY WEREN'T EVEN ABOUT REAL LIFE. THEY WERE ALL... FICTION.
ACTUALLY, THAT'S WHY WE LOVED THEM. I MEAN, HIS STORIES WERE BETTER THAN REAL LIFE.
DURING HIS LECTURES, HE'D ALWAYS GO OFF ON A TANGENT TO TELL SOME RANDOM, AMAZING STORY. NOT ONE PERSON IN CLASS EVER TRIED TO KEEP HIM ON TRACK.
HIS "DEMETRIOS" STORIES WERE EVERYONE'S FAVORITE. THEY WERE SO IMAGINATI--
WHAT STORIES?

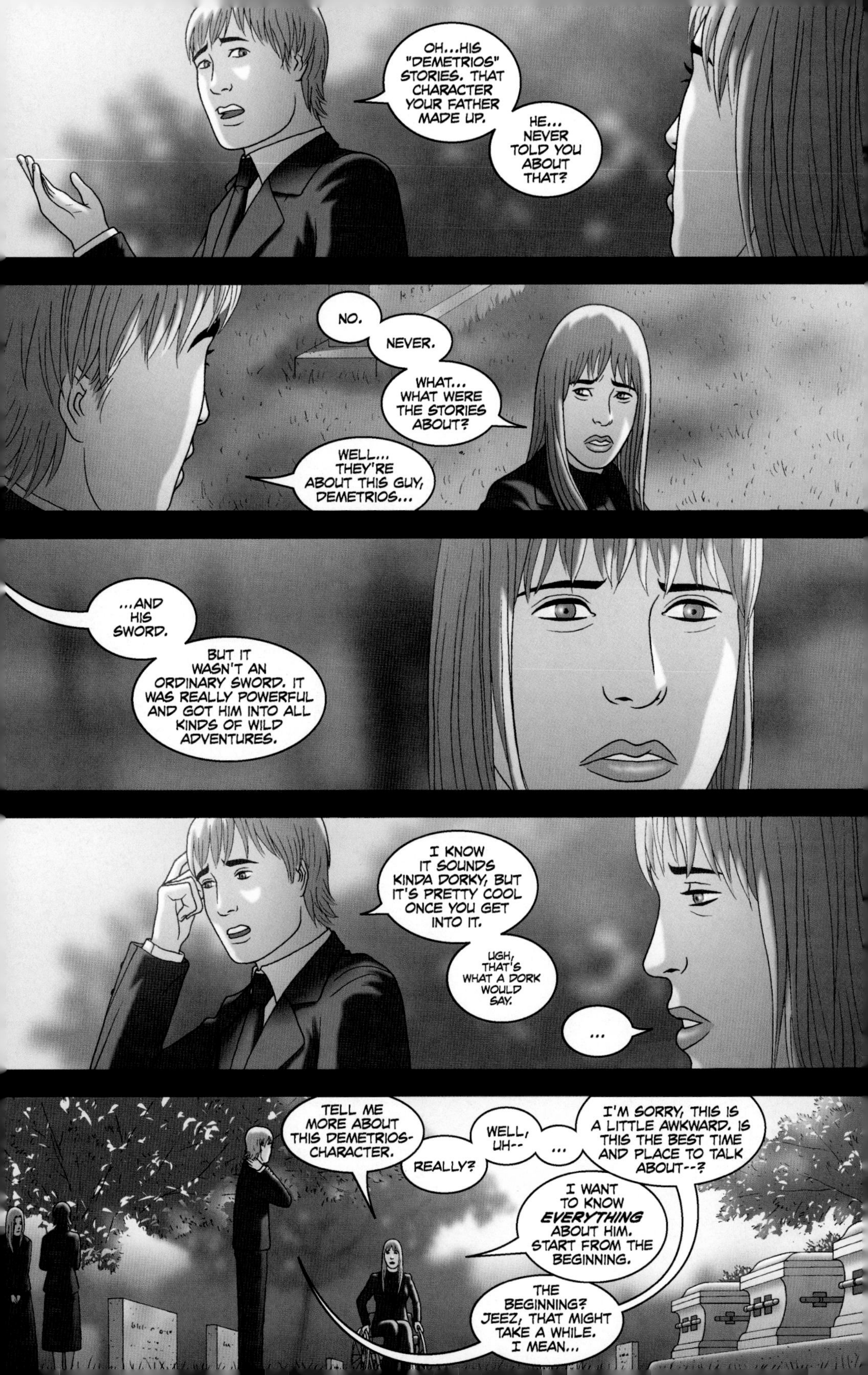
OH...HIS "DEMETRIOS" STORIES. THAT CHARACTER YOUR FATHER MADE UP.
HE... NEVER TOLD YOU ABOUT THAT?
NO.
NEVER.
WHAT... WHAT WERE THE STORIES ABOUT?
WELL... THEY'RE ABOUT THIS GUY, DEMETRIOS...
...AND HIS SWORD.
BUT IT WASN'T AN ORDINARY SWORD. IT WAS REALLY POWERFUL AND GOT HIM INTO ALL KINDS OF WILD ADVENTURES.
I KNOW IT SOUNDS KINDA DORKY, BUT IT'S PRETTY COOL ONCE YOU GET INTO IT.
UGH, THAT'S WHAT A DORK WOULD SAY.
...
TELL ME MORE ABOUT THIS DEMETRIOS-CHARACTER.
REALLY?
WELL, UH--
...
I'M SORRY, THIS IS A LITTLE AWKWARD. IS THIS THE BEST TIME AND PLACE TO TALK ABOUT--?
I WANT TO KNOW EVERYTHING ABOUT HIM. START FROM THE BEGINNING.
THE BEGINNING? JEEZ, THAT MIGHT TAKE A WHILE. I MEAN...

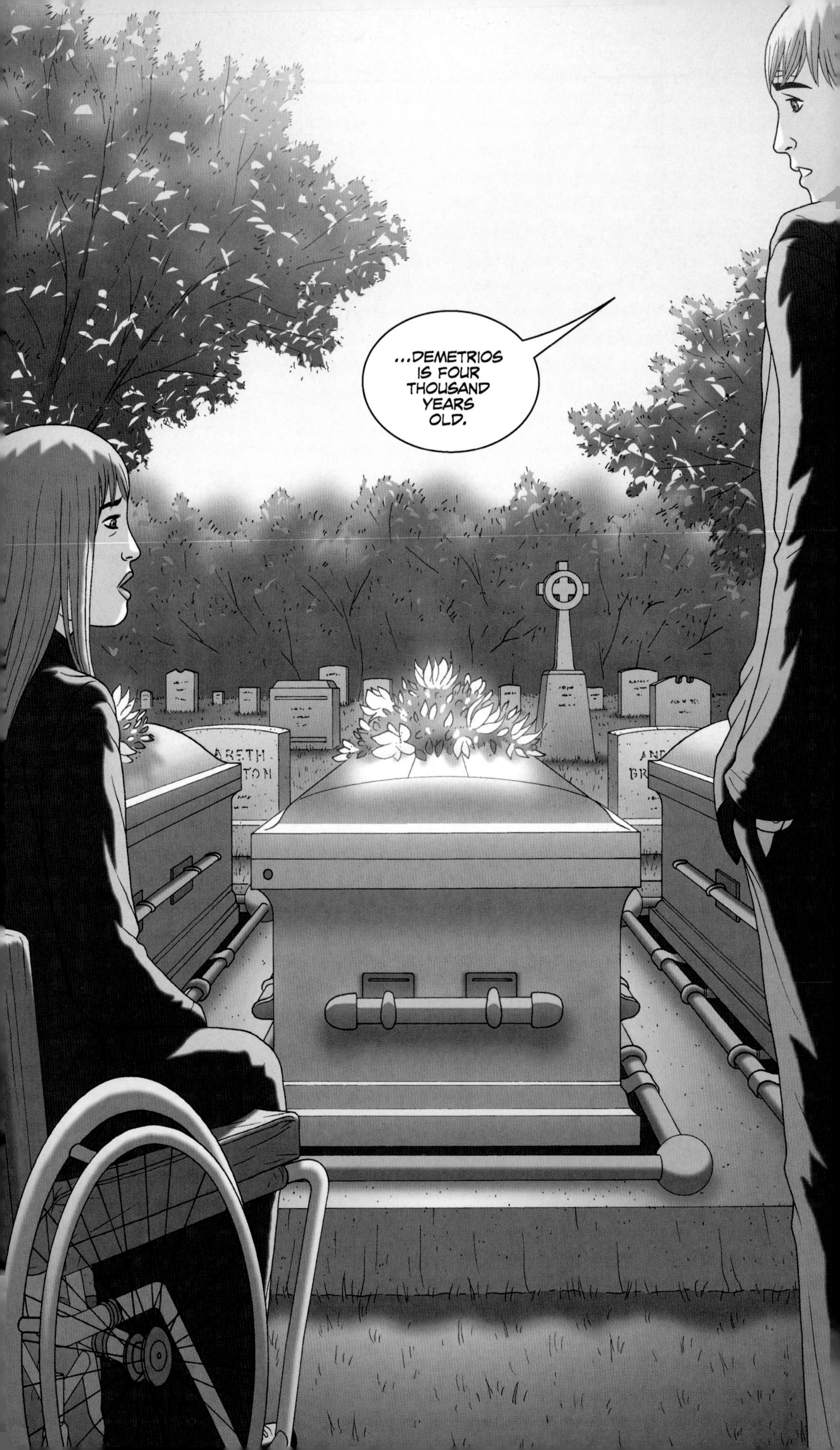
...DEMETRIOS IS FOUR THOUSAND YEARS OLD.

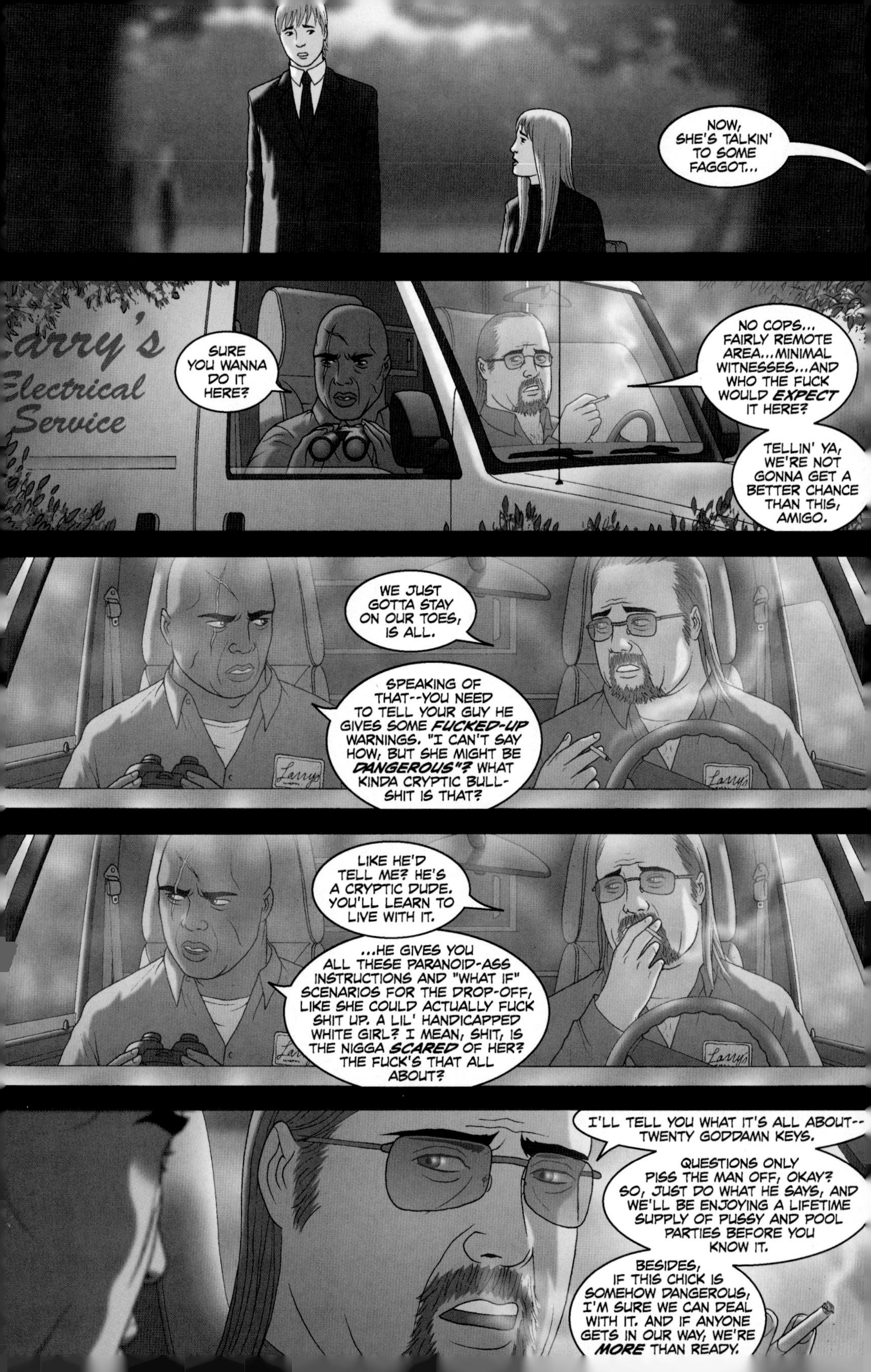
NOW, SHE'S TALKIN' TO SOME FAGGOT...
Larry's Electrical Service
SURE YOU WANNA DO IT HERE?
NO COPS... FAIRLY REMOTE AREA...MINIMAL WITNESSES...AND WHO THE FUCK WOULD EXPECT IT HERE?
TELLIN' YA, WE'RE NOT GONNA GET A BETTER CHANCE THAN THIS, AMIGO.
WE JUST GOTTA STAY ON OUR TOES, IS ALL.
SPEAKING OF THAT--YOU NEED TO TELL YOUR GUY HE GIVES SOME FUCKED-UP WARNINGS. "I CAN'T SAY HOW, BUT SHE MIGHT BE DANGEROUS"? WHAT KINDA CRYPTIC BULL-SHIT IS THAT?
LIKE HE'D TELL ME? HE'S A CRYPTIC DUDE. YOU'LL LEARN TO LIVE WITH IT.
...HE GIVES YOU ALL THESE PARANOID-ASS INSTRUCTIONS AND "WHAT IF" SCENARIOS FOR THE DROP-OFF, LIKE SHE COULD ACTUALLY FUCK SHIT UP. A LIL' HANDICAPPED WHITE GIRL? I MEAN, SHIT, IS THE NIGGA SCARED OF HER? THE FUCK'S THAT ALL ABOUT?
I'LL TELL YOU WHAT IT'S ALL ABOUT--TWENTY GODDAMN KEYS.
QUESTIONS ONLY PISS THE MAN OFF, OKAY? SO, JUST DO WHAT HE SAYS, AND WE'LL BE ENJOYING A LIFETIME SUPPLY OF PUSSY AND POOL PARTIES BEFORE YOU KNOW IT.
BESIDES, IF THIS CHICK IS SOMEHOW DANGEROUS, I'M SURE WE CAN DEAL WITH IT. AND IF ANYONE GETS IN OUR WAY, WE'RE MORE THAN READY.

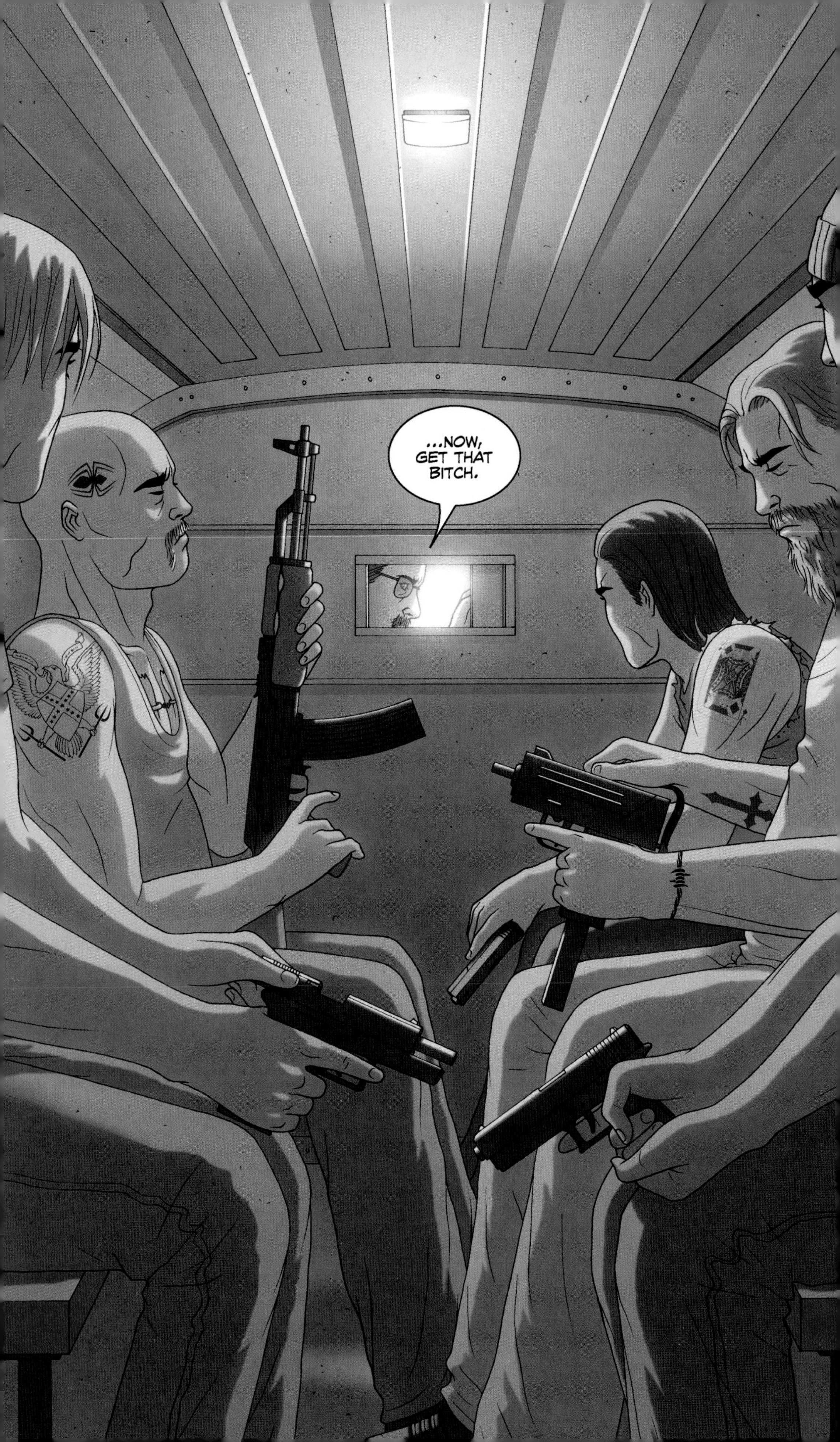
...NOW, GET THAT BITCH.

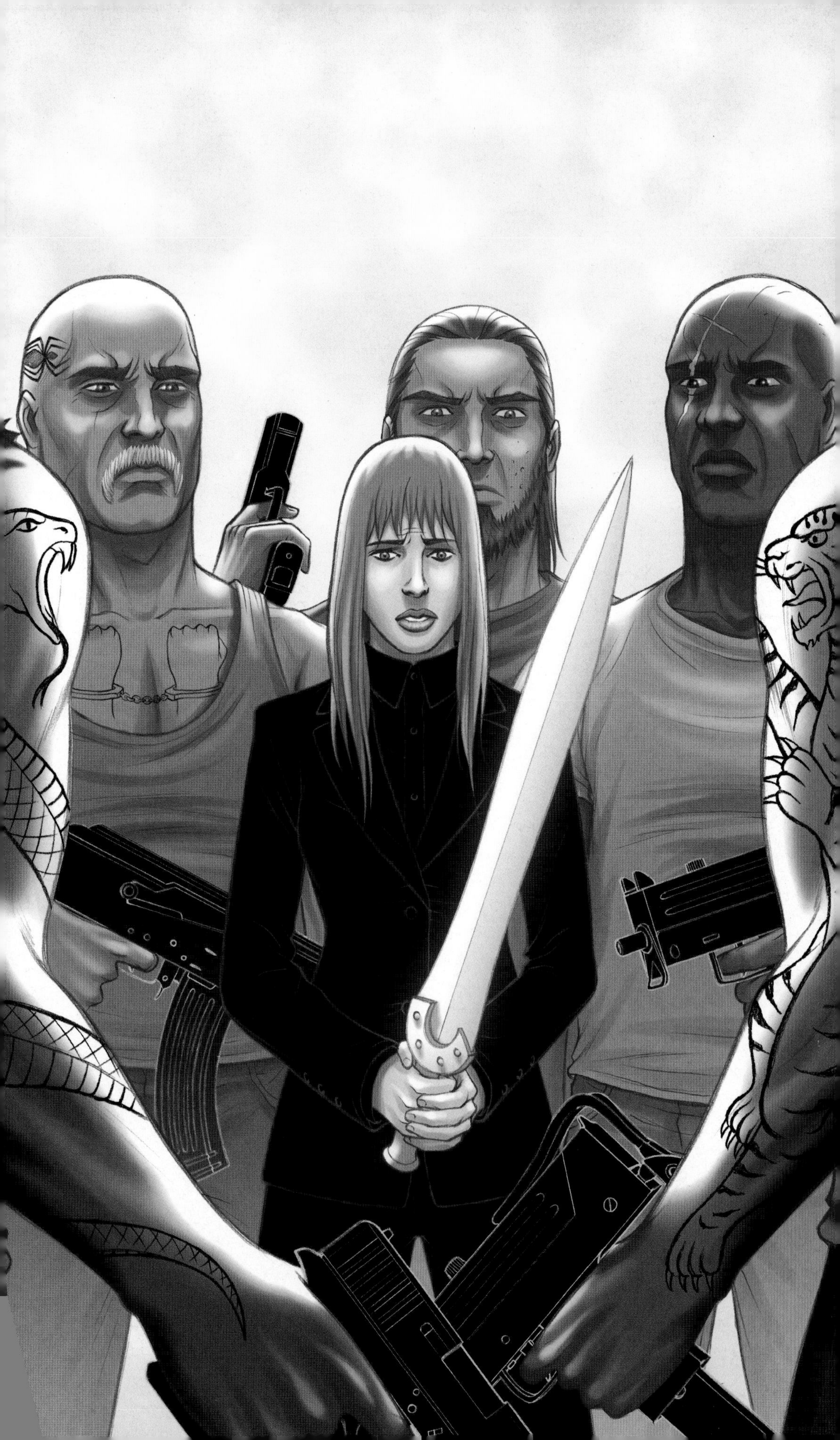

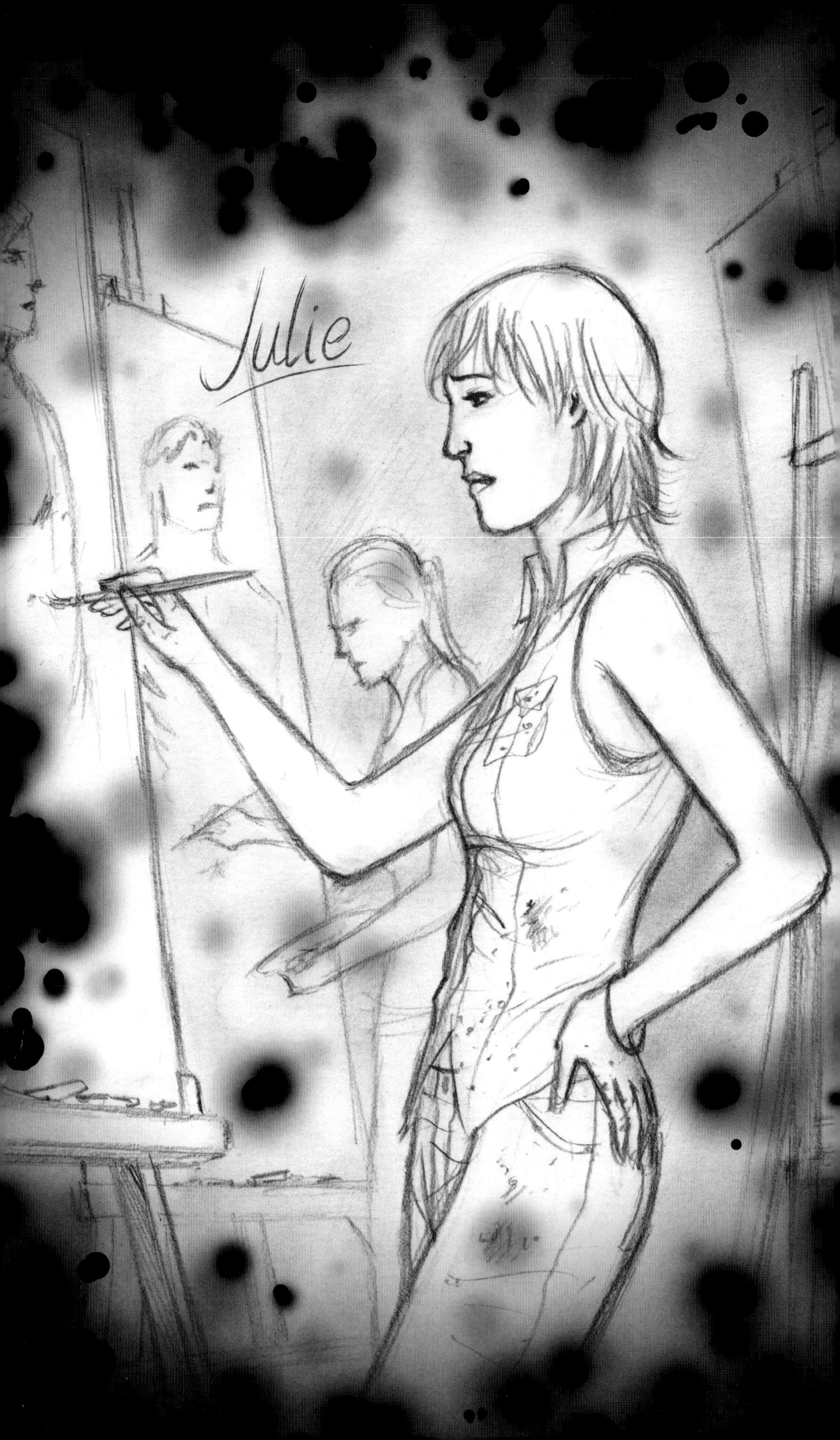
Julie

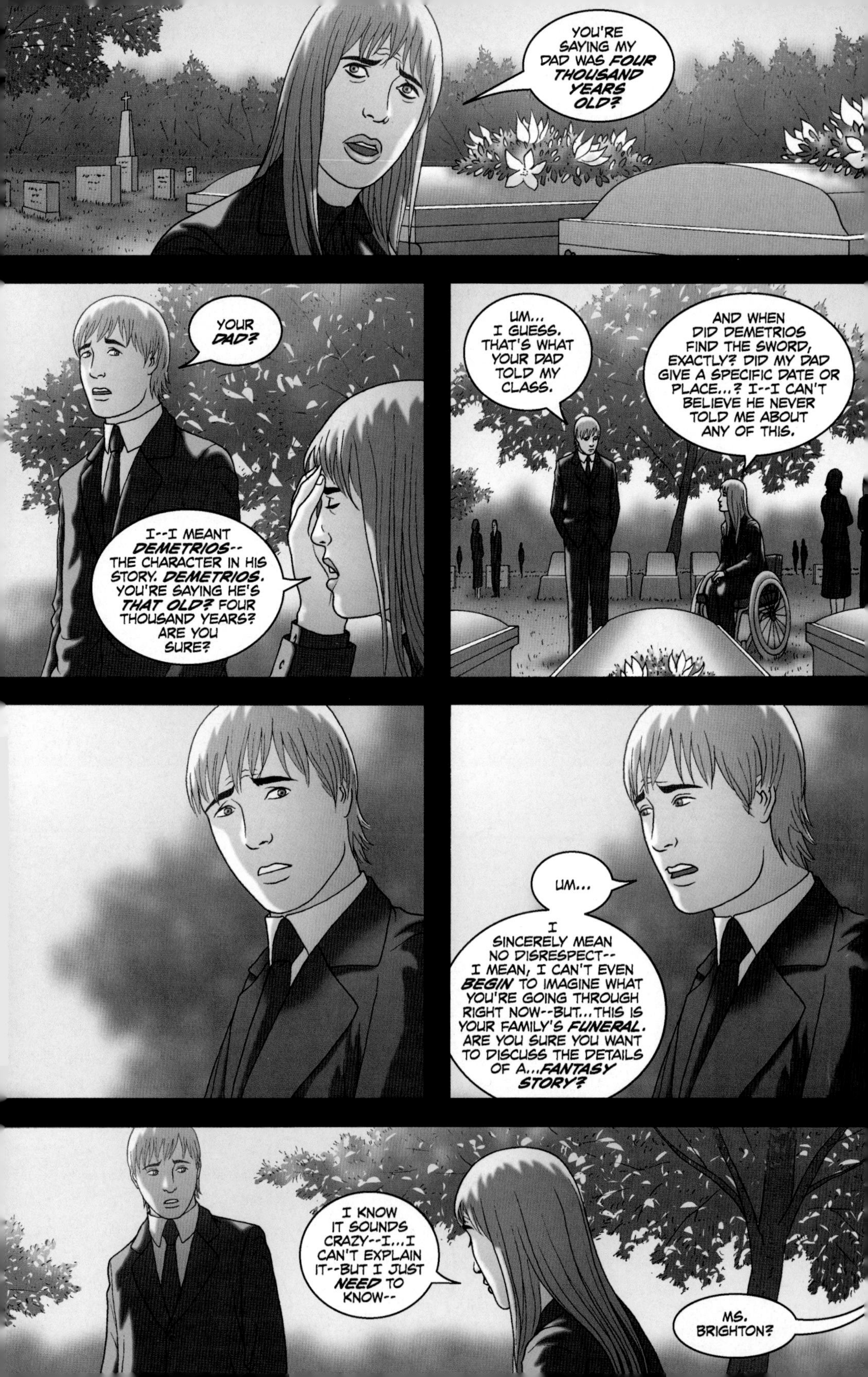
YOU'RE SAYING MY DAD WAS FOUR THOUSAND YEARS OLD?
YOUR DAD?
I--I MEANT DEMETRIOS-- THE CHARACTER IN HIS STORY. DEMETRIOS. YOU'RE SAYING HE'S THAT OLD? FOUR THOUSAND YEARS? ARE YOU SURE?
UM... I GUESS. THAT'S WHAT YOUR DAD TOLD MY CLASS.
AND WHEN DID DEMETRIOS FIND THE SWORD, EXACTLY? DID MY DAD GIVE A SPECIFIC DATE OR PLACE...? I--I CAN'T BELIEVE HE NEVER TOLD ME ABOUT ANY OF THIS.
UM...
I SINCERELY MEAN NO DISRESPECT-- I MEAN, I CAN'T EVEN BEGIN TO IMAGINE WHAT YOU'RE GOING THROUGH RIGHT NOW--BUT...THIS IS YOUR FAMILY'S FUNERAL. ARE YOU SURE YOU WANT TO DISCUSS THE DETAILS OF A...FANTASY STORY?
I KNOW IT SOUNDS CRAZY--I...I CAN'T EXPLAIN IT--BUT I JUST NEED TO KNOW--
MS. BRIGHTON?

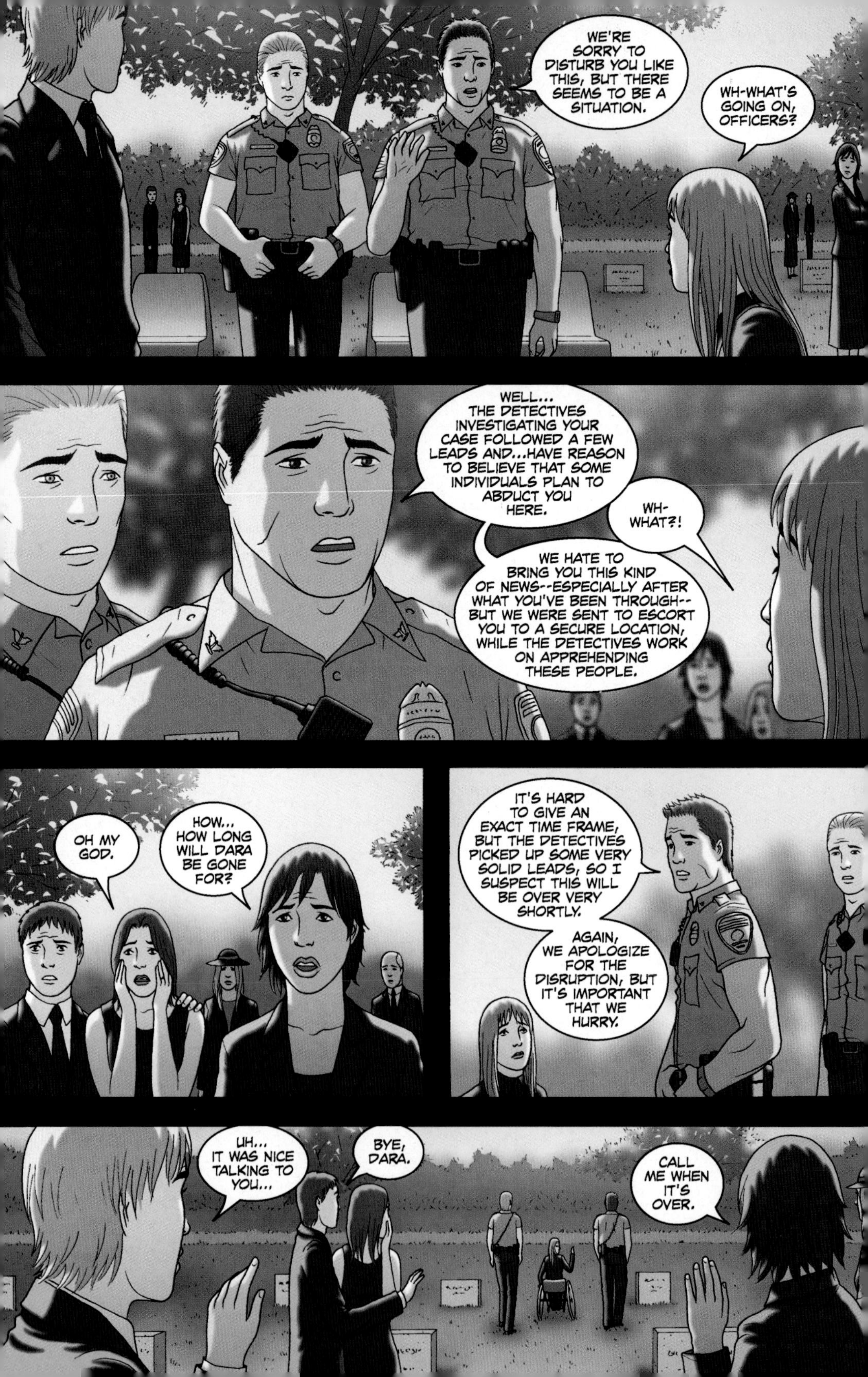
WE'RE SORRY TO DISTURB YOU LIKE THIS, BUT THERE SEEMS TO BE A SITUATION.
WH-WHAT'S GOING ON, OFFICERS?
WELL... THE DETECTIVES INVESTIGATING YOUR CASE FOLLOWED A FEW LEADS AND...HAVE REASON TO BELIEVE THAT SOME INDIVIDUALS PLAN TO ABDUCT YOU HERE.
WH- WHAT?!
WE HATE TO BRING YOU THIS KIND OF NEWS--ESPECIALLY AFTER WHAT YOU'VE BEEN THROUGH-- BUT WE WERE SENT TO ESCORT YOU TO A SECURE LOCATION, WHILE THE DETECTIVES WORK ON APPREHENDING THESE PEOPLE.
OH MY GOD.
HOW... HOW LONG WILL DARA BE GONE FOR?
IT'S HARD TO GIVE AN EXACT TIME FRAME, BUT THE DETECTIVES PICKED UP SOME VERY SOLID LEADS, SO I SUSPECT THIS WILL BE OVER VERY SHORTLY.
AGAIN, WE APOLOGIZE FOR THE DISRUPTION, BUT IT'S IMPORTANT THAT WE HURRY.
UH... IT WAS NICE TALKING TO YOU...
BYE, DARA.
CALL ME WHEN IT'S OVER.

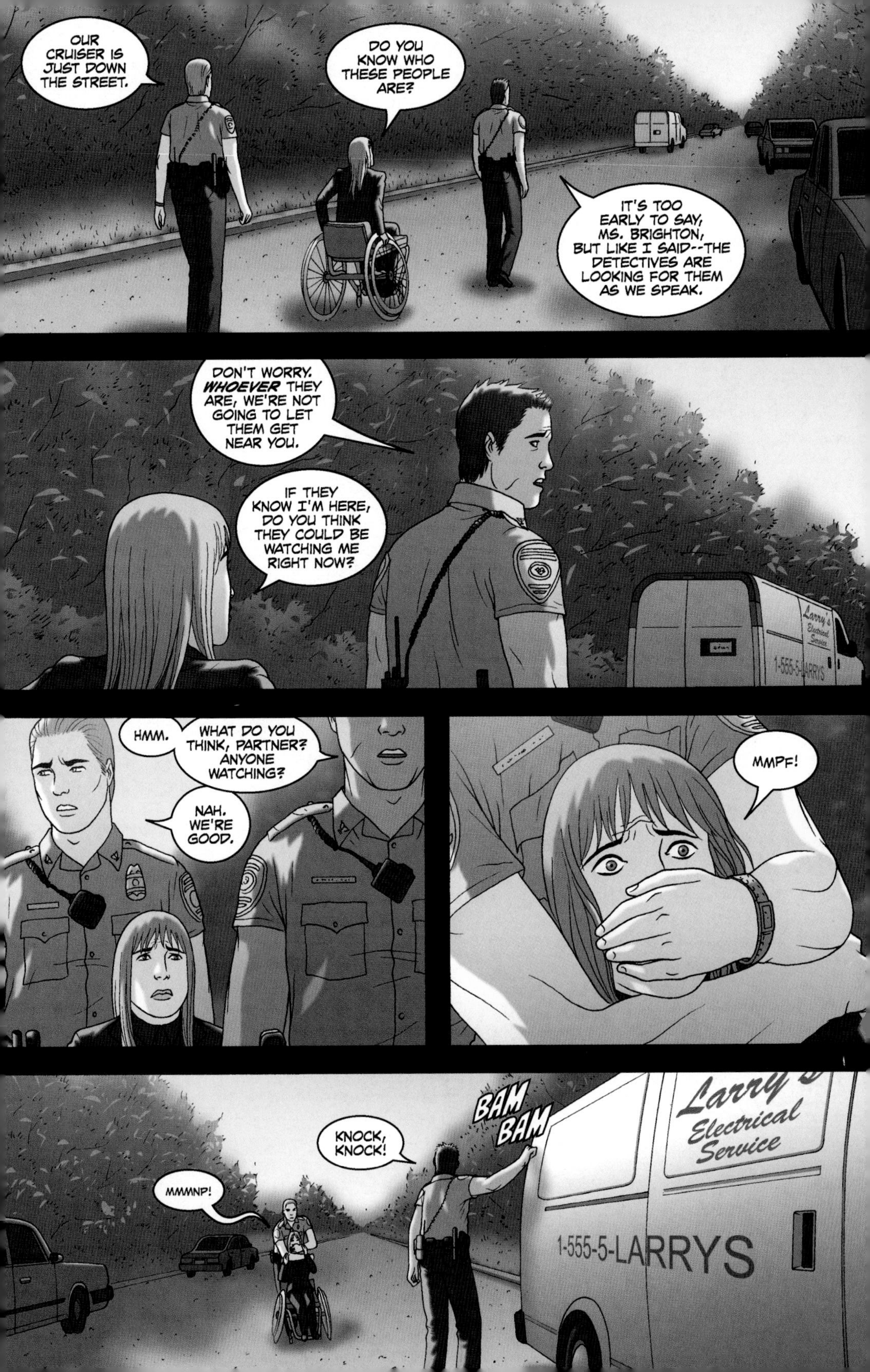
OUR CRUISER IS JUST DOWN THE STREET.
DO YOU KNOW WHO THESE PEOPLE ARE?
IT'S TOO EARLY TO SAY, MS. BRIGHTON, BUT LIKE I SAID--THE DETECTIVES ARE LOOKING FOR THEM AS WE SPEAK.
DON'T WORRY. WHOEVER THEY ARE, WE'RE NOT GOING TO LET THEM GET NEAR YOU.
IF THEY KNOW I'M HERE, DO YOU THINK THEY COULD BE WATCHING ME RIGHT NOW?
Larry's Electrical Service
1-555-5-LARRYS
HMM.
WHAT DO YOU THINK, PARTNER? ANYONE WATCHING?
NAH. WE'RE GOOD.
MMPF!
BAM BAM
KNOCK, KNOCK!
MMMNP!
Larry's Electrical Service
1-555-5-LARRYS

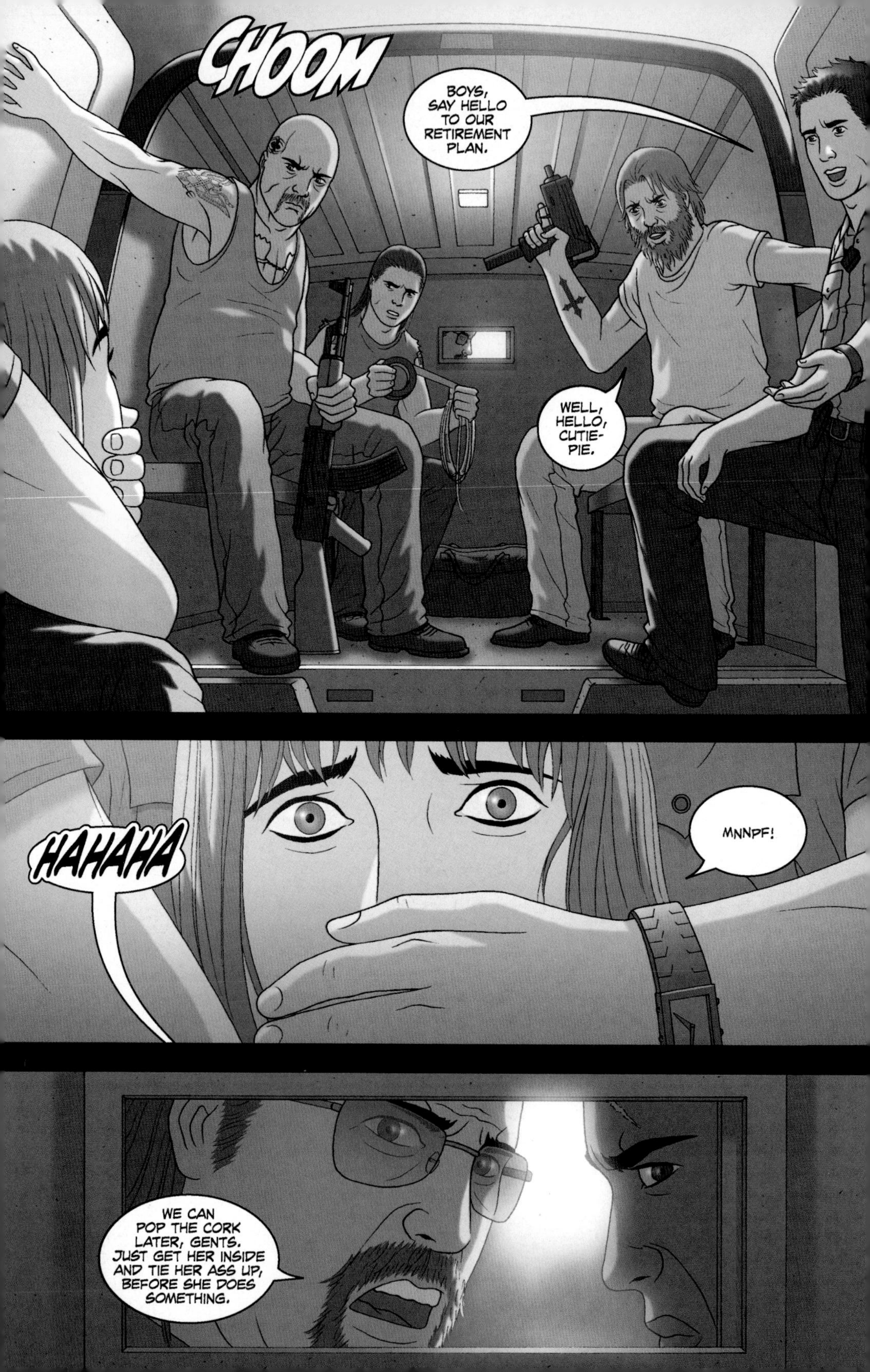
CHOOM
BOYS, SAY HELLO TO OUR RETIREMENT PLAN.
WELL, HELLO, CUTIE-PIE.
HAHAHA
MNNPF!
WE CAN POP THE CORK LATER, GENTS. JUST GET HER INSIDE AND TIE HER ASS UP, BEFORE SHE DOES SOMETHING.

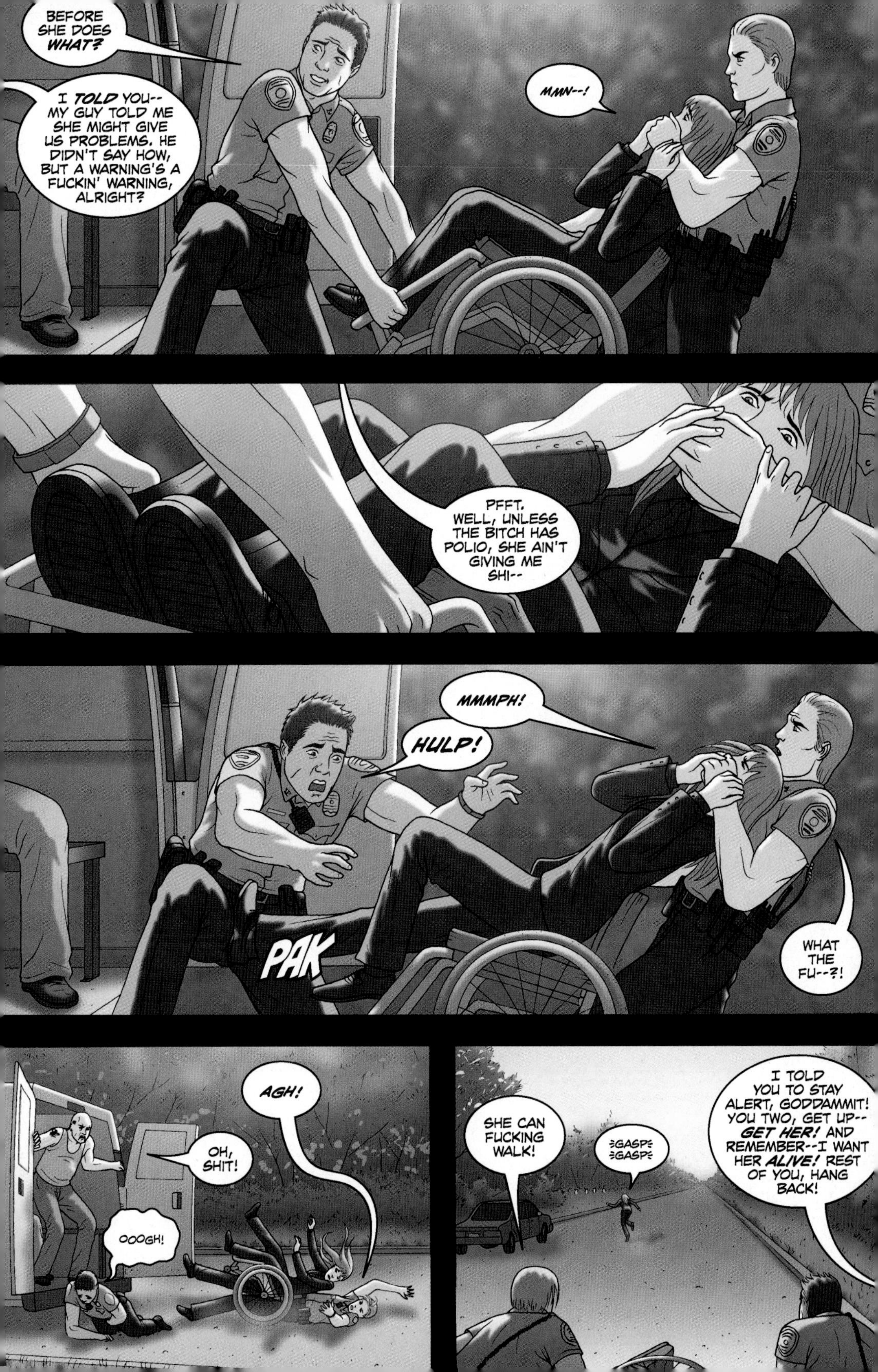
BEFORE SHE DOES WHAT?
I TOLD YOU-- MY GUY TOLD ME SHE MIGHT GIVE US PROBLEMS. HE DIDN'T SAY HOW, BUT A WARNING'S A FUCKIN' WARNING, ALRIGHT?
MMN--!
PFFT. WELL, UNLESS THE BITCH HAS POLIO, SHE AIN'T GIVING ME SHI--
MMMPH!
HULP!
PAK
WHAT THE FU--?!
AGH!
OH, SHIT!
OOOGH!
SHE CAN FUCKING WALK!
GASP GASP
I TOLD YOU TO STAY ALERT, GODDAMMIT! YOU TWO, GET UP-- GET HER! AND REMEMBER--I WANT HER ALIVE! REST OF YOU, HANG BACK!

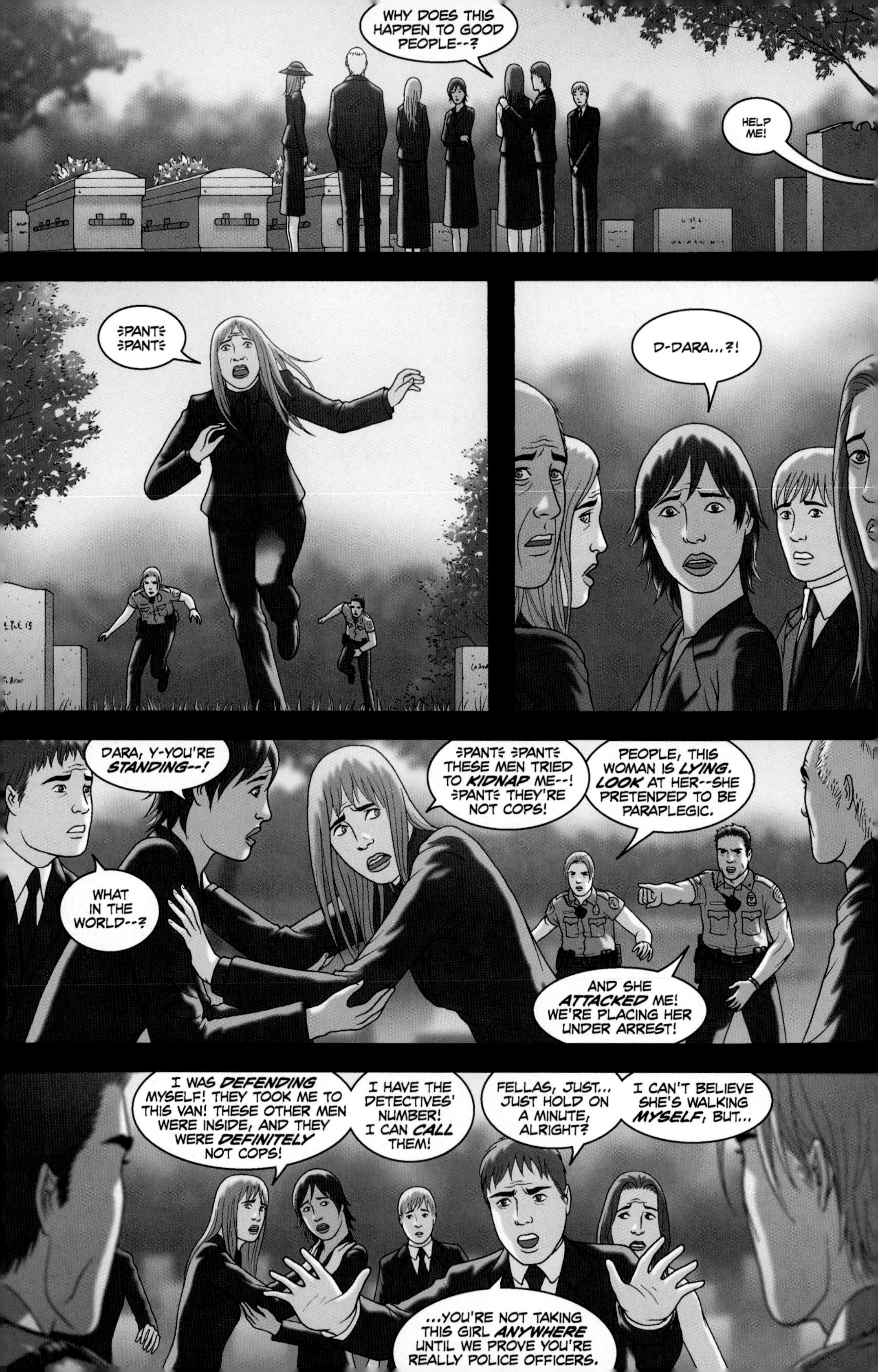
WHY DOES THIS HAPPEN TO GOOD PEOPLE--?
HELP ME!
≶PANT≶ ≶PANT≶
D-DARA...?!
DARA, Y-YOU'RE ***STANDING--!***
WHAT IN THE WORLD--?
≶PANT≶ ≶PANT≶ THESE MEN TRIED TO ***KIDNAP*** ME--! ≶PANT≶ THEY'RE NOT COPS!
PEOPLE, THIS WOMAN IS ***LYING. LOOK*** AT HER--SHE PRETENDED TO BE PARAPLEGIC.
AND SHE ***ATTACKED*** ME! WE'RE PLACING HER UNDER ARREST!
I WAS ***DEFENDING*** MYSELF! THEY TOOK ME TO THIS VAN! THESE OTHER MEN WERE INSIDE, AND THEY WERE ***DEFINITELY*** NOT COPS!
I HAVE THE DETECTIVES' NUMBER! I CAN ***CALL*** THEM!
FELLAS, JUST... JUST HOLD ON A MINUTE, ALRIGHT?
I CAN'T BELIEVE SHE'S WALKING ***MYSELF***, BUT...
...YOU'RE NOT TAKING THIS GIRL ***ANYWHERE*** UNTIL WE PROVE YOU'RE REALLY POLICE OFFICERS.

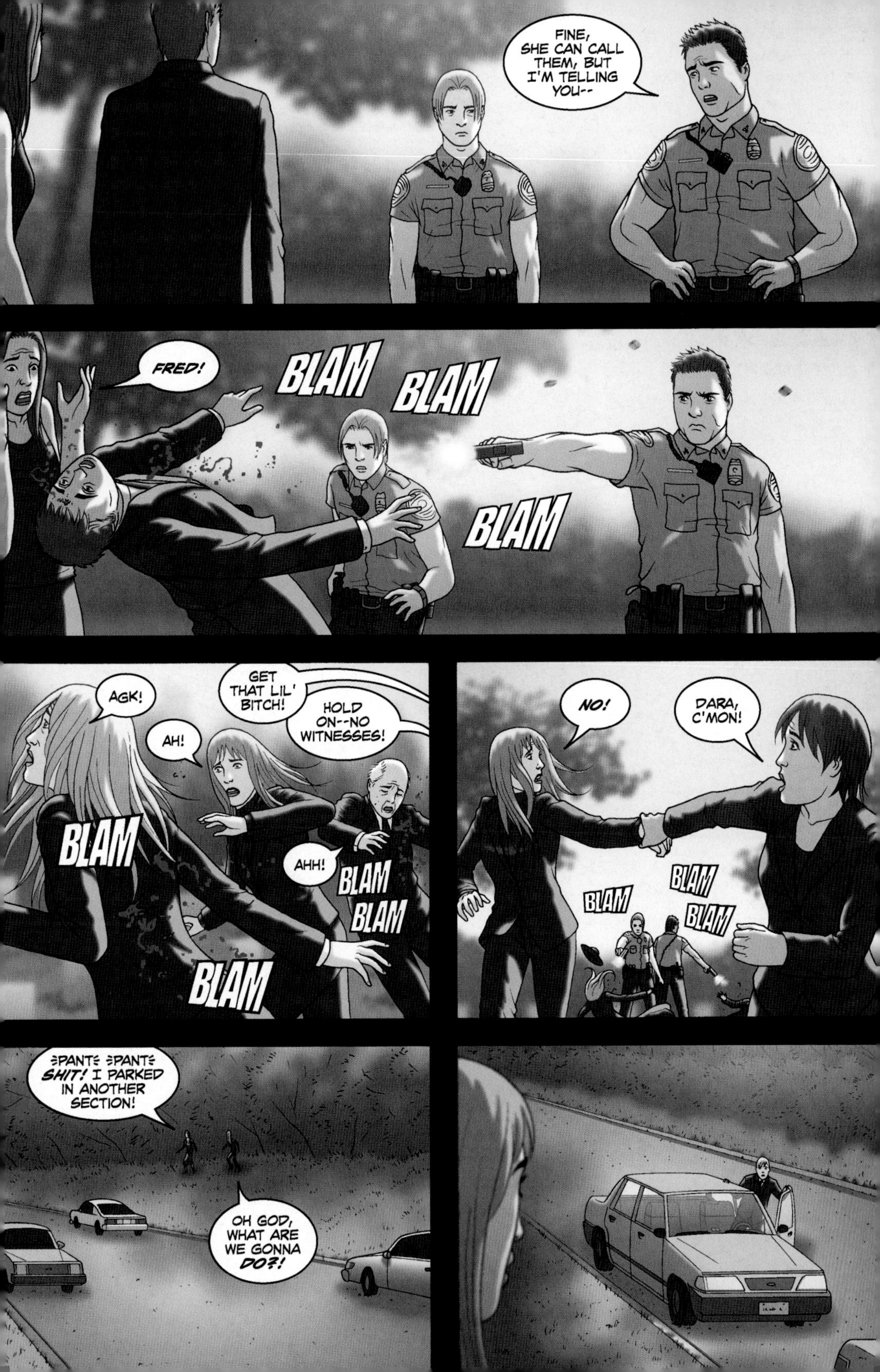

FINE, SHE CAN CALL THEM, BUT I'M TELLING YOU--
FRED!
BLAM
BLAM
BLAM
AGK!
GET THAT LIL' BITCH!
HOLD ON--NO WITNESSES!
AH!
BLAM
AHH!
BLAM
BLAM
BLAM
NO!
DARA, C'MON!
BLAM
BLAM
BLAM
≡PANT≡ ≡PANT≡ SHIT! I PARKED IN ANOTHER SECTION!
OH GOD, WHAT ARE WE GONNA DO?!

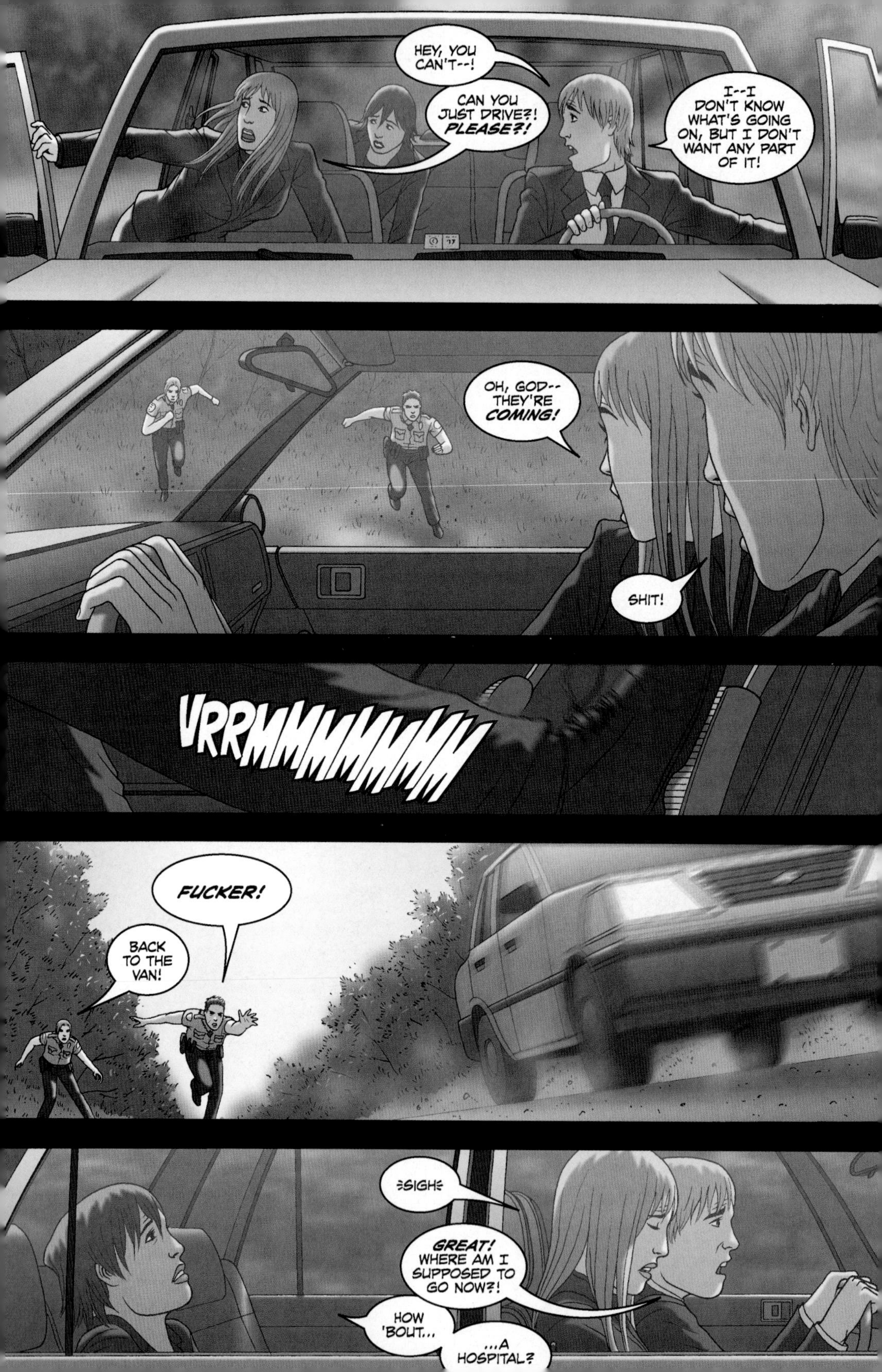

HEY, YOU CAN'T--!
CAN YOU JUST DRIVE?! PLEASE?!
I--I DON'T KNOW WHAT'S GOING ON, BUT I DON'T WANT ANY PART OF IT!
OH, GOD-- THEY'RE COMING!
SHIT!
VRRMMMMMMMH
FUCKER!
BACK TO THE VAN!
=SIGH=
GREAT! WHERE AM I SUPPOSED TO GO NOW?!
HOW 'BOUT...
...A HOSPITAL?

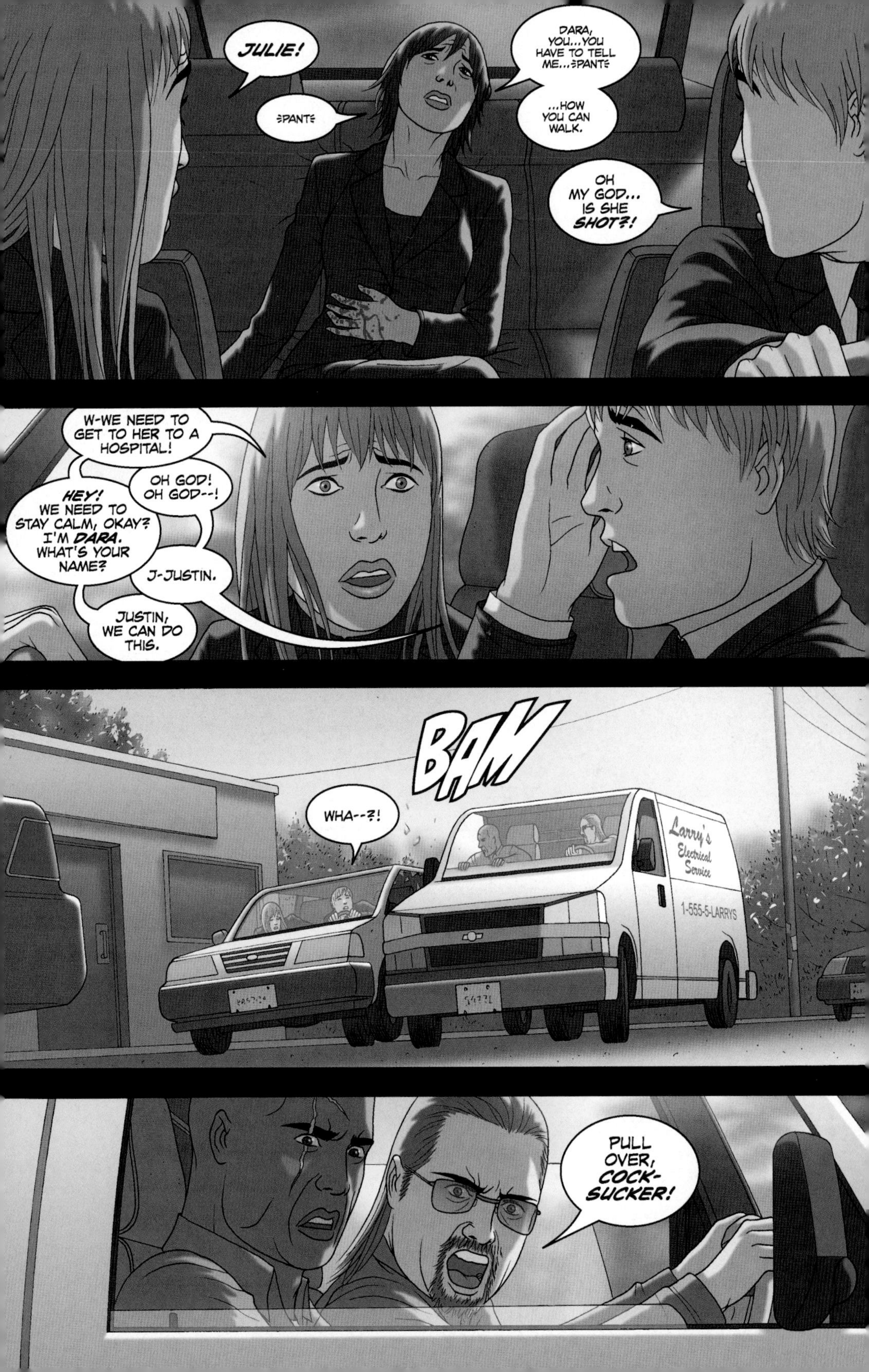
JULIE!
≠PANT≠
DARA, YOU...YOU HAVE TO TELL ME...≠PANT≠
...HOW YOU CAN WALK.
OH MY GOD... IS SHE SHOT?!
W-WE NEED TO GET TO HER TO A HOSPITAL!
OH GOD! OH GOD--!
HEY! WE NEED TO STAY CALM, OKAY? I'M DARA. WHAT'S YOUR NAME?
J-JUSTIN.
JUSTIN, WE CAN DO THIS.
BAM
WHA--?!
Larry's Electrical Service
1-555-5-LARRYS
PULL OVER, COCK-SUCKER!

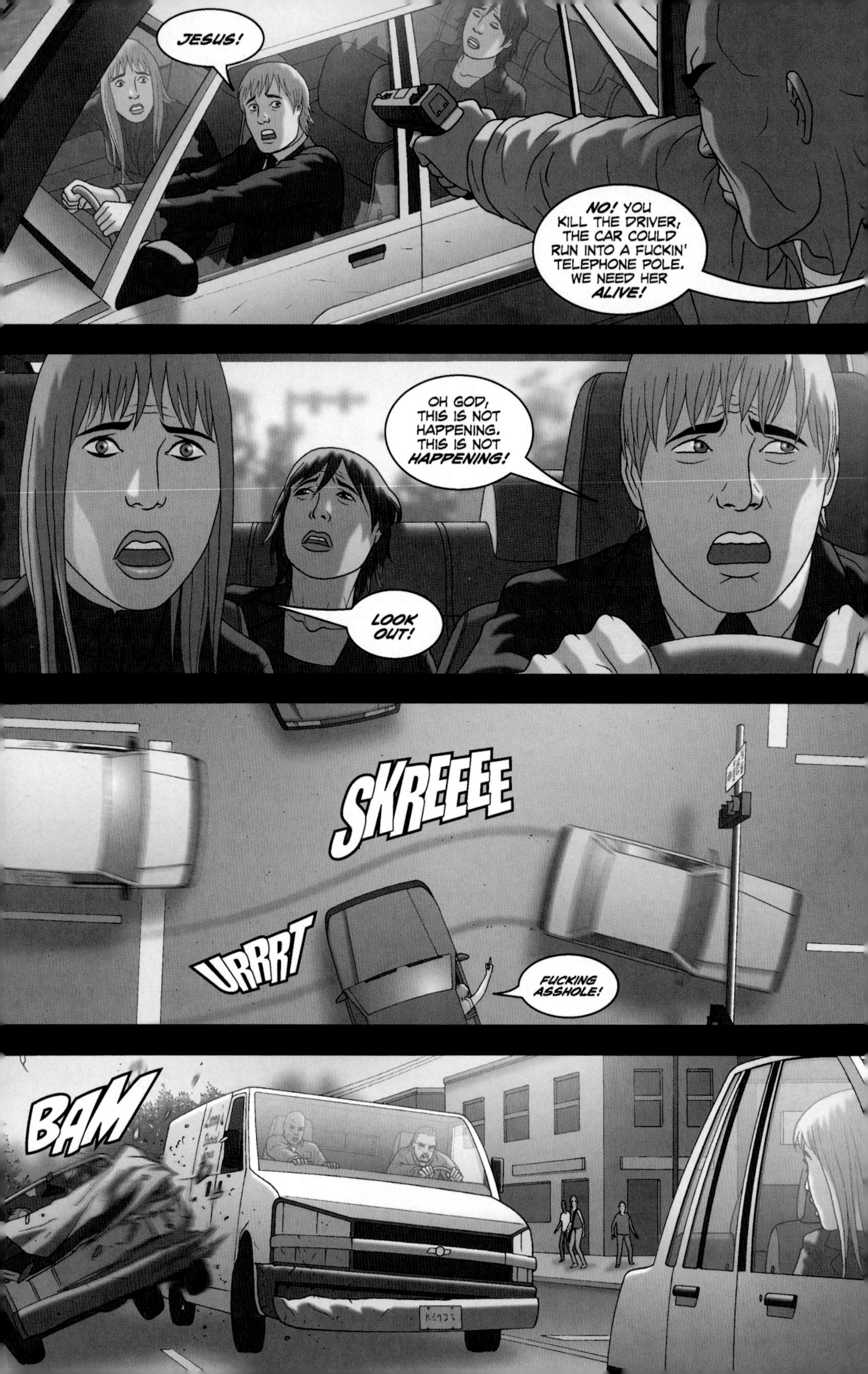
JESUS!
NO! YOU KILL THE DRIVER, THE CAR COULD RUN INTO A FUCKIN' TELEPHONE POLE. WE NEED HER ALIVE!
OH GOD, THIS IS NOT HAPPENING. THIS IS NOT HAPPENING!
LOOK OUT!
SKREEEE
URRRT
FUCKING ASSHOLE!
BAM

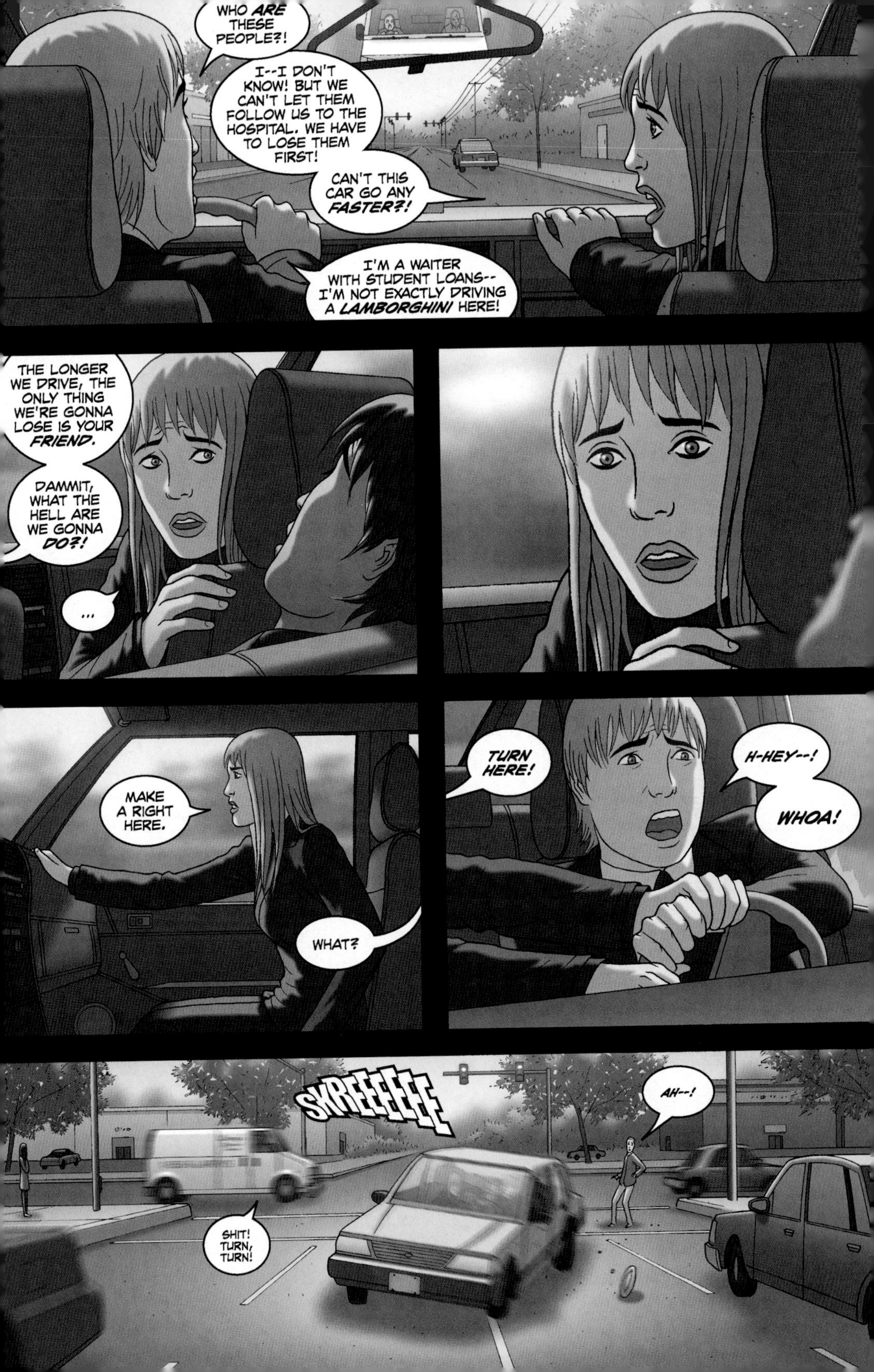
WHO ARE THESE PEOPLE?!
I--I DON'T KNOW! BUT WE CAN'T LET THEM FOLLOW US TO THE HOSPITAL. WE HAVE TO LOSE THEM FIRST!
CAN'T THIS CAR GO ANY FASTER?!
I'M A WAITER WITH STUDENT LOANS-- I'M NOT EXACTLY DRIVING A LAMBORGHINI HERE!
THE LONGER WE DRIVE, THE ONLY THING WE'RE GONNA LOSE IS YOUR FRIEND.
DAMMIT, WHAT THE HELL ARE WE GONNA DO?!
...
MAKE A RIGHT HERE.
WHAT?
TURN HERE!
H-HEY--!
WHOA!
SKREEEEEEE
AH--!
SHIT! TURN, TURN!

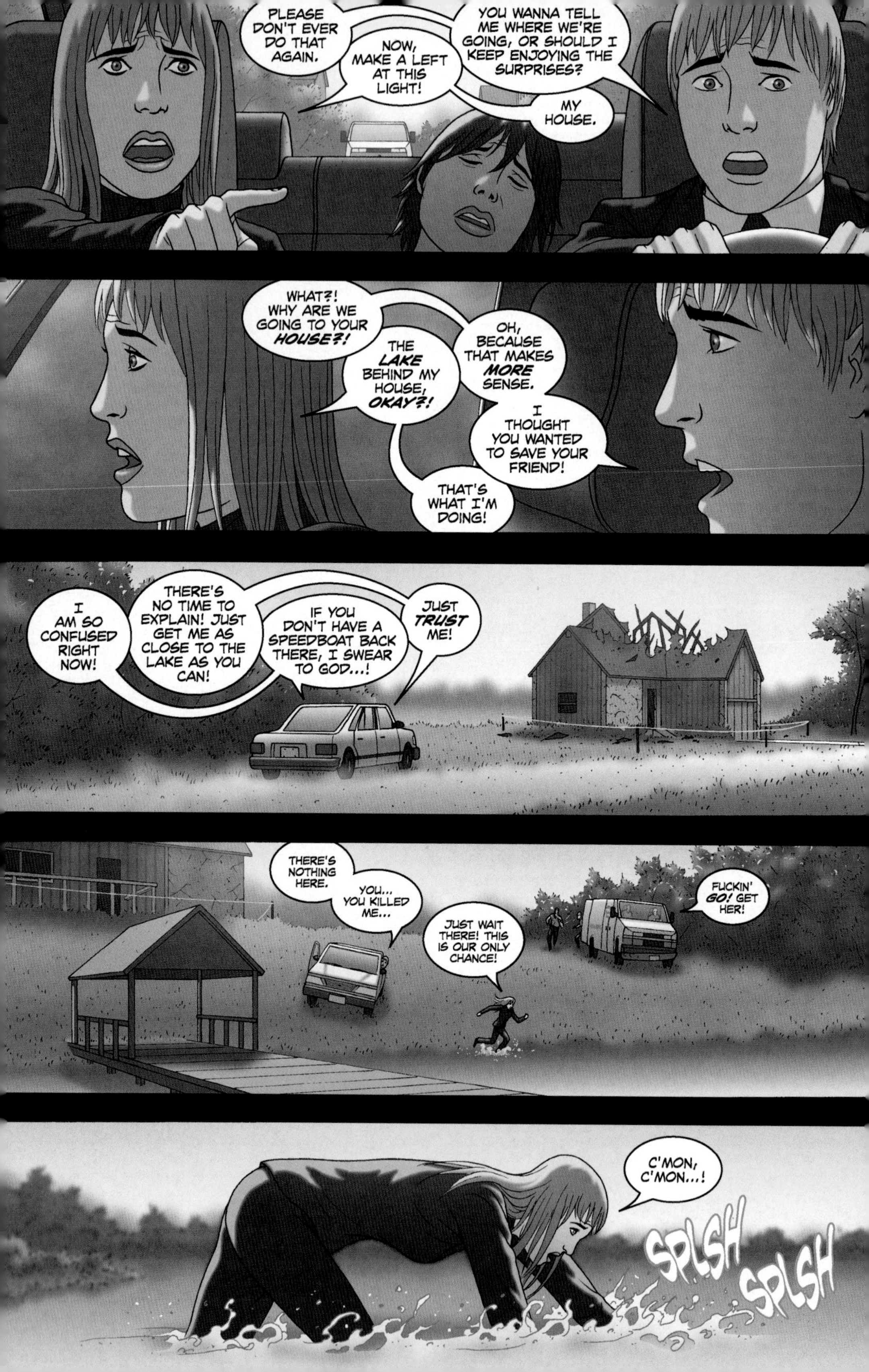
PLEASE DON'T EVER DO THAT AGAIN.
NOW, MAKE A LEFT AT THIS LIGHT!
YOU WANNA TELL ME WHERE WE'RE GOING, OR SHOULD I KEEP ENJOYING THE SURPRISES?
MY HOUSE.
WHAT?! WHY ARE WE GOING TO YOUR HOUSE?!
THE LAKE BEHIND MY HOUSE, OKAY?!
OH, BECAUSE THAT MAKES MORE SENSE.
I THOUGHT YOU WANTED TO SAVE YOUR FRIEND!
THAT'S WHAT I'M DOING!
I AM SO CONFUSED RIGHT NOW!
THERE'S NO TIME TO EXPLAIN! JUST GET ME AS CLOSE TO THE LAKE AS YOU CAN!
IF YOU DON'T HAVE A SPEEDBOAT BACK THERE, I SWEAR TO GOD...!
JUST TRUST ME!
THERE'S NOTHING HERE.
YOU... YOU KILLED ME...
JUST WAIT THERE! THIS IS OUR ONLY CHANCE!
FUCKIN' GO! GET HER!
C'MON, C'MON...!
SPLSH
SPLSH

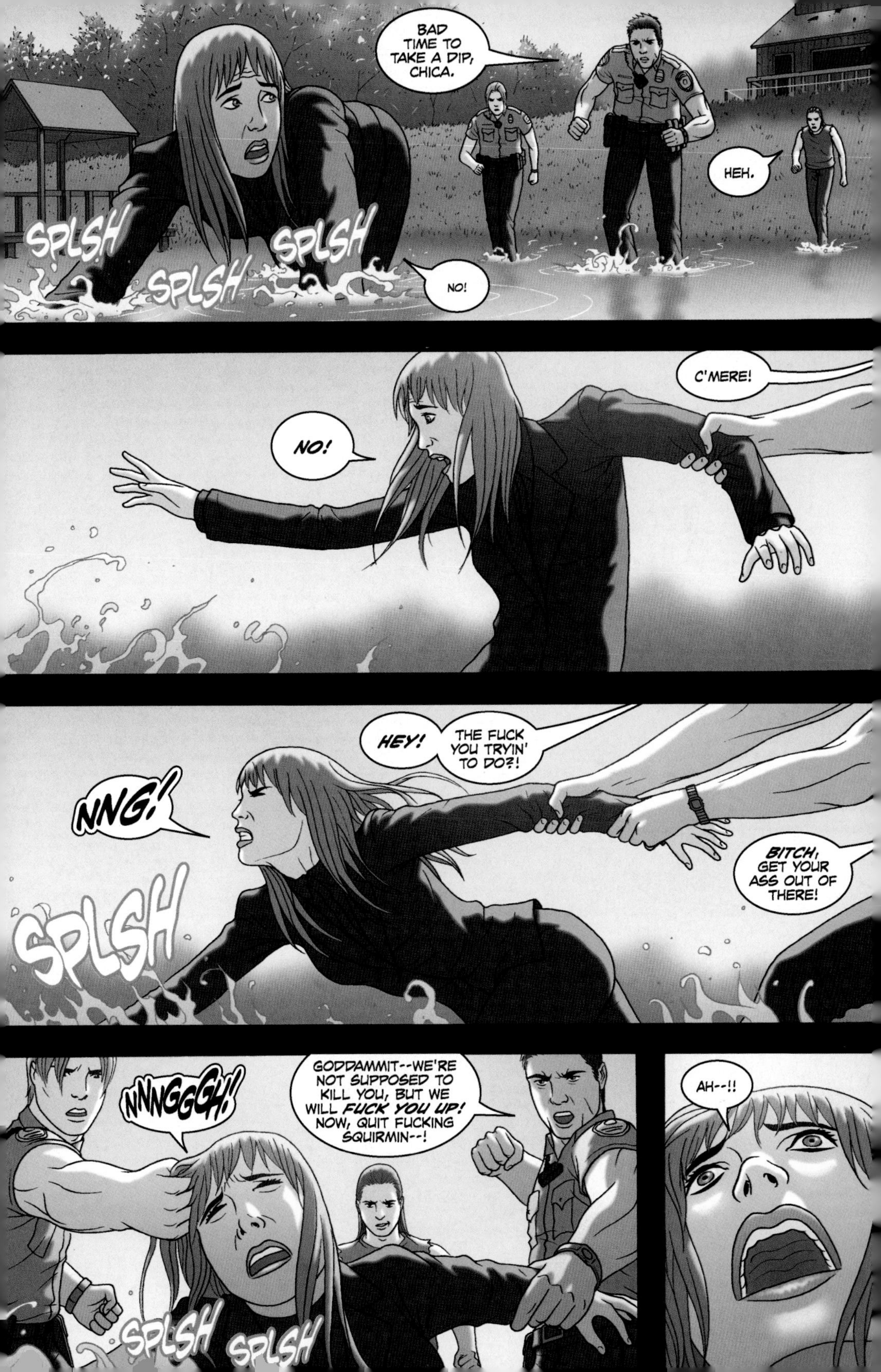
BAD TIME TO TAKE A DIP, CHICA.
HEH.
SPLSH
SPLSH
SPLSH
NO!
C'MERE!
NO!
HEY!
THE FUCK YOU TRYIN' TO DO?!
NNG!
BITCH, GET YOUR ASS OUT OF THERE!
SPLSH
NNNGGGH!
GODDAMMIT--WE'RE NOT SUPPOSED TO KILL YOU, BUT WE WILL FUCK YOU UP! NOW, QUIT FUCKING SQUIRMIN--!
SPLSH
SPLSH
AH--!!

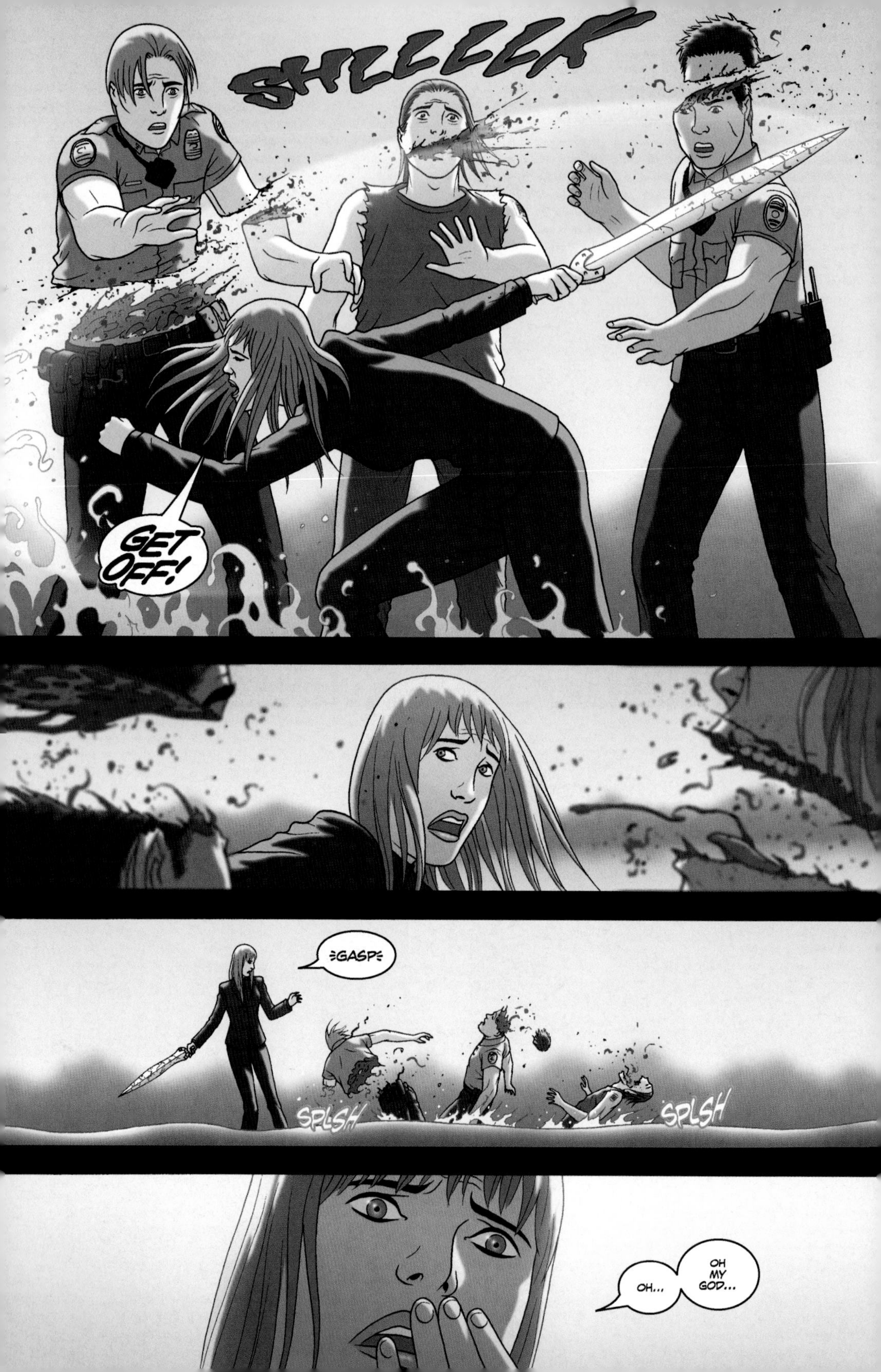
SHLLLLK
GET OFF!
GASP
SPLSH
SPLSH
OH...
OH MY GOD...

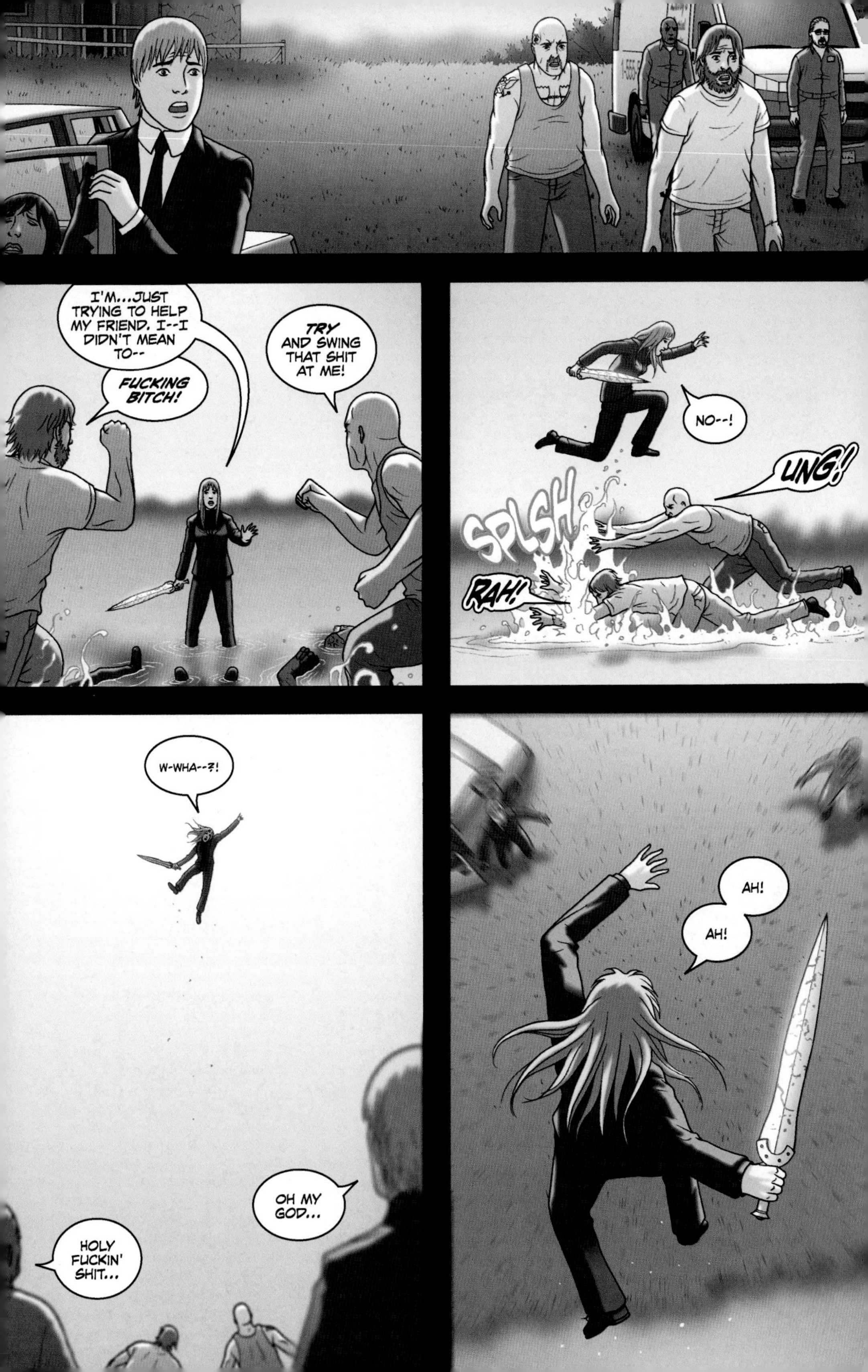
I'M...JUST TRYING TO HELP MY FRIEND. I--I DIDN'T MEAN TO--
FUCKING BITCH!
TRY AND SWING THAT SHIT AT ME!
NO--!
UNG!
SPLSH
RAH!
W-WHA--?!
OH MY GOD...
HOLY FUCKIN' SHIT...
AH!
AH!

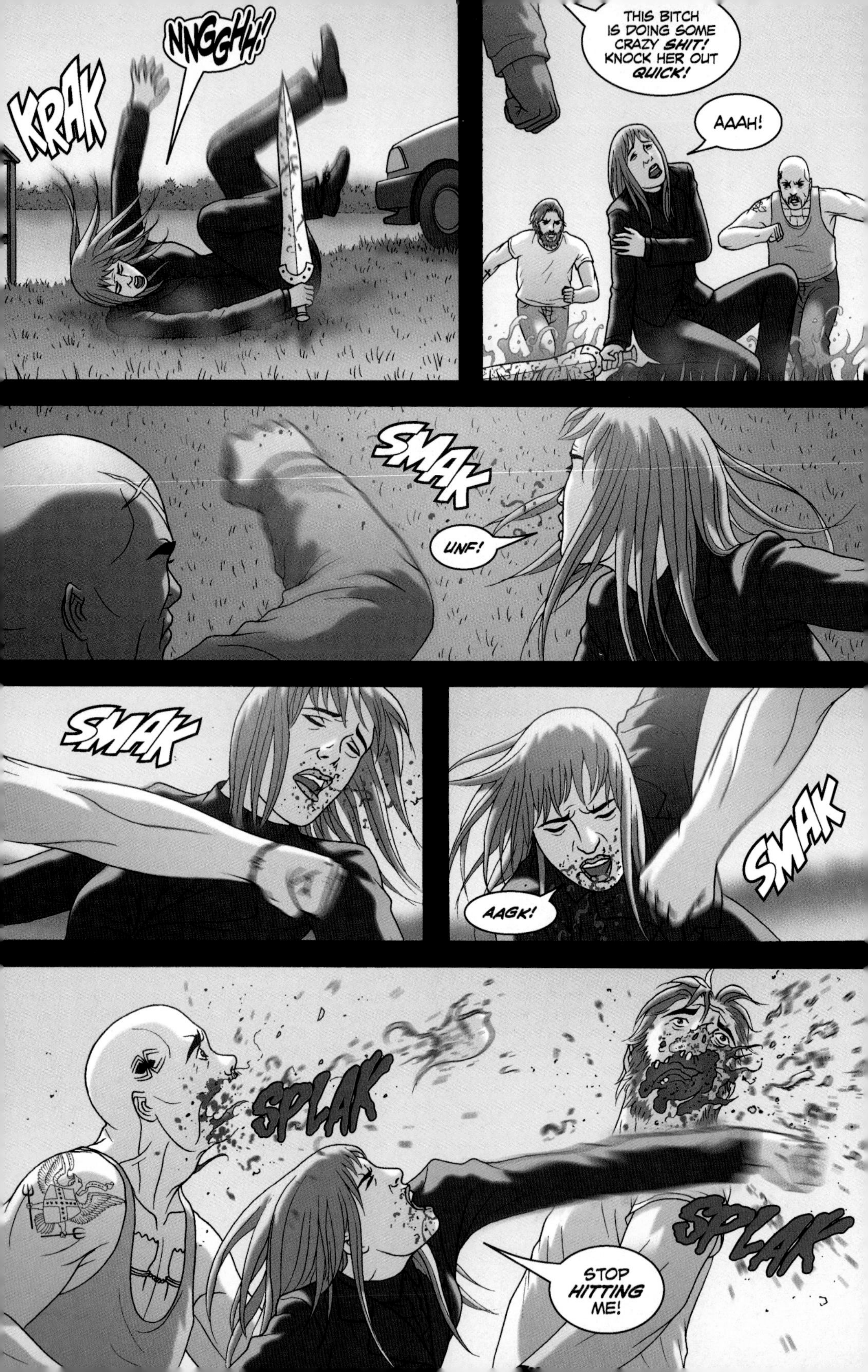
KRAK
NNGGHH!
THIS BITCH IS DOING SOME CRAZY SHIT! KNOCK HER OUT QUICK!
AAAH!
SMAK
UNF!
SMAK
SMAK
AAGK!
SPLAK
SPLAK
STOP HITTING ME!

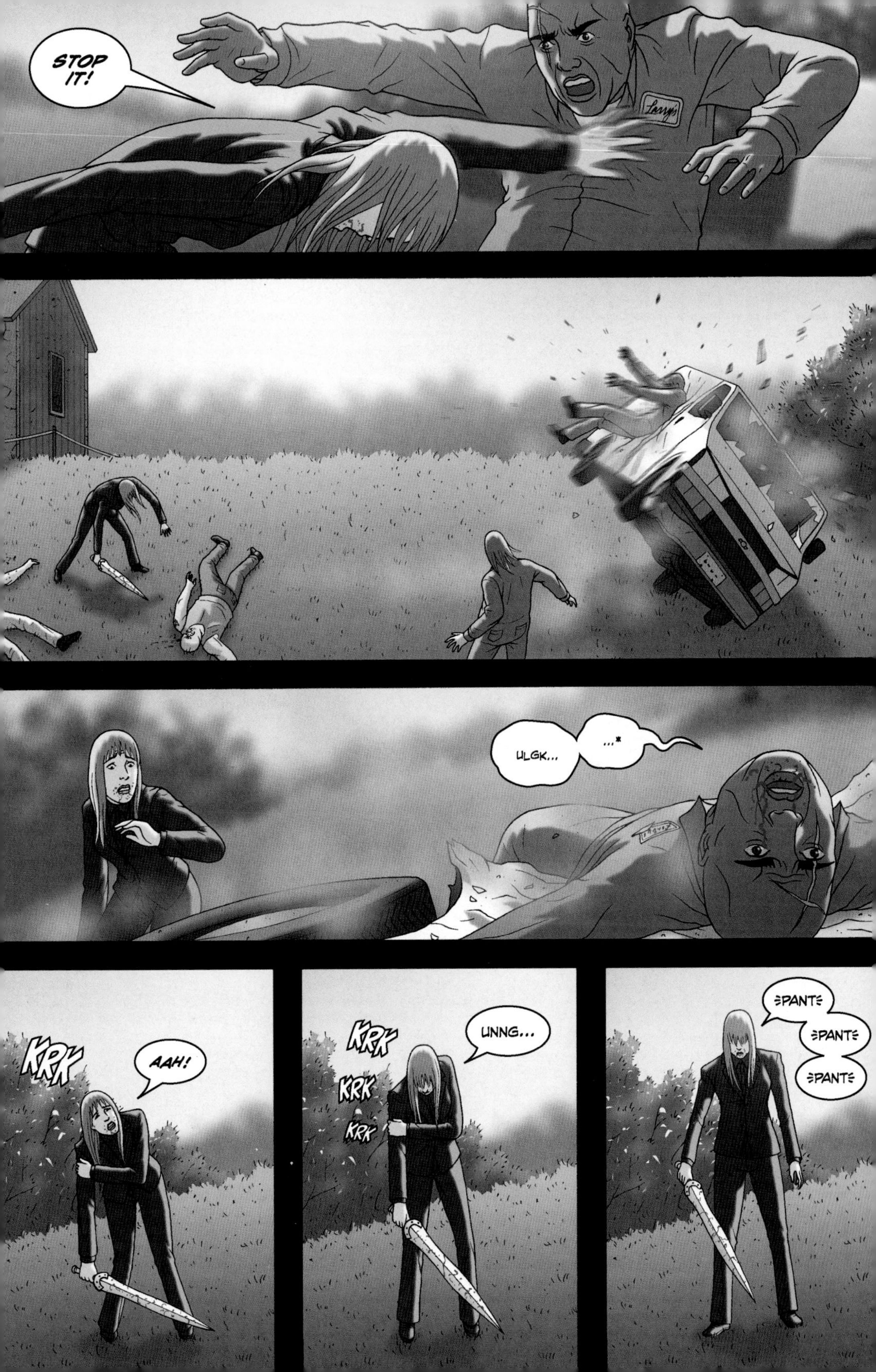
STOP IT!
ULGK...
...*
KRK
AAH!
KRK
KRK
KRK
UNNG...
PANT
PANT
PANT

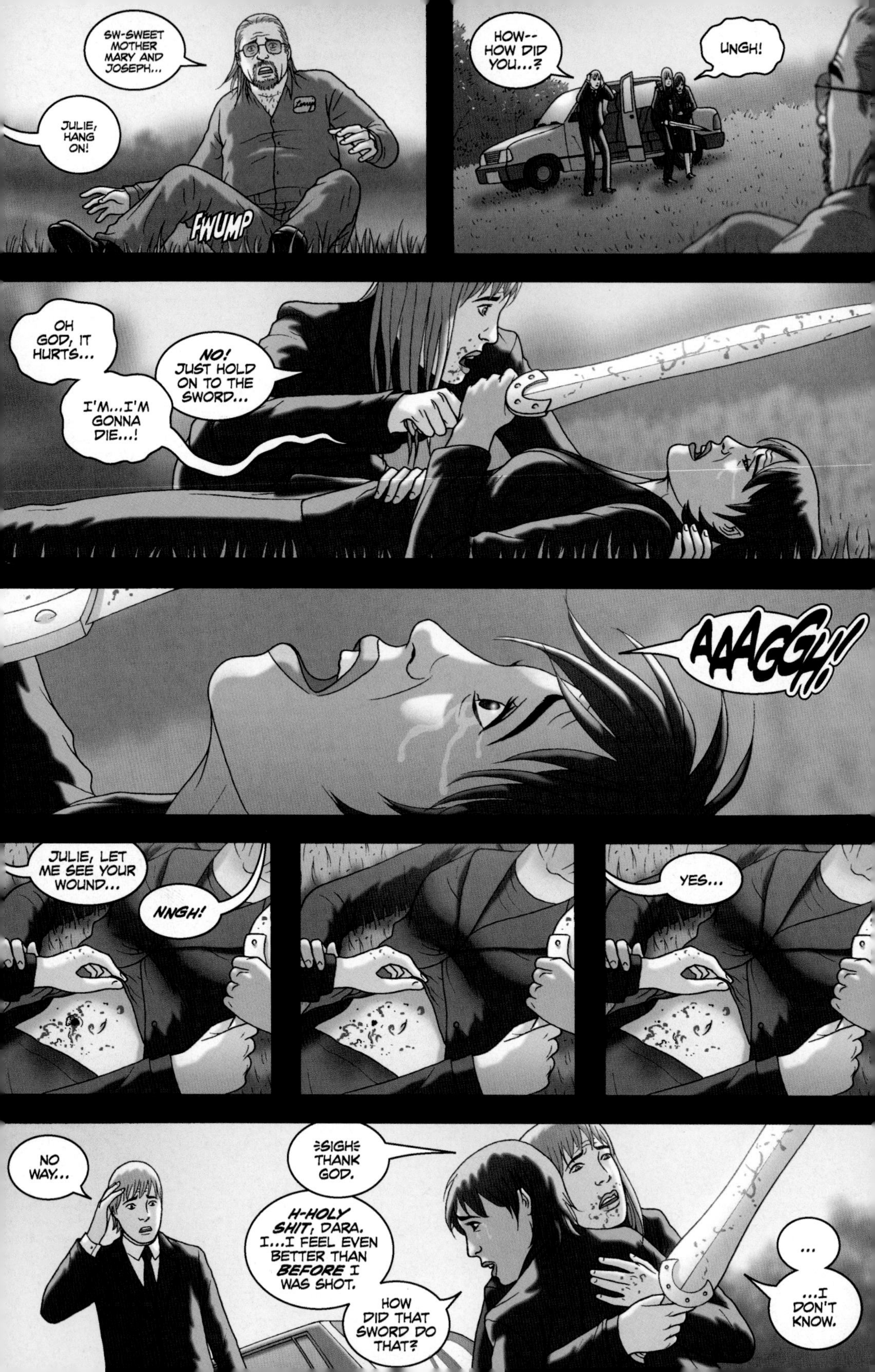
SW-SWEET MOTHER MARY AND JOSEPH...
JULIE, HANG ON!
FWUMP
HOW-- HOW DID YOU...?
UNGH!
OH GOD, IT HURTS...
I'M...I'M GONNA DIE...!
NO! JUST HOLD ON TO THE SWORD...
AAAGGH!!
JULIE, LET ME SEE YOUR WOUND...
NNGH!
YES...
NO WAY...
SIGH THANK GOD.
H-HOLY SHIT, DARA. I...I FEEL EVEN BETTER THAN BEFORE I WAS SHOT.
HOW DID THAT SWORD DO THAT?
...
...I DON'T KNOW.

AH--!

H-HOLD ON, NOW... IT WASN'T PERSONAL, *ALRIGHT?*

I WAS JUST HIRED TO NAB YOU.

WHO HIRED YOU?! THE PEOPLE WHO KILLED MY FAMILY?!

WHAT? I DON'T KNOW WHO DID THAT! I ANSWER TO *ONE* GUY, OKAY?

WHO?! WHAT'S HIS *NAME?!*

I DON'T EVEN KNOW THAT. HE'S MY ICE SUPPLIER. THAT'S *ALL* I KNOW, HONEST TO GOD. I DON'T KNOW WHERE HE *LIVES*, WHAT HE *LOOKS* LIKE. WE ONLY COMMUNICATE BY PHONE. HE SENDS ME PRODUCT, AND I SEND HIM MONEY OR DO ODD JOBS FOR HIM. IT'S JUST *BUSINESS.*

ICE CUBE BUSINESS?

JESUS, GIRL--*CRANK.* METH.

WHAT'S HIS PHONE NUMBER?

I NEVER CALL HIM, HE CALLS ME. HE'S A CAUTIOUS MOTHER-FUCKER.

YOU SAID YOU TWO SEND EACH OTHER THINGS. THAT MEANS THERE'S A *TRAIL.*

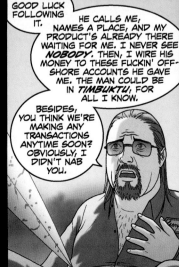

GOOD LUCK FOLLOWING IT.

HE CALLS ME, NAMES A PLACE, AND MY PRODUCT'S ALREADY THERE WAITING FOR ME. I NEVER SEE *NOBODY.* THEN, I WIRE HIS MONEY TO THESE FUCKIN' OFF-SHORE ACCOUNTS HE GAVE ME. THE MAN COULD BE IN *TIMBUKTU,* FOR ALL I KNOW.

BESIDES, YOU THINK WE'RE MAKING ANY TRANSACTIONS ANYTIME SOON? OBVIOUSLY, I DIDN'T NAB YOU.

WAIT.

SAY YOU *DID.* HOW WOULD YOU DELIVER ME TO HIM?

I'D DROP YOU OFF AT SOME PLACE, THEN HE'D PICK YOU UP.

BUT DON'T BOTHER. AS CAREFUL AS HIS ASS IS, HE'D BE A NO-SHOW UNLESS I FOLLOW THE SPECIFIC INSTRUCTIONS HE GAVE ME.

OKAY. SO, WHAT IF WE *PRETEND* TO FOLLOW THEM?

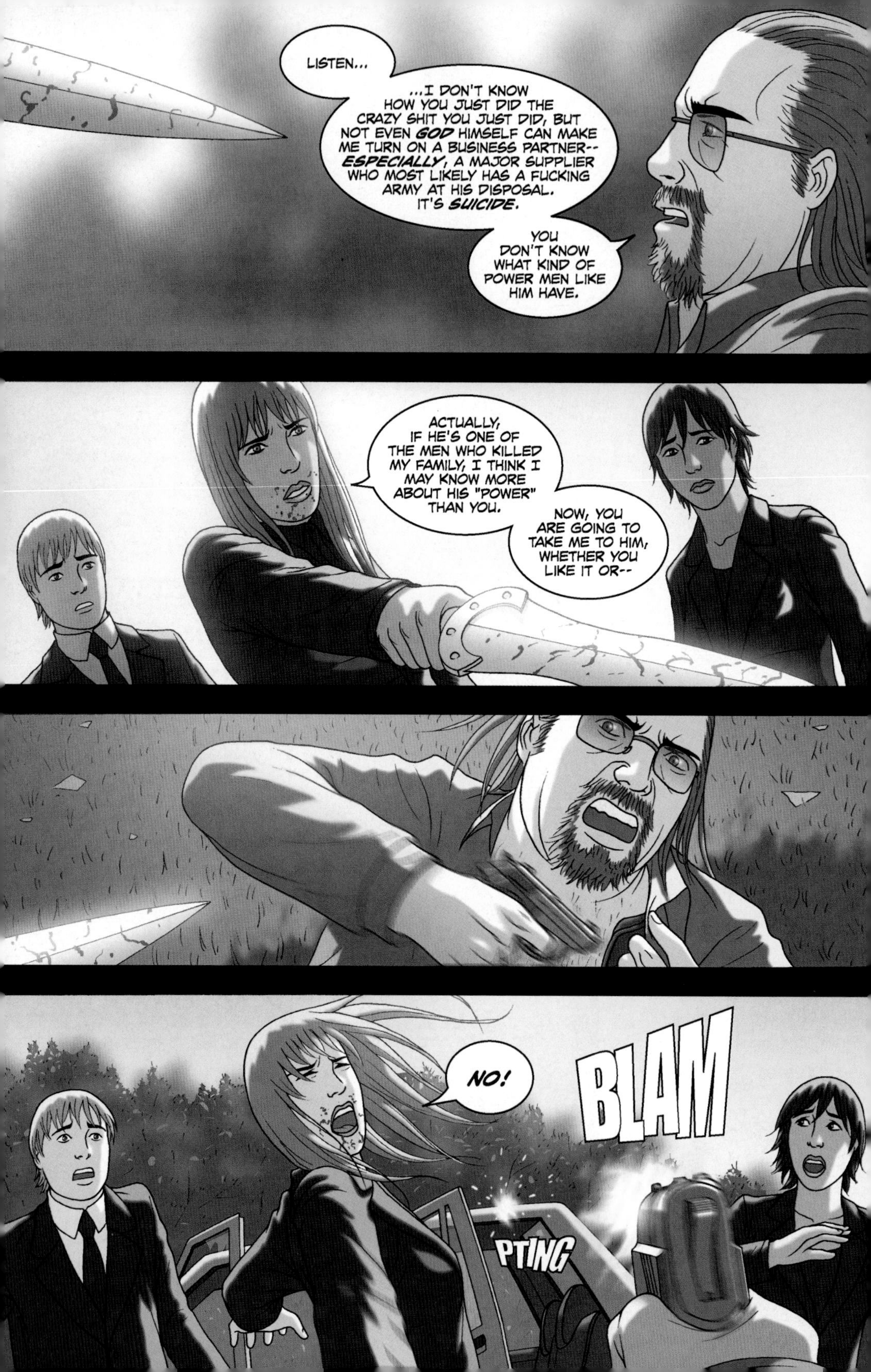

LISTEN...
...I DON'T KNOW HOW YOU JUST DID THE CRAZY SHIT YOU JUST DID, BUT NOT EVEN GOD HIMSELF CAN MAKE ME TURN ON A BUSINESS PARTNER-- ESPECIALLY, A MAJOR SUPPLIER WHO MOST LIKELY HAS A FUCKING ARMY AT HIS DISPOSAL. IT'S SUICIDE.
YOU DON'T KNOW WHAT KIND OF POWER MEN LIKE HIM HAVE.
ACTUALLY, IF HE'S ONE OF THE MEN WHO KILLED MY FAMILY, I THINK I MAY KNOW MORE ABOUT HIS "POWER" THAN YOU.
NOW, YOU ARE GOING TO TAKE ME TO HIM, WHETHER YOU LIKE IT OR--
NO!
BLAM
PTING

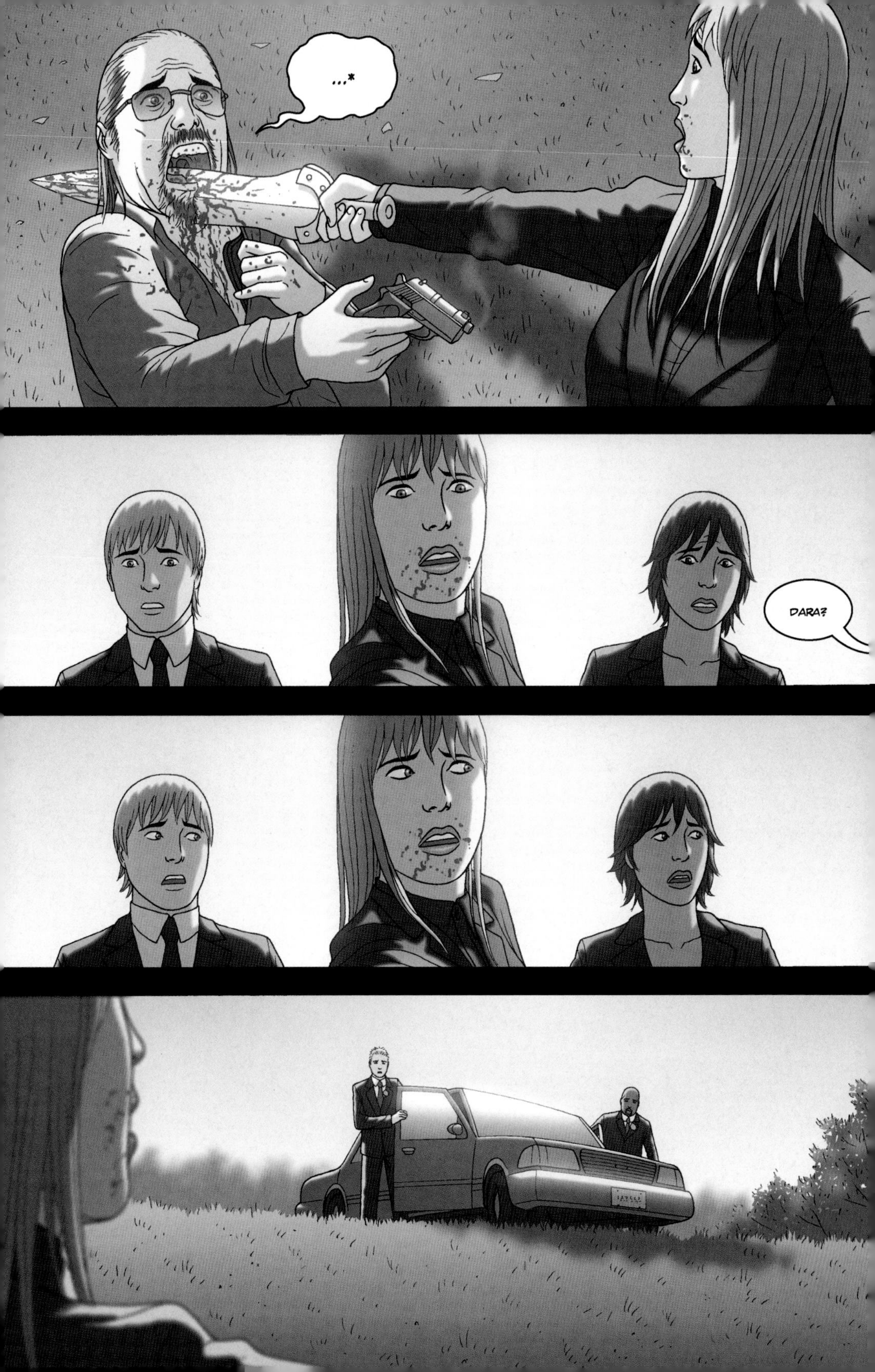

...*
DARA?

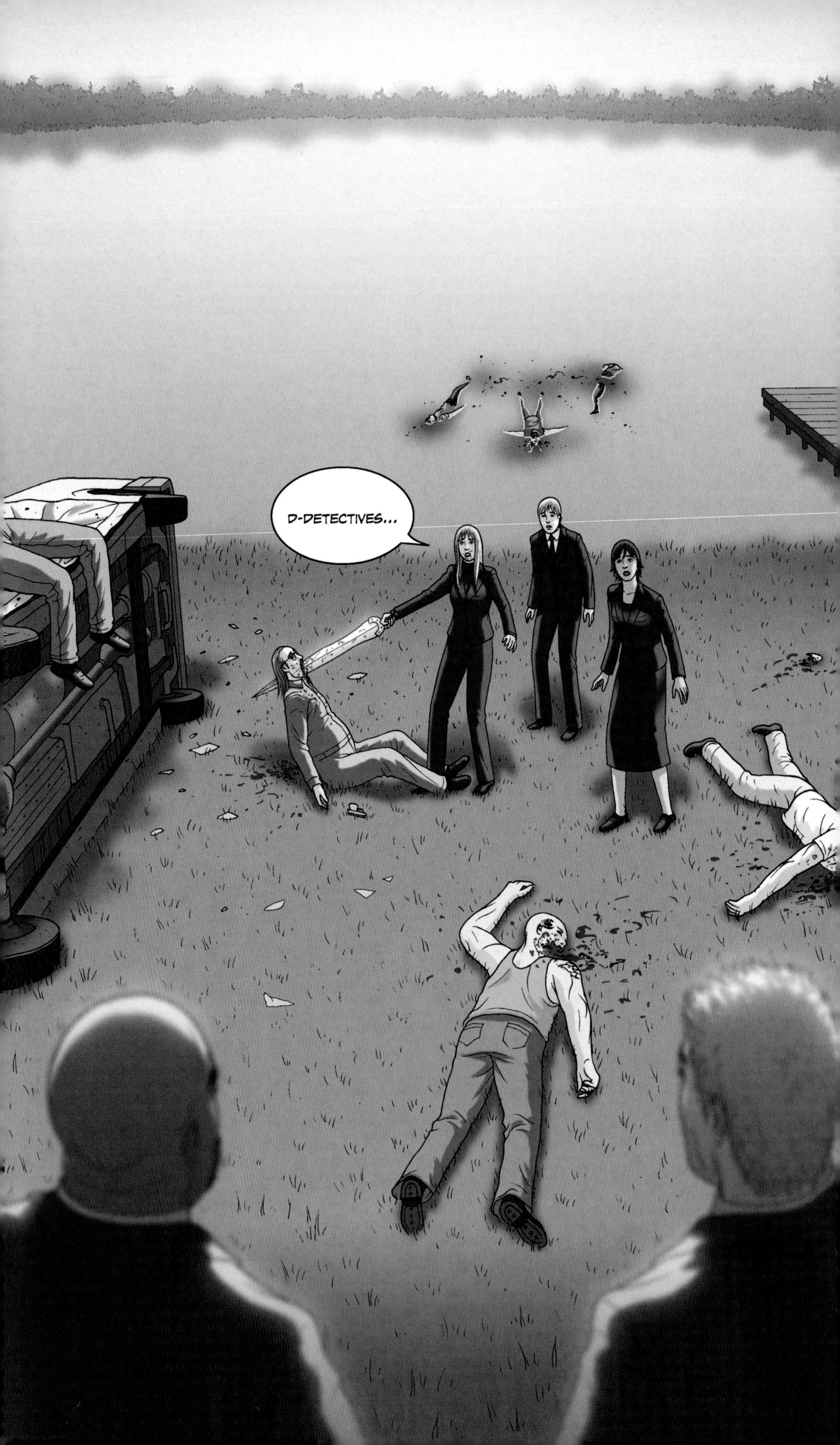
D-DETECTIVES...

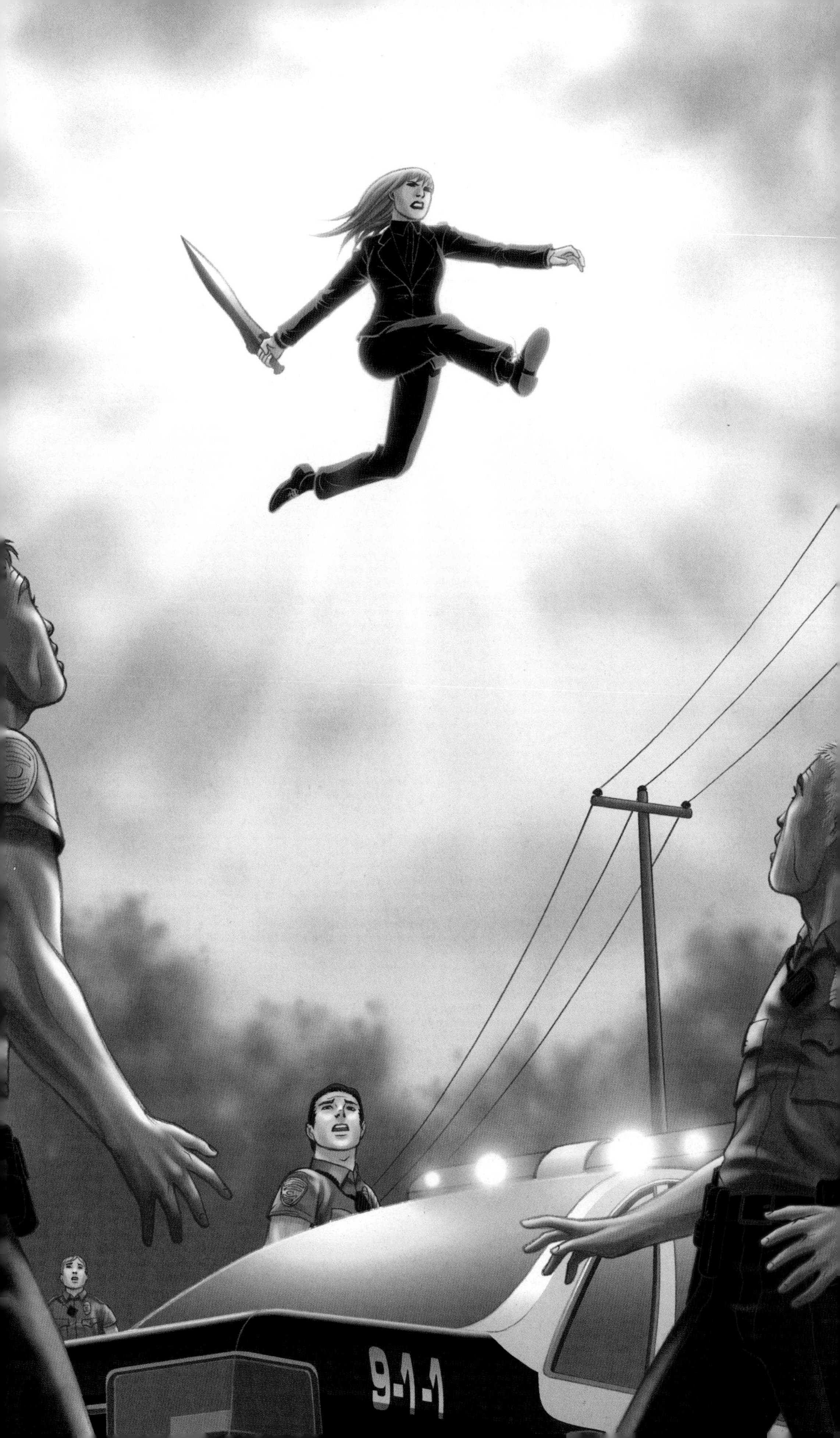
9-1-1

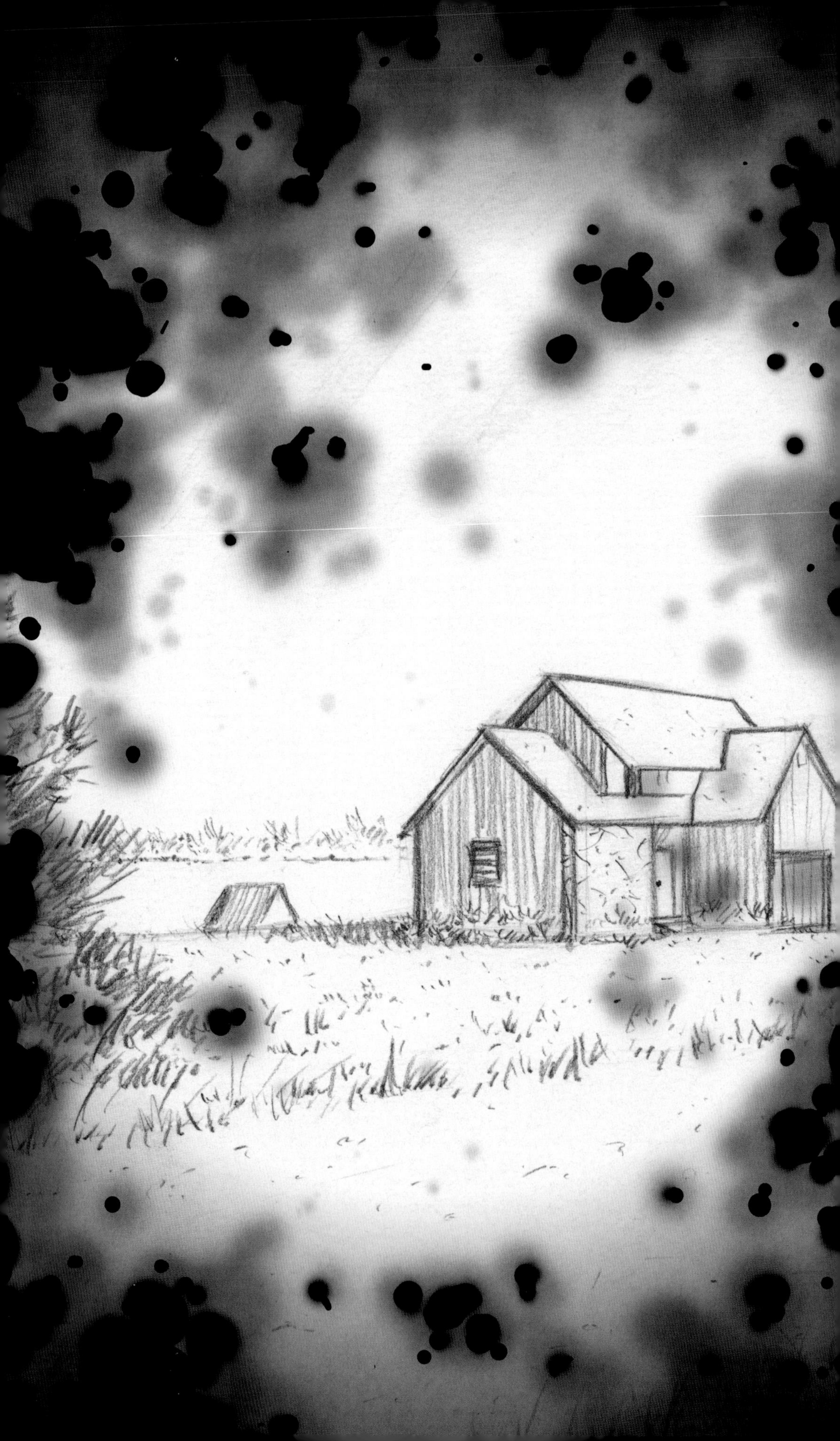

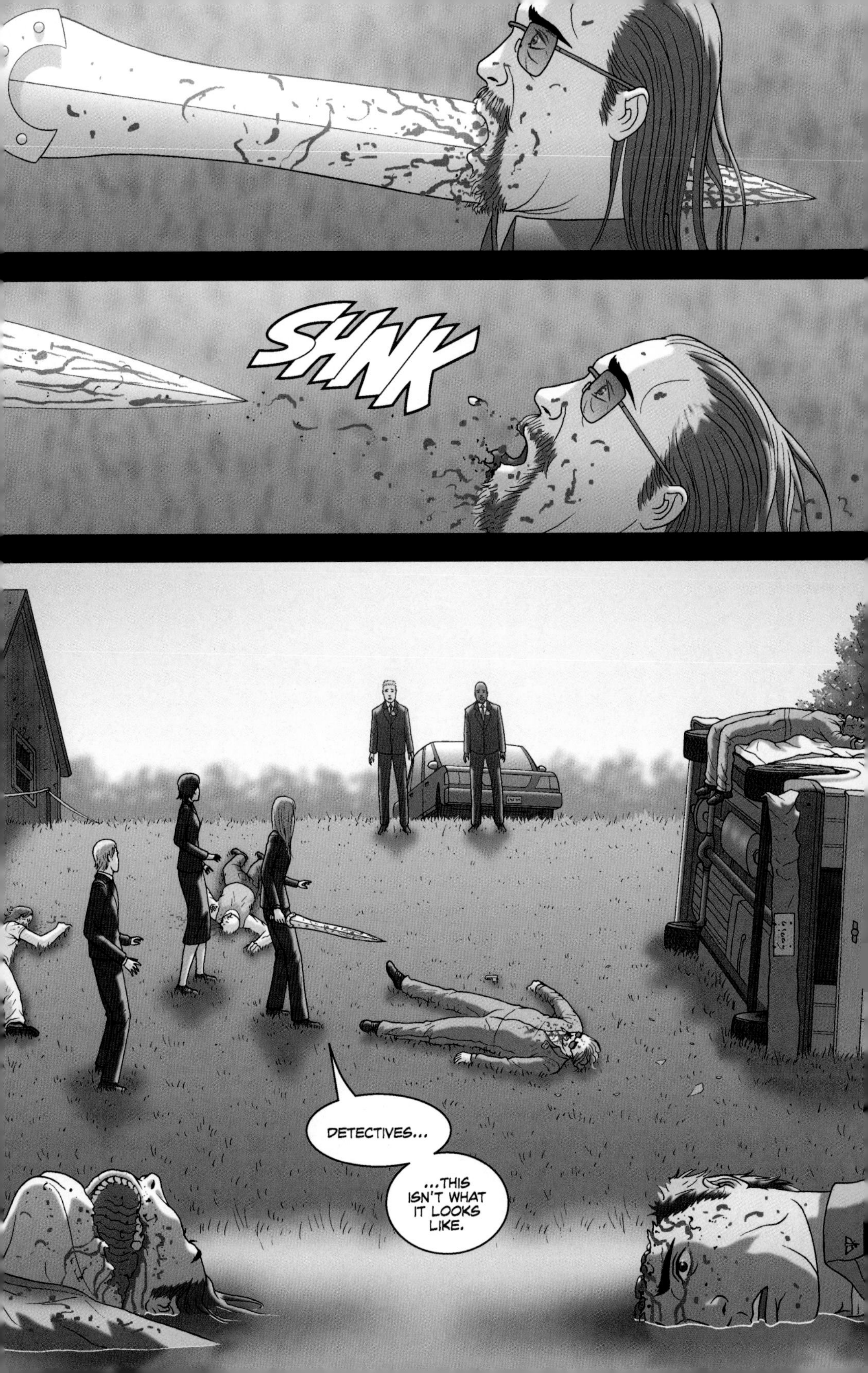
SHNK
DETECTIVES...
...THIS ISN'T WHAT IT LOOKS LIKE.

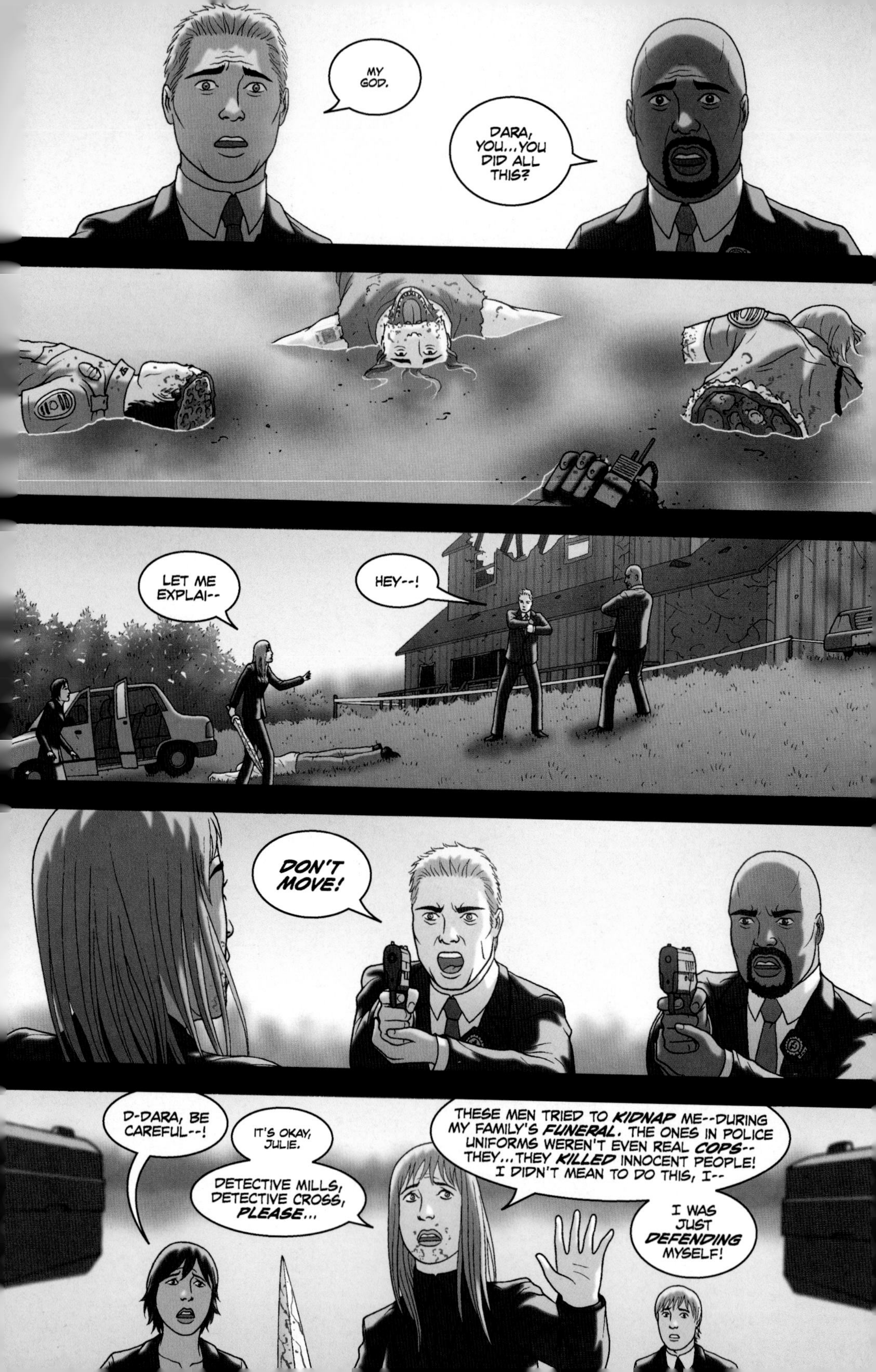
MY GOD.
DARA, YOU...YOU DID ALL THIS?
LET ME EXPLAI--
HEY--!
DON'T MOVE!
D-DARA, BE CAREFUL--!
IT'S OKAY, JULIE.
DETECTIVE MILLS, DETECTIVE CROSS, PLEASE...
THESE MEN TRIED TO KIDNAP ME--DURING MY FAMILY'S FUNERAL. THE ONES IN POLICE UNIFORMS WEREN'T EVEN REAL COPS--THEY...THEY KILLED INNOCENT PEOPLE! I DIDN'T MEAN TO DO THIS, I--
I WAS JUST DEFENDING MYSELF!

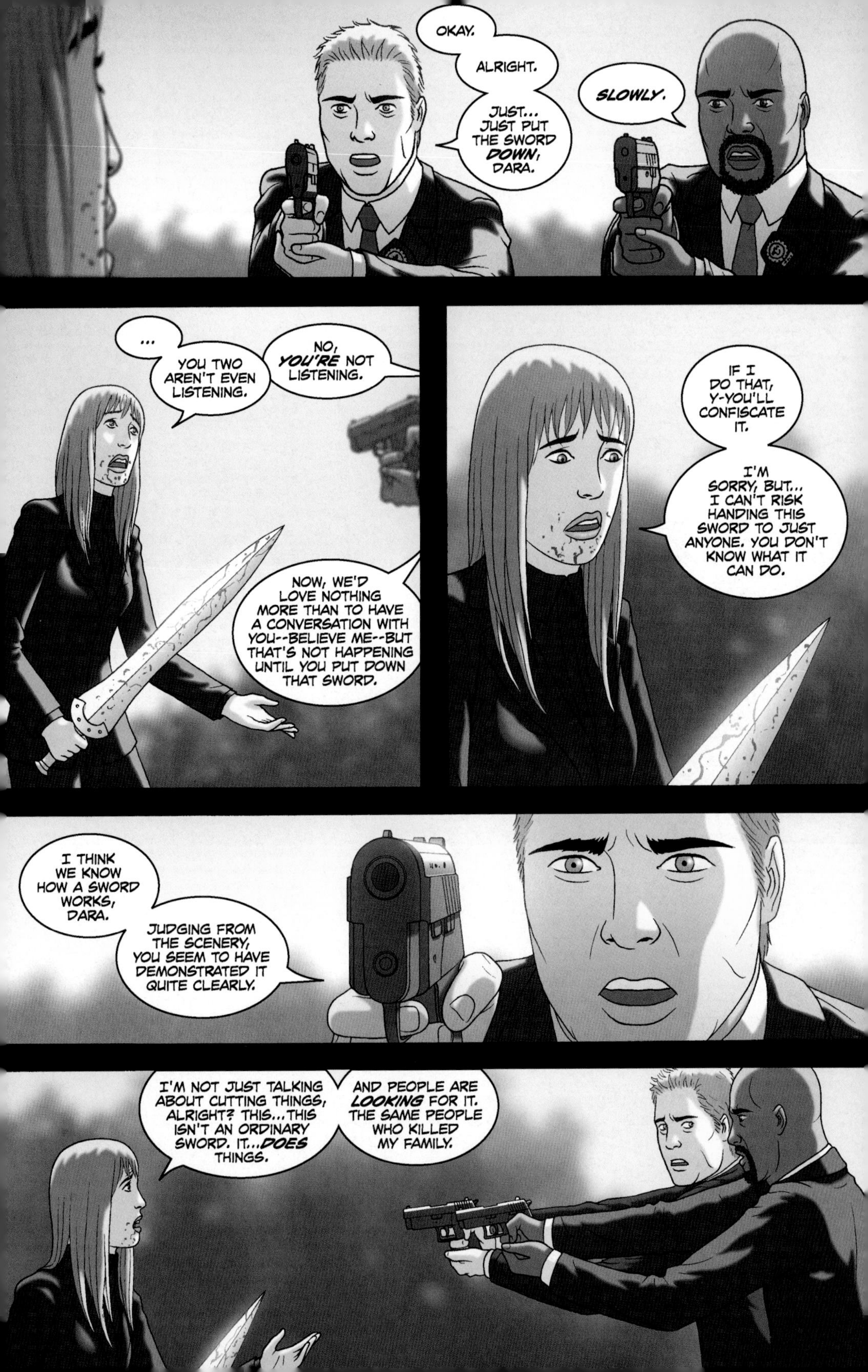
OKAY.
ALRIGHT.
JUST... JUST PUT THE SWORD DOWN, DARA.
SLOWLY.
...
YOU TWO AREN'T EVEN LISTENING.
NO, YOU'RE NOT LISTENING.
NOW, WE'D LOVE NOTHING MORE THAN TO HAVE A CONVERSATION WITH YOU--BELIEVE ME--BUT THAT'S NOT HAPPENING UNTIL YOU PUT DOWN THAT SWORD.
IF I DO THAT, Y-YOU'LL CONFISCATE IT.
I'M SORRY, BUT... I CAN'T RISK HANDING THIS SWORD TO JUST ANYONE. YOU DON'T KNOW WHAT IT CAN DO.
I THINK WE KNOW HOW A SWORD WORKS, DARA.
JUDGING FROM THE SCENERY, YOU SEEM TO HAVE DEMONSTRATED IT QUITE CLEARLY.
I'M NOT JUST TALKING ABOUT CUTTING THINGS, ALRIGHT? THIS...THIS ISN'T AN ORDINARY SWORD. IT...DOES THINGS.
AND PEOPLE ARE LOOKING FOR IT. THE SAME PEOPLE WHO KILLED MY FAMILY.

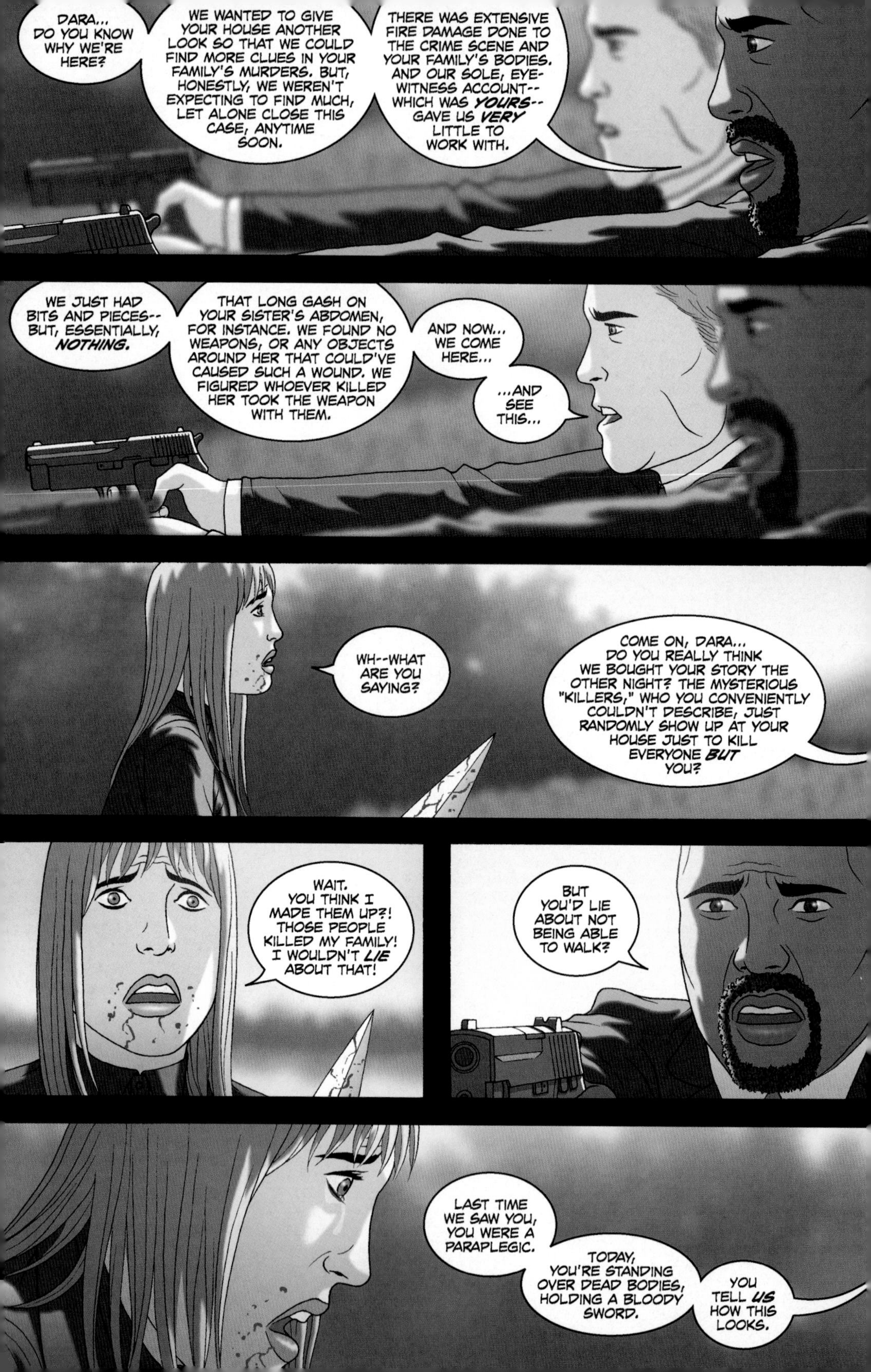
DARA... DO YOU KNOW WHY WE'RE HERE?
WE WANTED TO GIVE YOUR HOUSE ANOTHER LOOK SO THAT WE COULD FIND MORE CLUES IN YOUR FAMILY'S MURDERS. BUT, HONESTLY, WE WEREN'T EXPECTING TO FIND MUCH, LET ALONE CLOSE THIS CASE, ANYTIME SOON.
THERE WAS EXTENSIVE FIRE DAMAGE DONE TO THE CRIME SCENE AND YOUR FAMILY'S BODIES. AND OUR SOLE, EYE-WITNESS ACCOUNT-- WHICH WAS YOURS-- GAVE US VERY LITTLE TO WORK WITH.
WE JUST HAD BITS AND PIECES-- BUT, ESSENTIALLY, NOTHING.
THAT LONG GASH ON YOUR SISTER'S ABDOMEN, FOR INSTANCE. WE FOUND NO WEAPONS, OR ANY OBJECTS AROUND HER THAT COULD'VE CAUSED SUCH A WOUND. WE FIGURED WHOEVER KILLED HER TOOK THE WEAPON WITH THEM.
AND NOW... WE COME HERE...
...AND SEE THIS...
WH--WHAT ARE YOU SAYING?
COME ON, DARA... DO YOU REALLY THINK WE BOUGHT YOUR STORY THE OTHER NIGHT? THE MYSTERIOUS "KILLERS," WHO YOU CONVENIENTLY COULDN'T DESCRIBE, JUST RANDOMLY SHOW UP AT YOUR HOUSE JUST TO KILL EVERYONE BUT YOU?
WAIT. YOU THINK I MADE THEM UP?! THOSE PEOPLE KILLED MY FAMILY! I WOULDN'T LIE ABOUT THAT!
BUT YOU'D LIE ABOUT NOT BEING ABLE TO WALK?
LAST TIME WE SAW YOU, YOU WERE A PARAPLEGIC.
TODAY, YOU'RE STANDING OVER DEAD BODIES, HOLDING A BLOODY SWORD.
YOU TELL US HOW THIS LOOKS.

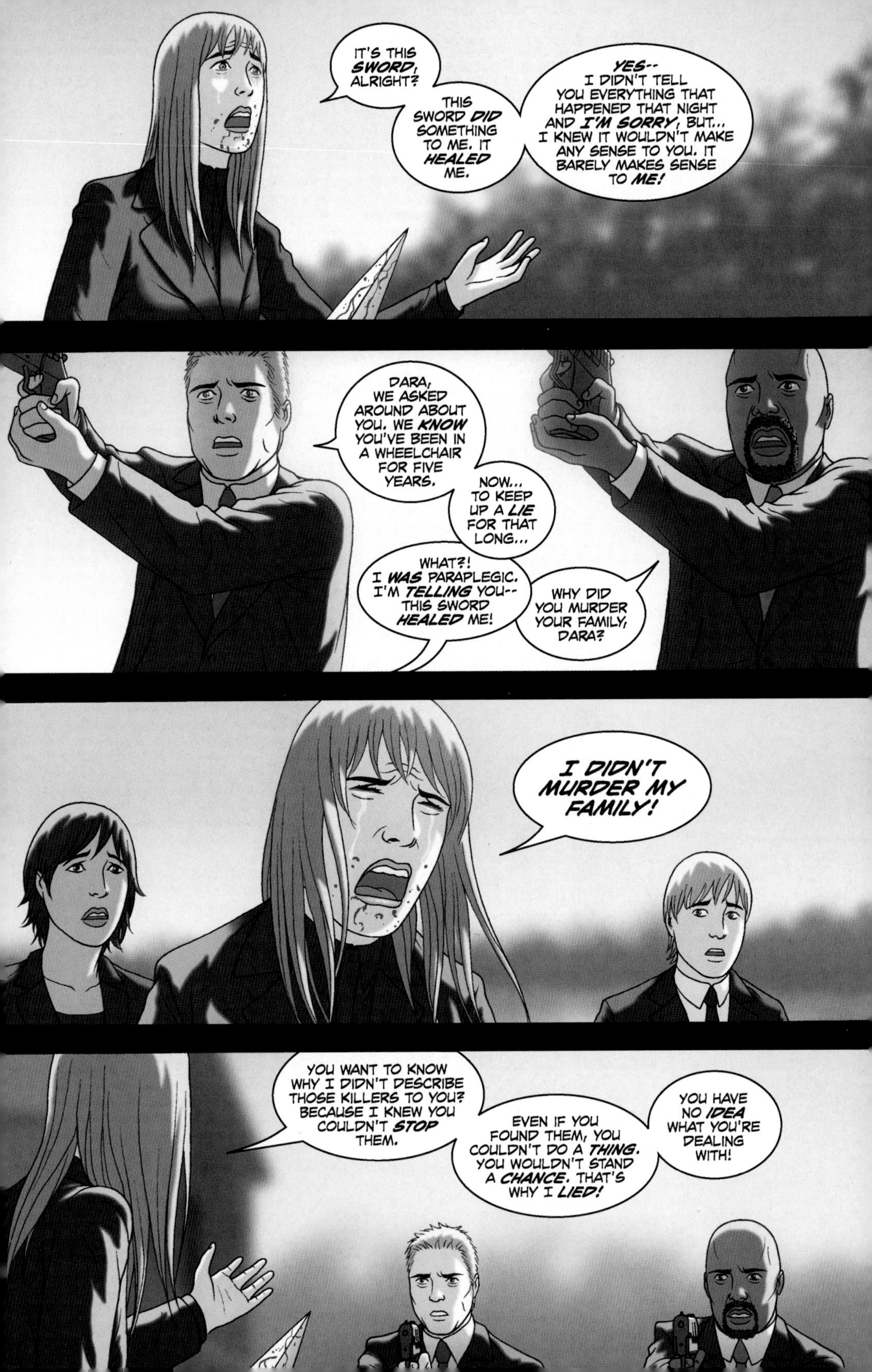
IT'S THIS SWORD, ALRIGHT?
THIS SWORD DID SOMETHING TO ME. IT HEALED ME.
YES-- I DIDN'T TELL YOU EVERYTHING THAT HAPPENED THAT NIGHT AND I'M SORRY, BUT... I KNEW IT WOULDN'T MAKE ANY SENSE TO YOU. IT BARELY MAKES SENSE TO ME!
DARA, WE ASKED AROUND ABOUT YOU. WE KNOW YOU'VE BEEN IN A WHEELCHAIR FOR FIVE YEARS.
NOW... TO KEEP UP A LIE FOR THAT LONG...
WHAT?! I WAS PARAPLEGIC. I'M TELLING YOU-- THIS SWORD HEALED ME!
WHY DID YOU MURDER YOUR FAMILY, DARA?
I DIDN'T MURDER MY FAMILY!
YOU WANT TO KNOW WHY I DIDN'T DESCRIBE THOSE KILLERS TO YOU? BECAUSE I KNEW YOU COULDN'T STOP THEM.
EVEN IF YOU FOUND THEM, YOU COULDN'T DO A THING. YOU WOULDN'T STAND A CHANCE. THAT'S WHY I LIED!
YOU HAVE NO IDEA WHAT YOU'RE DEALING WITH!

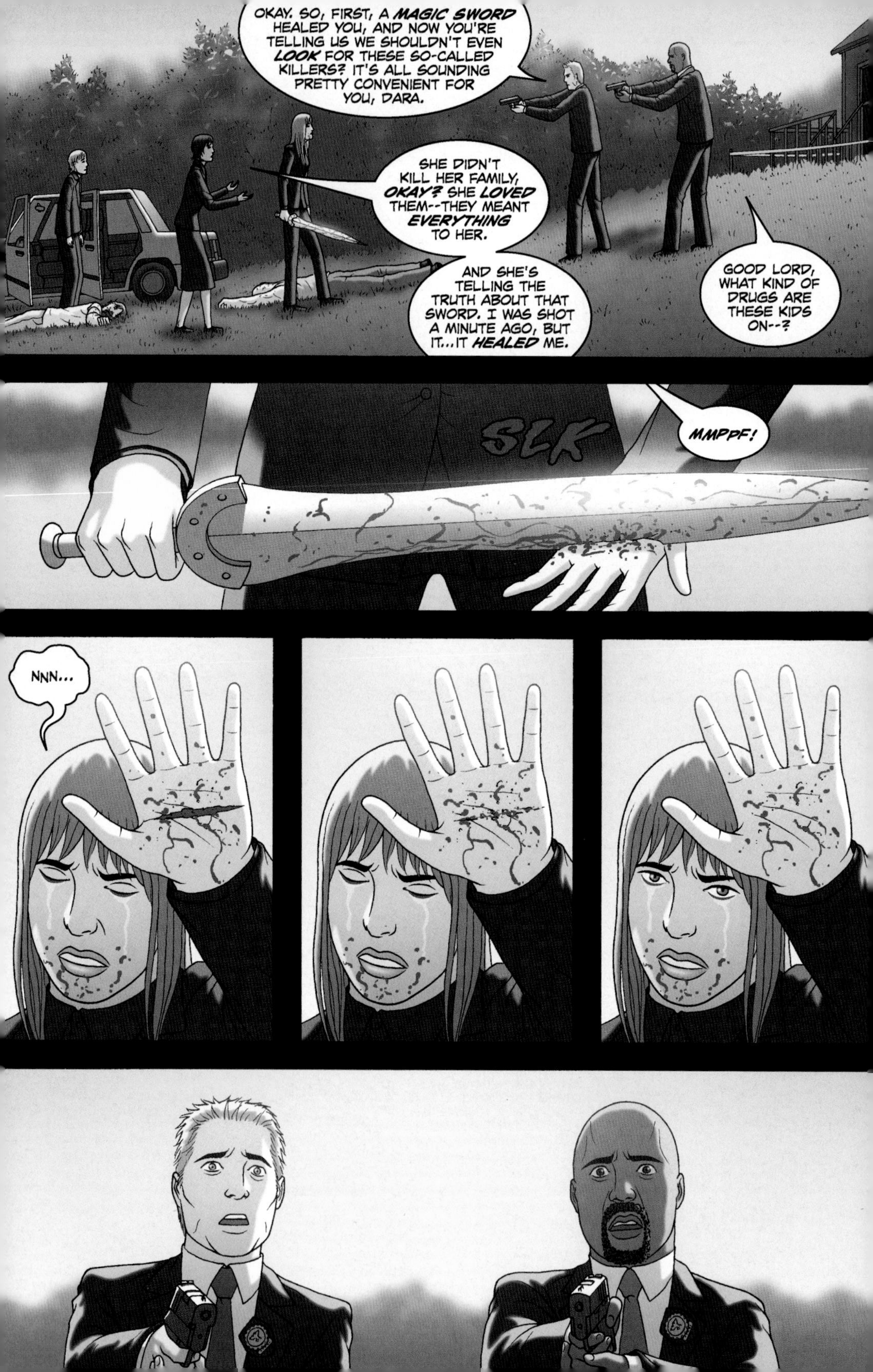
OKAY. SO, FIRST, A MAGIC SWORD HEALED YOU, AND NOW YOU'RE TELLING US WE SHOULDN'T EVEN LOOK FOR THESE SO-CALLED KILLERS? IT'S ALL SOUNDING PRETTY CONVENIENT FOR YOU, DARA.
SHE DIDN'T KILL HER FAMILY, OKAY? SHE LOVED THEM--THEY MEANT EVERYTHING TO HER.
AND SHE'S TELLING THE TRUTH ABOUT THAT SWORD. I WAS SHOT A MINUTE AGO, BUT IT...IT HEALED ME.
GOOD LORD, WHAT KIND OF DRUGS ARE THESE KIDS ON--?
SLK
MMPPF!
NNN...

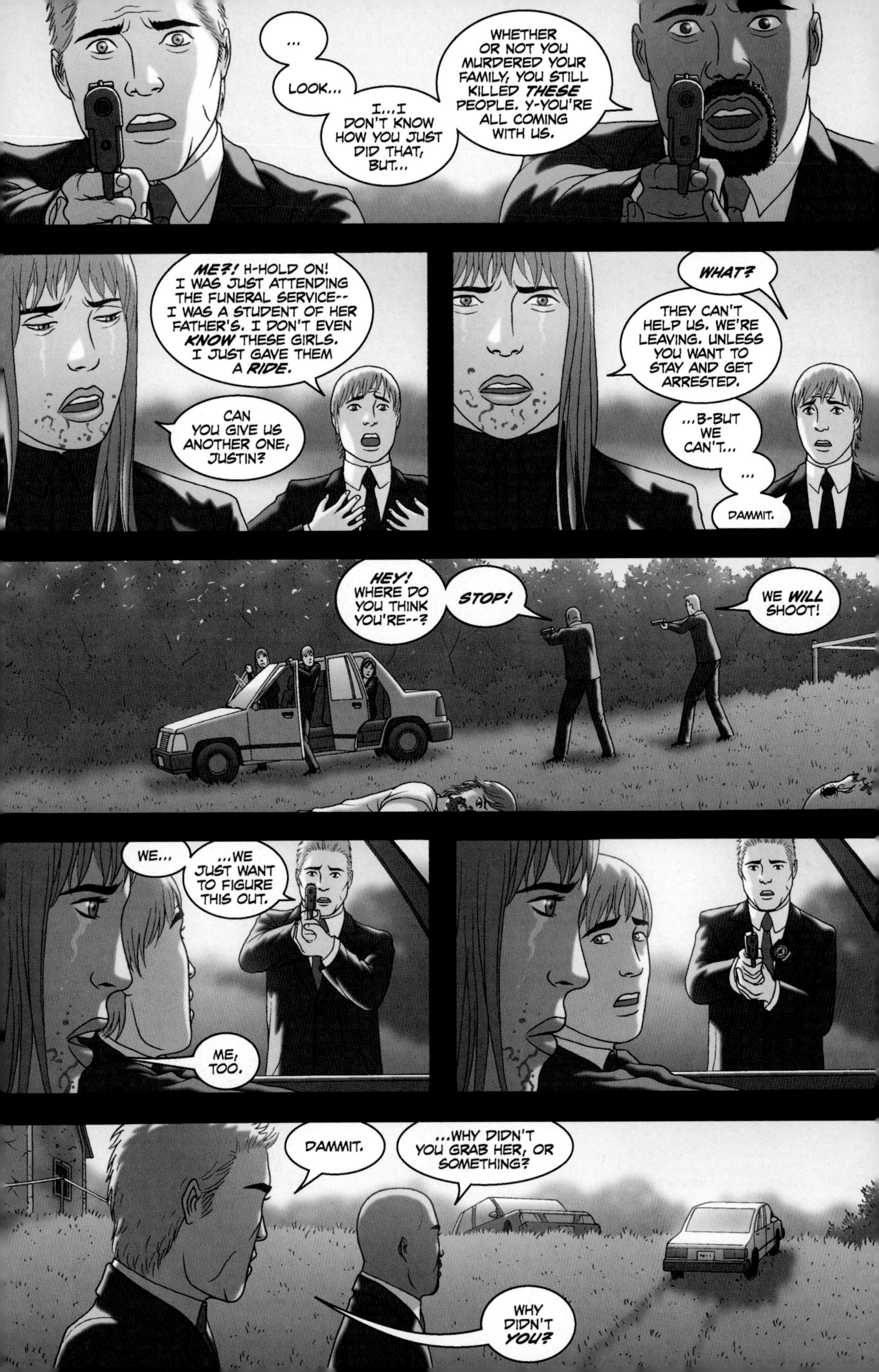
...
LOOK...
I...I DON'T KNOW HOW YOU JUST DID THAT, BUT...
WHETHER OR NOT YOU MURDERED YOUR FAMILY, YOU STILL KILLED THESE PEOPLE. Y-YOU'RE ALL COMING WITH US.
ME?! H-HOLD ON! I WAS JUST ATTENDING THE FUNERAL SERVICE-- I WAS A STUDENT OF HER FATHER'S. I DON'T EVEN KNOW THESE GIRLS. I JUST GAVE THEM A RIDE.
CAN YOU GIVE US ANOTHER ONE, JUSTIN?
WHAT?
THEY CAN'T HELP US. WE'RE LEAVING. UNLESS YOU WANT TO STAY AND GET ARRESTED.
...B-BUT WE CAN'T...
...
DAMMIT.
HEY! WHERE DO YOU THINK YOU'RE--?
STOP!
WE WILL SHOOT!
WE...
...WE JUST WANT TO FIGURE THIS OUT.
ME, TOO.
DAMMIT.
...WHY DIDN'T YOU GRAB HER, OR SOMETHING?
WHY DIDN'T YOU?

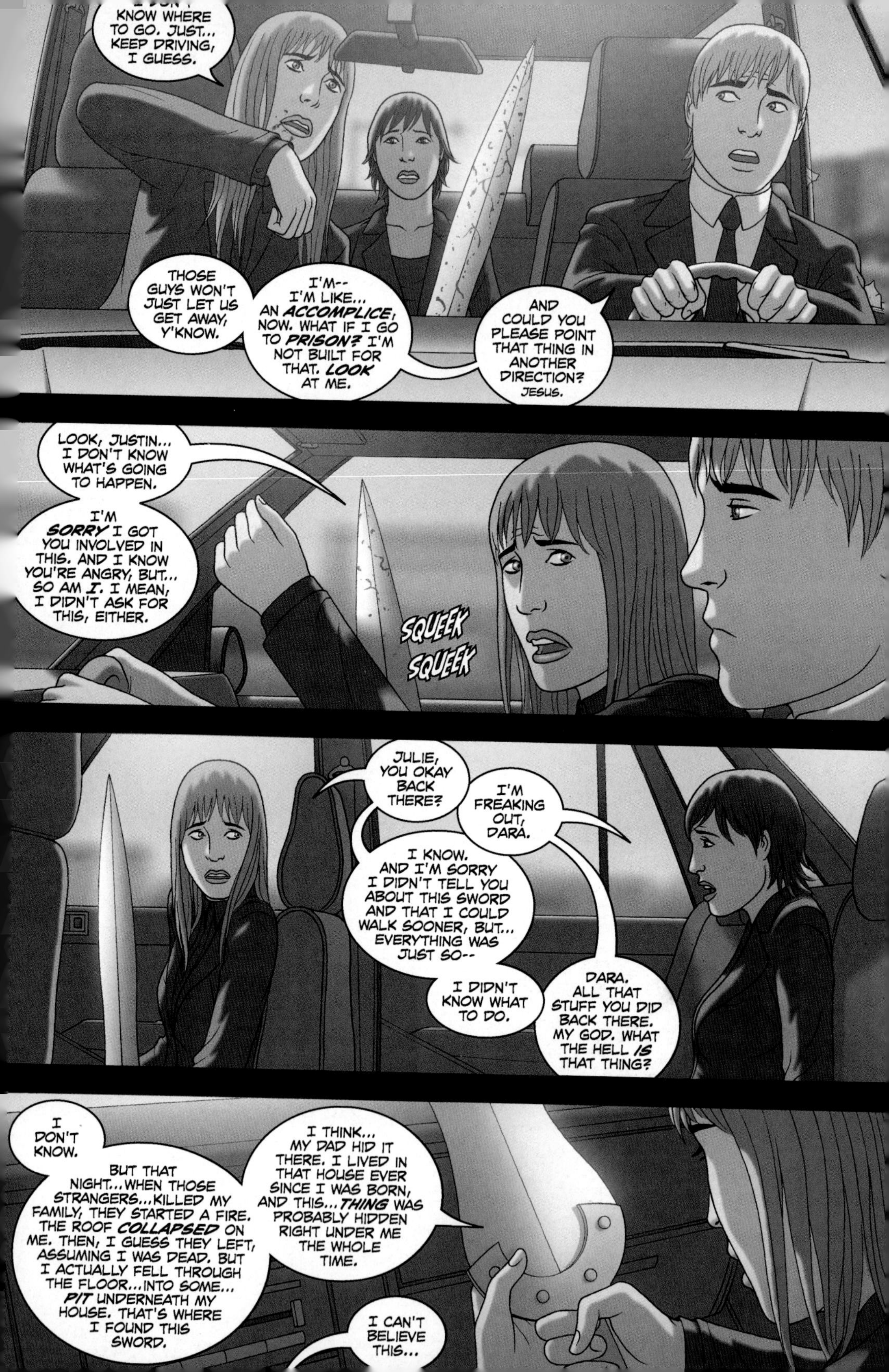
KNOW WHERE TO GO. JUST... KEEP DRIVING, I GUESS.
THOSE GUYS WON'T JUST LET US GET AWAY, Y'KNOW.
I'M-- I'M LIKE... AN ACCOMPLICE, NOW. WHAT IF I GO TO PRISON? I'M NOT BUILT FOR THAT. LOOK AT ME.
AND COULD YOU PLEASE POINT THAT THING IN ANOTHER DIRECTION? JESUS.
LOOK, JUSTIN... I DON'T KNOW WHAT'S GOING TO HAPPEN.
I'M SORRY I GOT YOU INVOLVED IN THIS. AND I KNOW YOU'RE ANGRY, BUT... SO AM I. I MEAN, I DIDN'T ASK FOR THIS, EITHER.
SQUEEK
SQUEEK
JULIE, YOU OKAY BACK THERE?
I'M FREAKING OUT, DARA.
I KNOW. AND I'M SORRY I DIDN'T TELL YOU ABOUT THIS SWORD AND THAT I COULD WALK SOONER, BUT... EVERYTHING WAS JUST SO--
I DIDN'T KNOW WHAT TO DO.
DARA. ALL THAT STUFF YOU DID BACK THERE. MY GOD. WHAT THE HELL IS THAT THING?
I DON'T KNOW.
BUT THAT NIGHT...WHEN THOSE STRANGERS...KILLED MY FAMILY, THEY STARTED A FIRE. THE ROOF COLLAPSED ON ME. THEN, I GUESS THEY LEFT, ASSUMING I WAS DEAD. BUT I ACTUALLY FELL THROUGH THE FLOOR...INTO SOME... PIT UNDERNEATH MY HOUSE. THAT'S WHERE I FOUND THIS SWORD.
I THINK... MY DAD HID IT THERE. I LIVED IN THAT HOUSE EVER SINCE I WAS BORN, AND THIS...THING WAS PROBABLY HIDDEN RIGHT UNDER ME THE WHOLE TIME.
I CAN'T BELIEVE THIS...

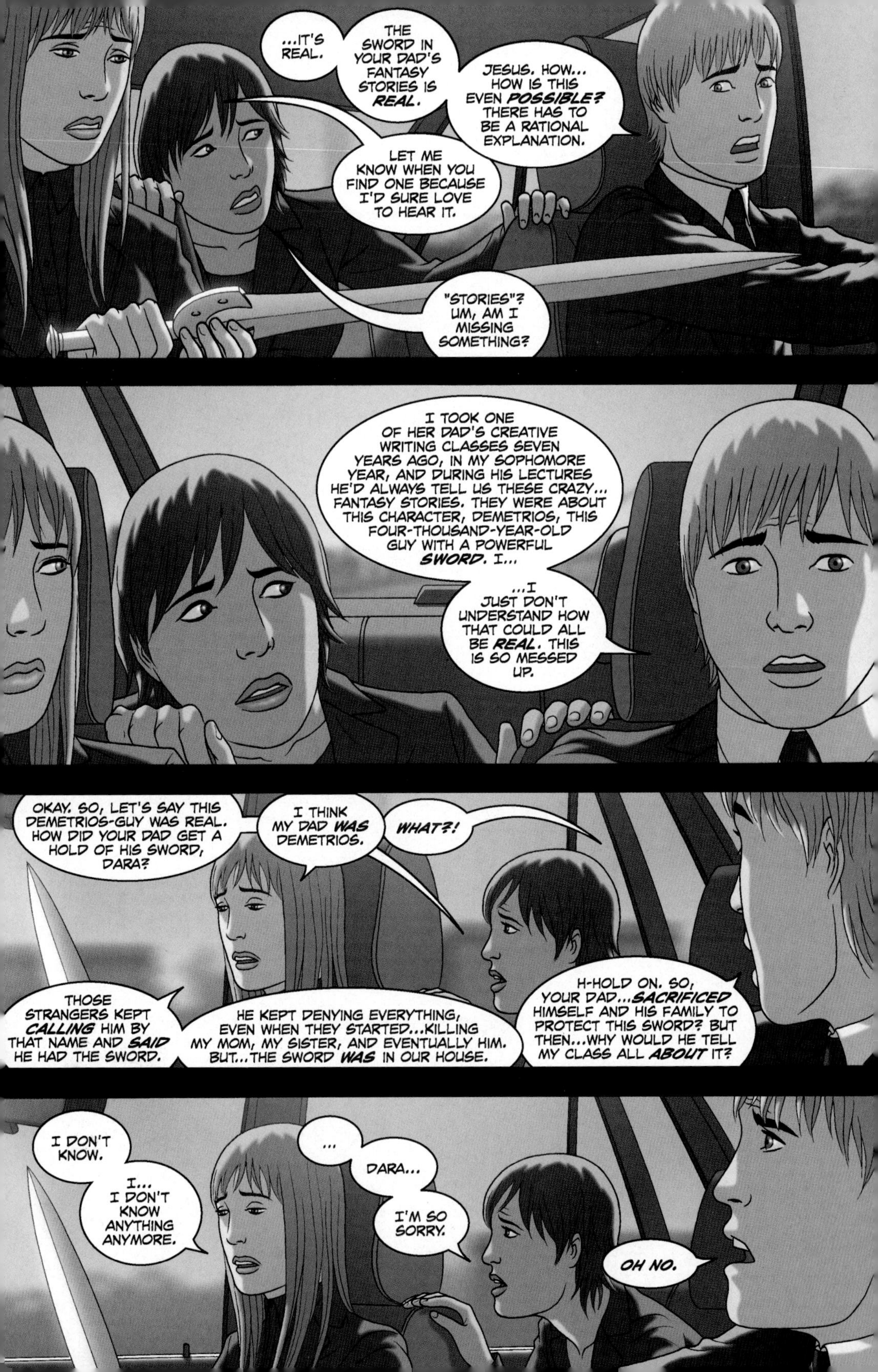
...IT'S REAL.
THE SWORD IN YOUR DAD'S FANTASY STORIES IS REAL.
JESUS. HOW... HOW IS THIS EVEN POSSIBLE? THERE HAS TO BE A RATIONAL EXPLANATION.
LET ME KNOW WHEN YOU FIND ONE BECAUSE I'D SURE LOVE TO HEAR IT.
"STORIES"? UM, AM I MISSING SOMETHING?
I TOOK ONE OF HER DAD'S CREATIVE WRITING CLASSES SEVEN YEARS AGO, IN MY SOPHOMORE YEAR, AND DURING HIS LECTURES HE'D ALWAYS TELL US THESE CRAZY... FANTASY STORIES. THEY WERE ABOUT THIS CHARACTER, DEMETRIOS, THIS FOUR-THOUSAND-YEAR-OLD GUY WITH A POWERFUL SWORD. I...
...I JUST DON'T UNDERSTAND HOW THAT COULD ALL BE REAL. THIS IS SO MESSED UP.
OKAY. SO, LET'S SAY THIS DEMETRIOS-GUY WAS REAL. HOW DID YOUR DAD GET A HOLD OF HIS SWORD, DARA?
I THINK MY DAD WAS DEMETRIOS.
WHAT?!
THOSE STRANGERS KEPT CALLING HIM BY THAT NAME AND SAID HE HAD THE SWORD.
HE KEPT DENYING EVERYTHING, EVEN WHEN THEY STARTED...KILLING MY MOM, MY SISTER, AND EVENTUALLY HIM. BUT...THE SWORD WAS IN OUR HOUSE.
H-HOLD ON. SO, YOUR DAD...SACRIFICED HIMSELF AND HIS FAMILY TO PROTECT THIS SWORD? BUT THEN...WHY WOULD HE TELL MY CLASS ALL ABOUT IT?
I DON'T KNOW.
I... I DON'T KNOW ANYTHING ANYMORE.
...
DARA...
I'M SO SORRY.
OH NO.

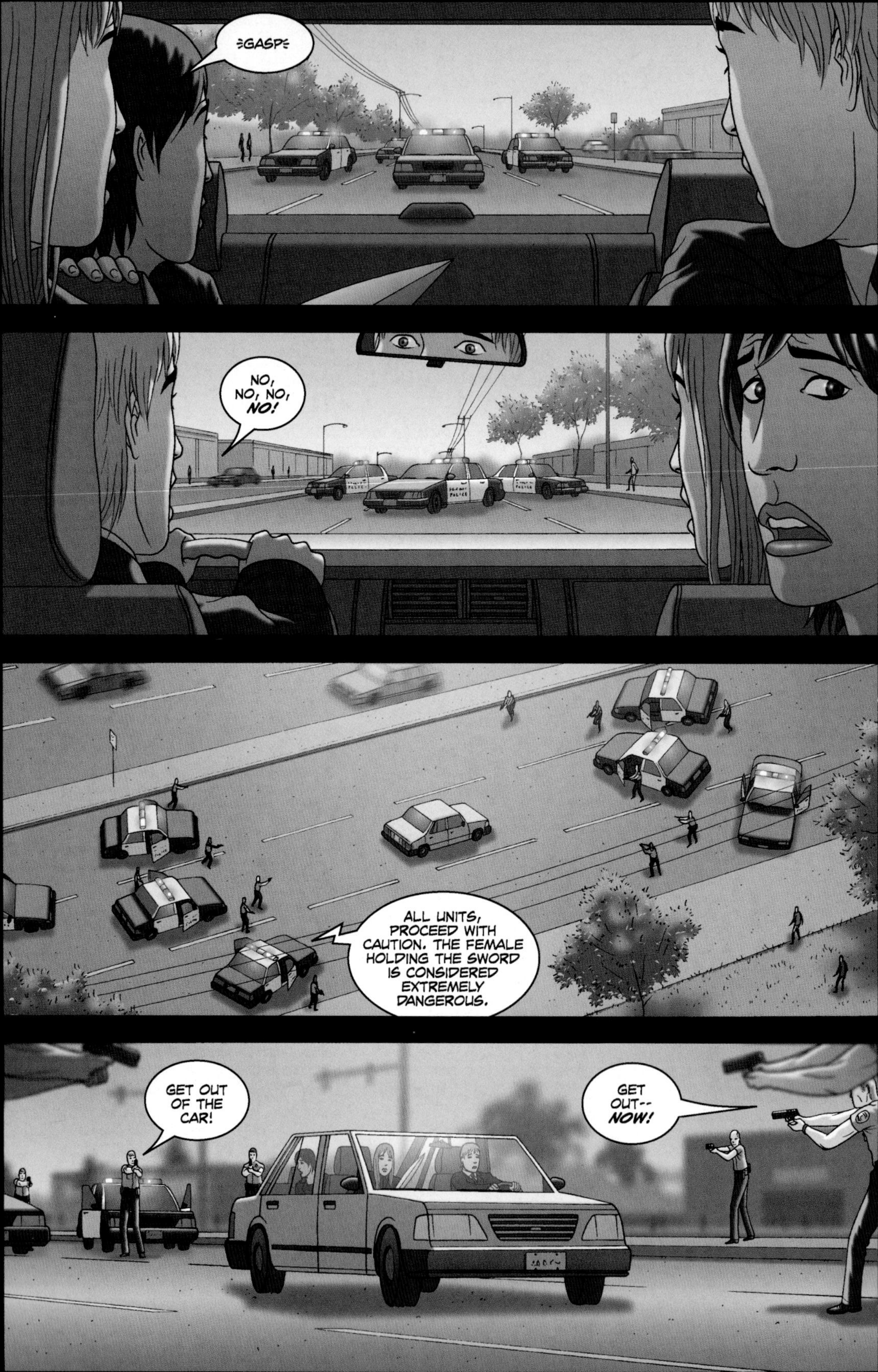

≡GASP≡
NO, NO, NO, NO!
ALL UNITS, PROCEED WITH CAUTION. THE FEMALE HOLDING THE SWORD IS CONSIDERED EXTREMELY DANGEROUS.
GET OUT OF THE CAR!
GET OUT-- NOW!

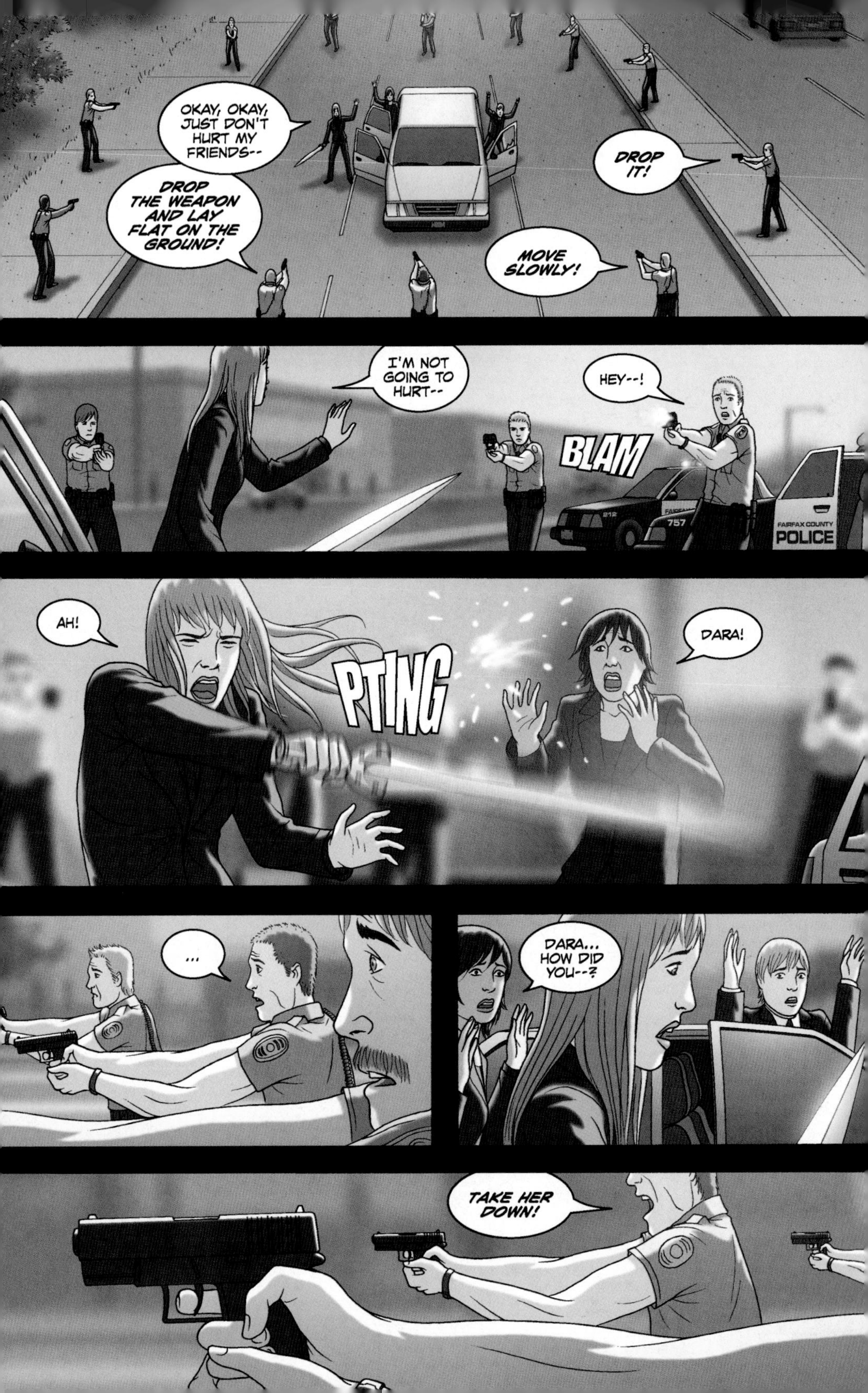
OKAY, OKAY, JUST DON'T HURT MY FRIENDS--
DROP THE WEAPON AND LAY FLAT ON THE GROUND!
DROP IT!
MOVE SLOWLY!
I'M NOT GOING TO HURT--
HEY--!
BLAM
757
FAIRFAX COUNTY
POLICE
AH!
PTING
DARA!
...
DARA... HOW DID YOU--?
TAKE HER DOWN!

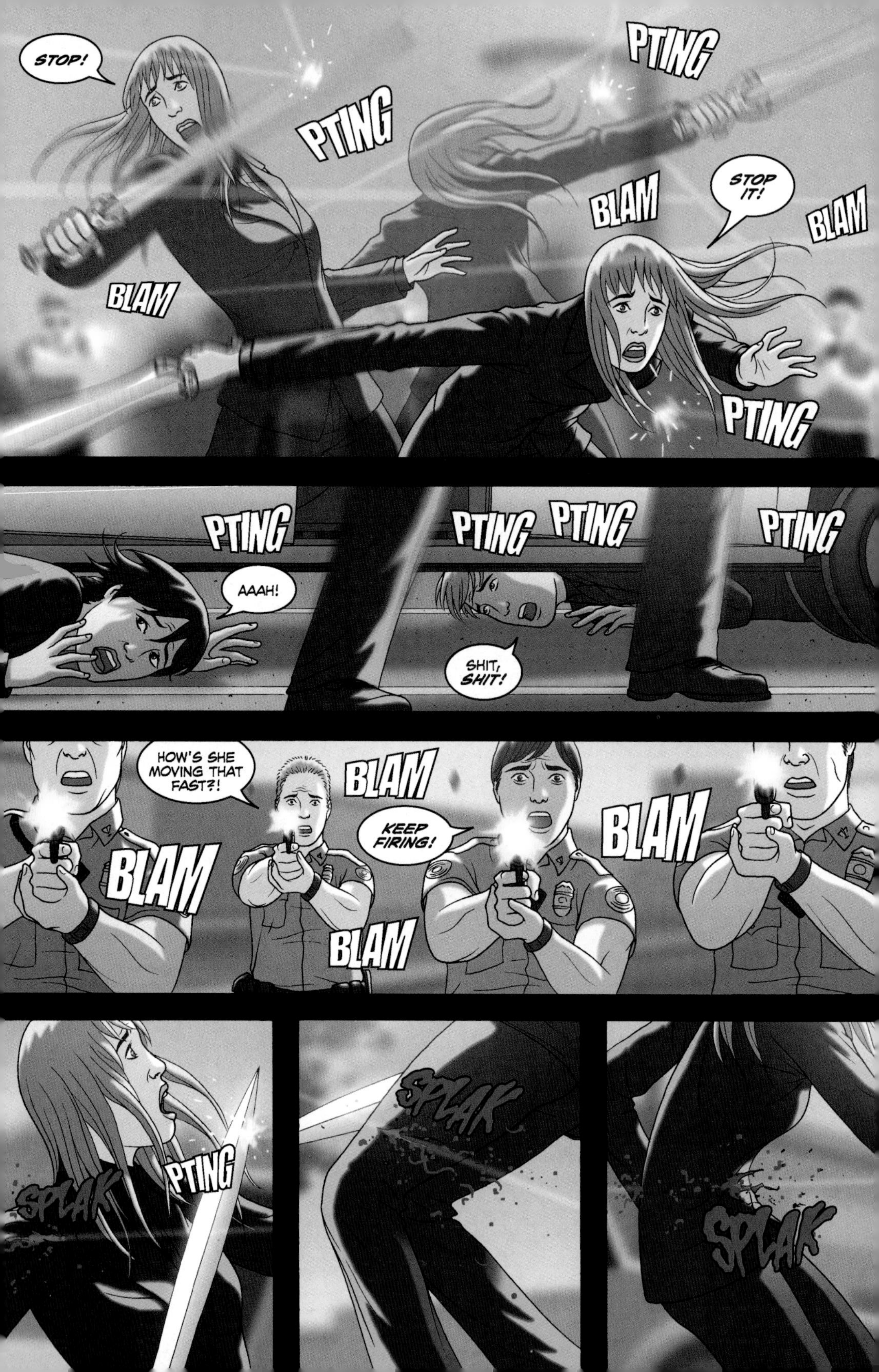
STOP!
PTING
PTING
BLAM
STOP IT!
BLAM
BLAM
PTING
PTING
PTING
PTING
PTING
AAAH!
SHIT, SHIT!
HOW'S SHE MOVING THAT FAST?!
BLAM
KEEP FIRING!
BLAM
BLAM
BLAM
SPLAK
PTING
SPLAK
SPLAK

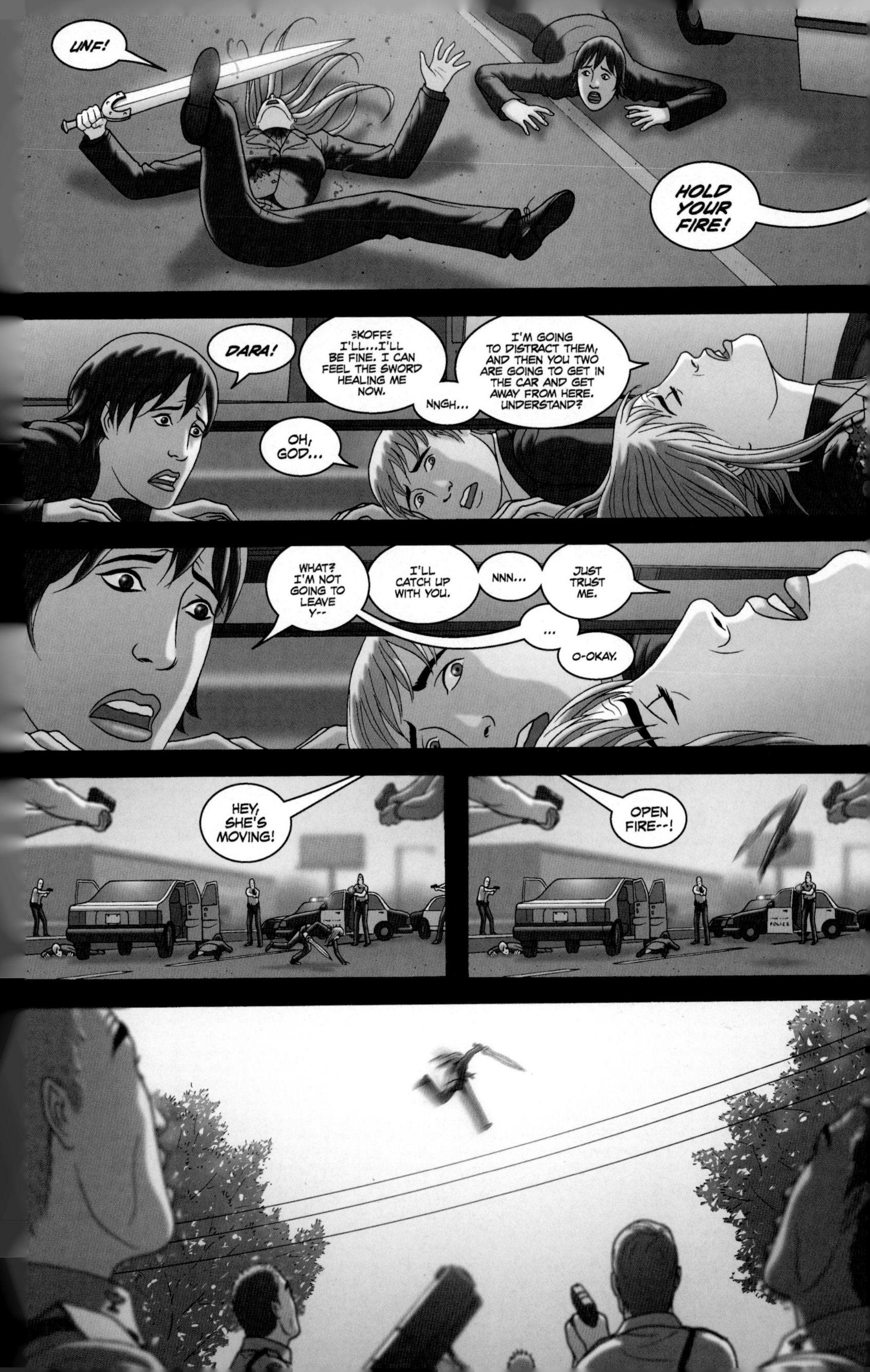
UNF!
HOLD YOUR FIRE!
DARA!
≠KOFF≠ I'LL...I'LL BE FINE. I CAN FEEL THE SWORD HEALING ME NOW.
NNGH...
I'M GOING TO DISTRACT THEM, AND THEN YOU TWO ARE GOING TO GET IN THE CAR AND GET AWAY FROM HERE. UNDERSTAND?
OH, GOD...
WHAT? I'M NOT GOING TO LEAVE Y--
I'LL CATCH UP WITH YOU.
NNN...
JUST TRUST ME.
...
O-OKAY.
HEY, SHE'S MOVING!
OPEN FIRE--!
POLICE

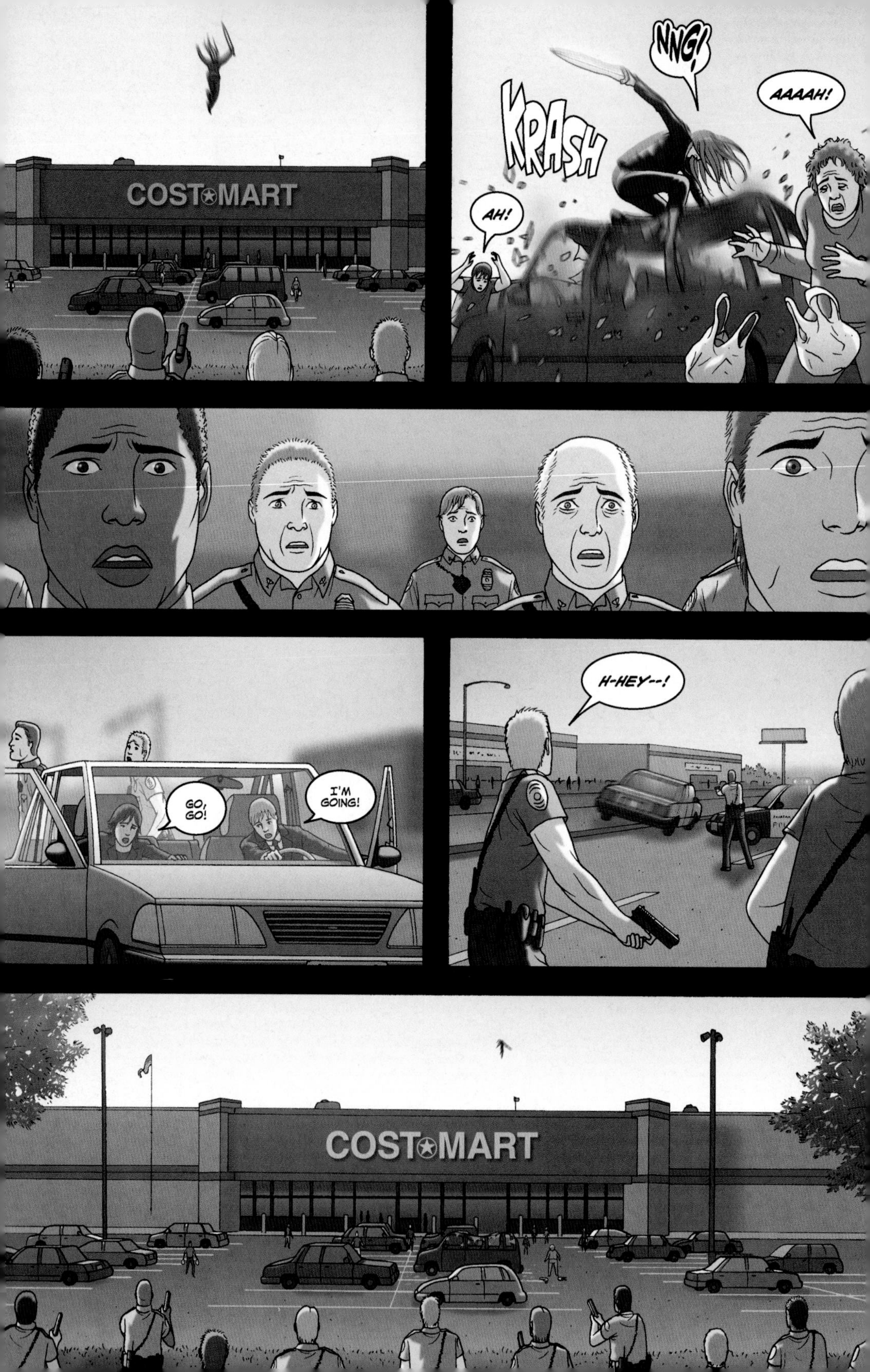
COST★MART
NNG!
KRASH
AAAAH!
AH!
GO, GO!
I'M GOING!
H-HEY--!
COST★MART

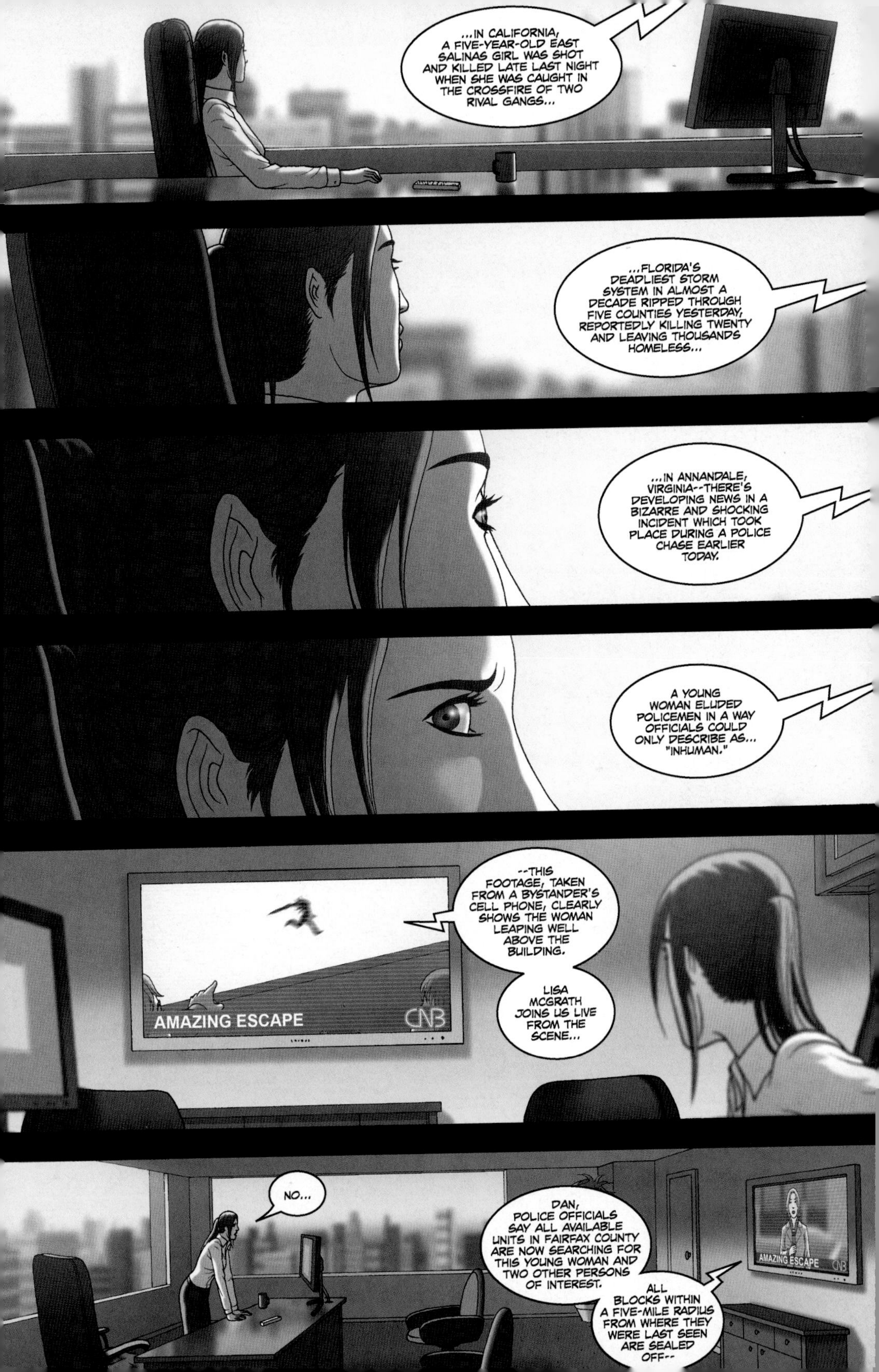
...IN CALIFORNIA, A FIVE-YEAR-OLD EAST SALINAS GIRL WAS SHOT AND KILLED LATE LAST NIGHT WHEN SHE WAS CAUGHT IN THE CROSSFIRE OF TWO RIVAL GANGS...
...FLORIDA'S DEADLIEST STORM SYSTEM IN ALMOST A DECADE RIPPED THROUGH FIVE COUNTIES YESTERDAY, REPORTEDLY KILLING TWENTY AND LEAVING THOUSANDS HOMELESS...
...IN ANNANDALE, VIRGINIA--THERE'S DEVELOPING NEWS IN A BIZARRE AND SHOCKING INCIDENT WHICH TOOK PLACE DURING A POLICE CHASE EARLIER TODAY.
A YOUNG WOMAN ELUDED POLICEMEN IN A WAY OFFICIALS COULD ONLY DESCRIBE AS... "INHUMAN."
AMAZING ESCAPE
CNB
--THIS FOOTAGE, TAKEN FROM A BYSTANDER'S CELL PHONE, CLEARLY SHOWS THE WOMAN LEAPING WELL ABOVE THE BUILDING.
LISA MCGRATH JOINS US LIVE FROM THE SCENE...
NO...
DAN, POLICE OFFICIALS SAY ALL AVAILABLE UNITS IN FAIRFAX COUNTY ARE NOW SEARCHING FOR THIS YOUNG WOMAN AND TWO OTHER PERSONS OF INTEREST.
AMAZING ESCAPE
CNB
ALL BLOCKS WITHIN A FIVE-MILE RADIUS FROM WHERE THEY WERE LAST SEEN ARE SEALED OFF--

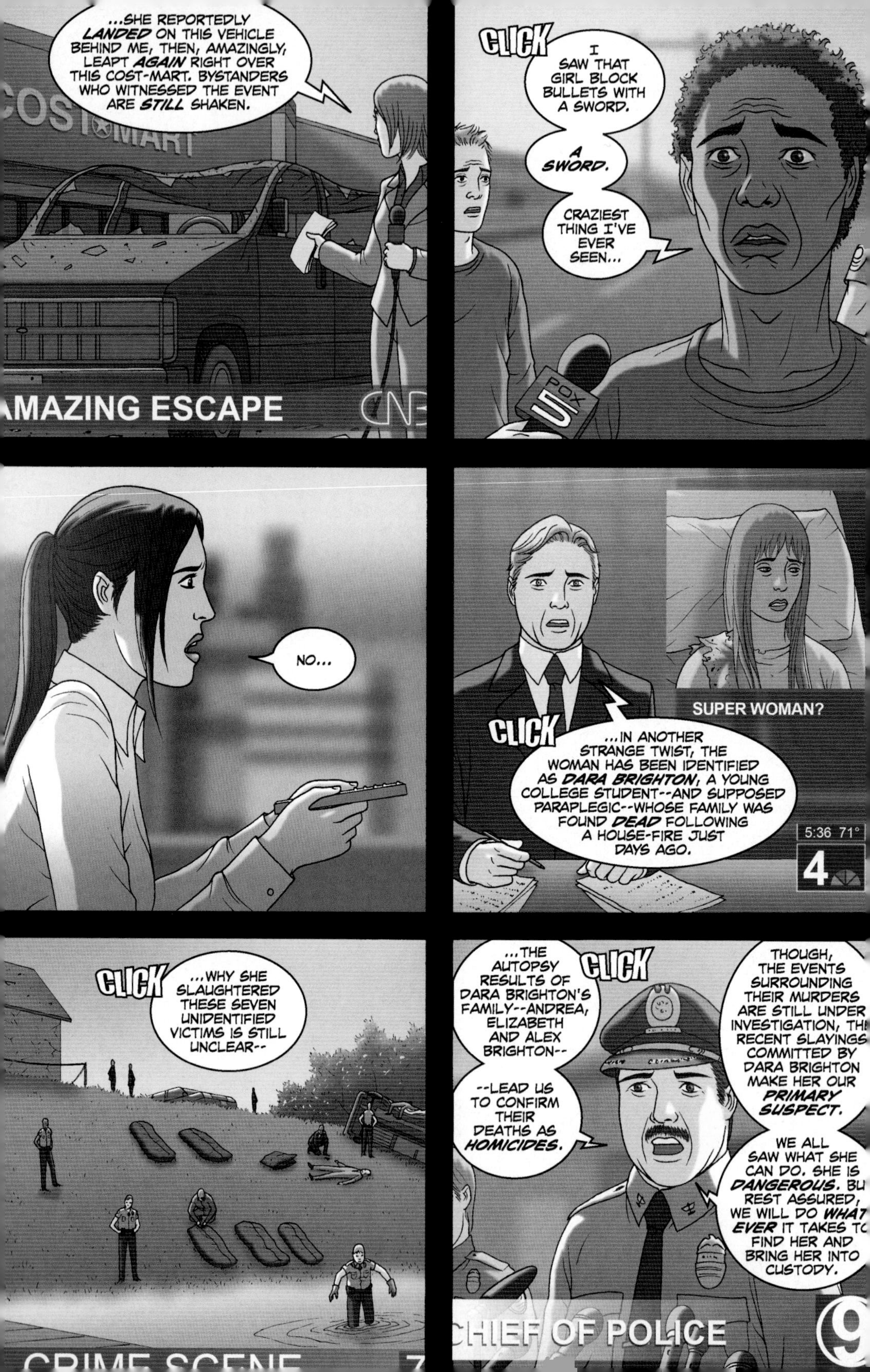
...SHE REPORTEDLY LANDED ON THIS VEHICLE BEHIND ME, THEN, AMAZINGLY, LEAPT AGAIN RIGHT OVER THIS COST-MART. BYSTANDERS WHO WITNESSED THE EVENT ARE STILL SHAKEN.
COST MART
AMAZING ESCAPE
CLICK
I SAW THAT GIRL BLOCK BULLETS WITH A SWORD.
A SWORD.
CRAZIEST THING I'VE EVER SEEN...
NO...
SUPER WOMAN?
CLICK
...IN ANOTHER STRANGE TWIST, THE WOMAN HAS BEEN IDENTIFIED AS DARA BRIGHTON, A YOUNG COLLEGE STUDENT--AND SUPPOSED PARAPLEGIC--WHOSE FAMILY WAS FOUND DEAD FOLLOWING A HOUSE-FIRE JUST DAYS AGO.
5:36 71°
4
CLICK
...WHY SHE SLAUGHTERED THESE SEVEN UNIDENTIFIED VICTIMS IS STILL UNCLEAR--
...THE AUTOPSY RESULTS OF DARA BRIGHTON'S FAMILY--ANDREA, ELIZABETH AND ALEX BRIGHTON--
CLICK
--LEAD US TO CONFIRM THEIR DEATHS AS HOMICIDES.
THOUGH, THE EVENTS SURROUNDING THEIR MURDERS ARE STILL UNDER INVESTIGATION, THE RECENT SLAYINGS COMMITTED BY DARA BRIGHTON MAKE HER OUR PRIMARY SUSPECT.
WE ALL SAW WHAT SHE CAN DO. SHE IS DANGEROUS. BUT REST ASSURED, WE WILL DO WHATEVER IT TAKES TO FIND HER AND BRING HER INTO CUSTODY.
CHIEF OF POLICE
9

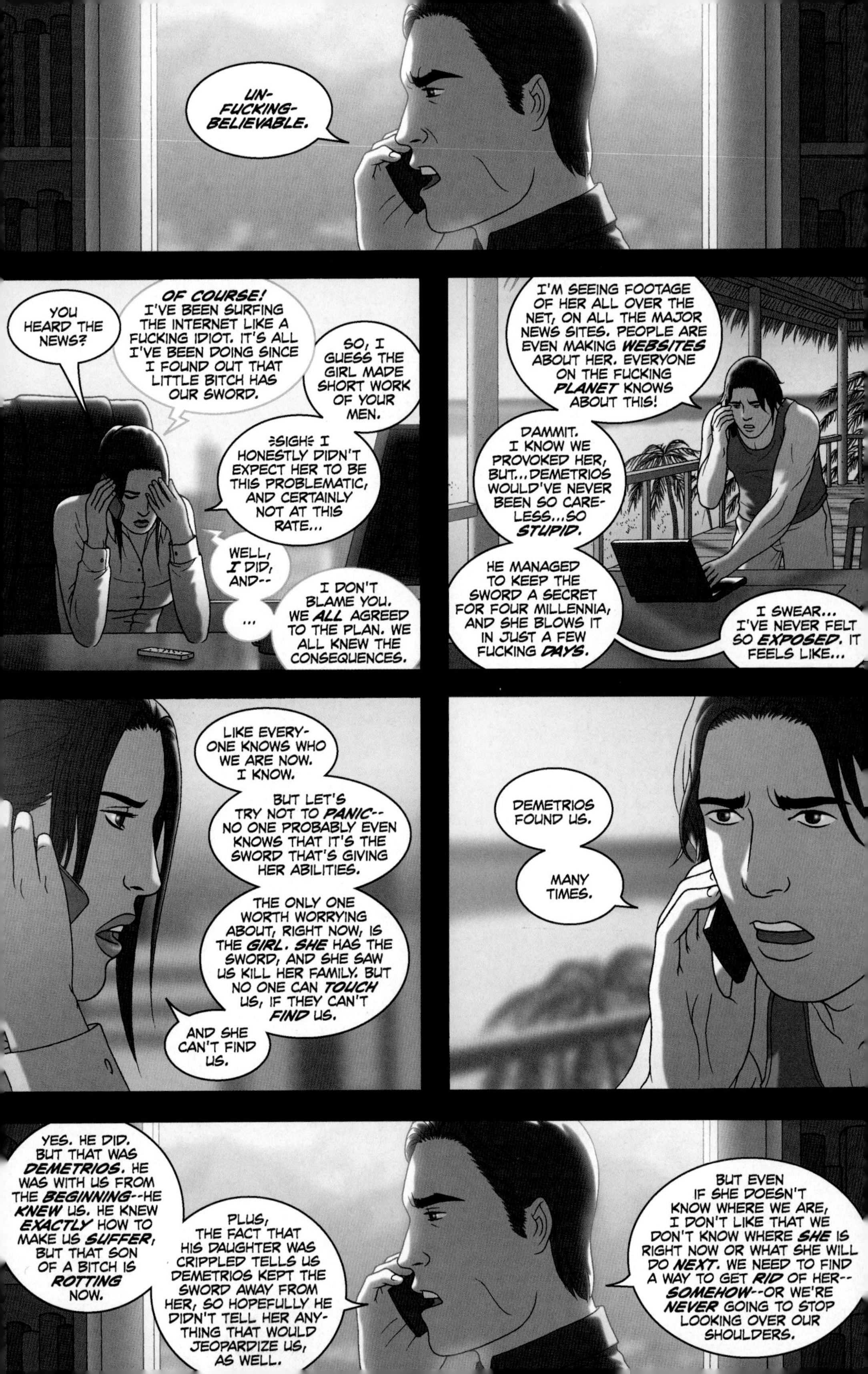
UN-FUCKING-BELIEVABLE.
YOU HEARD THE NEWS?
OF COURSE! I'VE BEEN SURFING THE INTERNET LIKE A FUCKING IDIOT. IT'S ALL I'VE BEEN DOING SINCE I FOUND OUT THAT LITTLE BITCH HAS OUR SWORD.
SO, I GUESS THE GIRL MADE SHORT WORK OF YOUR MEN.
SIGH I HONESTLY DIDN'T EXPECT HER TO BE THIS PROBLEMATIC, AND CERTAINLY NOT AT THIS RATE...
WELL, I DID, AND--
...
I DON'T BLAME YOU. WE ALL AGREED TO THE PLAN. WE ALL KNEW THE CONSEQUENCES.
I'M SEEING FOOTAGE OF HER ALL OVER THE NET, ON ALL THE MAJOR NEWS SITES. PEOPLE ARE EVEN MAKING WEBSITES ABOUT HER. EVERYONE ON THE FUCKING PLANET KNOWS ABOUT THIS!
DAMMIT. I KNOW WE PROVOKED HER, BUT...DEMETRIOS WOULD'VE NEVER BEEN SO CARE-LESS...SO STUPID.
HE MANAGED TO KEEP THE SWORD A SECRET FOR FOUR MILLENNIA, AND SHE BLOWS IT IN JUST A FEW FUCKING DAYS.
I SWEAR... I'VE NEVER FELT SO EXPOSED. IT FEELS LIKE...
LIKE EVERY-ONE KNOWS WHO WE ARE NOW. I KNOW.
BUT LET'S TRY NOT TO PANIC-- NO ONE PROBABLY EVEN KNOWS THAT IT'S THE SWORD THAT'S GIVING HER ABILITIES.
THE ONLY ONE WORTH WORRYING ABOUT, RIGHT NOW, IS THE GIRL. SHE HAS THE SWORD, AND SHE SAW US KILL HER FAMILY. BUT NO ONE CAN TOUCH US, IF THEY CAN'T FIND US.
AND SHE CAN'T FIND US.
DEMETRIOS FOUND US.
MANY TIMES.
YES. HE DID. BUT THAT WAS DEMETRIOS. HE WAS WITH US FROM THE BEGINNING--HE KNEW US. HE KNEW EXACTLY HOW TO MAKE US SUFFER, BUT THAT SON OF A BITCH IS ROTTING NOW.
PLUS, THE FACT THAT HIS DAUGHTER WAS CRIPPLED TELLS US DEMETRIOS KEPT THE SWORD AWAY FROM HER, SO HOPEFULLY HE DIDN'T TELL HER ANY-THING THAT WOULD JEOPARDIZE US, AS WELL.
BUT EVEN IF SHE DOESN'T KNOW WHERE WE ARE, I DON'T LIKE THAT WE DON'T KNOW WHERE SHE IS RIGHT NOW OR WHAT SHE WILL DO NEXT. WE NEED TO FIND A WAY TO GET RID OF HER-- SOMEHOW--OR WE'RE NEVER GOING TO STOP LOOKING OVER OUR SHOULDERS.

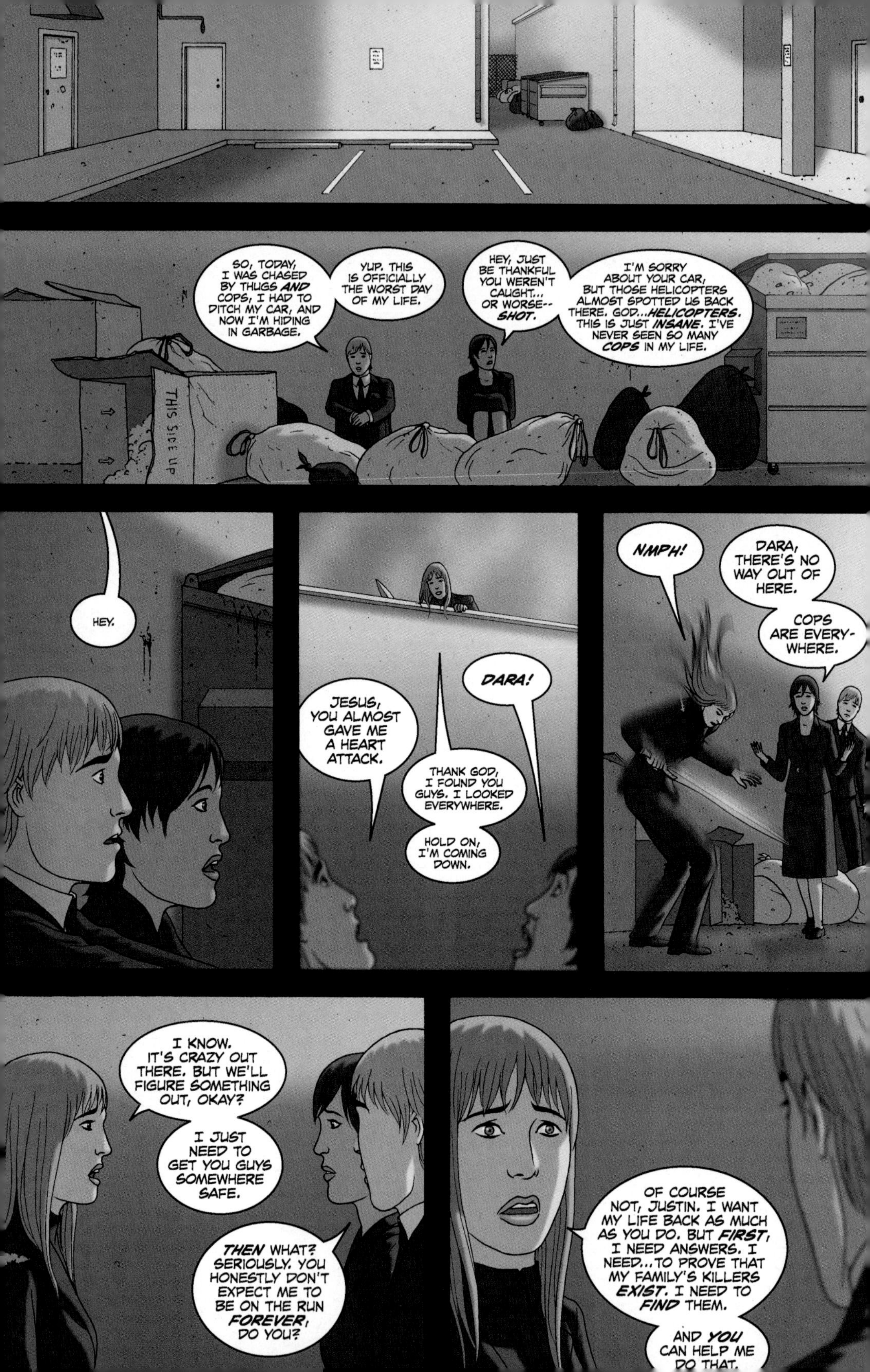
SO, TODAY, I WAS CHASED BY THUGS AND COPS, I HAD TO DITCH MY CAR, AND NOW I'M HIDING IN GARBAGE.
YUP. THIS IS OFFICIALLY THE WORST DAY OF MY LIFE.
HEY, JUST BE THANKFUL YOU WEREN'T CAUGHT... OR WORSE--SHOT.
I'M SORRY ABOUT YOUR CAR, BUT THOSE HELICOPTERS ALMOST SPOTTED US BACK THERE. GOD...HELICOPTERS. THIS IS JUST INSANE. I'VE NEVER SEEN SO MANY COPS IN MY LIFE.
THIS SIDE UP
HEY.
JESUS, YOU ALMOST GAVE ME A HEART ATTACK.
DARA!
THANK GOD, I FOUND YOU GUYS. I LOOKED EVERYWHERE.
HOLD ON, I'M COMING DOWN.
NMPH!
DARA, THERE'S NO WAY OUT OF HERE.
COPS ARE EVERYWHERE.
I KNOW. IT'S CRAZY OUT THERE. BUT WE'LL FIGURE SOMETHING OUT, OKAY?
I JUST NEED TO GET YOU GUYS SOMEWHERE SAFE.
THEN WHAT? SERIOUSLY. YOU HONESTLY DON'T EXPECT ME TO BE ON THE RUN FOREVER, DO YOU?
OF COURSE NOT, JUSTIN. I WANT MY LIFE BACK AS MUCH AS YOU DO. BUT FIRST, I NEED ANSWERS. I NEED...TO PROVE THAT MY FAMILY'S KILLERS EXIST. I NEED TO FIND THEM.
AND YOU CAN HELP ME DO THAT.

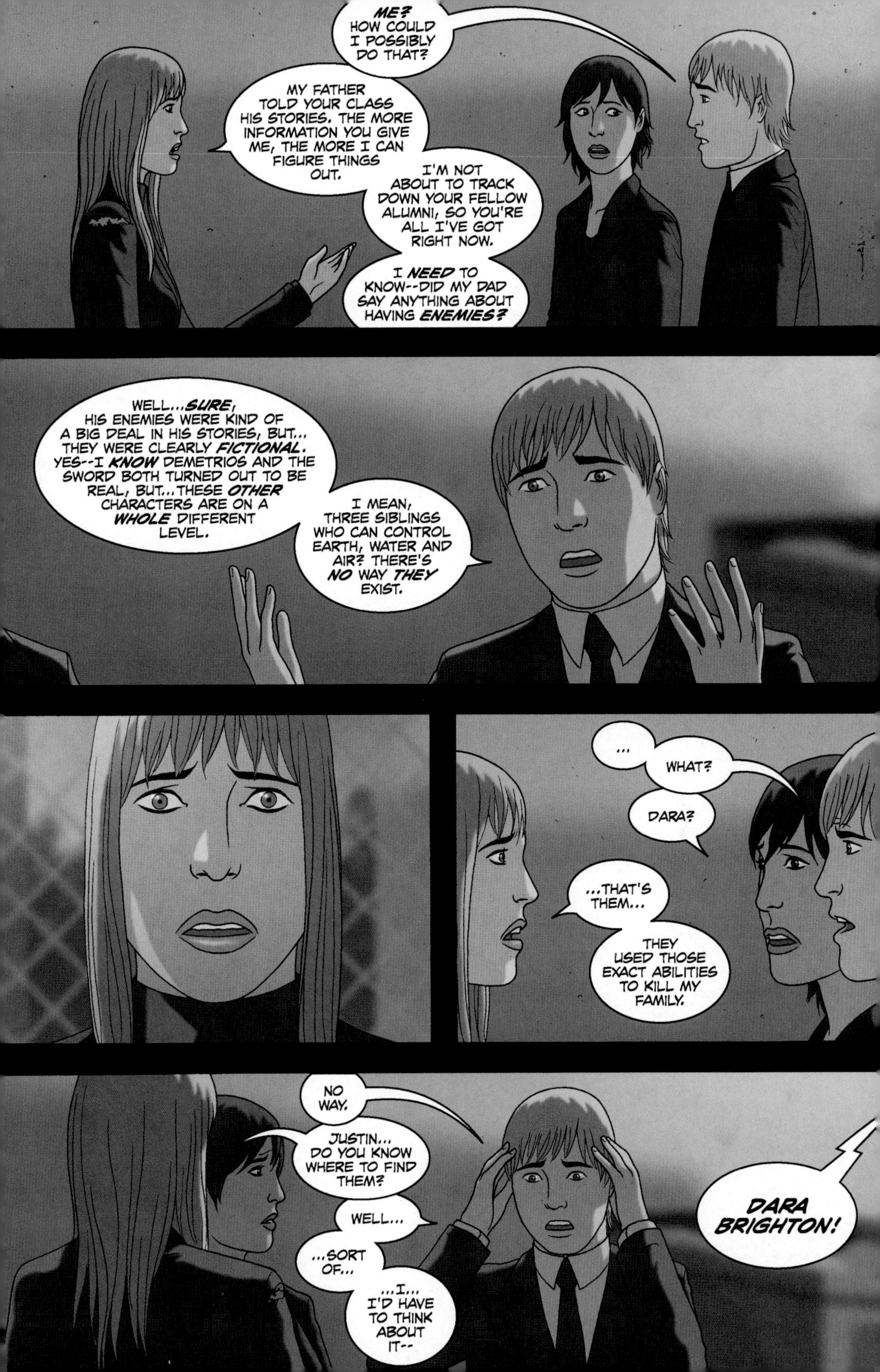
ME? HOW COULD I POSSIBLY DO THAT?
MY FATHER TOLD YOUR CLASS HIS STORIES. THE MORE INFORMATION YOU GIVE ME, THE MORE I CAN FIGURE THINGS OUT.
I'M NOT ABOUT TO TRACK DOWN YOUR FELLOW ALUMNI, SO YOU'RE ALL I'VE GOT RIGHT NOW.
I NEED TO KNOW--DID MY DAD SAY ANYTHING ABOUT HAVING ENEMIES?
WELL...SURE, HIS ENEMIES WERE KIND OF A BIG DEAL IN HIS STORIES, BUT... THEY WERE CLEARLY FICTIONAL. YES--I KNOW DEMETRIOS AND THE SWORD BOTH TURNED OUT TO BE REAL, BUT...THESE OTHER CHARACTERS ARE ON A WHOLE DIFFERENT LEVEL.
I MEAN, THREE SIBLINGS WHO CAN CONTROL EARTH, WATER AND AIR? THERE'S NO WAY THEY EXIST.
...
WHAT?
DARA?
...THAT'S THEM...
THEY USED THOSE EXACT ABILITIES TO KILL MY FAMILY.
NO WAY.
JUSTIN... DO YOU KNOW WHERE TO FIND THEM?
WELL...
...SORT OF...
...I... I'D HAVE TO THINK ABOUT IT--
DARA BRIGHTON!

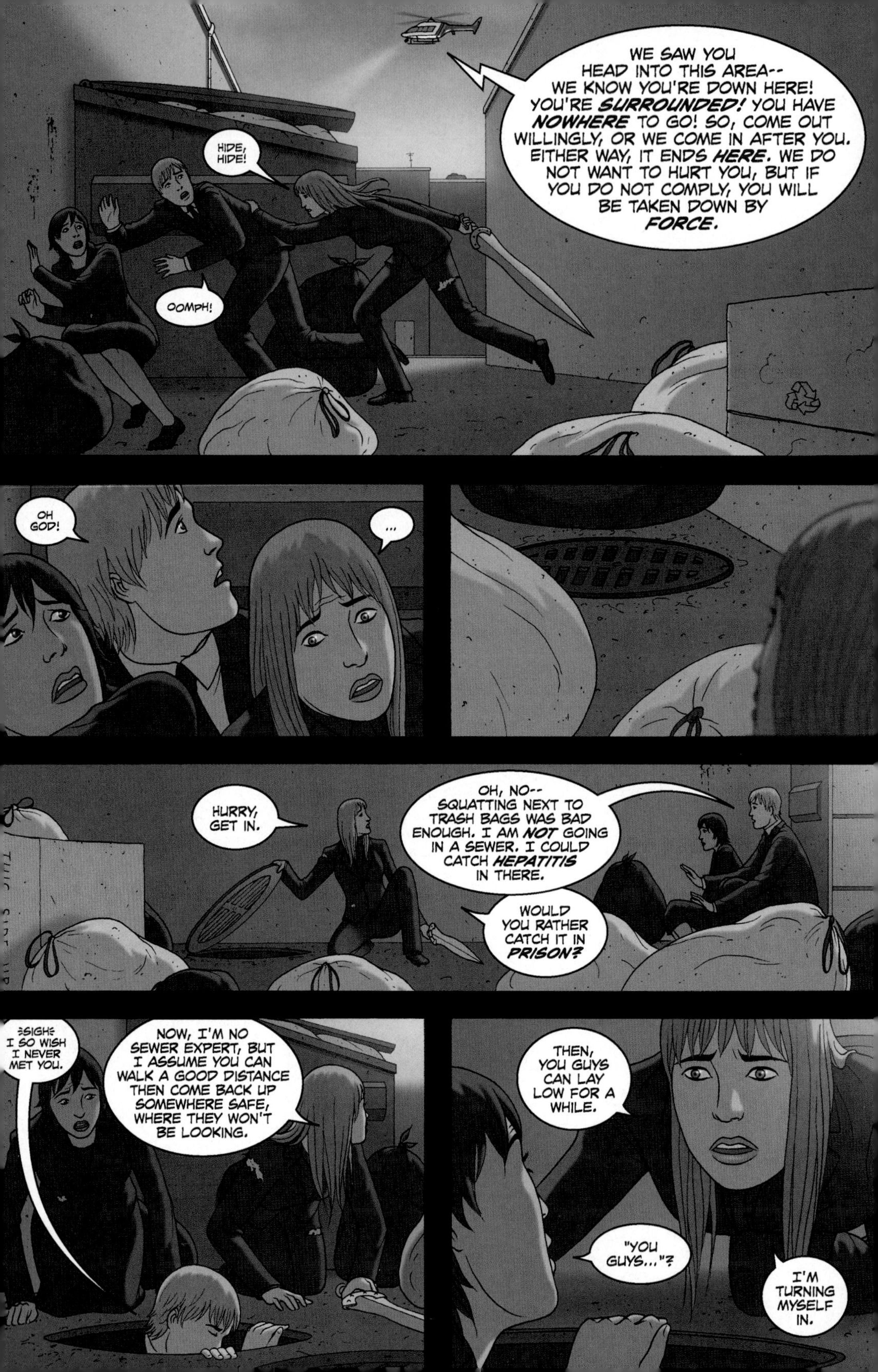
WE SAW YOU HEAD INTO THIS AREA-- WE KNOW YOU'RE DOWN HERE! YOU'RE SURROUNDED! YOU HAVE NOWHERE TO GO! SO, COME OUT WILLINGLY, OR WE COME IN AFTER YOU. EITHER WAY, IT ENDS HERE. WE DO NOT WANT TO HURT YOU, BUT IF YOU DO NOT COMPLY, YOU WILL BE TAKEN DOWN BY FORCE.
HIDE, HIDE!
OOMPH!
OH GOD!
...
HURRY, GET IN.
OH, NO-- SQUATTING NEXT TO TRASH BAGS WAS BAD ENOUGH. I AM NOT GOING IN A SEWER. I COULD CATCH HEPATITIS IN THERE.
WOULD YOU RATHER CATCH IT IN PRISON?
≡SIGH≡ I SO WISH I NEVER MET YOU.
NOW, I'M NO SEWER EXPERT, BUT I ASSUME YOU CAN WALK A GOOD DISTANCE THEN COME BACK UP SOMEWHERE SAFE, WHERE THEY WON'T BE LOOKING.
THEN, YOU GUYS CAN LAY LOW FOR A WHILE.
"YOU GUYS..."?
I'M TURNING MYSELF IN.

WHAT?! DARA...

THEY DON'T KNOW YOU TWO ARE DOWN HERE. *JUST ME.* IF THEY COME IN HERE AND SEE THAT I'M GONE--THEY'D *FIND* THIS MANHOLE AND TRACK US ALL DOWN. I'VE PUT YOU TWO THROUGH ENOUGH. I'M NOT LETTING YOU--OR ANYONE ELSE-- GET HURT BECAUSE OF ME. THIS IS YOUR CHANCE TO ESCAPE.

BUT...WHY DO YOU HAVE TO TURN YOURSELF *IN?* IF YOU'D JUST LET THEM SEE YOU JUMP AWAY, OR SOMETHING, WE COULD *ALL* ESCAPE.

JULIE...LOOK AT ME. I'M ACCUSED OF MURDERING MY *FAMILY*, AND I'M *RUNNING*. I EVEN...*KILLED* PEOPLE. I DON'T CARE IF THEY TRIED TO *KIDNAP* ME--I *KILLED* THEM. *OF COURSE* THE COPS ARE HUNTING ME DOWN LIKE AN *ANIMAL!* I HAVE TO STOP RUNNING, JULIE. THIS ISN'T *ME.*

A PART OF ME SAYS... THIS CAN ALL BE *FIXED*--THAT THE POLICE WILL *LISTEN* TO ME AND EVEN TAKE MY SIDE, IF I JUST TURN MYSELF IN. THEN, WE COULD ALL FIND MY FAMILY'S KILLERS... THE *RIGHT* WAY.

OKAY. SO, WHY CAN'T WE GO TO THE POLICE *TOGETHER?*

BECAUSE THE *OTHER* PART OF ME...ISN'T SO OPTIMISTIC.

BUT THAT'S A RISK I HAVE TO TAKE-- *ALONE.*

≈SIGH≈ GOD, DARA...

PLEASE BE CAREFUL.

I'LL CONTACT YOU WHEN--OR IF-- I CAN. NOW, *HURRY.*

HEY-- YOU!

STOP RIGHT THERE!

KLNK

CHNK

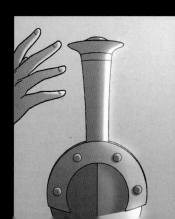

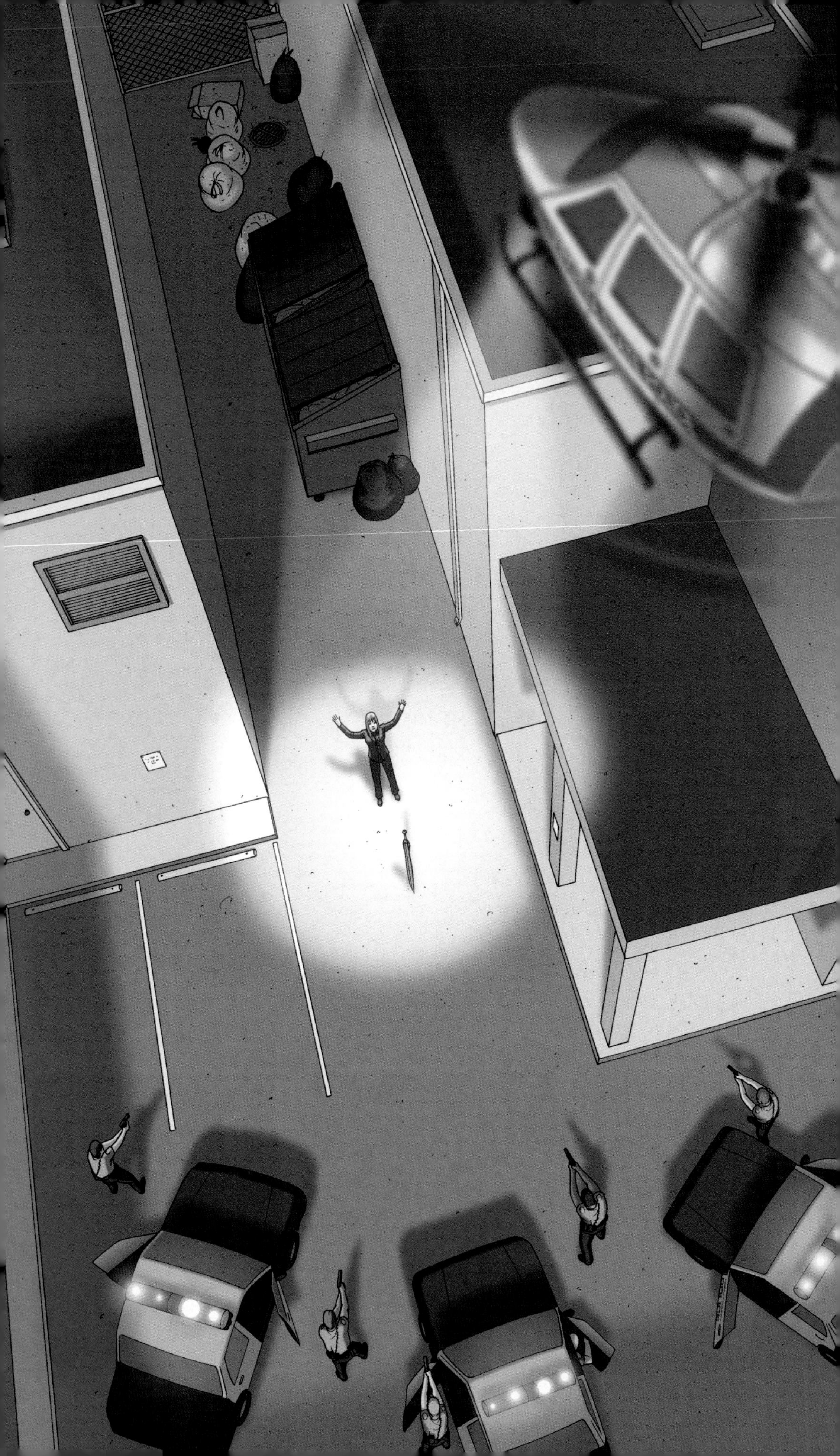

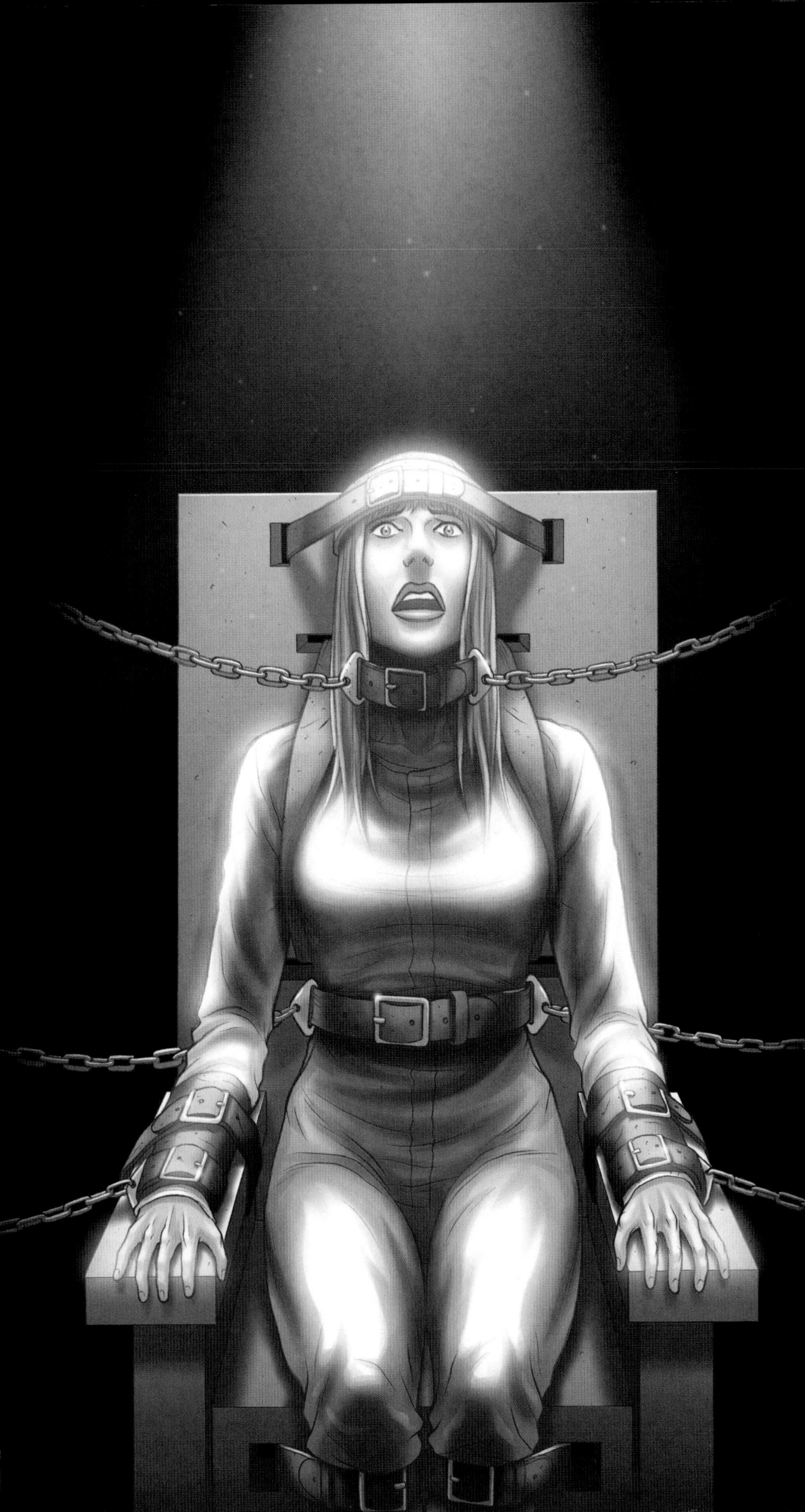

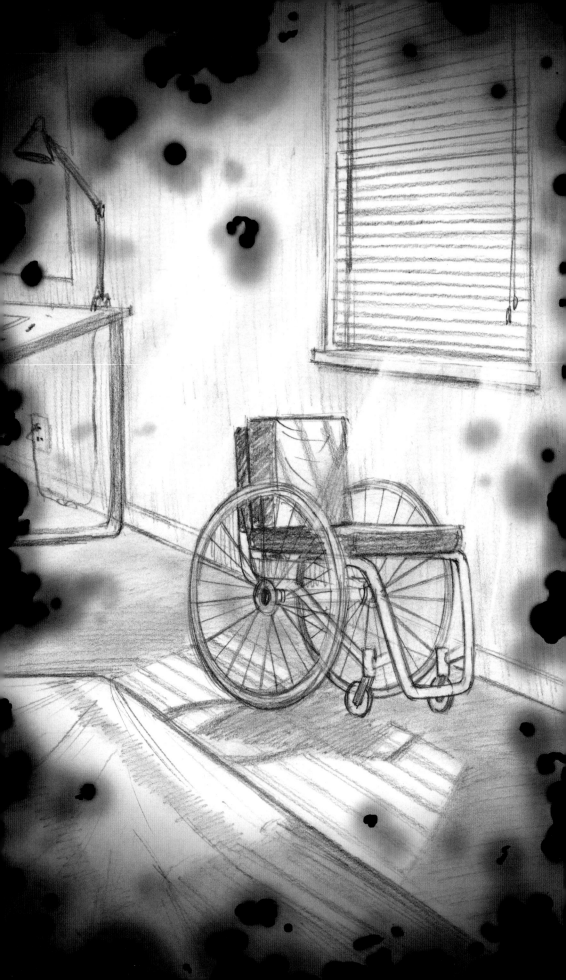

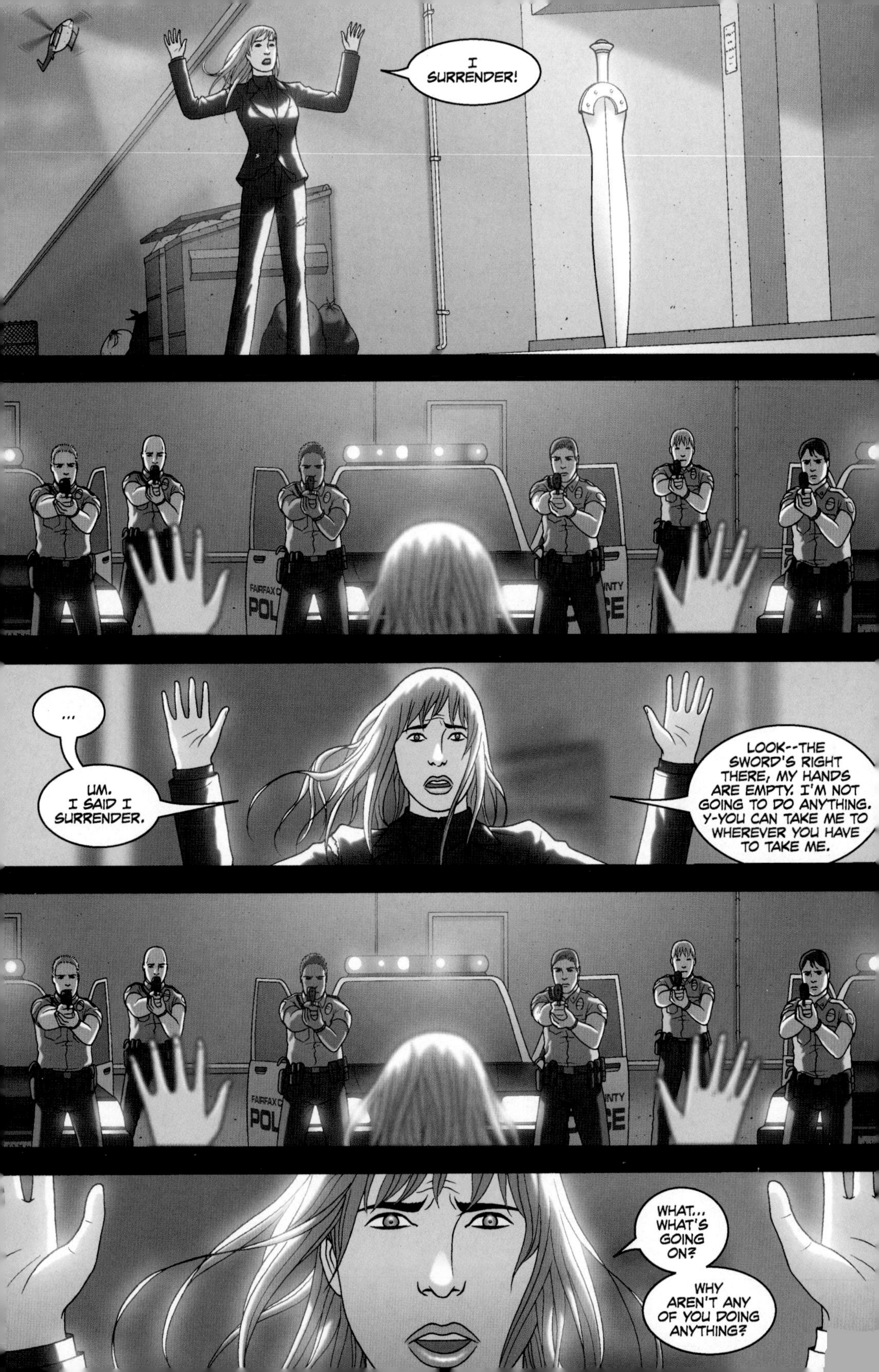
I SURRENDER!
FAIRFAX C
POL
NTY
CE
...
UM. I SAID I SURRENDER.
LOOK--THE SWORD'S RIGHT THERE, MY HANDS ARE EMPTY. I'M NOT GOING TO DO ANYTHING. Y-YOU CAN TAKE ME TO WHEREVER YOU HAVE TO TAKE ME.
WHAT... WHAT'S GOING ON?
WHY AREN'T ANY OF YOU DOING ANYTHING?

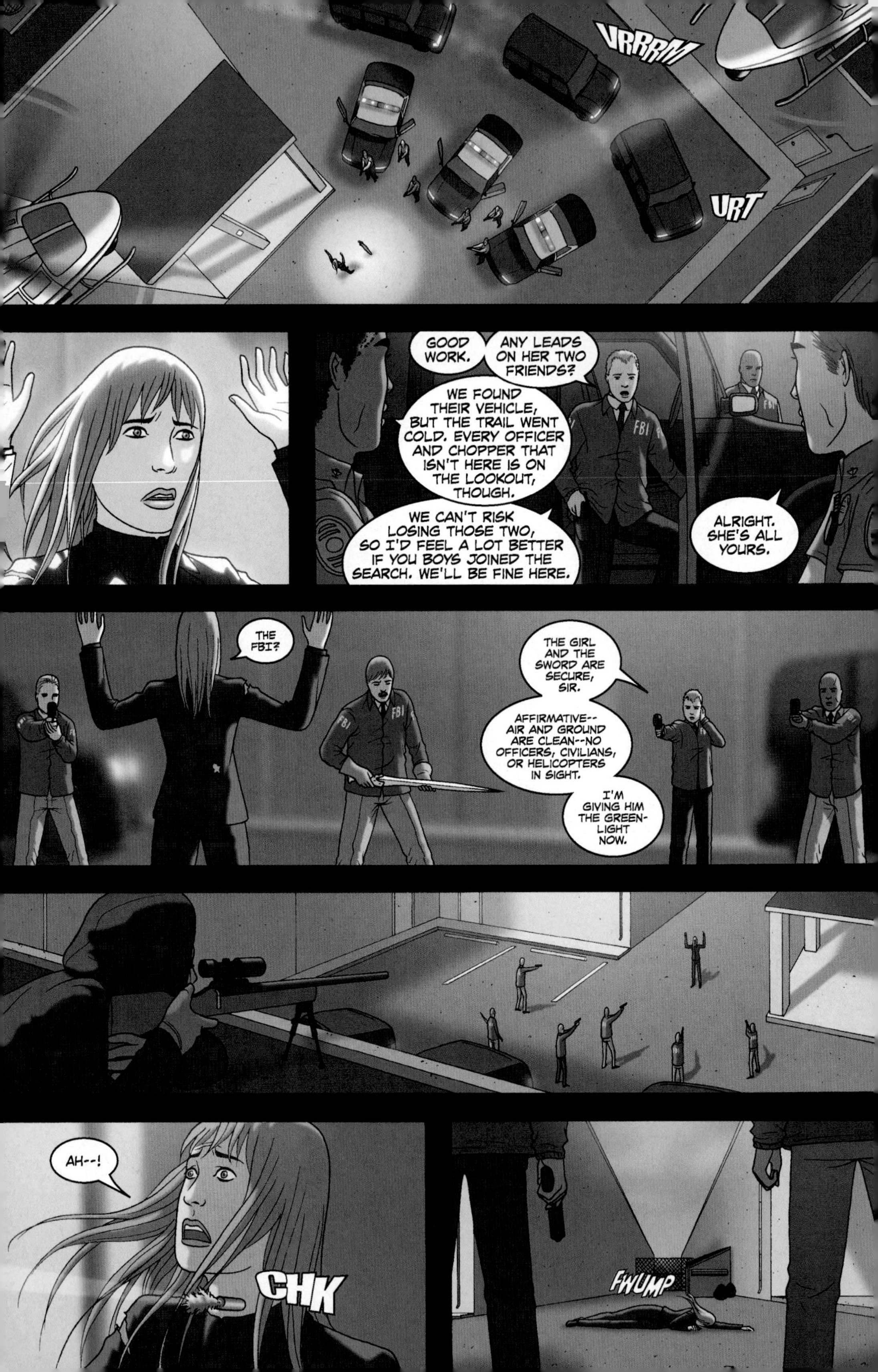
VRRRM
URT
GOOD WORK.
ANY LEADS ON HER TWO FRIENDS?
WE FOUND THEIR VEHICLE, BUT THE TRAIL WENT COLD. EVERY OFFICER AND CHOPPER THAT ISN'T HERE IS ON THE LOOKOUT, THOUGH.
WE CAN'T RISK LOSING THOSE TWO, SO I'D FEEL A LOT BETTER IF YOU BOYS JOINED THE SEARCH. WE'LL BE FINE HERE.
ALRIGHT. SHE'S ALL YOURS.
THE FBI?
THE GIRL AND THE SWORD ARE SECURE, SIR.
AFFIRMATIVE--AIR AND GROUND ARE CLEAN--NO OFFICERS, CIVILIANS, OR HELICOPTERS IN SIGHT.
I'M GIVING HIM THE GREEN-LIGHT NOW.
AH--!
CHK
FWUMP

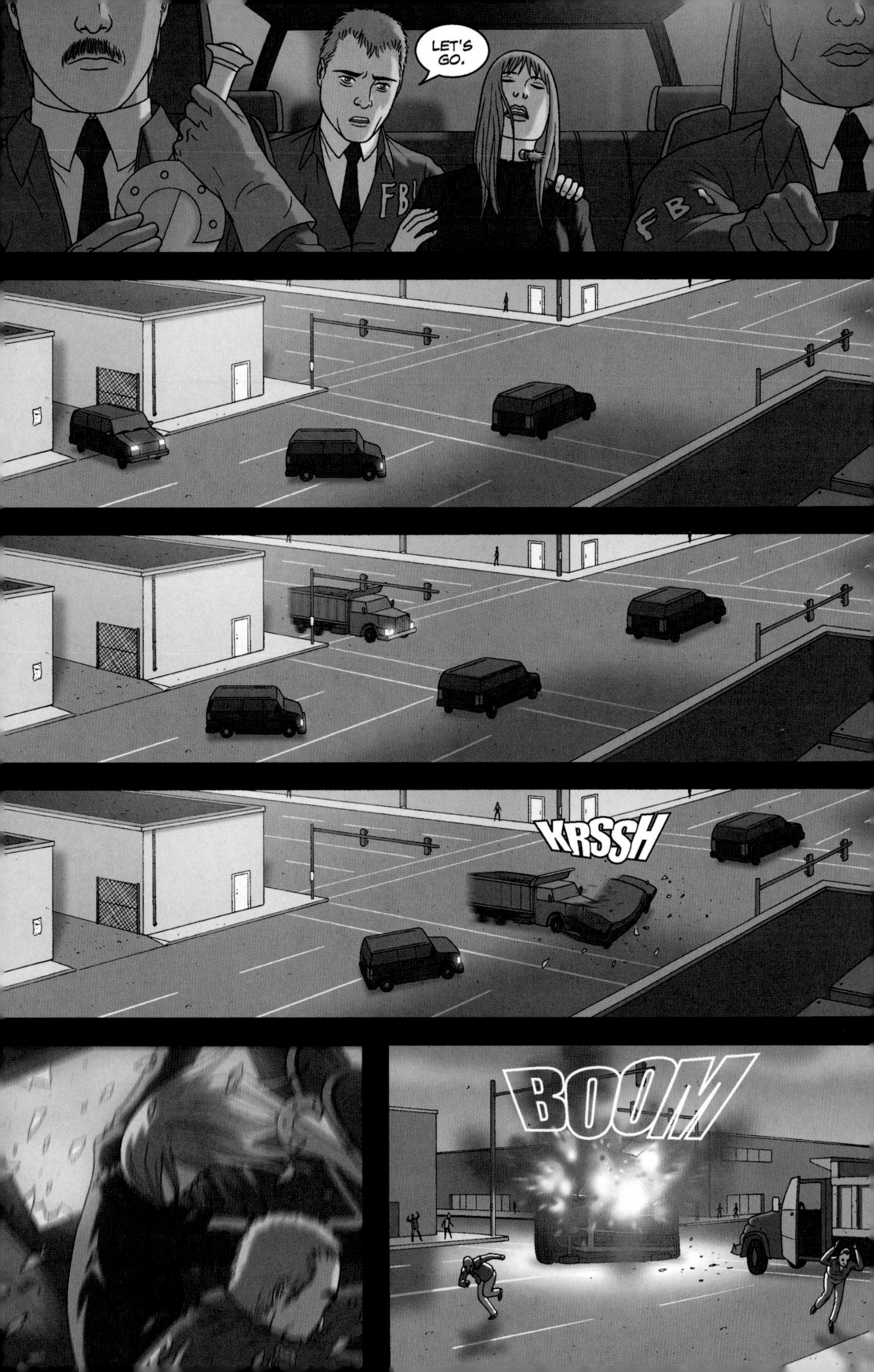
LET'S GO.
KRSSH
BOOM

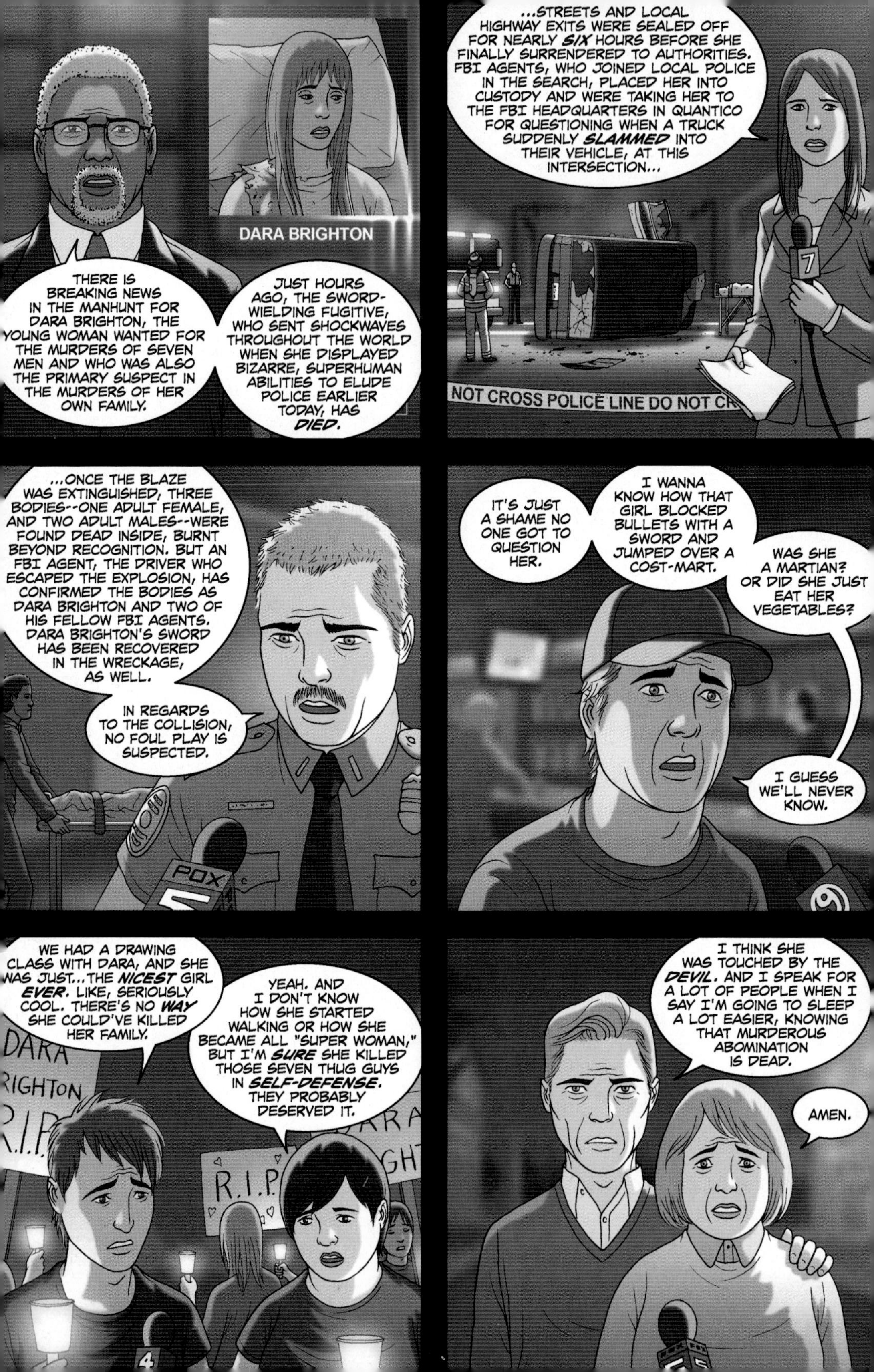
DARA BRIGHTON
THERE IS BREAKING NEWS IN THE MANHUNT FOR DARA BRIGHTON, THE YOUNG WOMAN WANTED FOR THE MURDERS OF SEVEN MEN AND WHO WAS ALSO THE PRIMARY SUSPECT IN THE MURDERS OF HER OWN FAMILY.
JUST HOURS AGO, THE SWORD-WIELDING FUGITIVE, WHO SENT SHOCKWAVES THROUGHOUT THE WORLD WHEN SHE DISPLAYED BIZARRE, SUPERHUMAN ABILITIES TO ELUDE POLICE EARLIER TODAY, HAS *DIED.*
...STREETS AND LOCAL HIGHWAY EXITS WERE SEALED OFF FOR NEARLY *SIX* HOURS BEFORE SHE FINALLY SURRENDERED TO AUTHORITIES. FBI AGENTS, WHO JOINED LOCAL POLICE IN THE SEARCH, PLACED HER INTO CUSTODY AND WERE TAKING HER TO THE FBI HEADQUARTERS IN QUANTICO FOR QUESTIONING WHEN A TRUCK SUDDENLY *SLAMMED* INTO THEIR VEHICLE, AT THIS INTERSECTION...
7
NOT CROSS POLICE LINE DO NOT CR
...ONCE THE BLAZE WAS EXTINGUISHED, THREE BODIES--ONE ADULT FEMALE, AND TWO ADULT MALES--WERE FOUND DEAD INSIDE, BURNT BEYOND RECOGNITION. BUT AN FBI AGENT, THE DRIVER WHO ESCAPED THE EXPLOSION, HAS CONFIRMED THE BODIES AS DARA BRIGHTON AND TWO OF HIS FELLOW FBI AGENTS. DARA BRIGHTON'S SWORD HAS BEEN RECOVERED IN THE WRECKAGE, AS WELL.
IN REGARDS TO THE COLLISION, NO FOUL PLAY IS SUSPECTED.
POX 5
IT'S JUST A SHAME NO ONE GOT TO QUESTION HER.
I WANNA KNOW HOW THAT GIRL BLOCKED BULLETS WITH A SWORD AND JUMPED OVER A COST-MART.
WAS SHE A MARTIAN? OR DID SHE JUST EAT HER VEGETABLES?
I GUESS WE'LL NEVER KNOW.
WE HAD A DRAWING CLASS WITH DARA, AND SHE WAS JUST...THE *NICEST* GIRL *EVER.* LIKE, SERIOUSLY COOL. THERE'S NO *WAY* SHE COULD'VE KILLED HER FAMILY.
YEAH. AND I DON'T KNOW HOW SHE STARTED WALKING OR HOW SHE BECAME ALL "SUPER WOMAN," BUT I'M *SURE* SHE KILLED THOSE SEVEN THUG GUYS IN *SELF-DEFENSE.* THEY PROBABLY DESERVED IT.
DARA BRIGHTON R.I.P.
R.I.P.
4
I THINK SHE WAS TOUCHED BY THE *DEVIL.* AND I SPEAK FOR A LOT OF PEOPLE WHEN I SAY I'M GOING TO SLEEP A LOT EASIER, KNOWING THAT MURDEROUS ABOMINATION IS DEAD.
AMEN.

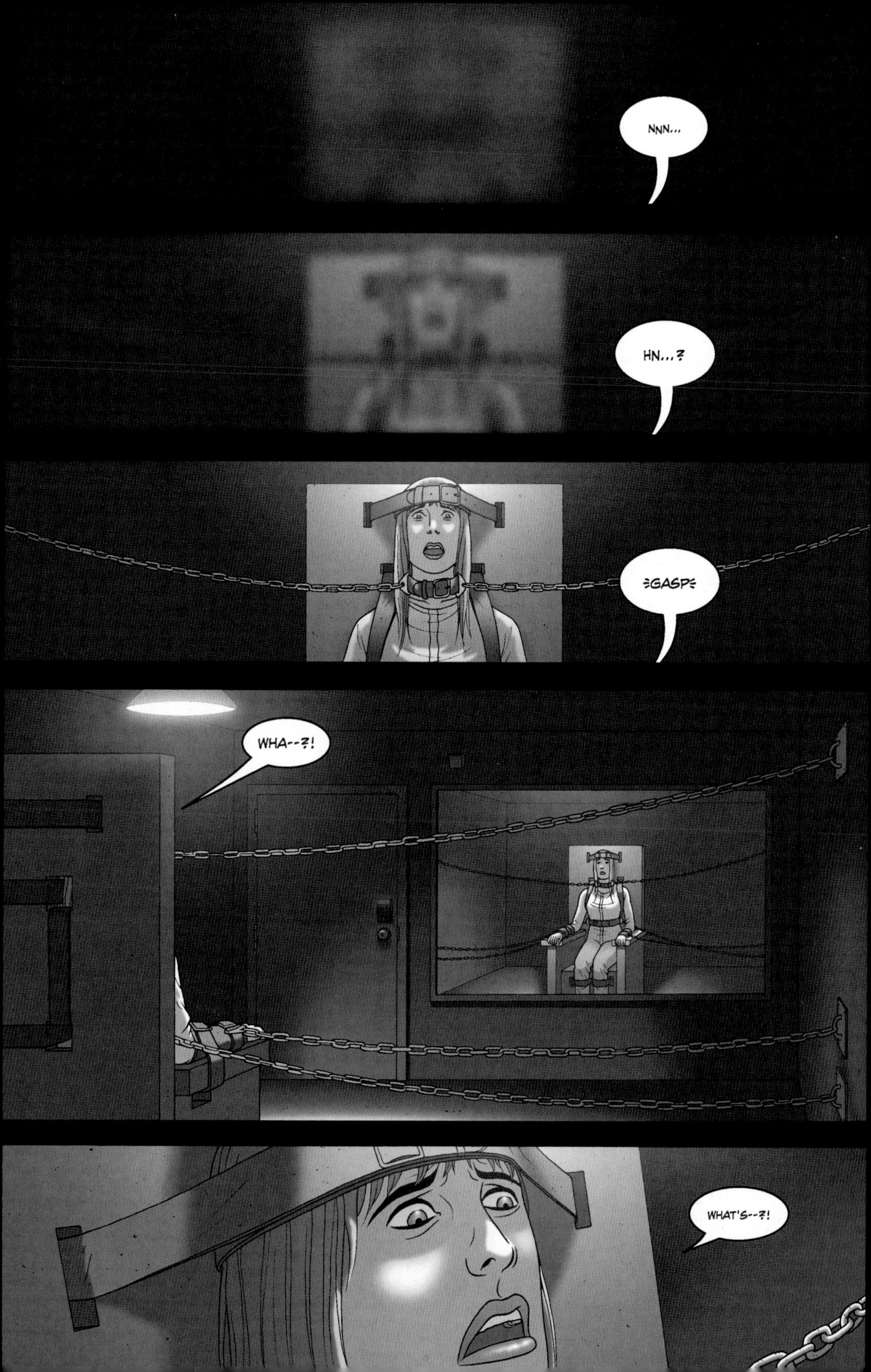
NNN...
HN...?
=GASP=
WHA--?!
WHAT'S--?!

NGGGH!
RNNNNG!
WHAT IS THIS?!!
RRRRAAH! LET ME... OUT!
WHO ARE YOU?!
WHERE AM I?!
I KNOW SOMEONE'S BACK THERE! ANSWER M--
BEEEEP
CLICK
GASP

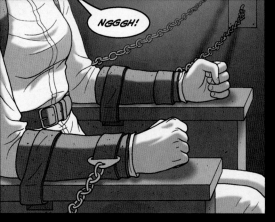

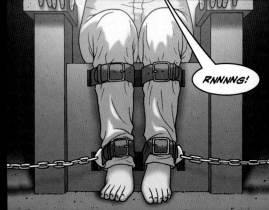

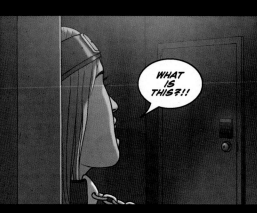

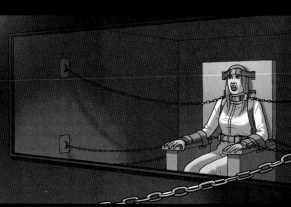

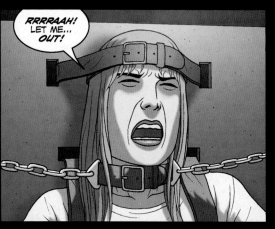

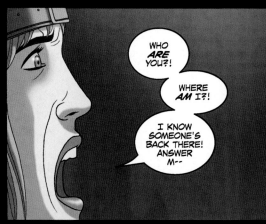

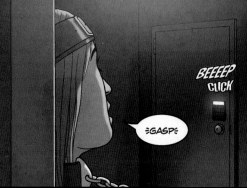

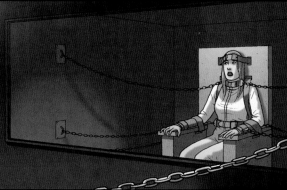

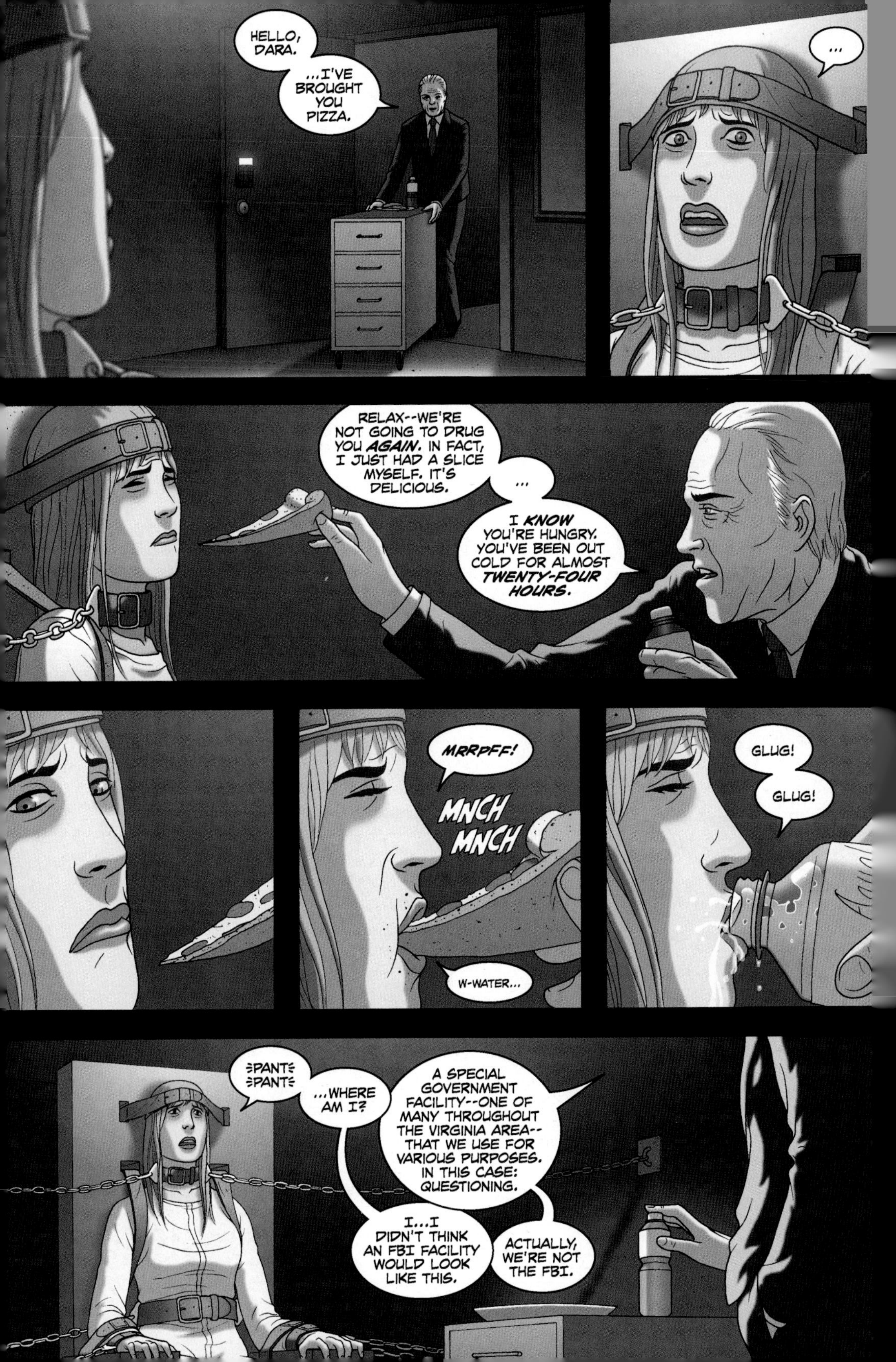
HELLO, DARA.
...I'VE BROUGHT YOU PIZZA.
...
RELAX--WE'RE NOT GOING TO DRUG YOU AGAIN. IN FACT, I JUST HAD A SLICE MYSELF. IT'S DELICIOUS.
...
I KNOW YOU'RE HUNGRY. YOU'VE BEEN OUT COLD FOR ALMOST TWENTY-FOUR HOURS.
MRRPFF!
MNCH MNCH
W-WATER...
GLUG!
GLUG!
PANT PANT
...WHERE AM I?
A SPECIAL GOVERNMENT FACILITY--ONE OF MANY THROUGHOUT THE VIRGINIA AREA--THAT WE USE FOR VARIOUS PURPOSES. IN THIS CASE: QUESTIONING.
I...I DIDN'T THINK AN FBI FACILITY WOULD LOOK LIKE THIS.
ACTUALLY, WE'RE NOT THE FBI.

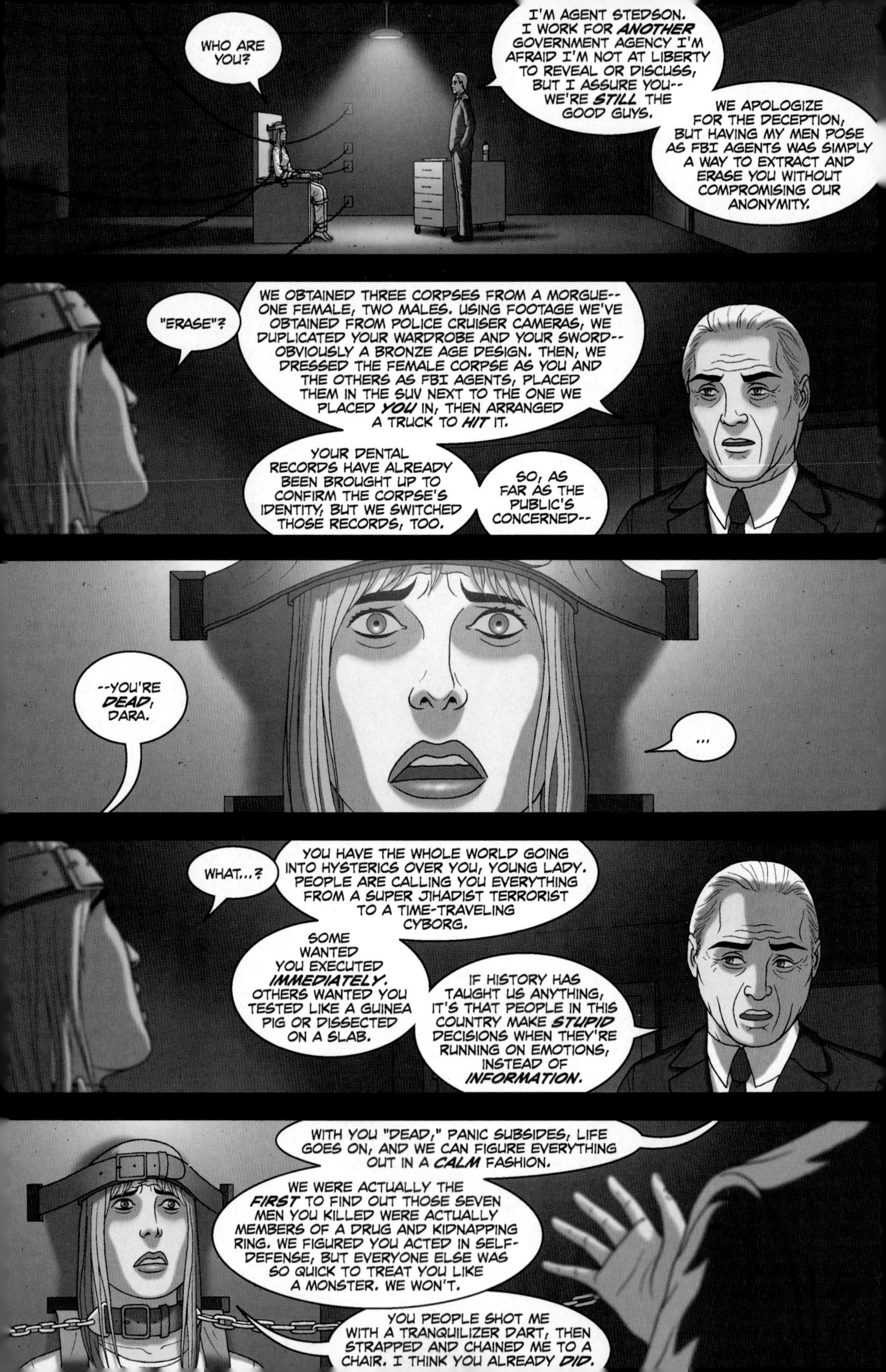
WHO ARE YOU?
I'M AGENT STEDSON. I WORK FOR ANOTHER GOVERNMENT AGENCY I'M AFRAID I'M NOT AT LIBERTY TO REVEAL OR DISCUSS, BUT I ASSURE YOU-- WE'RE STILL THE GOOD GUYS.
WE APOLOGIZE FOR THE DECEPTION, BUT HAVING MY MEN POSE AS FBI AGENTS WAS SIMPLY A WAY TO EXTRACT AND ERASE YOU WITHOUT COMPROMISING OUR ANONYMITY.
"ERASE"?
WE OBTAINED THREE CORPSES FROM A MORGUE-- ONE FEMALE, TWO MALES. USING FOOTAGE WE'VE OBTAINED FROM POLICE CRUISER CAMERAS, WE DUPLICATED YOUR WARDROBE AND YOUR SWORD-- OBVIOUSLY A BRONZE AGE DESIGN. THEN, WE DRESSED THE FEMALE CORPSE AS YOU AND THE OTHERS AS FBI AGENTS, PLACED THEM IN THE SUV NEXT TO THE ONE WE PLACED YOU IN, THEN ARRANGED A TRUCK TO HIT IT.
YOUR DENTAL RECORDS HAVE ALREADY BEEN BROUGHT UP TO CONFIRM THE CORPSE'S IDENTITY, BUT WE SWITCHED THOSE RECORDS, TOO.
SO, AS FAR AS THE PUBLIC'S CONCERNED--
--YOU'RE DEAD, DARA.
...
WHAT...?
YOU HAVE THE WHOLE WORLD GOING INTO HYSTERICS OVER YOU, YOUNG LADY. PEOPLE ARE CALLING YOU EVERYTHING FROM A SUPER JIHADIST TERRORIST TO A TIME-TRAVELING CYBORG.
SOME WANTED YOU EXECUTED IMMEDIATELY. OTHERS WANTED YOU TESTED LIKE A GUINEA PIG OR DISSECTED ON A SLAB.
IF HISTORY HAS TAUGHT US ANYTHING, IT'S THAT PEOPLE IN THIS COUNTRY MAKE STUPID DECISIONS WHEN THEY'RE RUNNING ON EMOTIONS, INSTEAD OF INFORMATION.
WITH YOU "DEAD," PANIC SUBSIDES, LIFE GOES ON, AND WE CAN FIGURE EVERYTHING OUT IN A CALM FASHION.
WE WERE ACTUALLY THE FIRST TO FIND OUT THOSE SEVEN MEN YOU KILLED WERE ACTUALLY MEMBERS OF A DRUG AND KIDNAPPING RING. WE FIGURED YOU ACTED IN SELF-DEFENSE, BUT EVERYONE ELSE WAS SO QUICK TO TREAT YOU LIKE A MONSTER. WE WON'T.
YOU PEOPLE SHOT ME WITH A TRANQUILIZER DART, THEN STRAPPED AND CHAINED ME TO A CHAIR. I THINK YOU ALREADY DID.

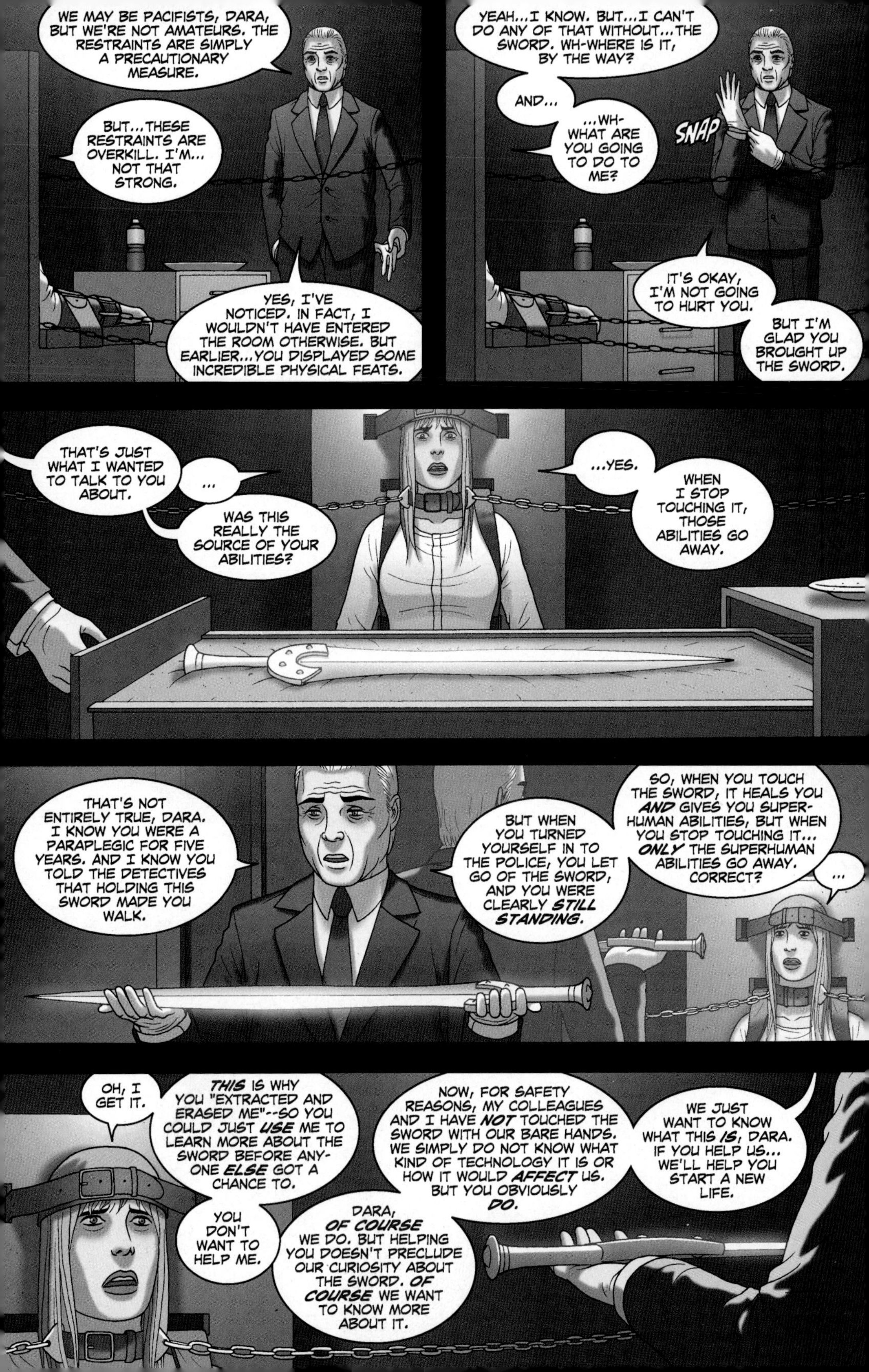
WE MAY BE PACIFISTS, DARA, BUT WE'RE NOT AMATEURS. THE RESTRAINTS ARE SIMPLY A PRECAUTIONARY MEASURE.
BUT...THESE RESTRAINTS ARE OVERKILL. I'M... NOT THAT STRONG.
YES, I'VE NOTICED. IN FACT, I WOULDN'T HAVE ENTERED THE ROOM OTHERWISE. BUT EARLIER...YOU DISPLAYED SOME INCREDIBLE PHYSICAL FEATS.
YEAH...I KNOW. BUT...I CAN'T DO ANY OF THAT WITHOUT...THE SWORD. WH-WHERE IS IT, BY THE WAY?
AND...
...WH- WHAT ARE YOU GOING TO DO TO ME?
SNAP
IT'S OKAY, I'M NOT GOING TO HURT YOU.
BUT I'M GLAD YOU BROUGHT UP THE SWORD.
THAT'S JUST WHAT I WANTED TO TALK TO YOU ABOUT.
...
WAS THIS REALLY THE SOURCE OF YOUR ABILITIES?
...YES.
WHEN I STOP TOUCHING IT, THOSE ABILITIES GO AWAY.
THAT'S NOT ENTIRELY TRUE, DARA. I KNOW YOU WERE A PARAPLEGIC FOR FIVE YEARS. AND I KNOW YOU TOLD THE DETECTIVES THAT HOLDING THIS SWORD MADE YOU WALK.
BUT WHEN YOU TURNED YOURSELF IN TO THE POLICE, YOU LET GO OF THE SWORD, AND YOU WERE CLEARLY STILL STANDING.
SO, WHEN YOU TOUCH THE SWORD, IT HEALS YOU AND GIVES YOU SUPER-HUMAN ABILITIES, BUT WHEN YOU STOP TOUCHING IT... ONLY THE SUPERHUMAN ABILITIES GO AWAY. CORRECT?
...
OH, I GET IT.
THIS IS WHY YOU "EXTRACTED AND ERASED ME"--SO YOU COULD JUST USE ME TO LEARN MORE ABOUT THE SWORD BEFORE ANY-ONE ELSE GOT A CHANCE TO.
YOU DON'T WANT TO HELP ME.
DARA, OF COURSE WE DO. BUT HELPING YOU DOESN'T PRECLUDE OUR CURIOSITY ABOUT THE SWORD. OF COURSE WE WANT TO KNOW MORE ABOUT IT.
NOW, FOR SAFETY REASONS, MY COLLEAGUES AND I HAVE NOT TOUCHED THE SWORD WITH OUR BARE HANDS. WE SIMPLY DO NOT KNOW WHAT KIND OF TECHNOLOGY IT IS OR HOW IT WOULD AFFECT US. BUT YOU OBVIOUSLY DO.
WE JUST WANT TO KNOW WHAT THIS IS, DARA. IF YOU HELP US... WE'LL HELP YOU START A NEW LIFE.

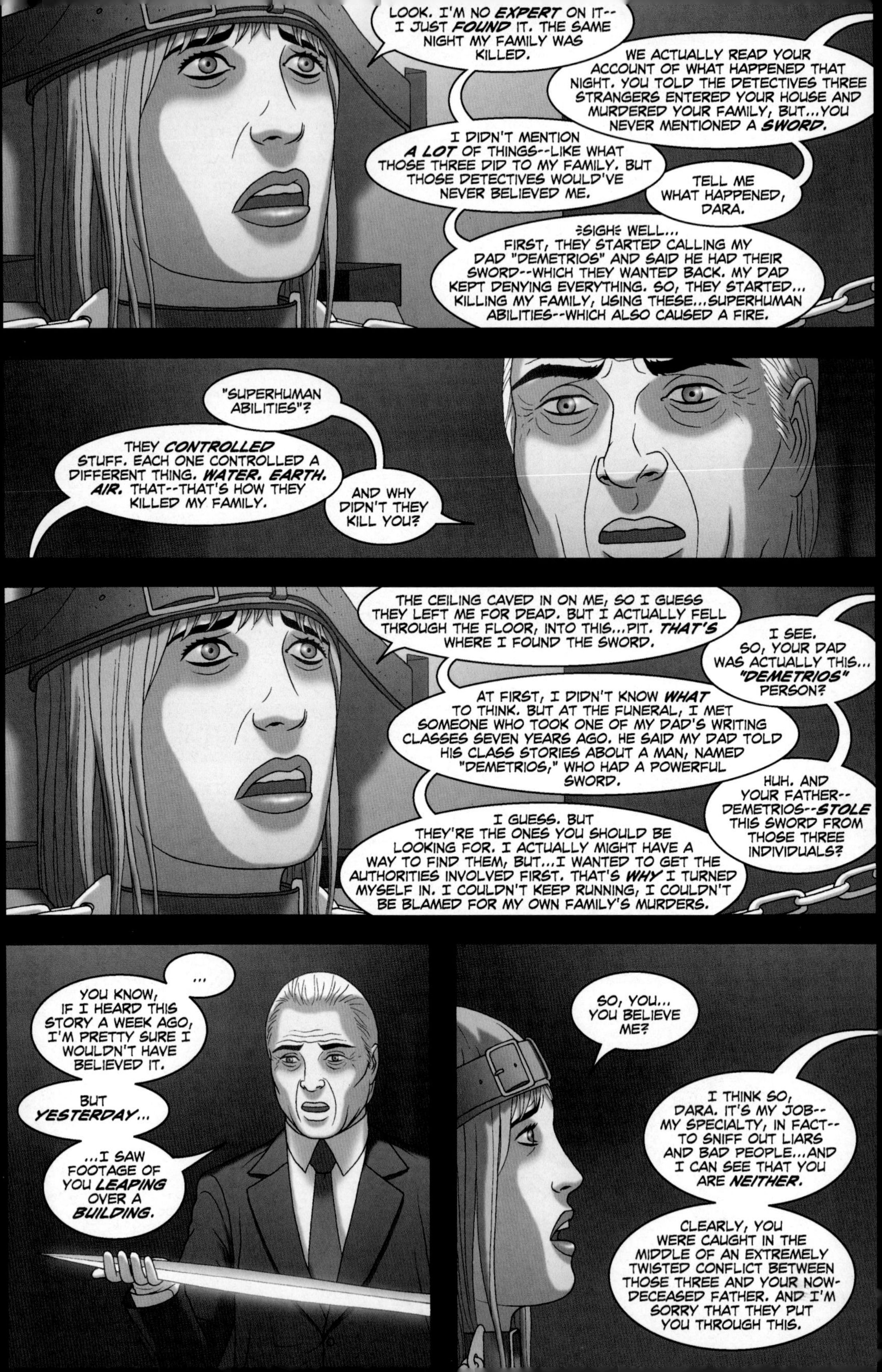
LOOK. I'M NO EXPERT ON IT-- I JUST FOUND IT. THE SAME NIGHT MY FAMILY WAS KILLED.
WE ACTUALLY READ YOUR ACCOUNT OF WHAT HAPPENED THAT NIGHT. YOU TOLD THE DETECTIVES THREE STRANGERS ENTERED YOUR HOUSE AND MURDERED YOUR FAMILY, BUT...YOU NEVER MENTIONED A SWORD.
I DIDN'T MENTION A LOT OF THINGS--LIKE WHAT THOSE THREE DID TO MY FAMILY. BUT THOSE DETECTIVES WOULD'VE NEVER BELIEVED ME.
TELL ME WHAT HAPPENED, DARA.
=SIGH= WELL... FIRST, THEY STARTED CALLING MY DAD "DEMETRIOS" AND SAID HE HAD THEIR SWORD--WHICH THEY WANTED BACK. MY DAD KEPT DENYING EVERYTHING. SO, THEY STARTED... KILLING MY FAMILY, USING THESE...SUPERHUMAN ABILITIES--WHICH ALSO CAUSED A FIRE.
"SUPERHUMAN ABILITIES"?
THEY CONTROLLED STUFF. EACH ONE CONTROLLED A DIFFERENT THING. WATER. EARTH. AIR. THAT--THAT'S HOW THEY KILLED MY FAMILY.
AND WHY DIDN'T THEY KILL YOU?
THE CEILING CAVED IN ON ME, SO I GUESS THEY LEFT ME FOR DEAD. BUT I ACTUALLY FELL THROUGH THE FLOOR, INTO THIS...PIT. THAT'S WHERE I FOUND THE SWORD.
I SEE. SO, YOUR DAD WAS ACTUALLY THIS... "DEMETRIOS" PERSON?
AT FIRST, I DIDN'T KNOW WHAT TO THINK. BUT AT THE FUNERAL, I MET SOMEONE WHO TOOK ONE OF MY DAD'S WRITING CLASSES SEVEN YEARS AGO. HE SAID MY DAD TOLD HIS CLASS STORIES ABOUT A MAN, NAMED "DEMETRIOS," WHO HAD A POWERFUL SWORD.
HUH. AND YOUR FATHER-- DEMETRIOS--STOLE THIS SWORD FROM THOSE THREE INDIVIDUALS?
I GUESS. BUT THEY'RE THE ONES YOU SHOULD BE LOOKING FOR. I ACTUALLY MIGHT HAVE A WAY TO FIND THEM, BUT...I WANTED TO GET THE AUTHORITIES INVOLVED FIRST. THAT'S WHY I TURNED MYSELF IN. I COULDN'T KEEP RUNNING, I COULDN'T BE BLAMED FOR MY OWN FAMILY'S MURDERS.
...
YOU KNOW, IF I HEARD THIS STORY A WEEK AGO, I'M PRETTY SURE I WOULDN'T HAVE BELIEVED IT.
BUT YESTERDAY...
...I SAW FOOTAGE OF YOU LEAPING OVER A BUILDING.
SO, YOU... YOU BELIEVE ME?
I THINK SO, DARA. IT'S MY JOB-- MY SPECIALTY, IN FACT-- TO SNIFF OUT LIARS AND BAD PEOPLE...AND I CAN SEE THAT YOU ARE NEITHER.
CLEARLY, YOU WERE CAUGHT IN THE MIDDLE OF AN EXTREMELY TWISTED CONFLICT BETWEEN THOSE THREE AND YOUR NOW-DECEASED FATHER. AND I'M SORRY THAT THEY PUT YOU THROUGH THIS.

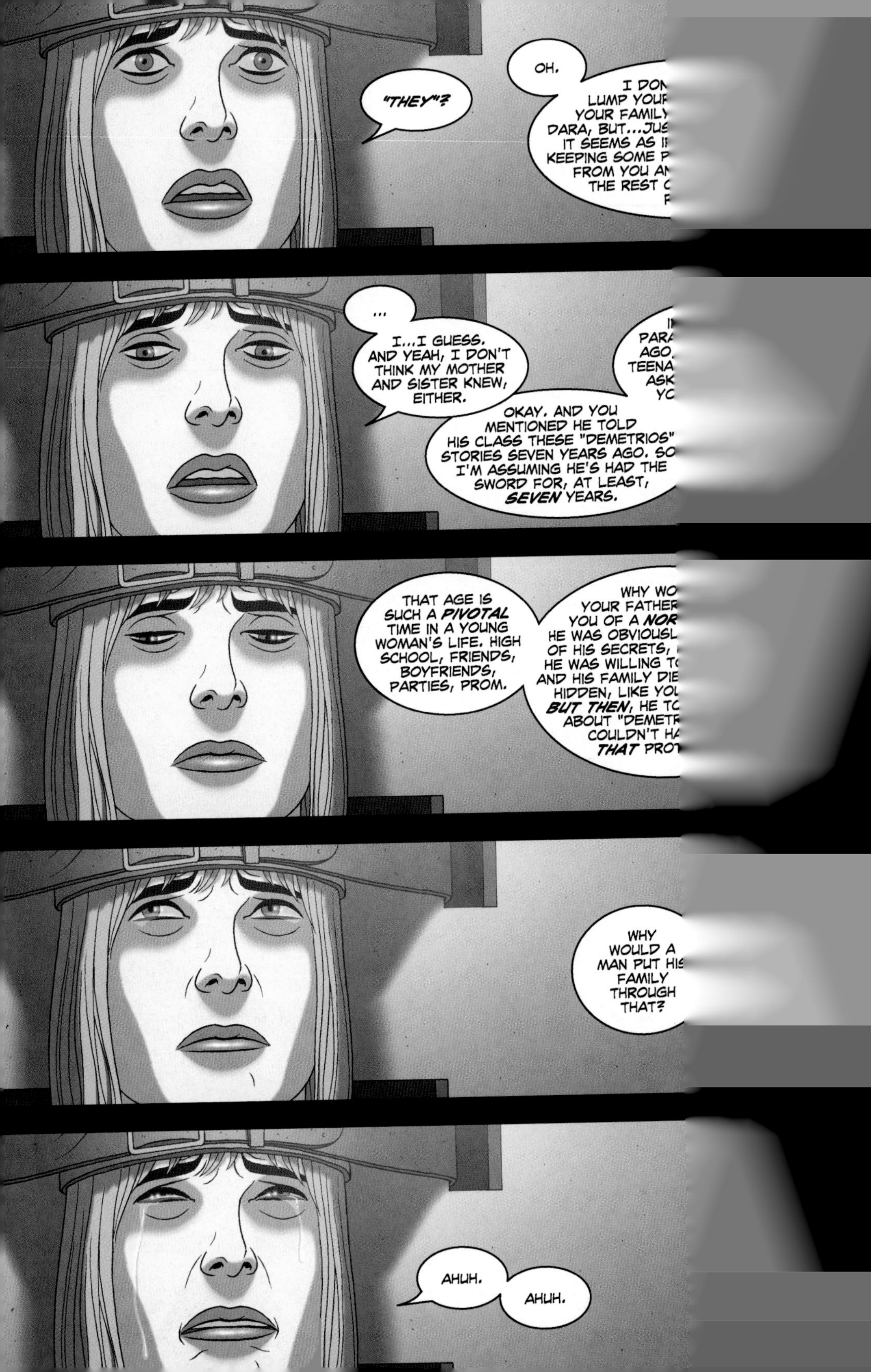
"THEY"?
OH.
I DON LUMP YOUR YOUR FAMILY DARA, BUT...JUS IT SEEMS AS I KEEPING SOME P FROM YOU AN THE REST C
...
I...I GUESS. AND YEAH, I DON'T THINK MY MOTHER AND SISTER KNEW, EITHER.
OKAY. AND YOU MENTIONED HE TOLD HIS CLASS THESE "DEMETRIOS" STORIES SEVEN YEARS AGO. SO I'M ASSUMING HE'S HAD THE SWORD FOR, AT LEAST, SEVEN YEARS.
PARA AGO. TEENA ASK YO
THAT AGE IS SUCH A PIVOTAL TIME IN A YOUNG WOMAN'S LIFE. HIGH SCHOOL, FRIENDS, BOYFRIENDS, PARTIES, PROM.
WHY WO YOUR FATHER YOU OF A NOR HE WAS OBVIOUSL OF HIS SECRETS, HE WAS WILLING TO AND HIS FAMILY DIE HIDDEN, LIKE YOU BUT THEN, HE TO ABOUT "DEMETR COULDN'T HA THAT PROT
WHY WOULD A MAN PUT HIS FAMILY THROUGH THAT?
AHUH.
AHUH.

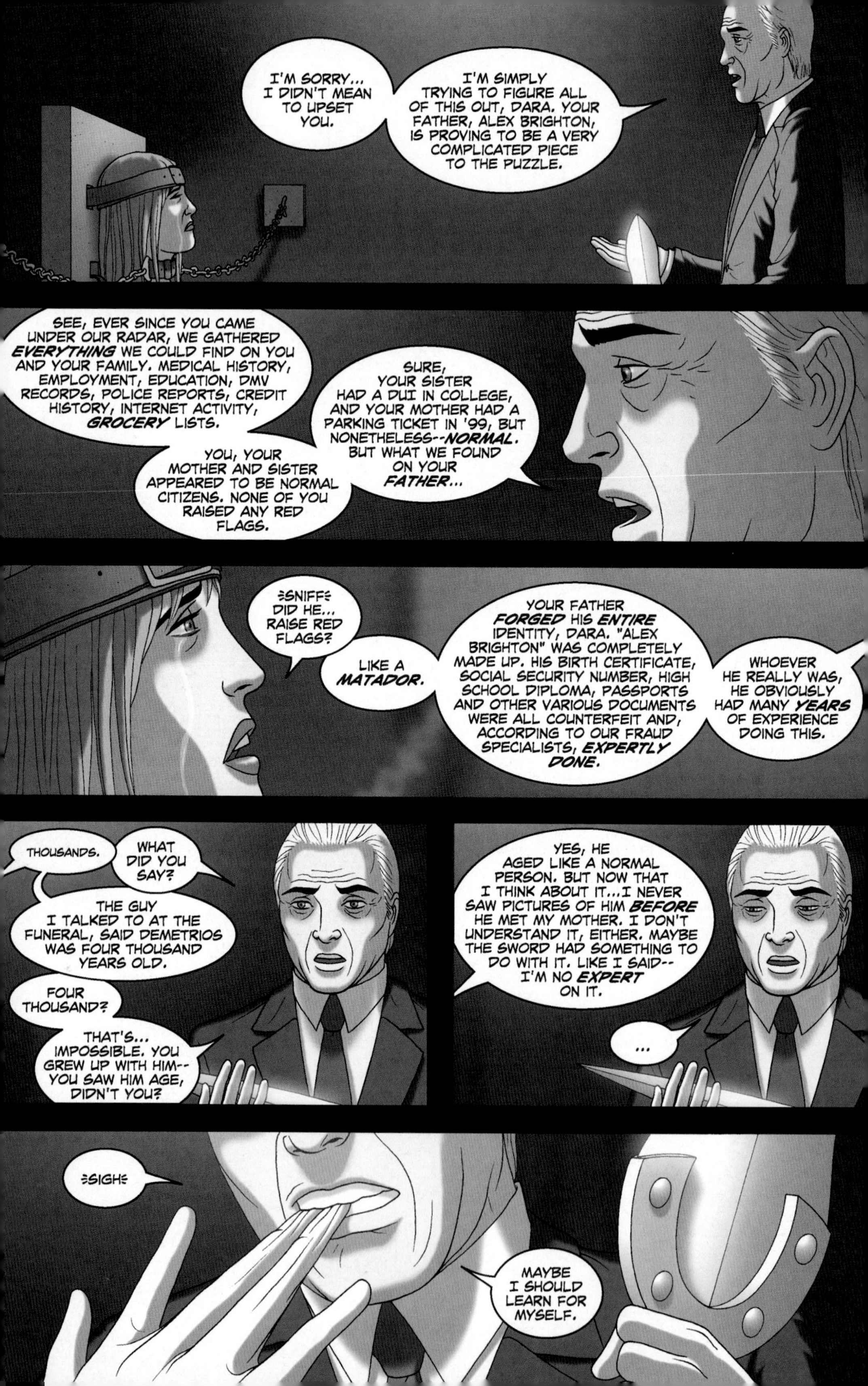
I'M SORRY... I DIDN'T MEAN TO UPSET YOU.
I'M SIMPLY TRYING TO FIGURE ALL OF THIS OUT, DARA. YOUR FATHER, ALEX BRIGHTON, IS PROVING TO BE A VERY COMPLICATED PIECE TO THE PUZZLE.
SEE, EVER SINCE YOU CAME UNDER OUR RADAR, WE GATHERED EVERYTHING WE COULD FIND ON YOU AND YOUR FAMILY. MEDICAL HISTORY, EMPLOYMENT, EDUCATION, DMV RECORDS, POLICE REPORTS, CREDIT HISTORY, INTERNET ACTIVITY, GROCERY LISTS.
YOU, YOUR MOTHER AND SISTER APPEARED TO BE NORMAL CITIZENS. NONE OF YOU RAISED ANY RED FLAGS.
SURE, YOUR SISTER HAD A DUI IN COLLEGE, AND YOUR MOTHER HAD A PARKING TICKET IN '99, BUT NONETHELESS--NORMAL. BUT WHAT WE FOUND ON YOUR FATHER...
SNIFF DID HE... RAISE RED FLAGS?
LIKE A MATADOR.
YOUR FATHER FORGED HIS ENTIRE IDENTITY, DARA. "ALEX BRIGHTON" WAS COMPLETELY MADE UP. HIS BIRTH CERTIFICATE, SOCIAL SECURITY NUMBER, HIGH SCHOOL DIPLOMA, PASSPORTS AND OTHER VARIOUS DOCUMENTS WERE ALL COUNTERFEIT AND, ACCORDING TO OUR FRAUD SPECIALISTS, EXPERTLY DONE.
WHOEVER HE REALLY WAS, HE OBVIOUSLY HAD MANY YEARS OF EXPERIENCE DOING THIS.
THOUSANDS.
WHAT DID YOU SAY?
THE GUY I TALKED TO AT THE FUNERAL, SAID DEMETRIOS WAS FOUR THOUSAND YEARS OLD.
FOUR THOUSAND?
THAT'S... IMPOSSIBLE. YOU GREW UP WITH HIM-- YOU SAW HIM AGE, DIDN'T YOU?
YES, HE AGED LIKE A NORMAL PERSON. BUT NOW THAT I THINK ABOUT IT...I NEVER SAW PICTURES OF HIM BEFORE HE MET MY MOTHER. I DON'T UNDERSTAND IT, EITHER. MAYBE THE SWORD HAD SOMETHING TO DO WITH IT. LIKE I SAID-- I'M NO EXPERT ON IT.
...
SIGH
MAYBE I SHOULD LEARN FOR MYSELF.

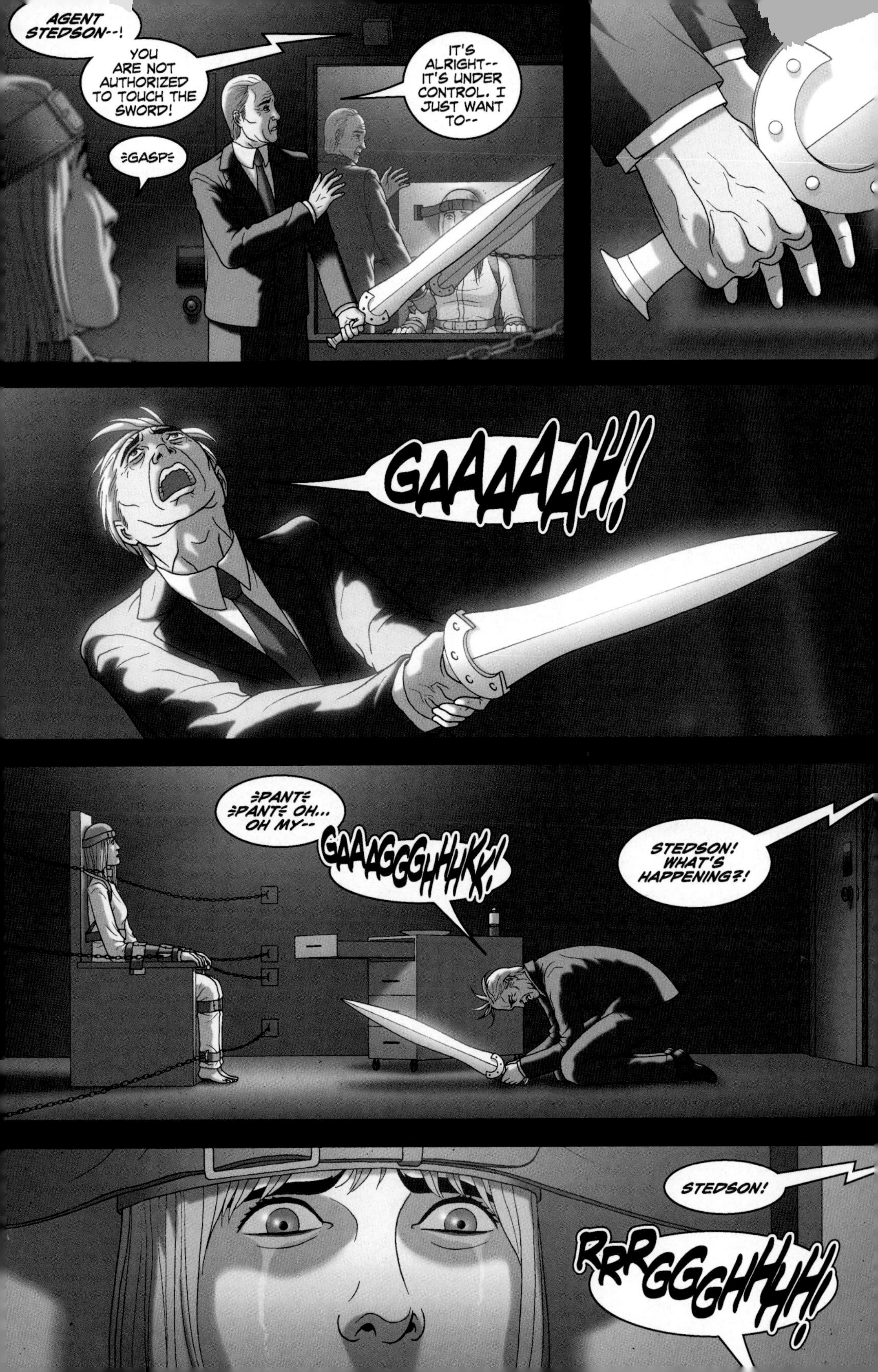
AGENT STEDSON--!
YOU ARE NOT AUTHORIZED TO TOUCH THE SWORD!
=GASP=
IT'S ALRIGHT-- IT'S UNDER CONTROL. I JUST WANT TO--
GAAAAAH!
=PANT= =PANT= OH... OH MY--
GAAAGGGHHUKK!
STEDSON! WHAT'S HAPPENING?!
STEDSON!
RRRGGGHHHH!

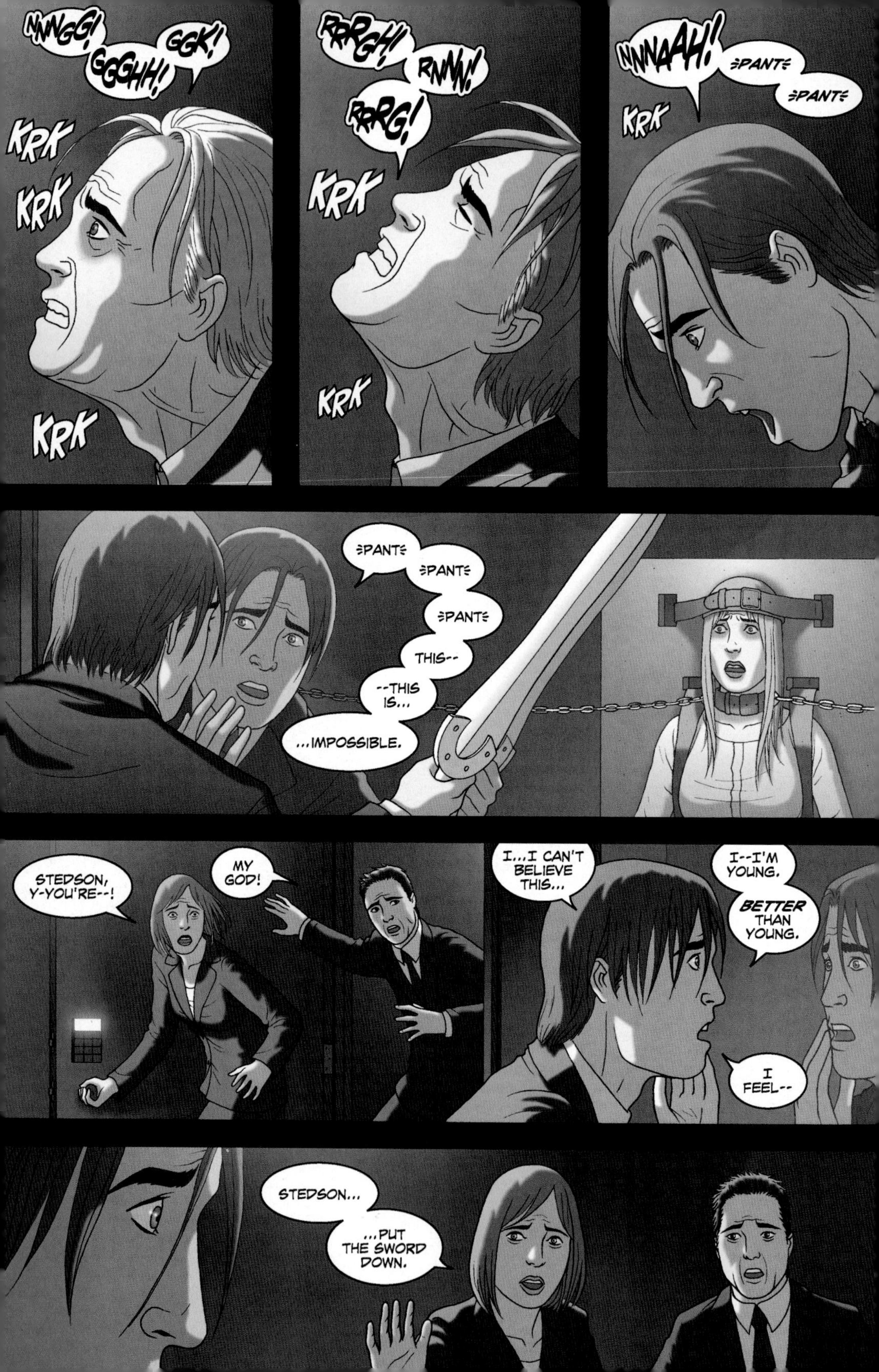
NNNGG!
GGGHH!
GGK!
KRK
KRK
KRK
RRRGH!
RNNN!
RRRG!
KRK
KRK
NNNAAH!
PANT
PANT
KRK
PANT
PANT
PANT
THIS--
--THIS IS...
...IMPOSSIBLE.
STEDSON, Y-YOU'RE--!
MY GOD!
I...I CAN'T BELIEVE THIS...
I--I'M YOUNG.
BETTER THAN YOUNG.
I FEEL--
STEDSON...
...PUT THE SWORD DOWN.

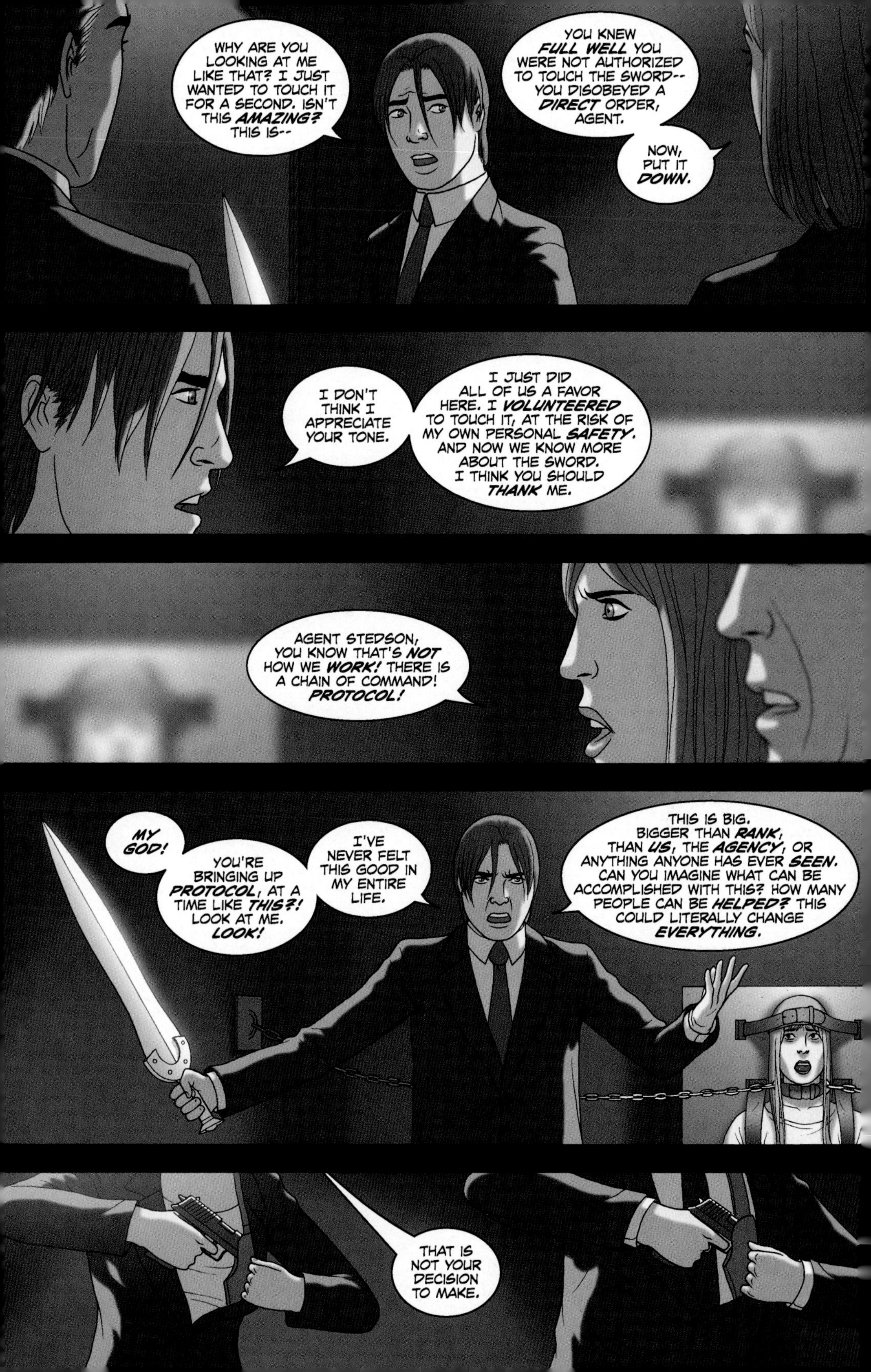
WHY ARE YOU LOOKING AT ME LIKE THAT? I JUST WANTED TO TOUCH IT FOR A SECOND. ISN'T THIS AMAZING? THIS IS--
YOU KNEW FULL WELL YOU WERE NOT AUTHORIZED TO TOUCH THE SWORD-- YOU DISOBEYED A DIRECT ORDER, AGENT.
NOW, PUT IT DOWN.
I DON'T THINK I APPRECIATE YOUR TONE.
I JUST DID ALL OF US A FAVOR HERE. I VOLUNTEERED TO TOUCH IT, AT THE RISK OF MY OWN PERSONAL SAFETY. AND NOW WE KNOW MORE ABOUT THE SWORD. I THINK YOU SHOULD THANK ME.
AGENT STEDSON, YOU KNOW THAT'S NOT HOW WE WORK! THERE IS A CHAIN OF COMMAND! PROTOCOL!
MY GOD!
YOU'RE BRINGING UP PROTOCOL, AT A TIME LIKE THIS?! LOOK AT ME. LOOK!
I'VE NEVER FELT THIS GOOD IN MY ENTIRE LIFE.
THIS IS BIG. BIGGER THAN RANK, THAN US, THE AGENCY, OR ANYTHING ANYONE HAS EVER SEEN. CAN YOU IMAGINE WHAT CAN BE ACCOMPLISHED WITH THIS? HOW MANY PEOPLE CAN BE HELPED? THIS COULD LITERALLY CHANGE EVERYTHING.
THAT IS NOT YOUR DECISION TO MAKE.

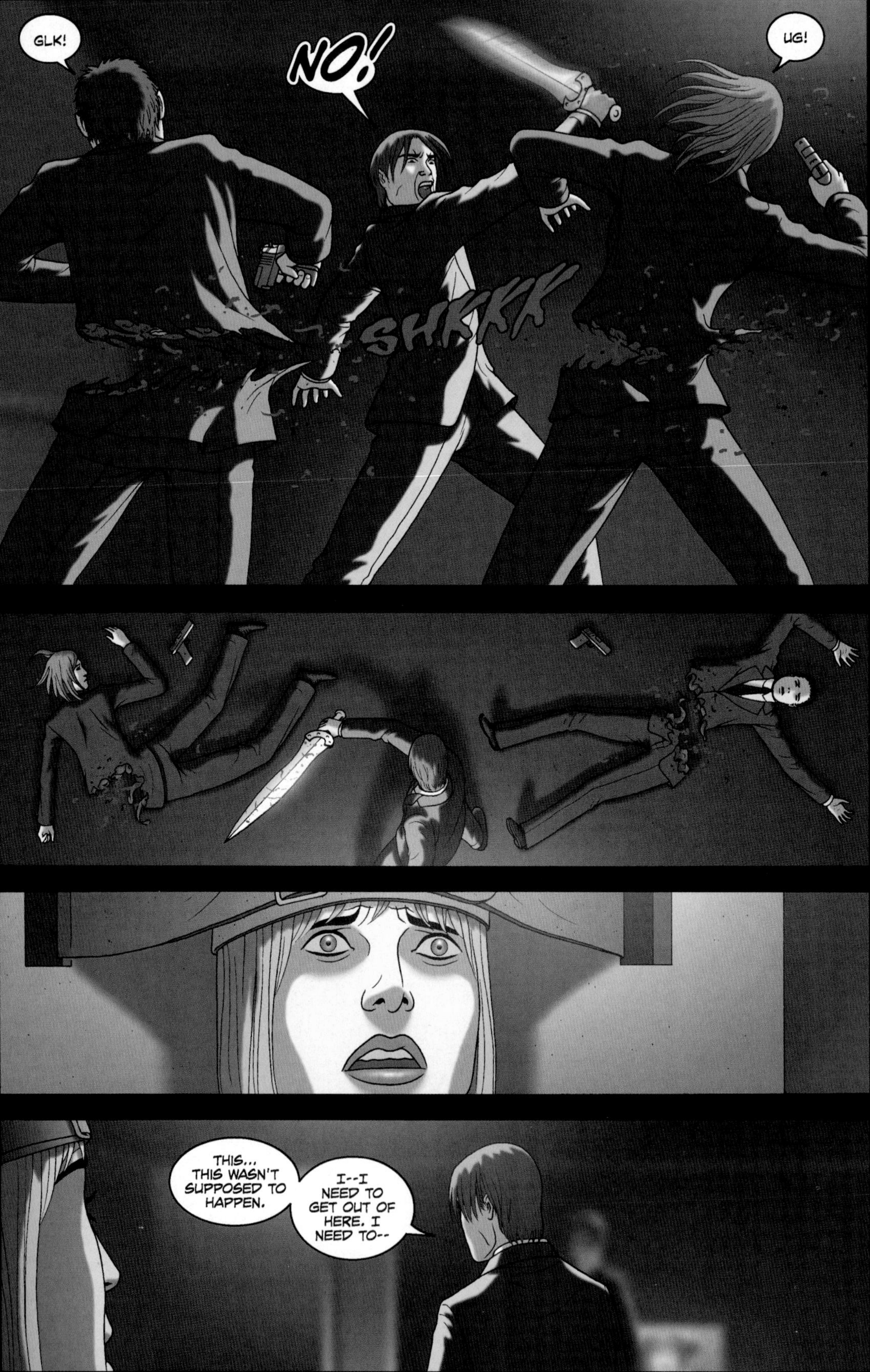
GLK!
NO!
UG!
SHKKK
THIS... THIS WASN'T SUPPOSED TO HAPPEN.
I--I NEED TO GET OUT OF HERE. I NEED TO--

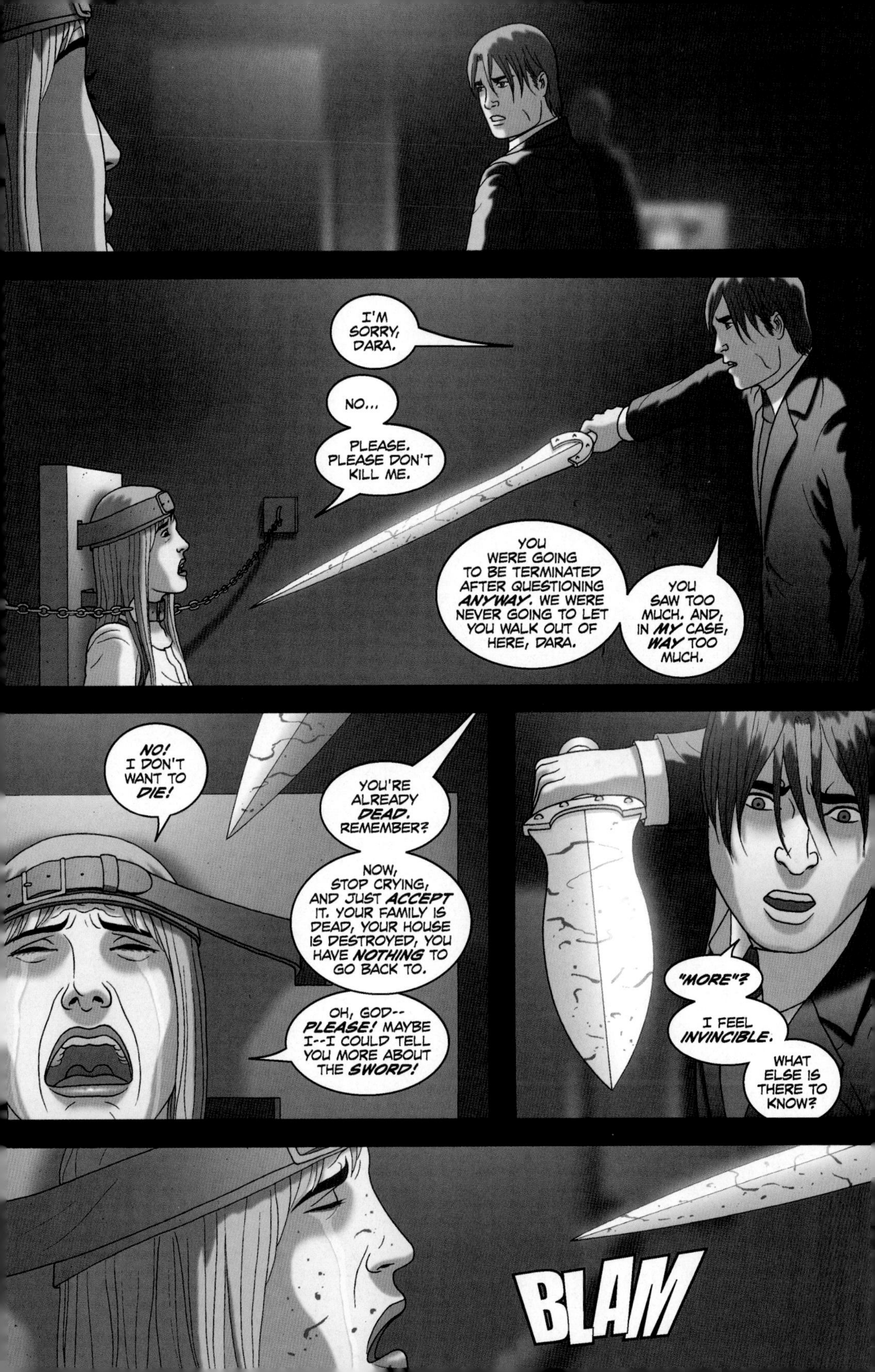
I'M SORRY, DARA.
NO...
PLEASE. PLEASE DON'T KILL ME.
YOU WERE GOING TO BE TERMINATED AFTER QUESTIONING ANYWAY. WE WERE NEVER GOING TO LET YOU WALK OUT OF HERE, DARA.
YOU SAW TOO MUCH. AND, IN MY CASE, WAY TOO MUCH.
NO! I DON'T WANT TO DIE!
YOU'RE ALREADY DEAD. REMEMBER?
NOW, STOP CRYING, AND JUST ACCEPT IT. YOUR FAMILY IS DEAD, YOUR HOUSE IS DESTROYED, YOU HAVE NOTHING TO GO BACK TO.
OH, GOD-- PLEASE! MAYBE I--I COULD TELL YOU MORE ABOUT THE SWORD!
"MORE"?
I FEEL INVINCIBLE.
WHAT ELSE IS THERE TO KNOW?
BLAM

NGK...

GK...

KLAK

KLANG

AGENTS?!
WE HEARD A
GUNSHOT! WHAT'S
YOUR STATUS?
AGENTS!

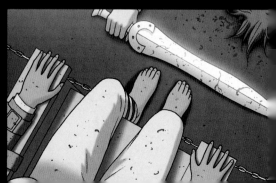

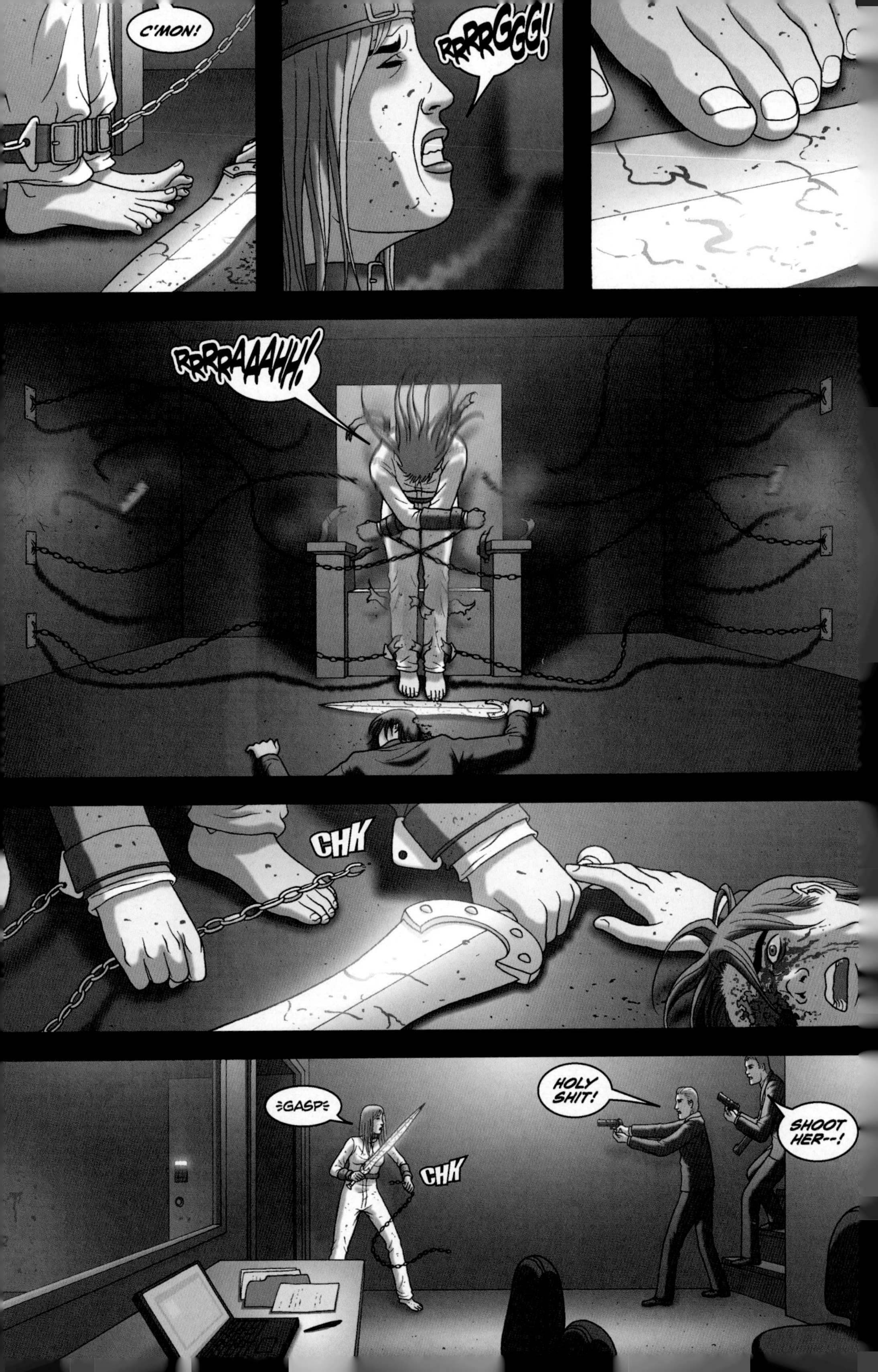
C'MON!
RRRRGGG!
RRRRAAAHH!
CHK
=GASP=
CHK
HOLY SHIT!
SHOOT HER--!

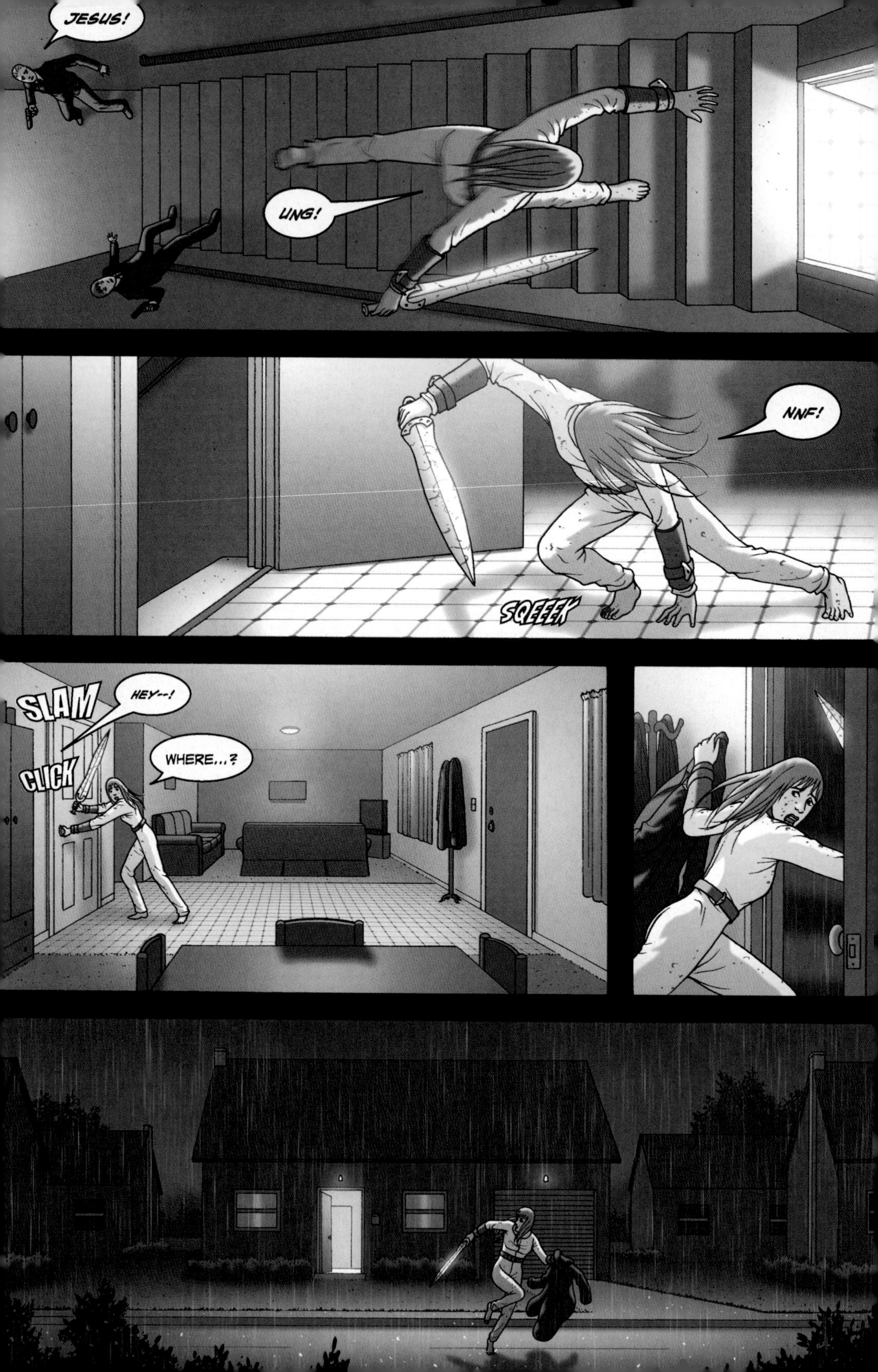
JESUS!
UNG!
NNF!
SQEEEK
SLAM
HEY--!
CLICK
WHERE...?

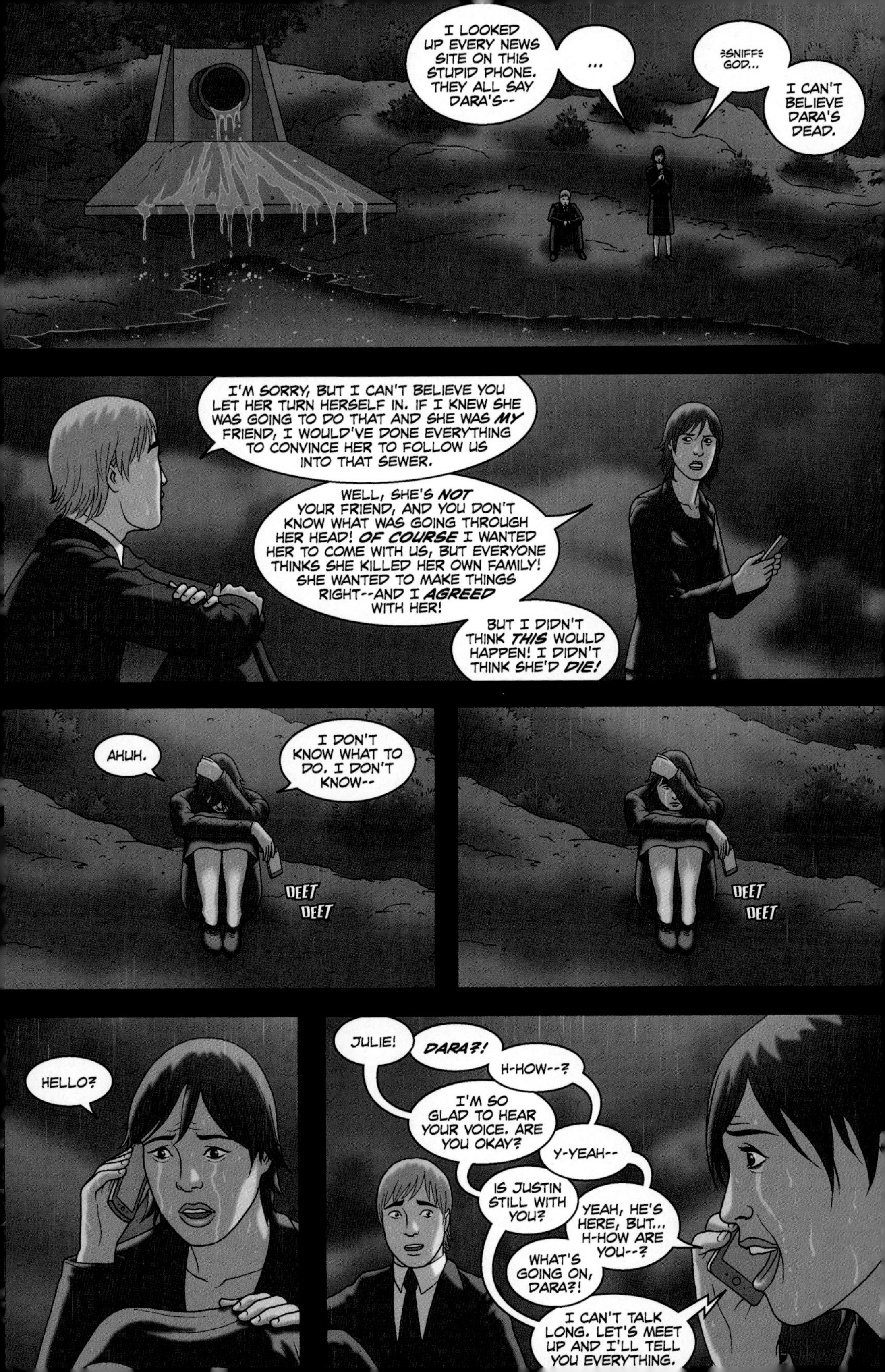
I LOOKED UP EVERY NEWS SITE ON THIS STUPID PHONE. THEY ALL SAY DARA'S--
...
SNIFF GOD...
I CAN'T BELIEVE DARA'S DEAD.
I'M SORRY, BUT I CAN'T BELIEVE YOU LET HER TURN HERSELF IN. IF I KNEW SHE WAS GOING TO DO THAT AND SHE WAS MY FRIEND, I WOULD'VE DONE EVERYTHING TO CONVINCE HER TO FOLLOW US INTO THAT SEWER.
WELL, SHE'S NOT YOUR FRIEND, AND YOU DON'T KNOW WHAT WAS GOING THROUGH HER HEAD! OF COURSE I WANTED HER TO COME WITH US, BUT EVERYONE THINKS SHE KILLED HER OWN FAMILY! SHE WANTED TO MAKE THINGS RIGHT--AND I AGREED WITH HER!
BUT I DIDN'T THINK THIS WOULD HAPPEN! I DIDN'T THINK SHE'D DIE!
AHUH.
I DON'T KNOW WHAT TO DO. I DON'T KNOW--
DEET
DEET
DEET
DEET
HELLO?
JULIE!
DARA?!
H-HOW--?
I'M SO GLAD TO HEAR YOUR VOICE. ARE YOU OKAY?
Y-YEAH--
IS JUSTIN STILL WITH YOU?
YEAH, HE'S HERE, BUT... H-HOW ARE YOU--?
WHAT'S GOING ON, DARA?!
I CAN'T TALK LONG. LET'S MEET UP AND I'LL TELL YOU EVERYTHING.

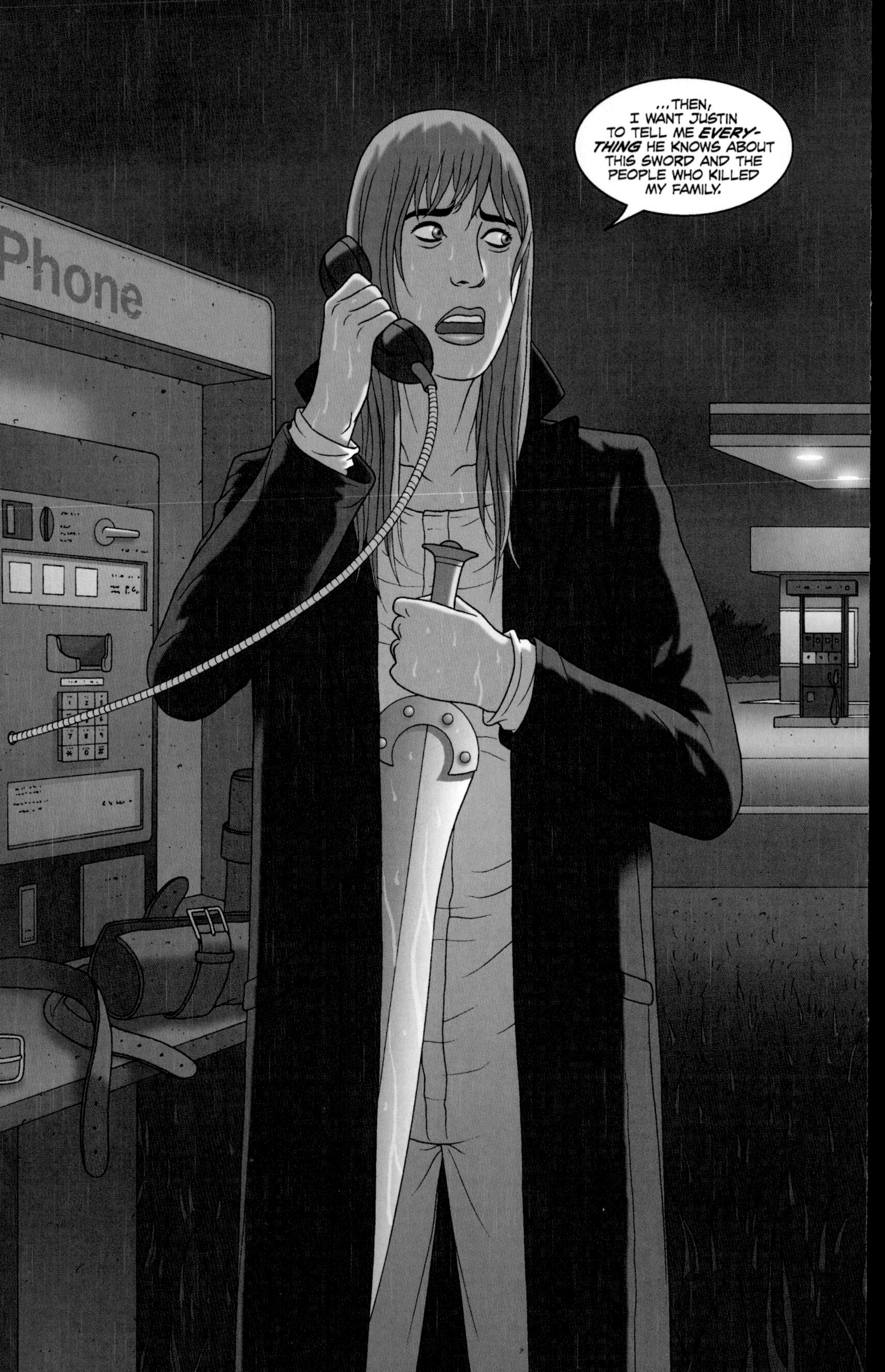
...THEN, I WANT JUSTIN TO TELL ME *EVERYTHING* HE KNOWS ABOUT THIS SWORD AND THE PEOPLE WHO KILLED MY FAMILY.
Phone

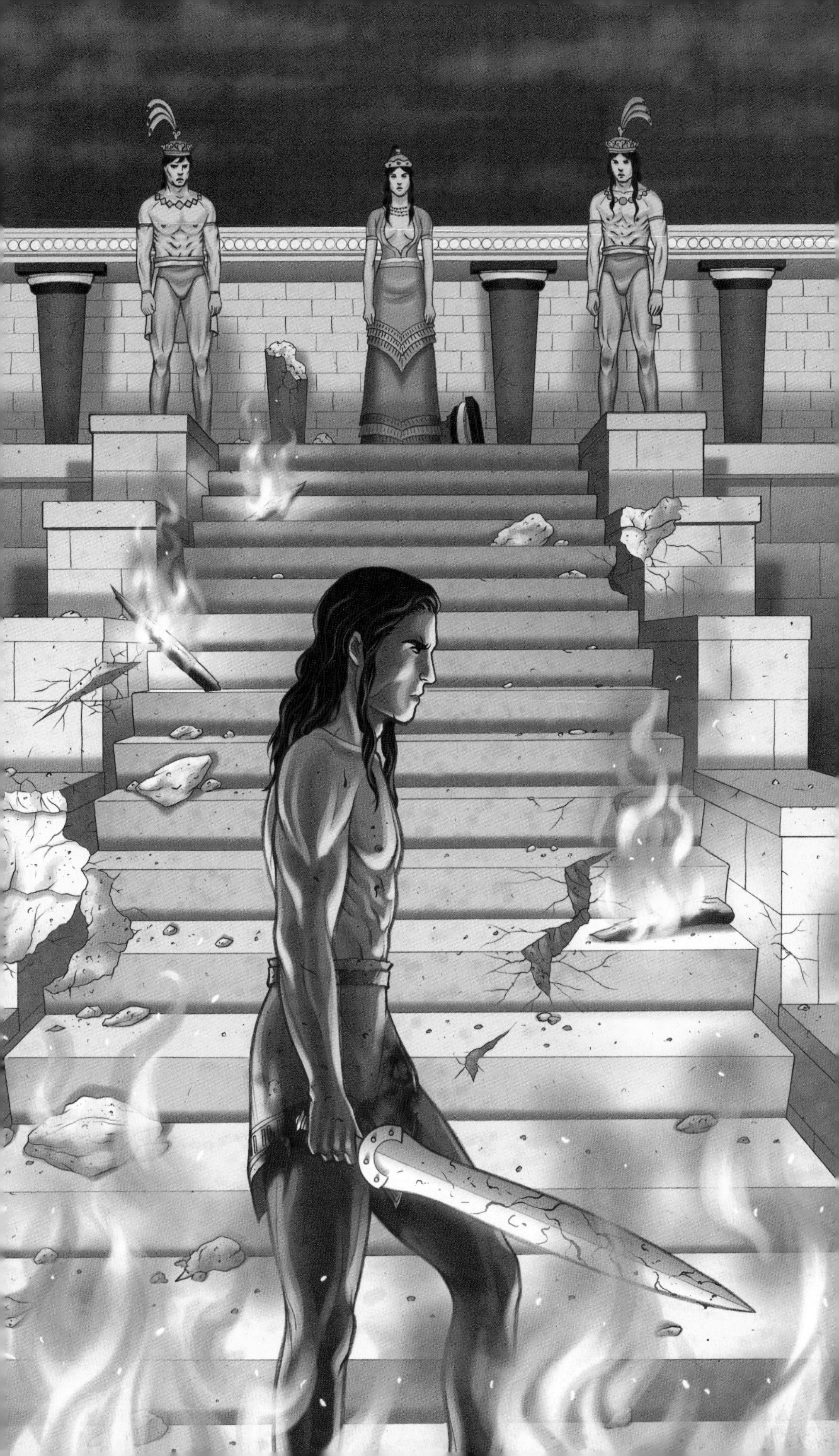

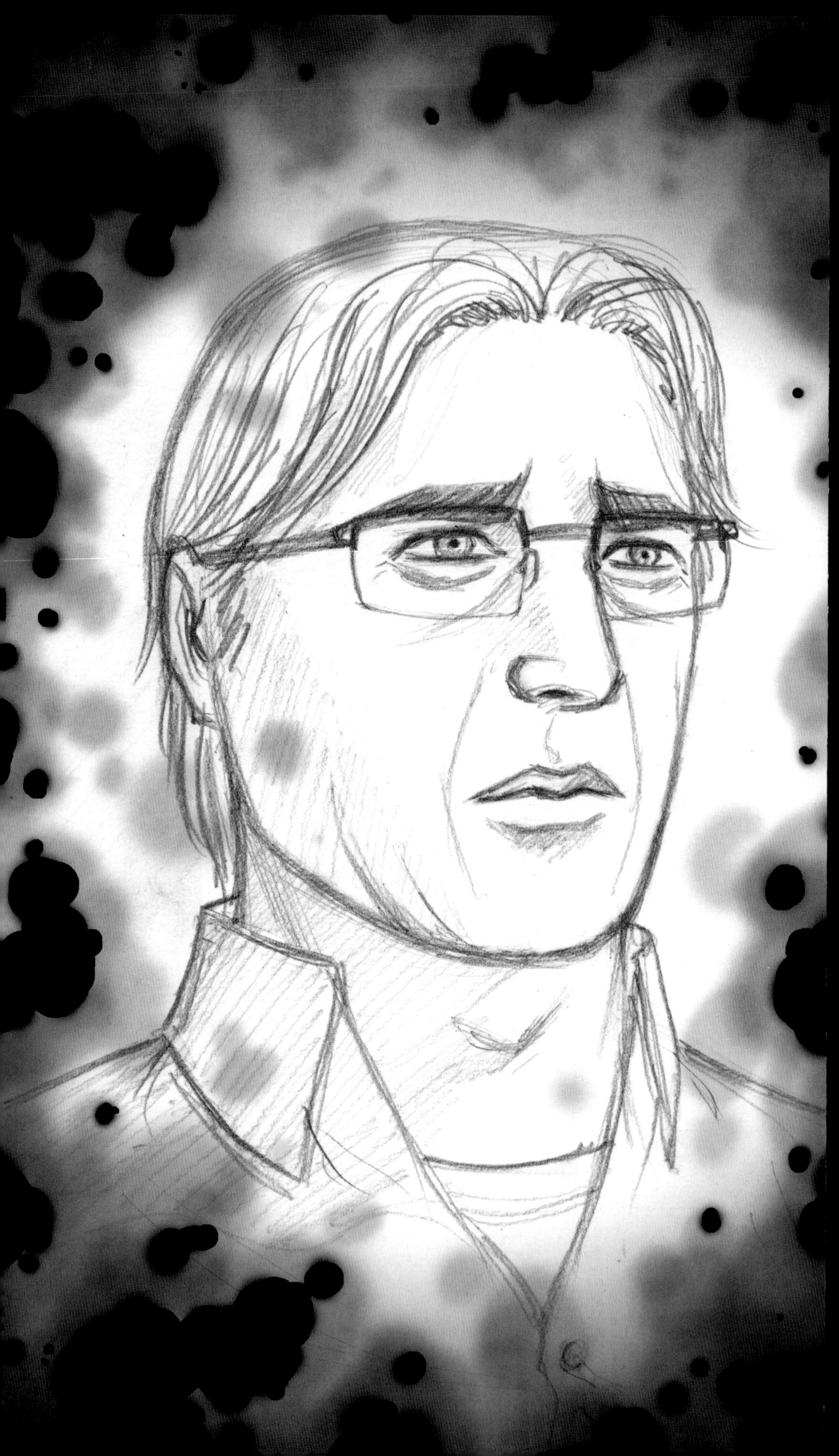

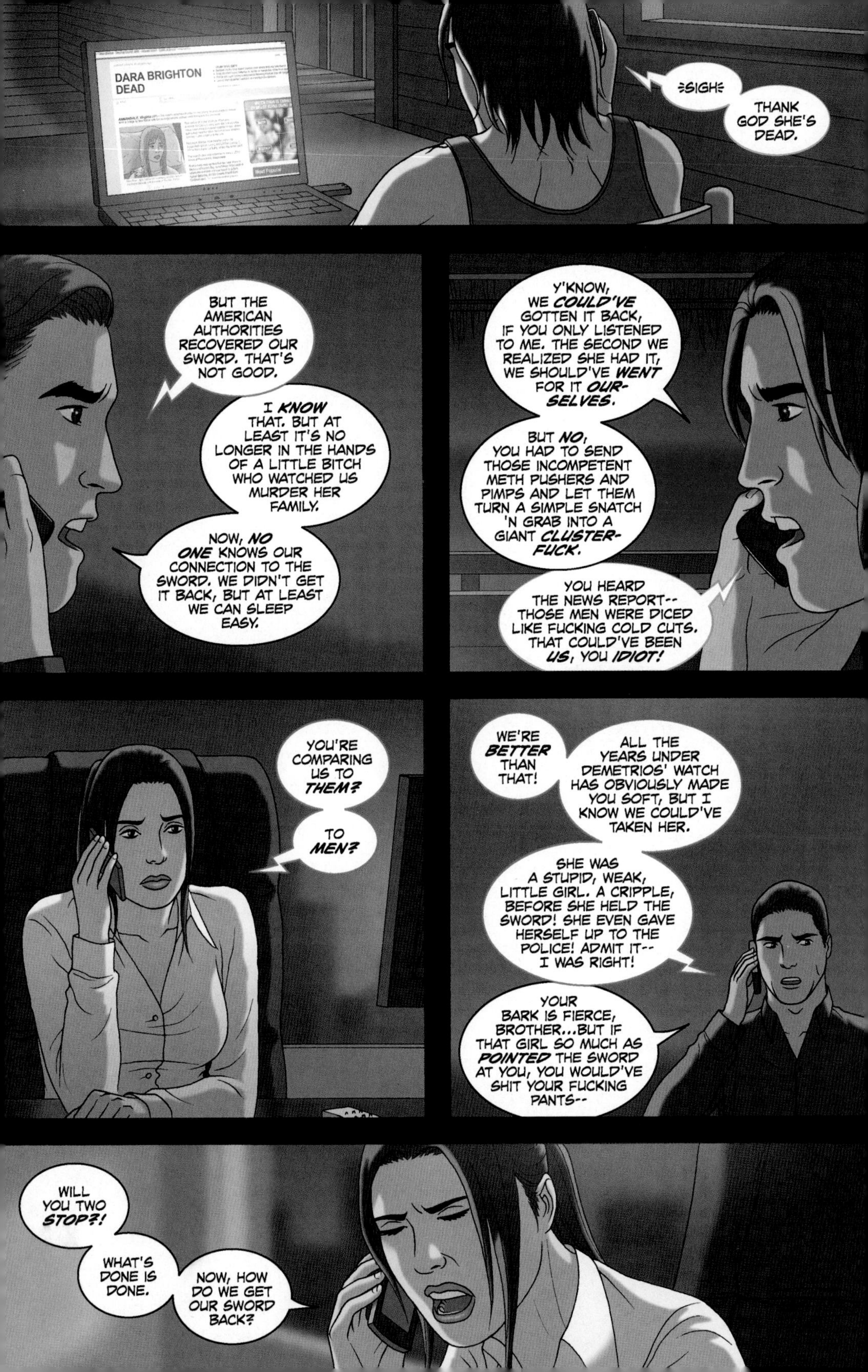
DARA BRIGHTON DEAD
≶SIGH≷
THANK GOD SHE'S DEAD.
BUT THE AMERICAN AUTHORITIES RECOVERED OUR SWORD. THAT'S NOT GOOD.
I KNOW THAT. BUT AT LEAST IT'S NO LONGER IN THE HANDS OF A LITTLE BITCH WHO WATCHED US MURDER HER FAMILY.
NOW, NO ONE KNOWS OUR CONNECTION TO THE SWORD. WE DIDN'T GET IT BACK, BUT AT LEAST WE CAN SLEEP EASY.
Y'KNOW, WE COULD'VE GOTTEN IT BACK, IF YOU ONLY LISTENED TO ME. THE SECOND WE REALIZED SHE HAD IT, WE SHOULD'VE WENT FOR IT OURSELVES.
BUT NO, YOU HAD TO SEND THOSE INCOMPETENT METH PUSHERS AND PIMPS AND LET THEM TURN A SIMPLE SNATCH 'N GRAB INTO A GIANT CLUSTER-FUCK.
YOU HEARD THE NEWS REPORT-- THOSE MEN WERE DICED LIKE FUCKING COLD CUTS. THAT COULD'VE BEEN US, YOU IDIOT!
YOU'RE COMPARING US TO THEM?
TO MEN?
WE'RE BETTER THAN THAT!
ALL THE YEARS UNDER DEMETRIOS' WATCH HAS OBVIOUSLY MADE YOU SOFT, BUT I KNOW WE COULD'VE TAKEN HER.
SHE WAS A STUPID, WEAK, LITTLE GIRL. A CRIPPLE, BEFORE SHE HELD THE SWORD! SHE EVEN GAVE HERSELF UP TO THE POLICE! ADMIT IT-- I WAS RIGHT!
YOUR BARK IS FIERCE, BROTHER...BUT IF THAT GIRL SO MUCH AS POINTED THE SWORD AT YOU, YOU WOULD'VE SHIT YOUR FUCKING PANTS--
WILL YOU TWO STOP?!
WHAT'S DONE IS DONE.
NOW, HOW DO WE GET OUR SWORD BACK?

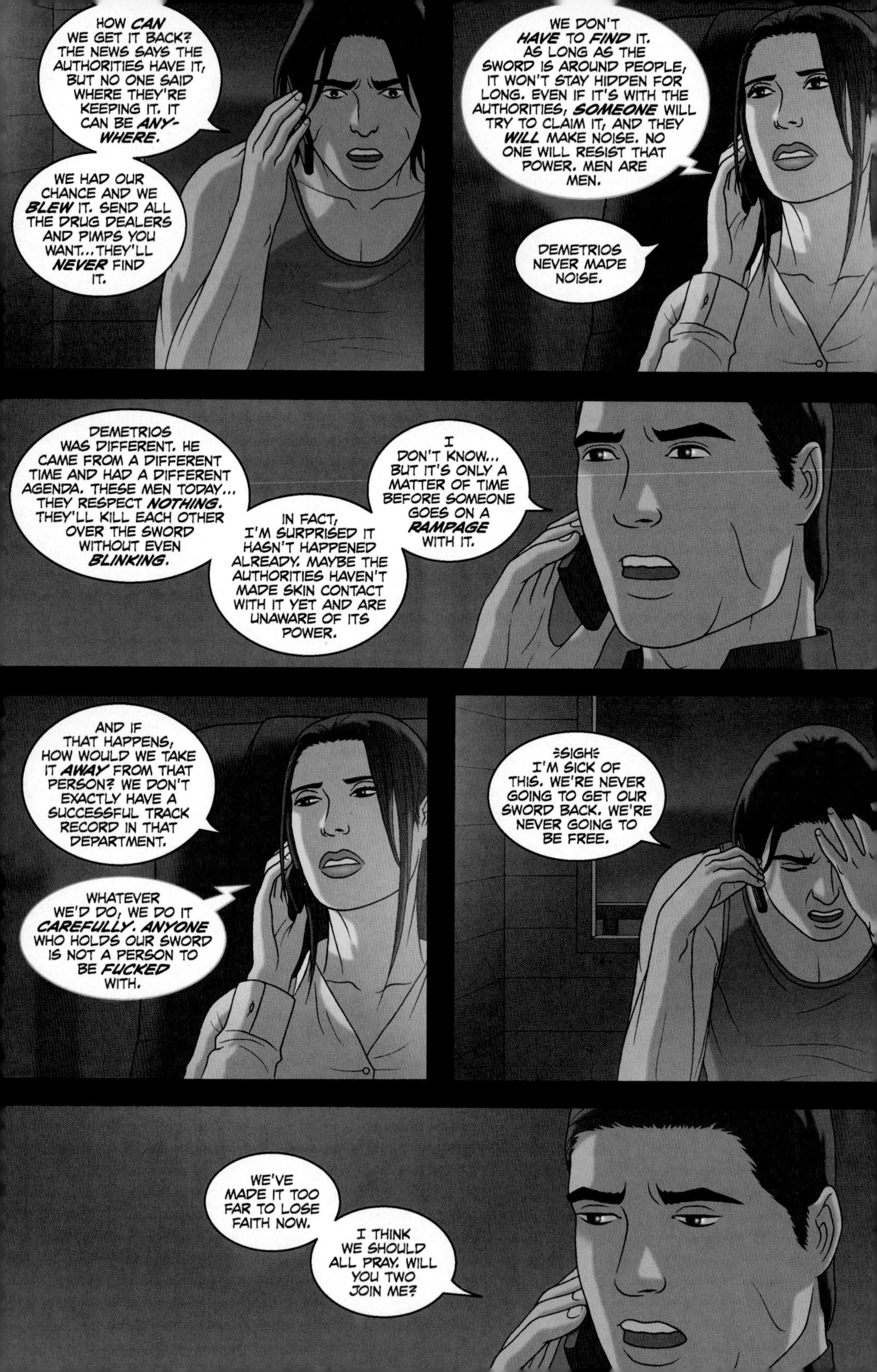
HOW CAN WE GET IT BACK? THE NEWS SAYS THE AUTHORITIES HAVE IT, BUT NO ONE SAID WHERE THEY'RE KEEPING IT. IT CAN BE ANY-WHERE.
WE HAD OUR CHANCE AND WE BLEW IT. SEND ALL THE DRUG DEALERS AND PIMPS YOU WANT...THEY'LL NEVER FIND IT.
WE DON'T HAVE TO FIND IT. AS LONG AS THE SWORD IS AROUND PEOPLE, IT WON'T STAY HIDDEN FOR LONG. EVEN IF IT'S WITH THE AUTHORITIES, SOMEONE WILL TRY TO CLAIM IT, AND THEY WILL MAKE NOISE. NO ONE WILL RESIST THAT POWER. MEN ARE MEN.
DEMETRIOS NEVER MADE NOISE.
DEMETRIOS WAS DIFFERENT. HE CAME FROM A DIFFERENT TIME AND HAD A DIFFERENT AGENDA. THESE MEN TODAY... THEY RESPECT NOTHING. THEY'LL KILL EACH OTHER OVER THE SWORD WITHOUT EVEN BLINKING.
IN FACT, I'M SURPRISED IT HASN'T HAPPENED ALREADY. MAYBE THE AUTHORITIES HAVEN'T MADE SKIN CONTACT WITH IT YET AND ARE UNAWARE OF ITS POWER.
I DON'T KNOW... BUT IT'S ONLY A MATTER OF TIME BEFORE SOMEONE GOES ON A RAMPAGE WITH IT.
AND IF THAT HAPPENS, HOW WOULD WE TAKE IT AWAY FROM THAT PERSON? WE DON'T EXACTLY HAVE A SUCCESSFUL TRACK RECORD IN THAT DEPARTMENT.
WHATEVER WE'D DO, WE DO IT CAREFULLY. ANYONE WHO HOLDS OUR SWORD IS NOT A PERSON TO BE FUCKED WITH.
≈SIGH≈ I'M SICK OF THIS. WE'RE NEVER GOING TO GET OUR SWORD BACK. WE'RE NEVER GOING TO BE FREE.
WE'VE MADE IT TOO FAR TO LOSE FAITH NOW.
I THINK WE SHOULD ALL PRAY. WILL YOU TWO JOIN ME?

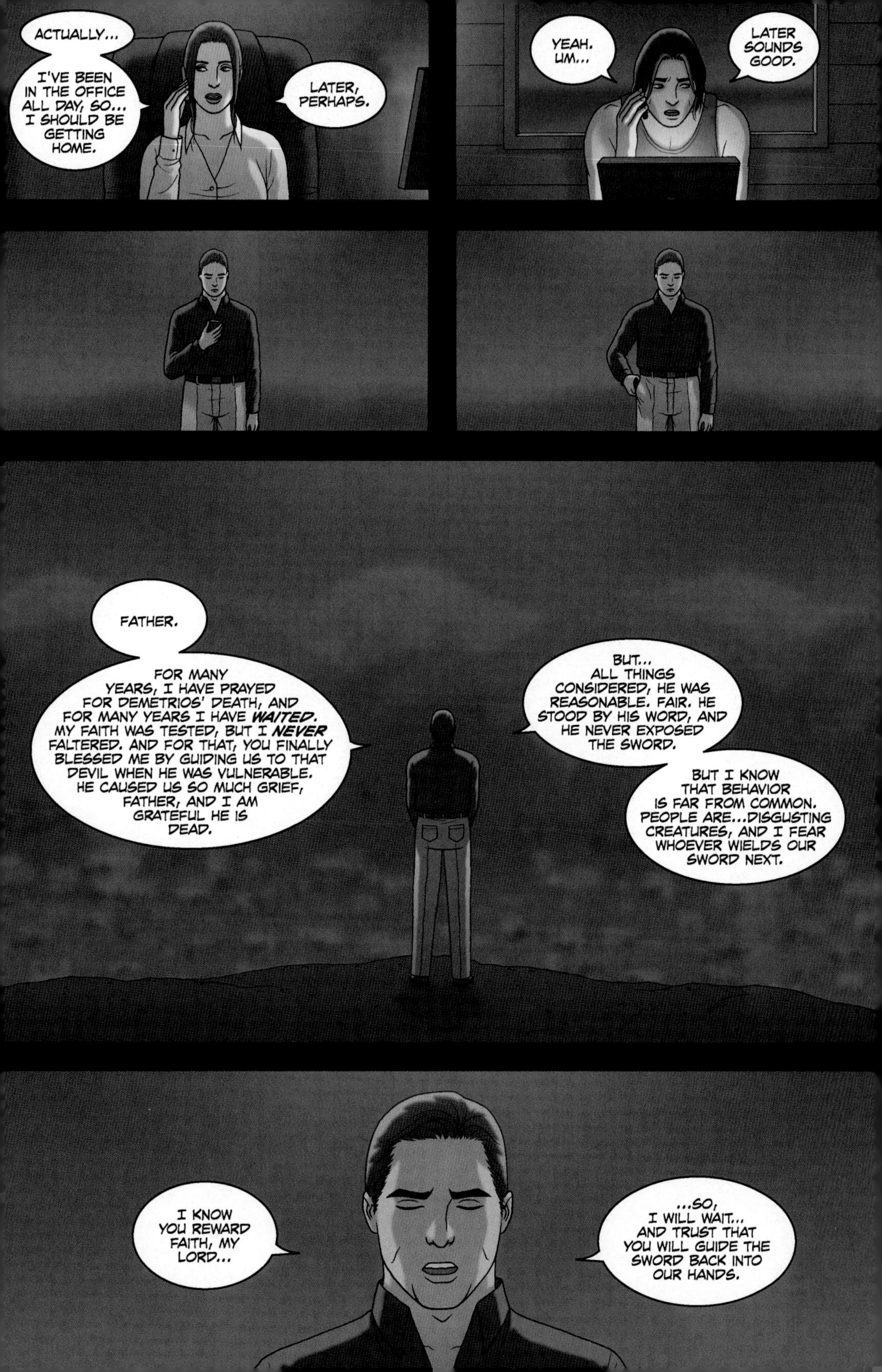
ACTUALLY...
I'VE BEEN IN THE OFFICE ALL DAY, SO... I SHOULD BE GETTING HOME.
LATER, PERHAPS.
YEAH. UM...
LATER SOUNDS GOOD.
FATHER.
FOR MANY YEARS, I HAVE PRAYED FOR DEMETRIOS' DEATH, AND FOR MANY YEARS I HAVE *WAITED*. MY FAITH WAS TESTED, BUT I *NEVER* FALTERED. AND FOR THAT, YOU FINALLY BLESSED ME BY GUIDING US TO THAT DEVIL WHEN HE WAS VULNERABLE. HE CAUSED US SO MUCH GRIEF, FATHER, AND I AM GRATEFUL HE IS DEAD.
BUT... ALL THINGS CONSIDERED, HE WAS REASONABLE. FAIR. HE STOOD BY HIS WORD, AND HE NEVER EXPOSED THE SWORD.
BUT I KNOW THAT BEHAVIOR IS FAR FROM COMMON. PEOPLE ARE...DISGUSTING CREATURES, AND I FEAR WHOEVER WIELDS OUR SWORD NEXT.
I KNOW YOU REWARD FAITH, MY LORD...
...SO, I WILL WAIT... AND TRUST THAT YOU WILL GUIDE THE SWORD BACK INTO OUR HANDS.

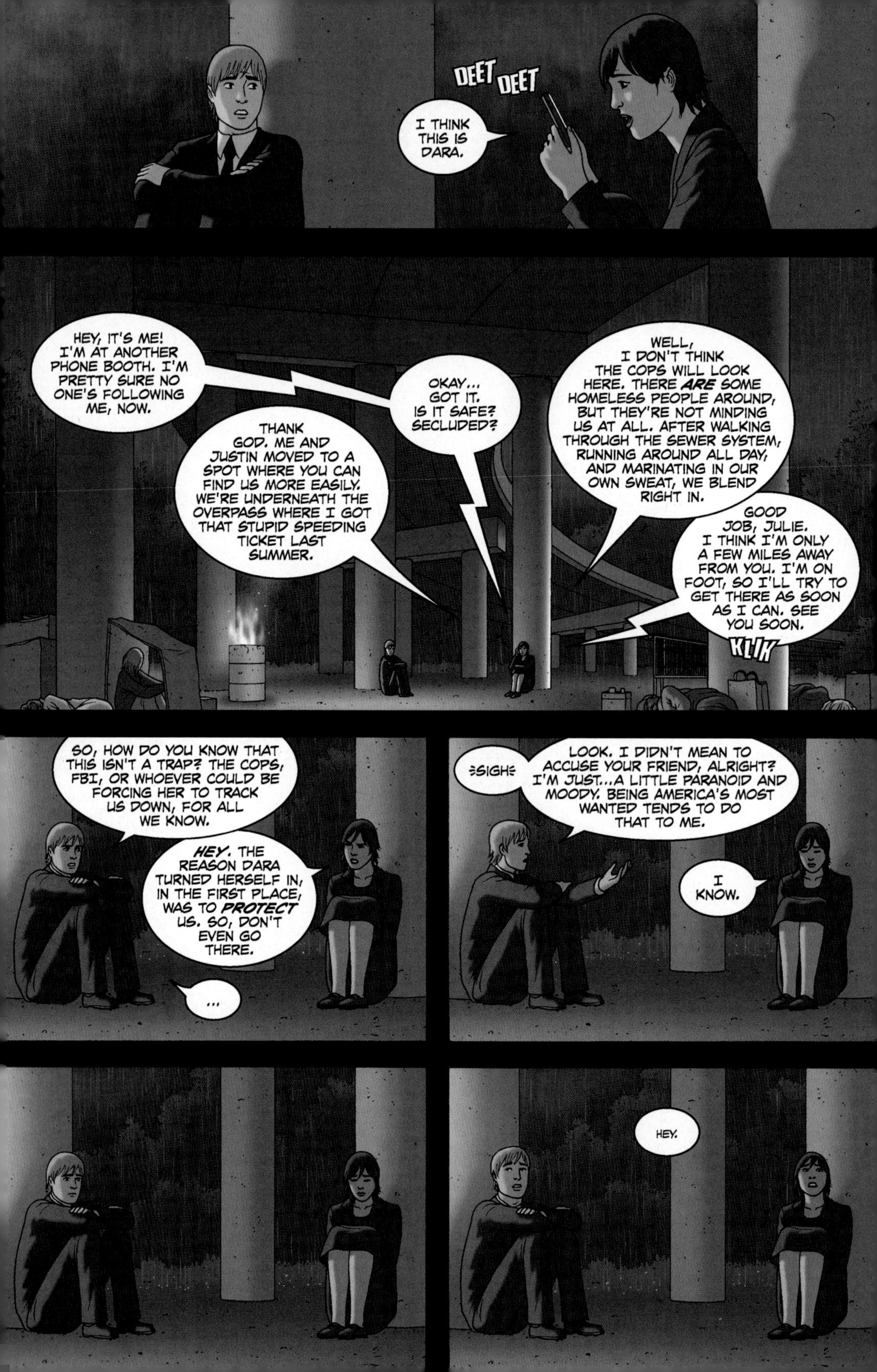
DEET DEET
I THINK THIS IS DARA.
HEY, IT'S ME! I'M AT ANOTHER PHONE BOOTH. I'M PRETTY SURE NO ONE'S FOLLOWING ME, NOW.
THANK GOD. ME AND JUSTIN MOVED TO A SPOT WHERE YOU CAN FIND US MORE EASILY. WE'RE UNDERNEATH THE OVERPASS WHERE I GOT THAT STUPID SPEEDING TICKET LAST SUMMER.
OKAY... GOT IT. IS IT SAFE? SECLUDED?
WELL, I DON'T THINK THE COPS WILL LOOK HERE. THERE *ARE* SOME HOMELESS PEOPLE AROUND, BUT THEY'RE NOT MINDING US AT ALL. AFTER WALKING THROUGH THE SEWER SYSTEM, RUNNING AROUND ALL DAY, AND MARINATING IN OUR OWN SWEAT, WE BLEND RIGHT IN.
GOOD JOB, JULIE. I THINK I'M ONLY A FEW MILES AWAY FROM YOU. I'M ON FOOT, SO I'LL TRY TO GET THERE AS SOON AS I CAN. SEE YOU SOON.
KLIK
SO, HOW DO YOU KNOW THAT THIS ISN'T A TRAP? THE COPS, FBI, OR WHOEVER COULD BE FORCING HER TO TRACK US DOWN, FOR ALL WE KNOW.
HEY. THE REASON DARA TURNED HERSELF IN, IN THE FIRST PLACE, WAS TO *PROTECT* US. SO, DON'T EVEN GO THERE.
...
SIGH
LOOK. I DIDN'T MEAN TO ACCUSE YOUR FRIEND, ALRIGHT? I'M JUST...A LITTLE PARANOID AND MOODY. BEING AMERICA'S MOST WANTED TENDS TO DO THAT TO ME.
I KNOW.
HEY.

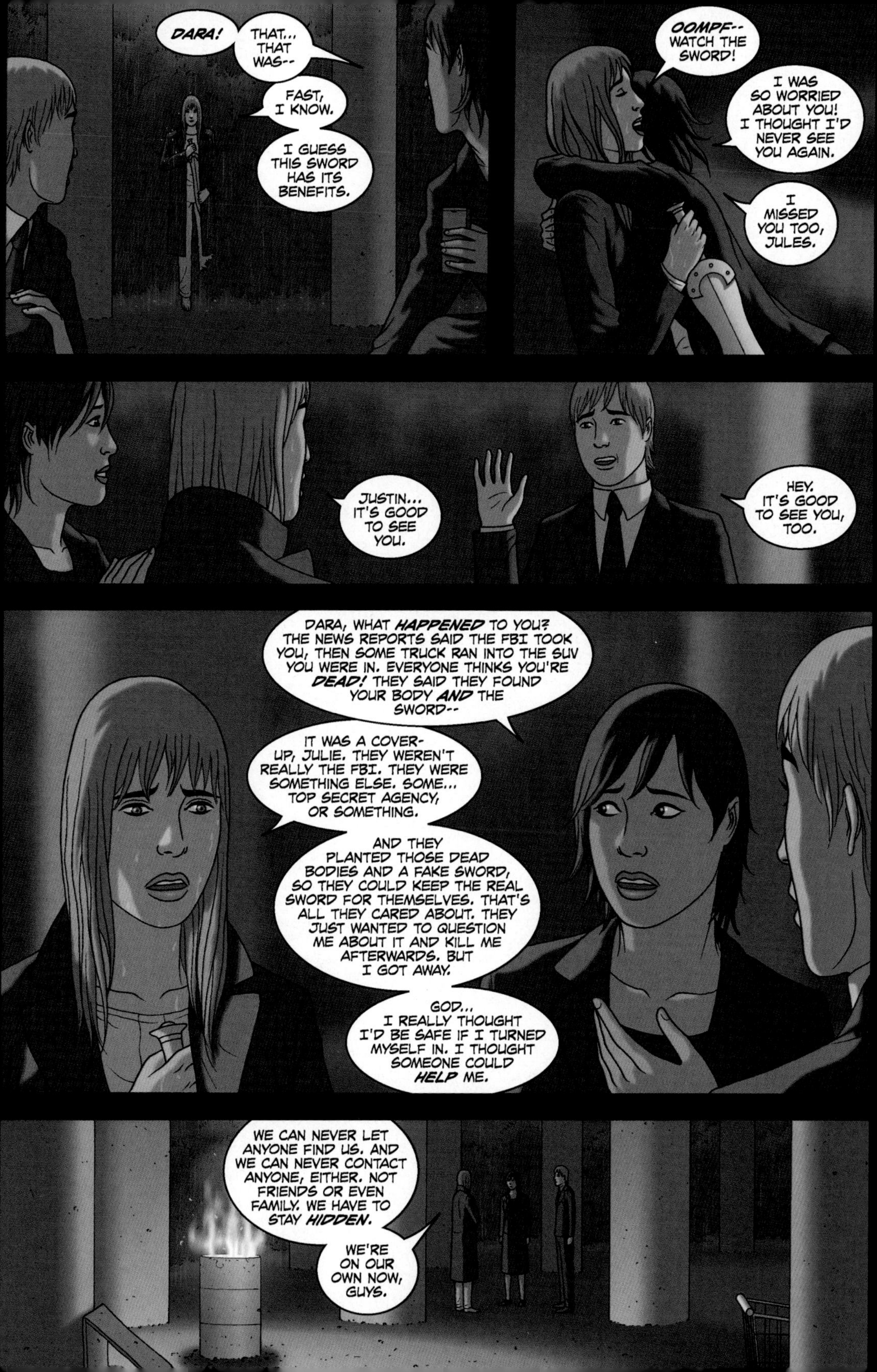
DARA!
THAT... THAT WAS--
FAST, I KNOW.
I GUESS THIS SWORD HAS ITS BENEFITS.
OOMPF-- WATCH THE SWORD!
I WAS SO WORRIED ABOUT YOU! I THOUGHT I'D NEVER SEE YOU AGAIN.
I MISSED YOU TOO, JULES.
JUSTIN... IT'S GOOD TO SEE YOU.
HEY. IT'S GOOD TO SEE YOU, TOO.
DARA, WHAT HAPPENED TO YOU? THE NEWS REPORTS SAID THE FBI TOOK YOU, THEN SOME TRUCK RAN INTO THE SUV YOU WERE IN. EVERYONE THINKS YOU'RE DEAD! THEY SAID THEY FOUND YOUR BODY AND THE SWORD--
IT WAS A COVER-UP, JULIE. THEY WEREN'T REALLY THE FBI. THEY WERE SOMETHING ELSE. SOME... TOP SECRET AGENCY, OR SOMETHING.
AND THEY PLANTED THOSE DEAD BODIES AND A FAKE SWORD, SO THEY COULD KEEP THE REAL SWORD FOR THEMSELVES. THAT'S ALL THEY CARED ABOUT. THEY JUST WANTED TO QUESTION ME ABOUT IT AND KILL ME AFTERWARDS. BUT I GOT AWAY.
GOD... I REALLY THOUGHT I'D BE SAFE IF I TURNED MYSELF IN. I THOUGHT SOMEONE COULD HELP ME.
WE CAN NEVER LET ANYONE FIND US. AND WE CAN NEVER CONTACT ANYONE, EITHER. NOT FRIENDS OR EVEN FAMILY. WE HAVE TO STAY HIDDEN.
WE'RE ON OUR OWN NOW, GUYS.

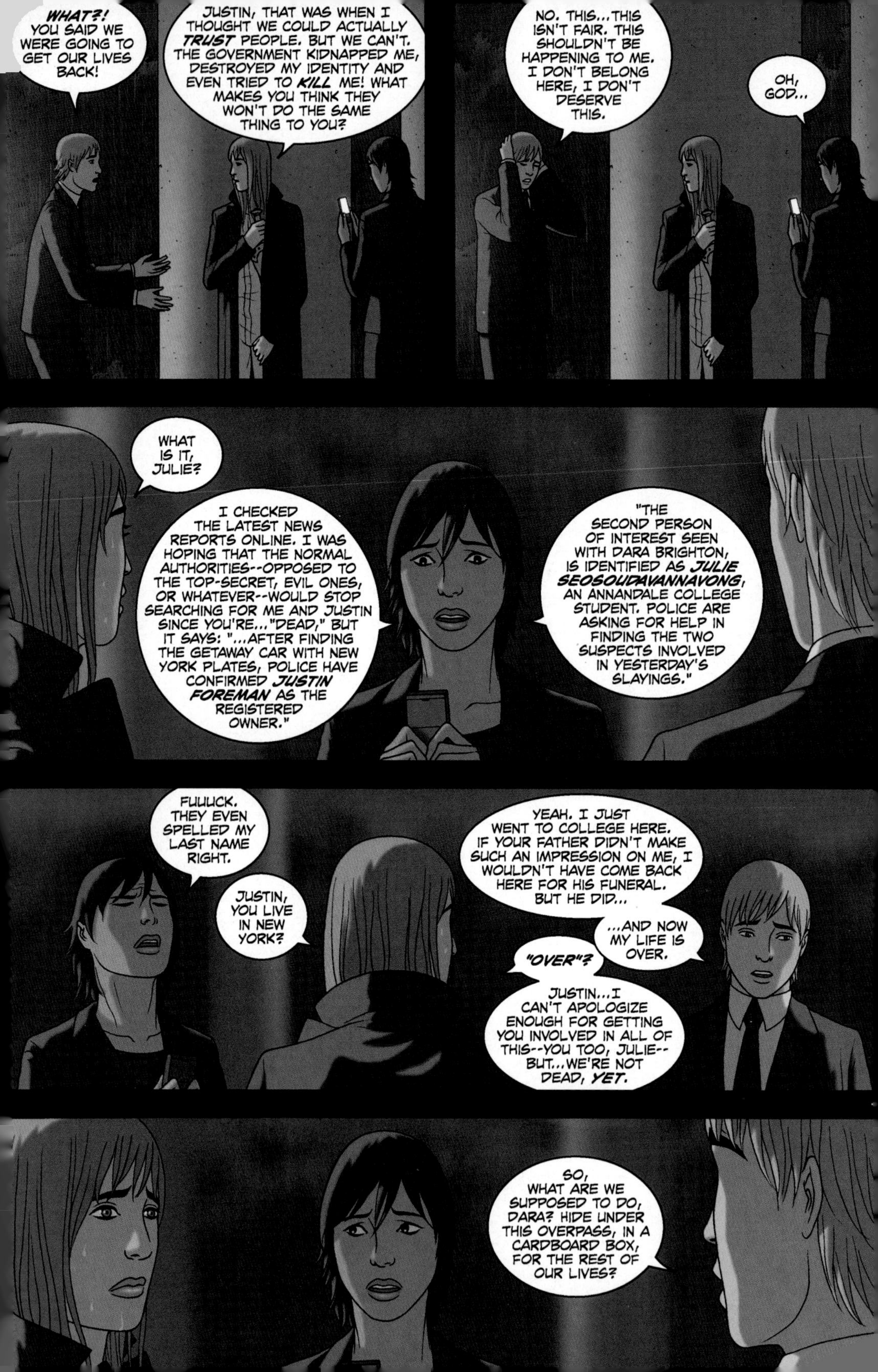
WHAT?! YOU SAID WE WERE GOING TO GET OUR LIVES BACK!
JUSTIN, THAT WAS WHEN I THOUGHT WE COULD ACTUALLY TRUST PEOPLE. BUT WE CAN'T. THE GOVERNMENT KIDNAPPED ME, DESTROYED MY IDENTITY AND EVEN TRIED TO KILL ME! WHAT MAKES YOU THINK THEY WON'T DO THE SAME THING TO YOU?
NO. THIS...THIS ISN'T FAIR. THIS SHOULDN'T BE HAPPENING TO ME. I DON'T BELONG HERE, I DON'T DESERVE THIS.
OH, GOD...
WHAT IS IT, JULIE?
I CHECKED THE LATEST NEWS REPORTS ONLINE. I WAS HOPING THAT THE NORMAL AUTHORITIES--OPPOSED TO THE TOP-SECRET, EVIL ONES, OR WHATEVER--WOULD STOP SEARCHING FOR ME AND JUSTIN SINCE YOU'RE..."DEAD," BUT IT SAYS: "...AFTER FINDING THE GETAWAY CAR WITH NEW YORK PLATES, POLICE HAVE CONFIRMED JUSTIN FOREMAN AS THE REGISTERED OWNER."
"THE SECOND PERSON OF INTEREST SEEN WITH DARA BRIGHTON, IS IDENTIFIED AS JULIE SEOSOUDAVANNAVONG, AN ANNANDALE COLLEGE STUDENT. POLICE ARE ASKING FOR HELP IN FINDING THE TWO SUSPECTS INVOLVED IN YESTERDAY'S SLAYINGS."
FUUUCK. THEY EVEN SPELLED MY LAST NAME RIGHT.
JUSTIN, YOU LIVE IN NEW YORK?
YEAH. I JUST WENT TO COLLEGE HERE. IF YOUR FATHER DIDN'T MAKE SUCH AN IMPRESSION ON ME, I WOULDN'T HAVE COME BACK HERE FOR HIS FUNERAL. BUT HE DID...
...AND NOW MY LIFE IS OVER.
"OVER"?
JUSTIN...I CAN'T APOLOGIZE ENOUGH FOR GETTING YOU INVOLVED IN ALL OF THIS--YOU TOO, JULIE--BUT...WE'RE NOT DEAD, YET.
SO, WHAT ARE WE SUPPOSED TO DO, DARA? HIDE UNDER THIS OVERPASS, IN A CARDBOARD BOX, FOR THE REST OF OUR LIVES?

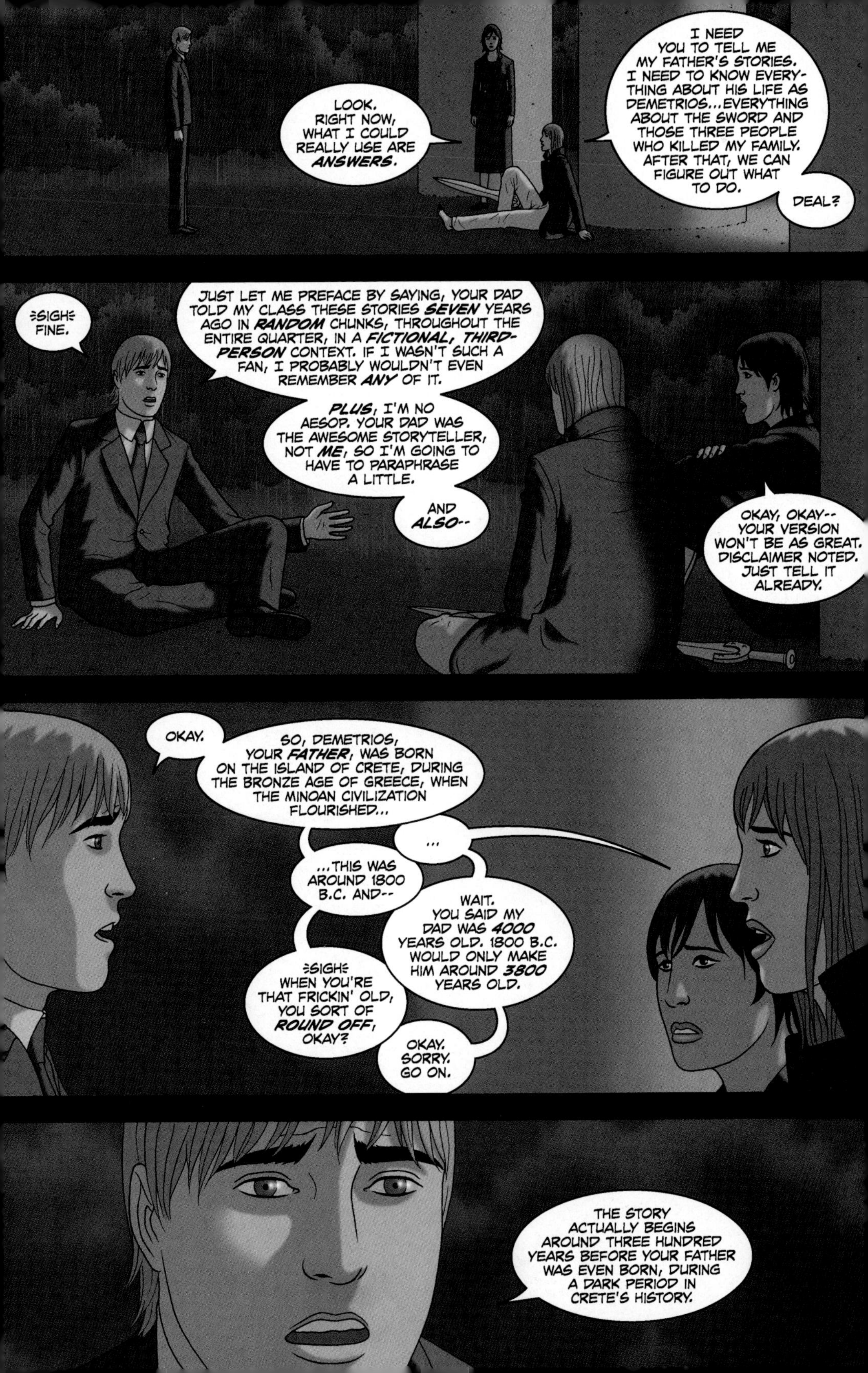
LOOK. RIGHT NOW, WHAT I COULD REALLY USE ARE ANSWERS.
I NEED YOU TO TELL ME MY FATHER'S STORIES. I NEED TO KNOW EVERY-THING ABOUT HIS LIFE AS DEMETRIOS...EVERYTHING ABOUT THE SWORD AND THOSE THREE PEOPLE WHO KILLED MY FAMILY. AFTER THAT, WE CAN FIGURE OUT WHAT TO DO.
DEAL?
=SIGH= FINE.
JUST LET ME PREFACE BY SAYING, YOUR DAD TOLD MY CLASS THESE STORIES SEVEN YEARS AGO IN RANDOM CHUNKS, THROUGHOUT THE ENTIRE QUARTER, IN A FICTIONAL, THIRD-PERSON CONTEXT. IF I WASN'T SUCH A FAN, I PROBABLY WOULDN'T EVEN REMEMBER ANY OF IT.
PLUS, I'M NO AESOP. YOUR DAD WAS THE AWESOME STORYTELLER, NOT ME, SO I'M GOING TO HAVE TO PARAPHRASE A LITTLE.
AND ALSO--
OKAY, OKAY-- YOUR VERSION WON'T BE AS GREAT. DISCLAIMER NOTED. JUST TELL IT ALREADY.
OKAY.
SO, DEMETRIOS, YOUR FATHER, WAS BORN ON THE ISLAND OF CRETE, DURING THE BRONZE AGE OF GREECE, WHEN THE MINOAN CIVILIZATION FLOURISHED...
...
...THIS WAS AROUND 1800 B.C. AND--
WAIT. YOU SAID MY DAD WAS 4000 YEARS OLD. 1800 B.C. WOULD ONLY MAKE HIM AROUND 3800 YEARS OLD.
=SIGH= WHEN YOU'RE THAT FRICKIN' OLD, YOU SORT OF ROUND OFF, OKAY?
OKAY. SORRY. GO ON.
THE STORY ACTUALLY BEGINS AROUND THREE HUNDRED YEARS BEFORE YOUR FATHER WAS EVEN BORN, DURING A DARK PERIOD IN CRETE'S HISTORY.

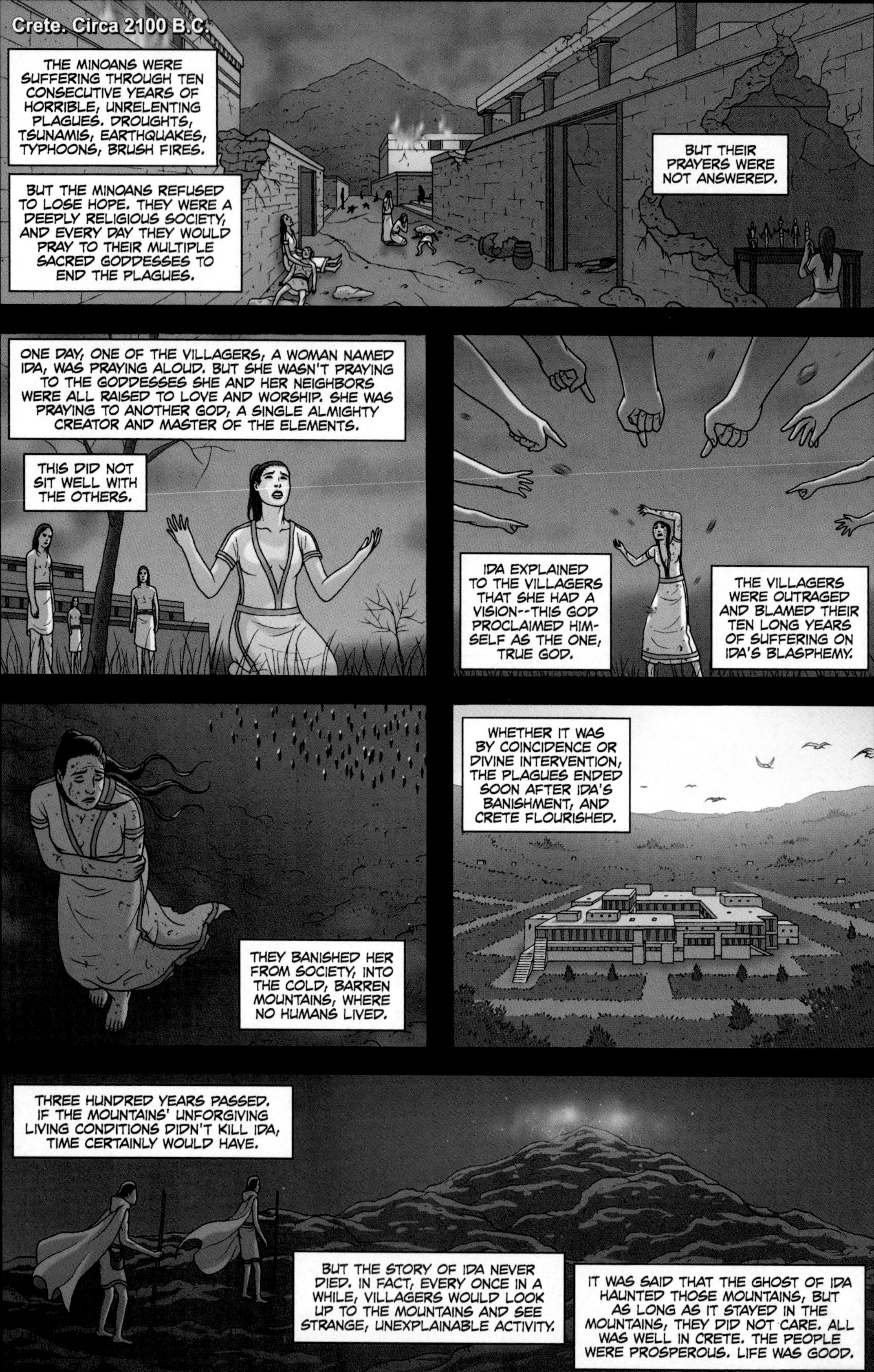

Crete. Circa 2100 B.C.
THE MINOANS WERE SUFFERING THROUGH TEN CONSECUTIVE YEARS OF HORRIBLE, UNRELENTING PLAGUES. DROUGHTS, TSUNAMIS, EARTHQUAKES, TYPHOONS, BRUSH FIRES.
BUT THE MINOANS REFUSED TO LOSE HOPE. THEY WERE A DEEPLY RELIGIOUS SOCIETY, AND EVERY DAY THEY WOULD PRAY TO THEIR MULTIPLE SACRED GODDESSES TO END THE PLAGUES.
BUT THEIR PRAYERS WERE NOT ANSWERED.
ONE DAY, ONE OF THE VILLAGERS, A WOMAN NAMED IDA, WAS PRAYING ALOUD. BUT SHE WASN'T PRAYING TO THE GODDESSES SHE AND HER NEIGHBORS WERE ALL RAISED TO LOVE AND WORSHIP. SHE WAS PRAYING TO ANOTHER GOD, A SINGLE ALMIGHTY CREATOR AND MASTER OF THE ELEMENTS.
THIS DID NOT SIT WELL WITH THE OTHERS.
IDA EXPLAINED TO THE VILLAGERS THAT SHE HAD A VISION--THIS GOD PROCLAIMED HIMSELF AS THE ONE, TRUE GOD.
THE VILLAGERS WERE OUTRAGED AND BLAMED THEIR TEN LONG YEARS OF SUFFERING ON IDA'S BLASPHEMY.
THEY BANISHED HER FROM SOCIETY, INTO THE COLD, BARREN MOUNTAINS, WHERE NO HUMANS LIVED.
WHETHER IT WAS BY COINCIDENCE OR DIVINE INTERVENTION, THE PLAGUES ENDED SOON AFTER IDA'S BANISHMENT, AND CRETE FLOURISHED.
THREE HUNDRED YEARS PASSED. IF THE MOUNTAINS' UNFORGIVING LIVING CONDITIONS DIDN'T KILL IDA, TIME CERTAINLY WOULD HAVE.
BUT THE STORY OF IDA NEVER DIED. IN FACT, EVERY ONCE IN A WHILE, VILLAGERS WOULD LOOK UP TO THE MOUNTAINS AND SEE STRANGE, UNEXPLAINABLE ACTIVITY.
IT WAS SAID THAT THE GHOST OF IDA HAUNTED THOSE MOUNTAINS, BUT AS LONG AS IT STAYED IN THE MOUNTAINS, THEY DID NOT CARE. ALL WAS WELL IN CRETE. THE PEOPLE WERE PROSPEROUS. LIFE WAS GOOD.

HNN?

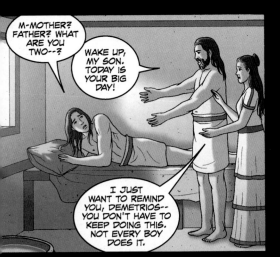

M-MOTHER? FATHER? WHAT ARE YOU TWO--?

WAKE UP, MY SON. TODAY IS YOUR BIG DAY!

I JUST WANT TO REMIND YOU, DEMETRIOS-- YOU DON'T HAVE TO KEEP DOING THIS. NOT EVERY BOY DOES IT.

AND NOT EVERY BOY BECOMES A *MAN*, MY LOVE. BUT OUR SON IS DESTINED FOR GREATNESS.

THE GODDESSES WILL WATCH OVER HIM. HE WILL BE FINE.

BUT DON'T THINK YOU CAN IGNORE YOUR LESSONS. YOU CAN BE A MAN, BUT I WILL *NOT* LET MY SON BE A *BRAINLESS* MAN.

AND YOUR LITTLE BROTHER LOOKS UP TO YOU, DEMETRIOS. YOU NEED TO SET AN EXAMPLE.

YES, MOTHER.

SPEAKING OF THE LITTLE BUGGER...

TODAY'S THE DAY, DUDE!

"DUDE"?

HEY, I TOLD YOU THIS STORY WOULDN'T BE COMPLETELY ACCURATE. AND IT'S NOT LIKE THESE PEOPLE EVEN USED *ENGLISH*, TO BEGIN WITH, ALRIGHT?

IN FACT, NO ONE EVEN KNOWS HOW THE MINOANS SPOKE. THE ONLY RECORDS OF THEIR LANGUAGE, FOR THIS PARTICULAR TIME PERIOD, COMES FROM ANCIENT TABLETS WHICH, TO THIS DAY, HASN'T EVEN BEEN *DECIPHERED*. SO, BASICALLY, I'M ALL YOU GOT.

SORRY. I'LL SHUT UP.

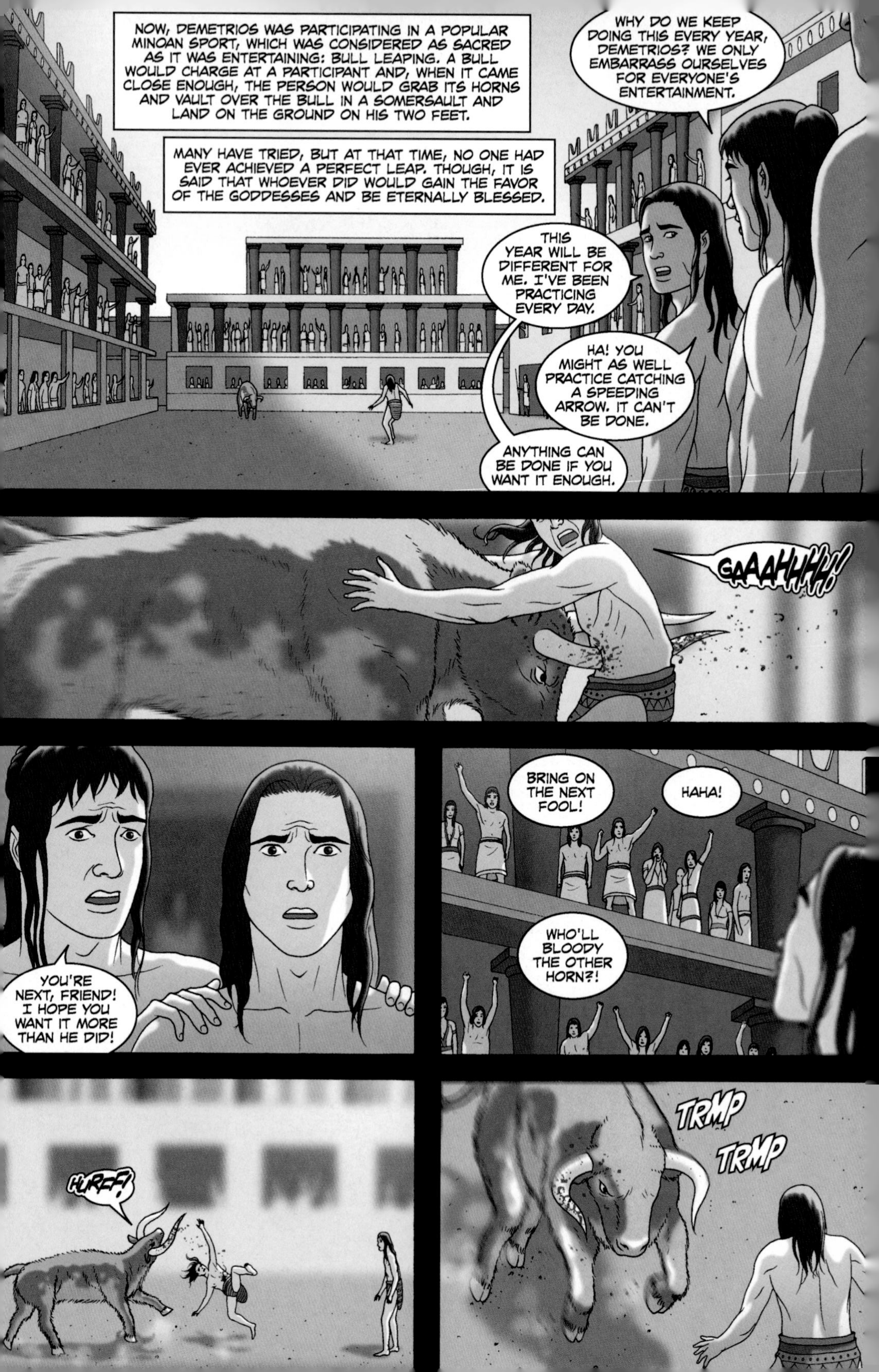
NOW, DEMETRIOS WAS PARTICIPATING IN A POPULAR MINOAN SPORT, WHICH WAS CONSIDERED AS SACRED AS IT WAS ENTERTAINING: BULL LEAPING. A BULL WOULD CHARGE AT A PARTICIPANT AND, WHEN IT CAME CLOSE ENOUGH, THE PERSON WOULD GRAB ITS HORNS AND VAULT OVER THE BULL IN A SOMERSAULT AND LAND ON THE GROUND ON HIS TWO FEET.
MANY HAVE TRIED, BUT AT THAT TIME, NO ONE HAD EVER ACHIEVED A PERFECT LEAP. THOUGH, IT IS SAID THAT WHOEVER DID WOULD GAIN THE FAVOR OF THE GODDESSES AND BE ETERNALLY BLESSED.
WHY DO WE KEEP DOING THIS EVERY YEAR, DEMETRIOS? WE ONLY EMBARRASS OURSELVES FOR EVERYONE'S ENTERTAINMENT.
THIS YEAR WILL BE DIFFERENT FOR ME. I'VE BEEN PRACTICING EVERY DAY.
HA! YOU MIGHT AS WELL PRACTICE CATCHING A SPEEDING ARROW. IT CAN'T BE DONE.
ANYTHING CAN BE DONE IF YOU WANT IT ENOUGH.
GAAAHHHH!
YOU'RE NEXT, FRIEND! I HOPE YOU WANT IT MORE THAN HE DID!
BRING ON THE NEXT FOOL!
HAHA!
WHO'LL BLOODY THE OTHER HORN?!
HURFF!
TRMP
TRMP

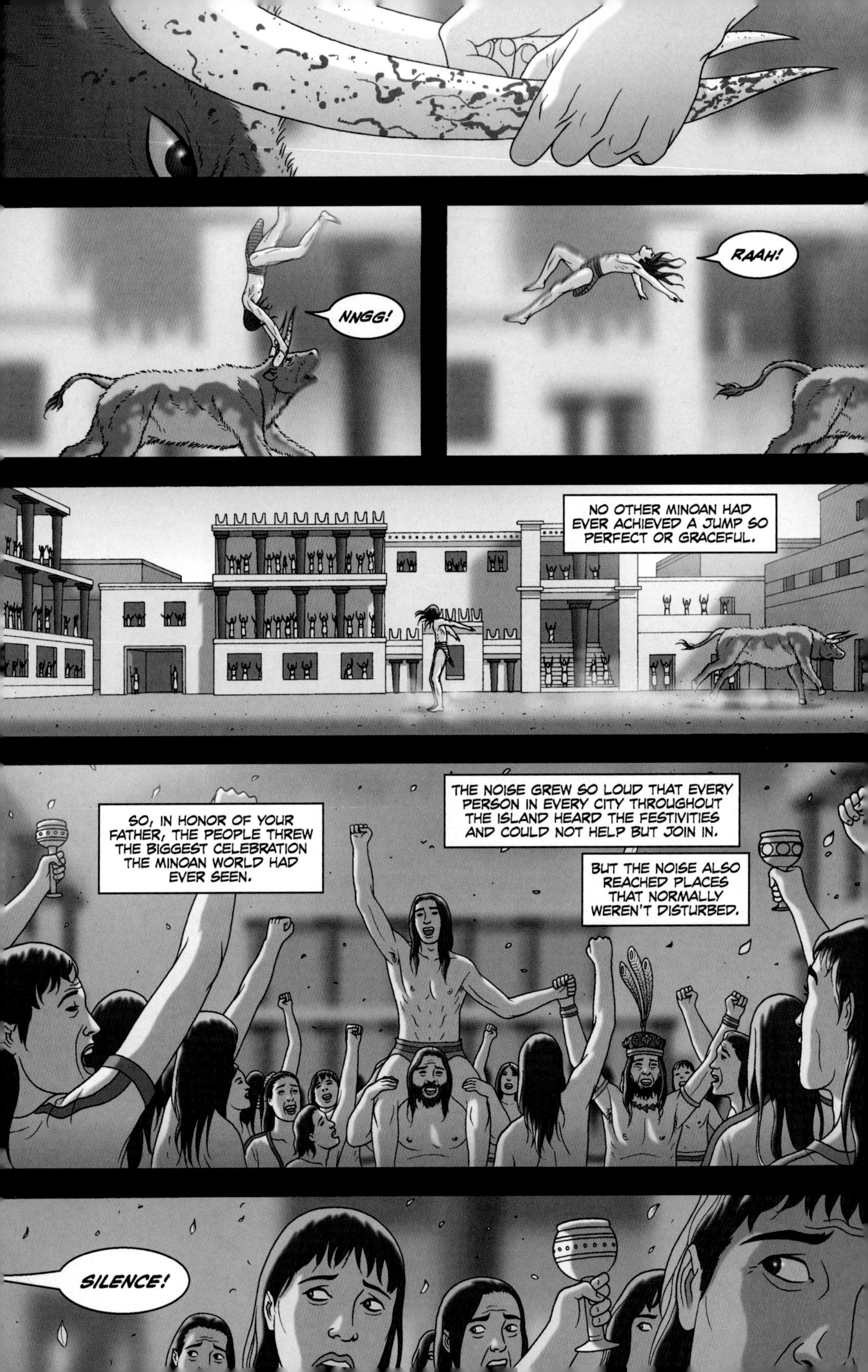
NNGG!
RAAH!
NO OTHER MINOAN HAD EVER ACHIEVED A JUMP SO PERFECT OR GRACEFUL.
SO, IN HONOR OF YOUR FATHER, THE PEOPLE THREW THE BIGGEST CELEBRATION THE MINOAN WORLD HAD EVER SEEN.
THE NOISE GREW SO LOUD THAT EVERY PERSON IN EVERY CITY THROUGHOUT THE ISLAND HEARD THE FESTIVITIES AND COULD NOT HELP BUT JOIN IN.
BUT THE NOISE ALSO REACHED PLACES THAT NORMALLY WEREN'T DISTURBED.
SILENCE!

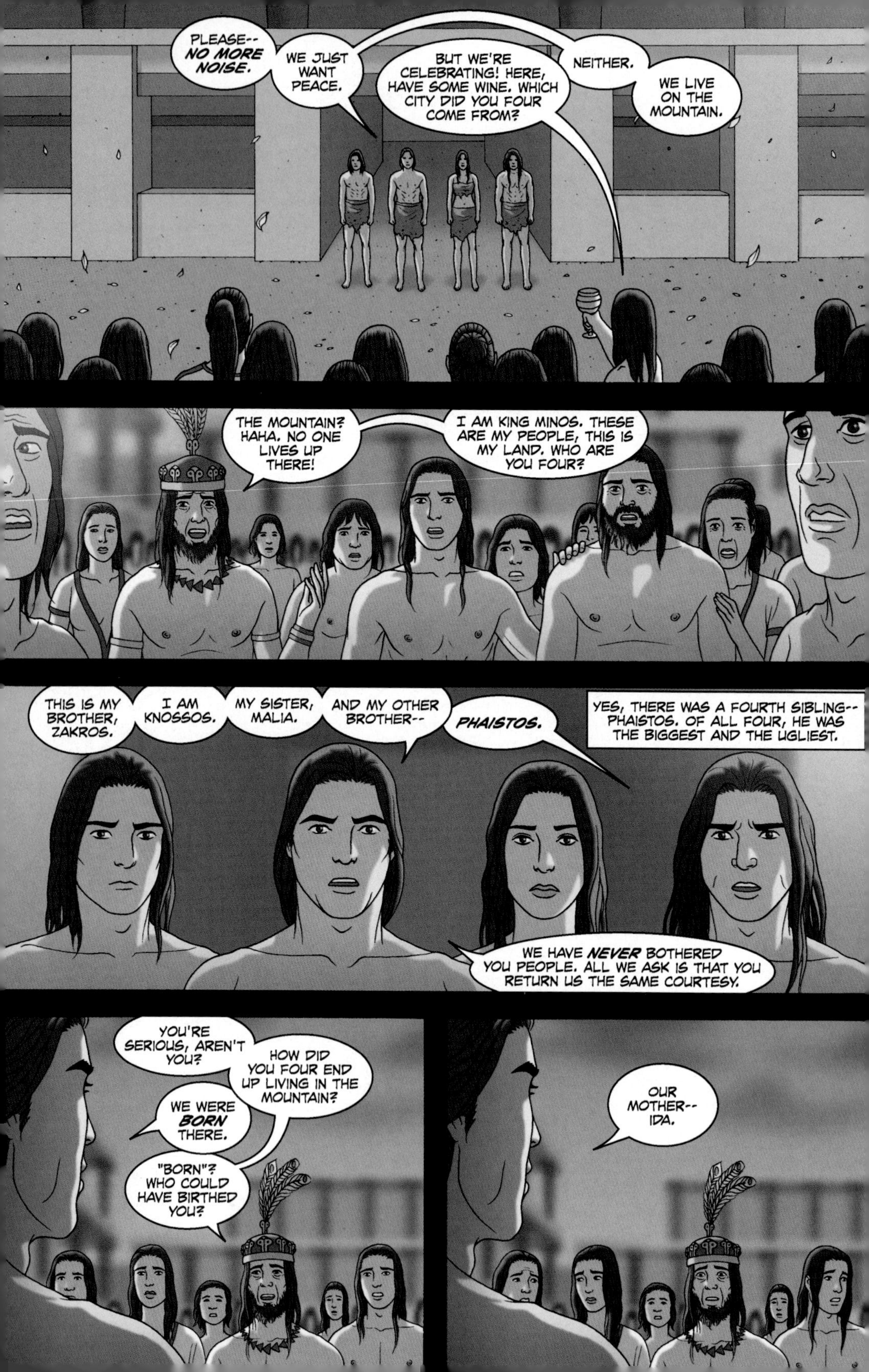
PLEASE-- NO MORE NOISE.
WE JUST WANT PEACE.
BUT WE'RE CELEBRATING! HERE, HAVE SOME WINE. WHICH CITY DID YOU FOUR COME FROM?
NEITHER.
WE LIVE ON THE MOUNTAIN.
THE MOUNTAIN? HAHA. NO ONE LIVES UP THERE!
I AM KING MINOS. THESE ARE MY PEOPLE, THIS IS MY LAND. WHO ARE YOU FOUR?
THIS IS MY BROTHER, ZAKROS.
I AM KNOSSOS.
MY SISTER, MALIA.
AND MY OTHER BROTHER--
PHAISTOS.
YES, THERE WAS A FOURTH SIBLING-- PHAISTOS. OF ALL FOUR, HE WAS THE BIGGEST AND THE UGLIEST.
WE HAVE NEVER BOTHERED YOU PEOPLE. ALL WE ASK IS THAT YOU RETURN US THE SAME COURTESY.
YOU'RE SERIOUS, AREN'T YOU?
HOW DID YOU FOUR END UP LIVING IN THE MOUNTAIN?
WE WERE BORN THERE.
"BORN"? WHO COULD HAVE BIRTHED YOU?
OUR MOTHER-- IDA.

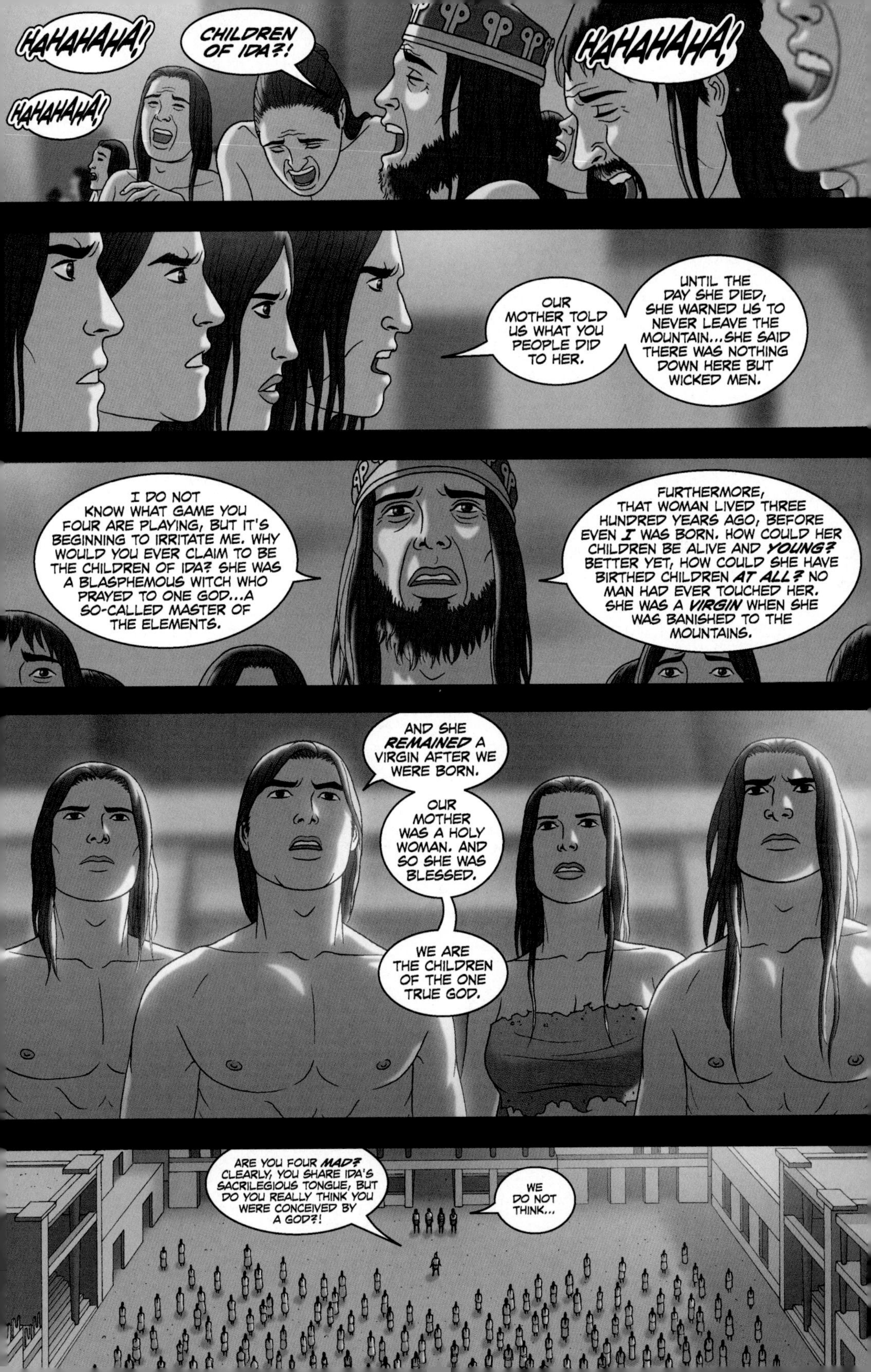
HAHAHAHA!
CHILDREN OF IDA?!
HAHAHAHA!
HAHAHAHA!
OUR MOTHER TOLD US WHAT YOU PEOPLE DID TO HER.
UNTIL THE DAY SHE DIED, SHE WARNED US TO NEVER LEAVE THE MOUNTAIN...SHE SAID THERE WAS NOTHING DOWN HERE BUT WICKED MEN.
I DO NOT KNOW WHAT GAME YOU FOUR ARE PLAYING, BUT IT'S BEGINNING TO IRRITATE ME. WHY WOULD YOU EVER CLAIM TO BE THE CHILDREN OF IDA? SHE WAS A BLASPHEMOUS WITCH WHO PRAYED TO ONE GOD...A SO-CALLED MASTER OF THE ELEMENTS.
FURTHERMORE, THAT WOMAN LIVED THREE HUNDRED YEARS AGO, BEFORE EVEN *I* WAS BORN. HOW COULD HER CHILDREN BE ALIVE AND ***YOUNG?*** BETTER YET, HOW COULD SHE HAVE BIRTHED CHILDREN ***AT ALL?*** NO MAN HAD EVER TOUCHED HER. SHE WAS A ***VIRGIN*** WHEN SHE WAS BANISHED TO THE MOUNTAINS.
AND SHE ***REMAINED*** A VIRGIN AFTER WE WERE BORN.
OUR MOTHER WAS A HOLY WOMAN. AND SO SHE WAS BLESSED.
WE ARE THE CHILDREN OF THE ONE TRUE GOD.
ARE YOU FOUR ***MAD?*** CLEARLY, YOU SHARE IDA'S SACRILEGIOUS TONGUE, BUT DO YOU REALLY THINK YOU WERE CONCEIVED BY A GOD?!
WE DO NOT THINK...

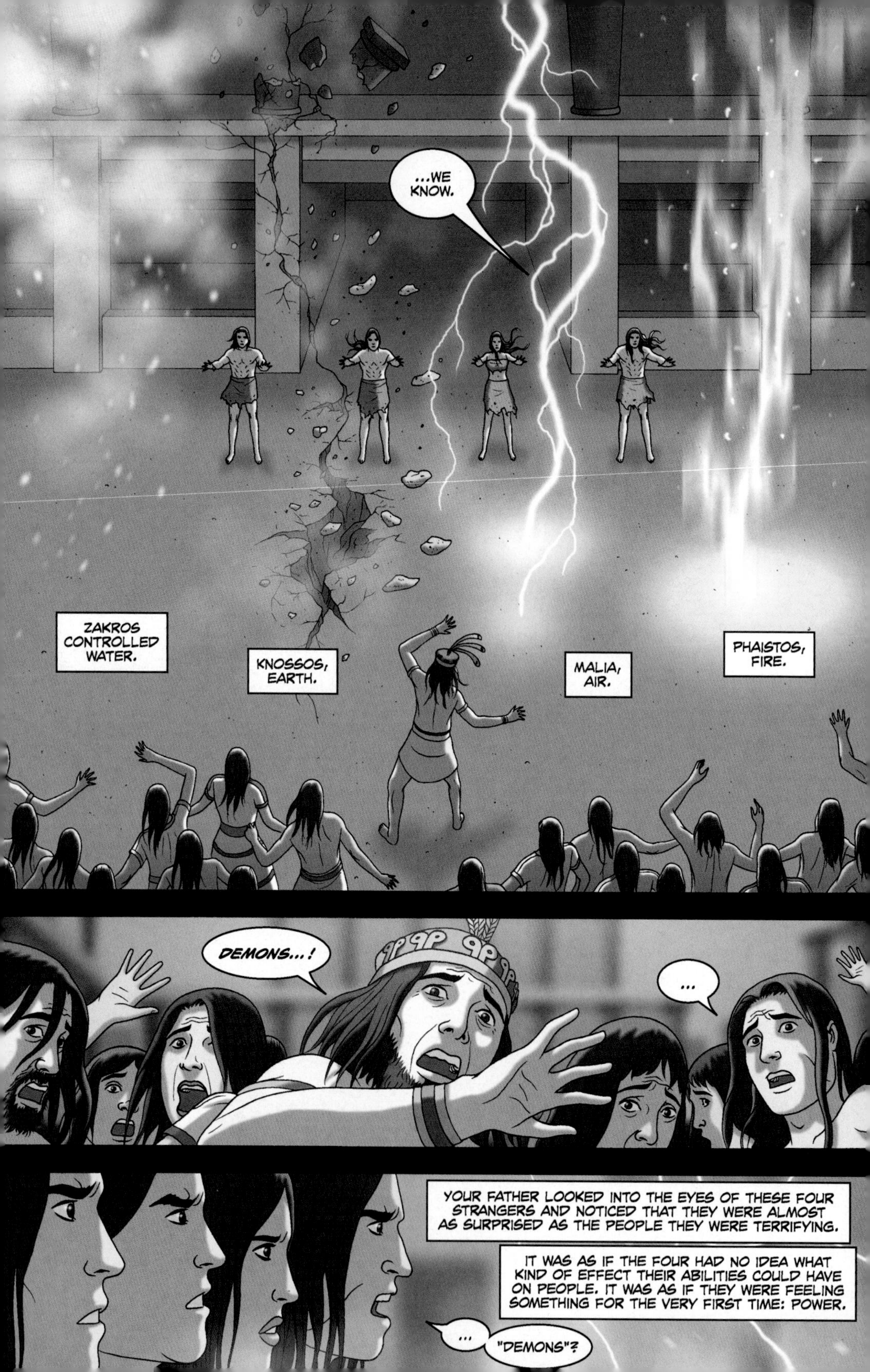
...WE KNOW.
ZAKROS CONTROLLED WATER.
KNOSSOS, EARTH.
MALIA, AIR.
PHAISTOS, FIRE.
DEMONS...!
...
YOUR FATHER LOOKED INTO THE EYES OF THESE FOUR STRANGERS AND NOTICED THAT THEY WERE ALMOST AS SURPRISED AS THE PEOPLE THEY WERE TERRIFYING.
IT WAS AS IF THE FOUR HAD NO IDEA WHAT KIND OF EFFECT THEIR ABILITIES COULD HAVE ON PEOPLE. IT WAS AS IF THEY WERE FEELING SOMETHING FOR THE VERY FIRST TIME: POWER.
...
"DEMONS"?

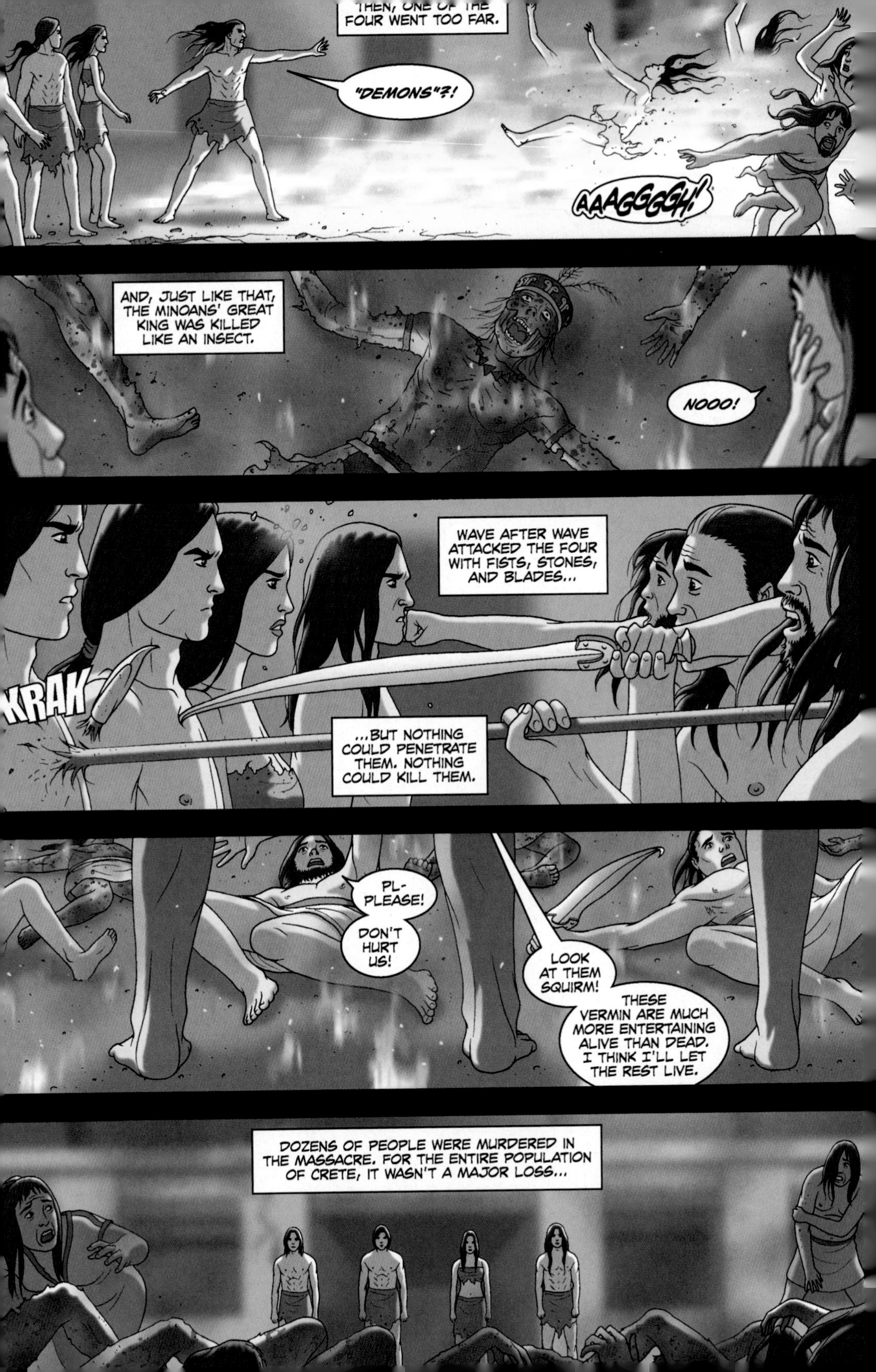
THEN, ONE OF THE FOUR WENT TOO FAR.
"DEMONS"?!
AAAGGGGH!
AND, JUST LIKE THAT, THE MINOANS' GREAT KING WAS KILLED LIKE AN INSECT.
NOOO!
WAVE AFTER WAVE ATTACKED THE FOUR WITH FISTS, STONES, AND BLADES...
KRAK
...BUT NOTHING COULD PENETRATE THEM. NOTHING COULD KILL THEM.
PL- PLEASE!
DON'T HURT US!
LOOK AT THEM SQUIRM!
THESE VERMIN ARE MUCH MORE ENTERTAINING ALIVE THAN DEAD. I THINK I'LL LET THE REST LIVE.
DOZENS OF PEOPLE WERE MURDERED IN THE MASSACRE. FOR THE ENTIRE POPULATION OF CRETE, IT WASN'T A MAJOR LOSS...

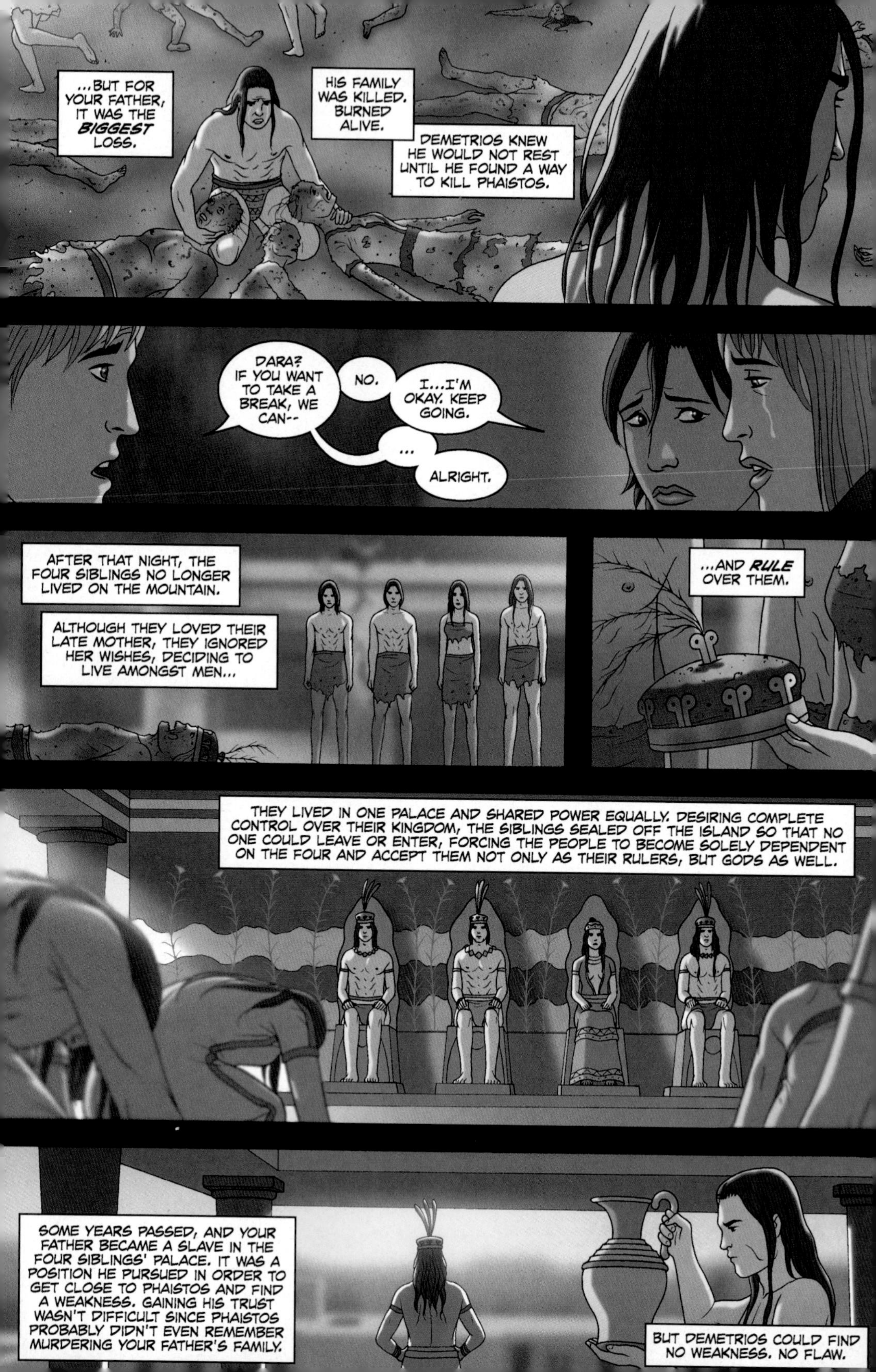
...BUT FOR YOUR FATHER, IT WAS THE *BIGGEST* LOSS.
HIS FAMILY WAS KILLED. BURNED ALIVE.
DEMETRIOS KNEW HE WOULD NOT REST UNTIL HE FOUND A WAY TO KILL PHAISTOS.
DARA? IF YOU WANT TO TAKE A BREAK, WE CAN--
NO.
I...I'M OKAY. KEEP GOING.
...
ALRIGHT.
AFTER THAT NIGHT, THE FOUR SIBLINGS NO LONGER LIVED ON THE MOUNTAIN.
ALTHOUGH THEY LOVED THEIR LATE MOTHER, THEY IGNORED HER WISHES, DECIDING TO LIVE AMONGST MEN...
...AND *RULE* OVER THEM.
THEY LIVED IN ONE PALACE AND SHARED POWER EQUALLY. DESIRING COMPLETE CONTROL OVER THEIR KINGDOM, THE SIBLINGS SEALED OFF THE ISLAND SO THAT NO ONE COULD LEAVE OR ENTER, FORCING THE PEOPLE TO BECOME SOLELY DEPENDENT ON THE FOUR AND ACCEPT THEM NOT ONLY AS THEIR RULERS, BUT GODS AS WELL.
SOME YEARS PASSED, AND YOUR FATHER BECAME A SLAVE IN THE FOUR SIBLINGS' PALACE. IT WAS A POSITION HE PURSUED IN ORDER TO GET CLOSE TO PHAISTOS AND FIND A WEAKNESS. GAINING HIS TRUST WASN'T DIFFICULT SINCE PHAISTOS PROBABLY DIDN'T EVEN REMEMBER MURDERING YOUR FATHER'S FAMILY.
BUT DEMETRIOS COULD FIND NO WEAKNESS. NO FLAW.

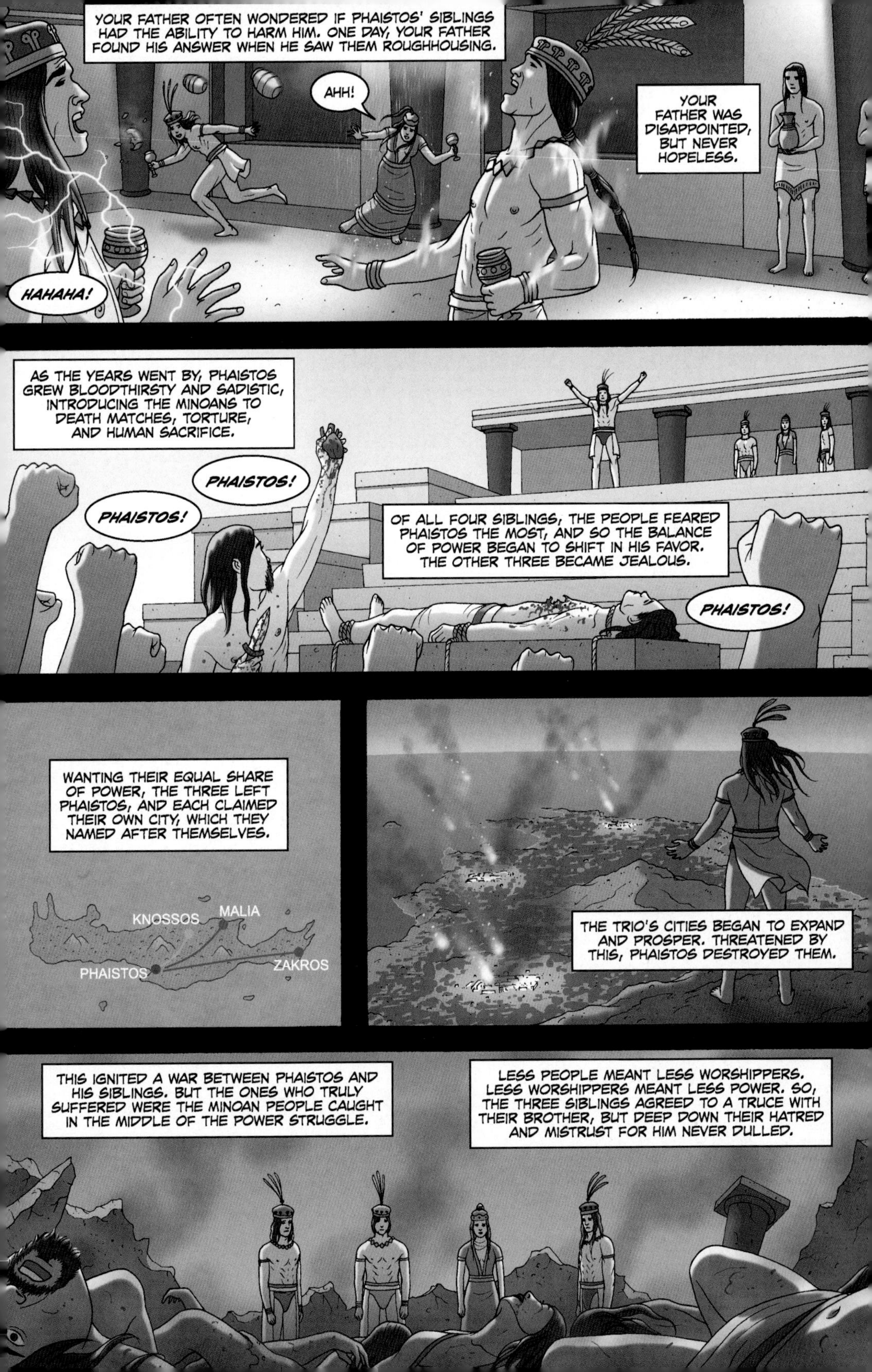

YOUR FATHER OFTEN WONDERED IF PHAISTOS' SIBLINGS HAD THE ABILITY TO HARM HIM. ONE DAY, YOUR FATHER FOUND HIS ANSWER WHEN HE SAW THEM ROUGHHOUSING.
AHH!
YOUR FATHER WAS DISAPPOINTED, BUT NEVER HOPELESS.
HAHAHA!
AS THE YEARS WENT BY, PHAISTOS GREW BLOODTHIRSTY AND SADISTIC, INTRODUCING THE MINOANS TO DEATH MATCHES, TORTURE, AND HUMAN SACRIFICE.
PHAISTOS!
PHAISTOS!
OF ALL FOUR SIBLINGS, THE PEOPLE FEARED PHAISTOS THE MOST, AND SO THE BALANCE OF POWER BEGAN TO SHIFT IN HIS FAVOR. THE OTHER THREE BECAME JEALOUS.
PHAISTOS!
WANTING THEIR EQUAL SHARE OF POWER, THE THREE LEFT PHAISTOS, AND EACH CLAIMED THEIR OWN CITY, WHICH THEY NAMED AFTER THEMSELVES.
KNOSSOS
MALIA
PHAISTOS
ZAKROS
THE TRIO'S CITIES BEGAN TO EXPAND AND PROSPER. THREATENED BY THIS, PHAISTOS DESTROYED THEM.
THIS IGNITED A WAR BETWEEN PHAISTOS AND HIS SIBLINGS. BUT THE ONES WHO TRULY SUFFERED WERE THE MINOAN PEOPLE CAUGHT IN THE MIDDLE OF THE POWER STRUGGLE.
LESS PEOPLE MEANT LESS WORSHIPPERS. LESS WORSHIPPERS MEANT LESS POWER. SO, THE THREE SIBLINGS AGREED TO A TRUCE WITH THEIR BROTHER, BUT DEEP DOWN THEIR HATRED AND MISTRUST FOR HIM NEVER DULLED.

TO SYMBOLIZE THEIR EQUAL SHARE OF POWER, THE FOUR SIBLINGS HAD A MONUMENT ERECTED IN A NEUTRAL AREA. EACH STATUE REPRESENTED THEIR INDIVIDUAL REIGN, SO THE FOUR USED SLAVES FROM THEIR RESPECTIVE CITIES TO BUILD IT.

AN OBJECT WAS TO BE PLACED WHERE THEIR HANDS MET--SOMETHING TO SYMBOLIZE THEIR POWER. THEIR STRENGTH.

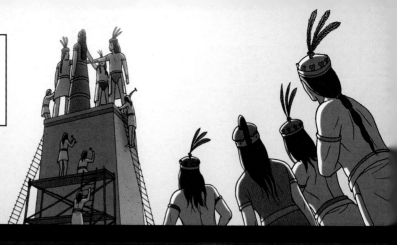

THEY CHOSE A *SWORD*.

SINCE THE SWORD WAS GOING TO REPRESENT THEIR POWER, THEY REFUSED MORTAL ASSISTANCE AND DECIDED TO BUILD IT THEMSELVES ON THE MOUNTAIN WHERE THEY WERE BORN.

FOR THE FIRST TIME, THEY COMBINED THEIR ELEMENTAL ABILITIES.

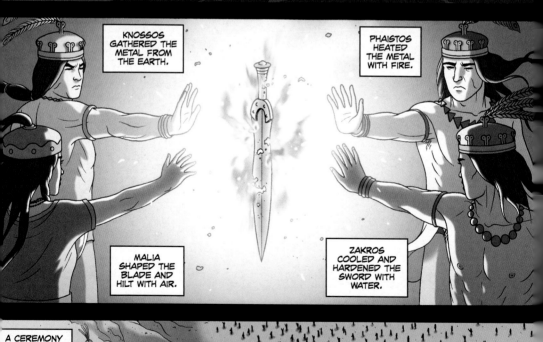

KNOSSOS GATHERED THE METAL FROM THE EARTH.

PHAISTOS HEATED THE METAL WITH FIRE.

MALIA SHAPED THE BLADE AND HILT WITH AIR.

ZAKROS COOLED AND HARDENED THE SWORD WITH WATER.

A CEREMONY WAS HELD THE DAY THE SWORD WAS UNVEILED.

THE PEOPLE OF CRETE GATHERED TO WATCH THE FOUR SIBLINGS PLACE IT ON THE MONUMENT.

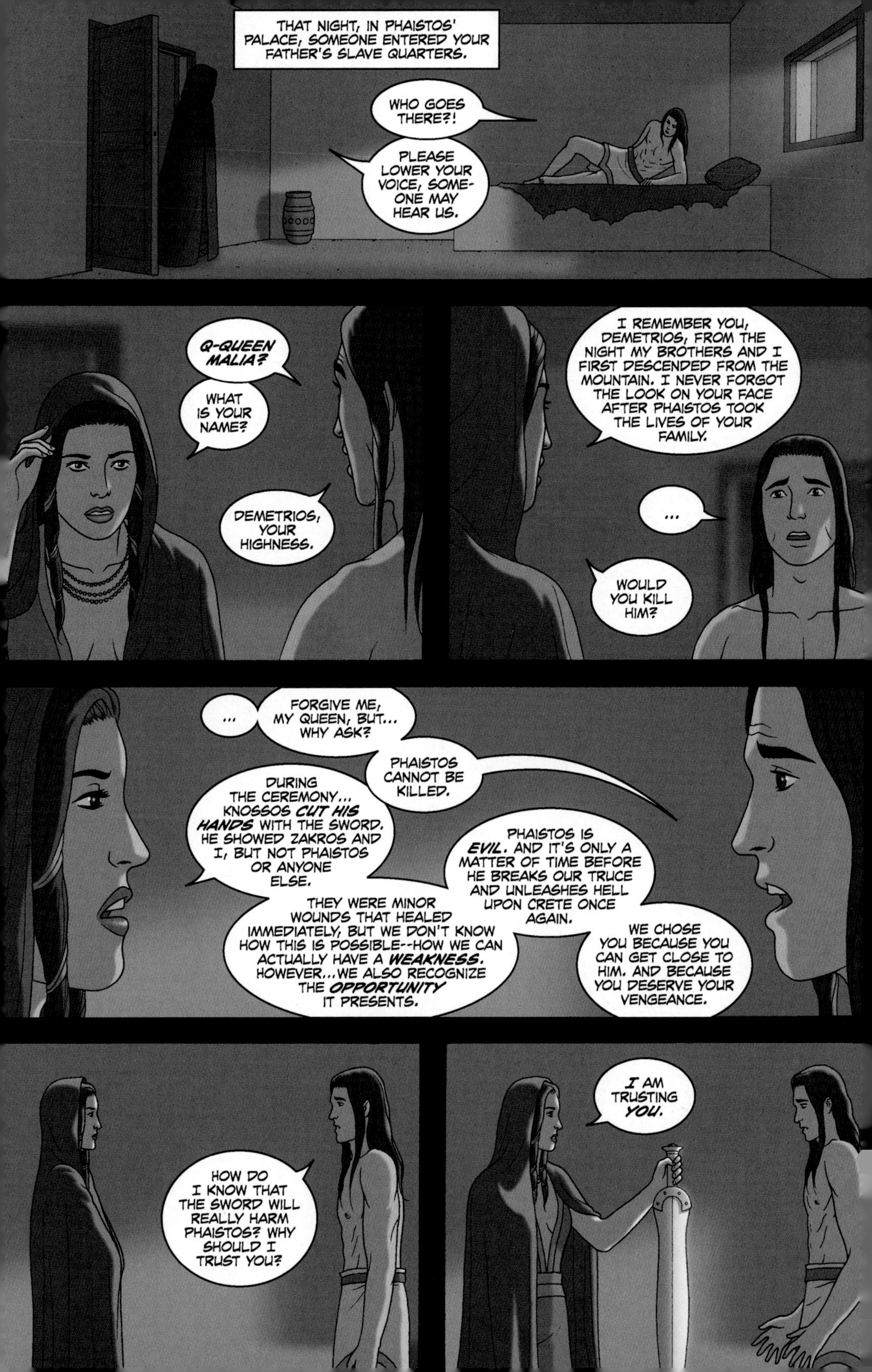
THAT NIGHT, IN PHAISTOS' PALACE, SOMEONE ENTERED YOUR FATHER'S SLAVE QUARTERS.
WHO GOES THERE?!
PLEASE LOWER YOUR VOICE, SOMEONE MAY HEAR US.
Q-QUEEN MALIA?
WHAT IS YOUR NAME?
DEMETRIOS, YOUR HIGHNESS.
I REMEMBER YOU, DEMETRIOS, FROM THE NIGHT MY BROTHERS AND I FIRST DESCENDED FROM THE MOUNTAIN. I NEVER FORGOT THE LOOK ON YOUR FACE AFTER PHAISTOS TOOK THE LIVES OF YOUR FAMILY.
...
WOULD YOU KILL HIM?
...
FORGIVE ME, MY QUEEN, BUT... WHY ASK?
PHAISTOS CANNOT BE KILLED.
DURING THE CEREMONY... KNOSSOS CUT HIS HANDS WITH THE SWORD. HE SHOWED ZAKROS AND I, BUT NOT PHAISTOS OR ANYONE ELSE.
THEY WERE MINOR WOUNDS THAT HEALED IMMEDIATELY, BUT WE DON'T KNOW HOW THIS IS POSSIBLE--HOW WE CAN ACTUALLY HAVE A WEAKNESS. HOWEVER...WE ALSO RECOGNIZE THE OPPORTUNITY IT PRESENTS.
PHAISTOS IS EVIL. AND IT'S ONLY A MATTER OF TIME BEFORE HE BREAKS OUR TRUCE AND UNLEASHES HELL UPON CRETE ONCE AGAIN.
WE CHOSE YOU BECAUSE YOU CAN GET CLOSE TO HIM. AND BECAUSE YOU DESERVE YOUR VENGEANCE.
HOW DO I KNOW THAT THE SWORD WILL REALLY HARM PHAISTOS? WHY SHOULD I TRUST YOU?
I AM TRUSTING YOU.

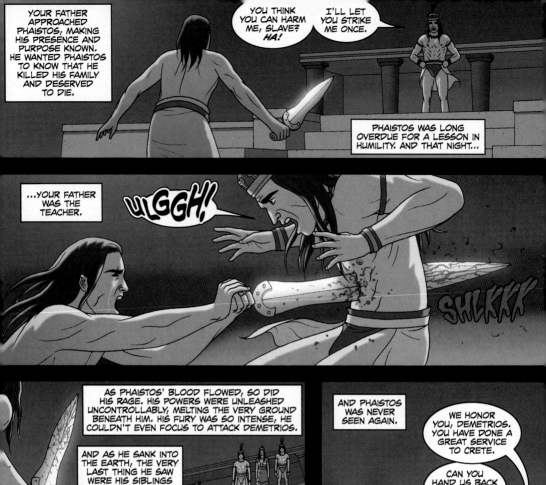

YOUR FATHER APPROACHED PHAISTOS, MAKING HIS PRESENCE AND PURPOSE KNOWN. HE WANTED PHAISTOS TO KNOW THAT HE KILLED HIS FAMILY AND DESERVED TO DIE.

YOU THINK YOU CAN HARM ME, SLAVE? *HA!*

I'LL LET YOU STRIKE ME ONCE.

PHAISTOS WAS LONG OVERDUE FOR A LESSON IN HUMILITY. AND THAT NIGHT...

...YOUR FATHER WAS THE TEACHER.

ULGGH!

SHLKKK

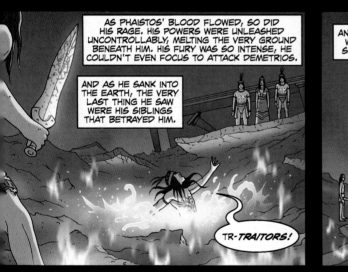

AS PHAISTOS' BLOOD FLOWED, SO DID HIS RAGE. HIS POWERS WERE UNLEASHED UNCONTROLLABLY, MELTING THE VERY GROUND BENEATH HIM. HIS FURY WAS SO INTENSE, HE COULDN'T EVEN FOCUS TO ATTACK DEMETRIOS.

AND AS HE SANK INTO THE EARTH, THE VERY LAST THING HE SAW WERE HIS SIBLINGS THAT BETRAYED HIM.

TR-*TRAITORS!*

AND PHAISTOS WAS NEVER SEEN AGAIN.

WE HONOR YOU, DEMETRIOS. YOU HAVE DONE A GREAT SERVICE TO CRETE.

CAN YOU HAND US BACK THE SWORD, DEMETRIOS?

NO.

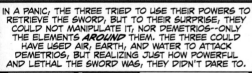

IN A PANIC, THE THREE TRIED TO USE THEIR POWERS TO RETRIEVE THE SWORD, BUT TO THEIR SURPRISE, THEY COULD NOT MANIPULATE IT, NOR DEMETRIOS--ONLY THE ELEMENTS *AROUND* THEM. THE THREE COULD HAVE USED AIR, EARTH, AND WATER TO ATTACK DEMETRIOS, BUT REALIZING JUST HOW POWERFUL AND LETHAL THE SWORD WAS, THEY DIDN'T DARE TO.

ALL FOUR OF YOU HAVE CAUSED SO MUCH DEATH AND DESTRUCTION IN CRETE.

HOWEVER, YOU THREE GAVE ME MY REVENGE. IN RETURN, I WILL LET YOU LIVE.

BUT FROM THIS DAY FORTH, YOU WILL STEP DOWN AS RULERS AND FOREVER LIVE AS COMMONERS. MORTALS. AND I WILL DO EVERYTHING IN MY POWER TO MAKE SURE YOU NEVER RULE OR USE YOUR ABILITIES EVER AGAIN.

I'LL BE WATCHING... AND WAITING.

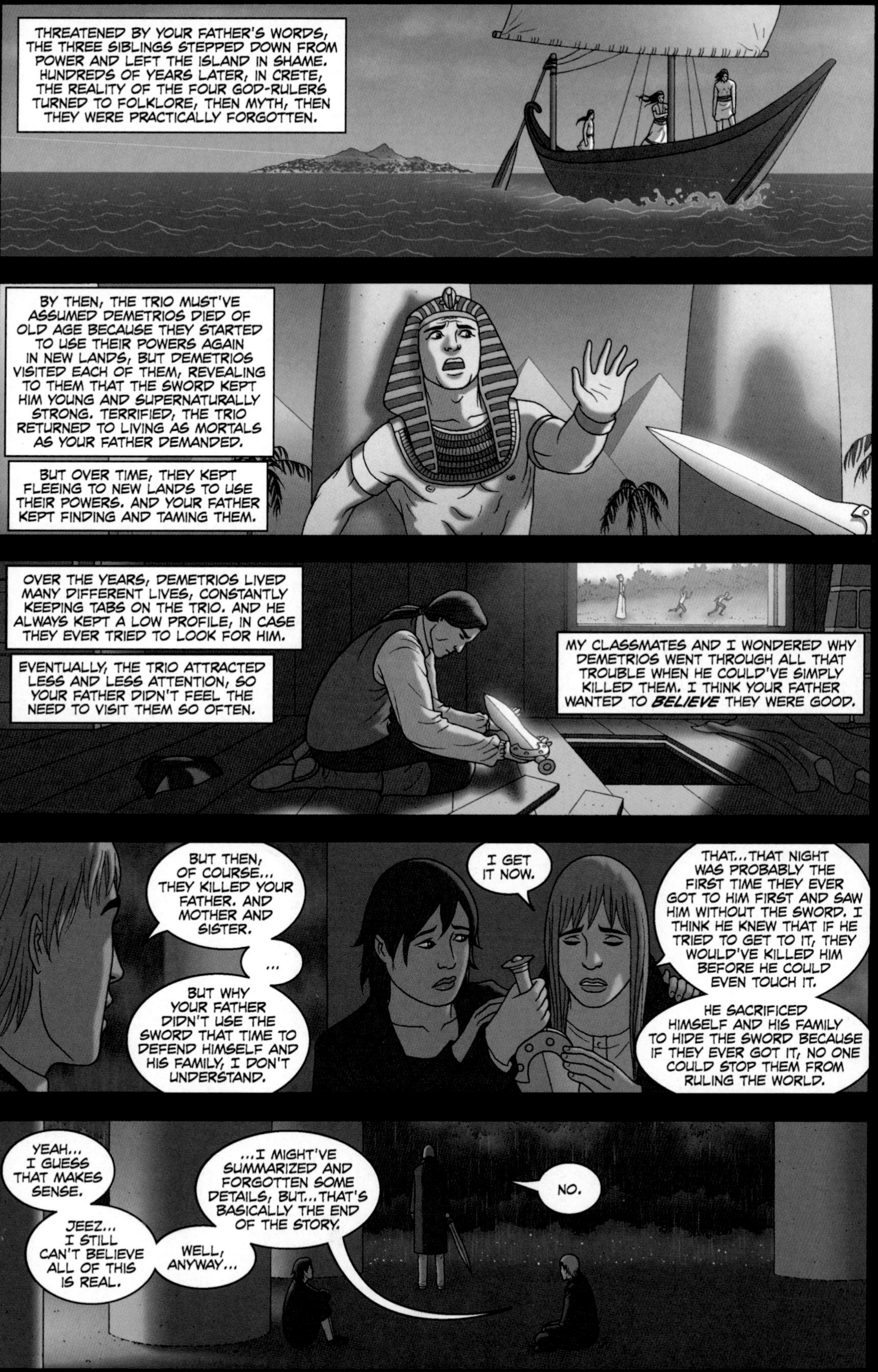

THREATENED BY YOUR FATHER'S WORDS, THE THREE SIBLINGS STEPPED DOWN FROM POWER AND LEFT THE ISLAND IN SHAME. HUNDREDS OF YEARS LATER, IN CRETE, THE REALITY OF THE FOUR GOD-RULERS TURNED TO FOLKLORE, THEN MYTH, THEN THEY WERE PRACTICALLY FORGOTTEN.
BY THEN, THE TRIO MUST'VE ASSUMED DEMETRIOS DIED OF OLD AGE BECAUSE THEY STARTED TO USE THEIR POWERS AGAIN IN NEW LANDS, BUT DEMETRIOS VISITED EACH OF THEM, REVEALING TO THEM THAT THE SWORD KEPT HIM YOUNG AND SUPERNATURALLY STRONG. TERRIFIED, THE TRIO RETURNED TO LIVING AS MORTALS AS YOUR FATHER DEMANDED.
BUT OVER TIME, THEY KEPT FLEEING TO NEW LANDS TO USE THEIR POWERS. AND YOUR FATHER KEPT FINDING AND TAMING THEM.
OVER THE YEARS, DEMETRIOS LIVED MANY DIFFERENT LIVES, CONSTANTLY KEEPING TABS ON THE TRIO. AND HE ALWAYS KEPT A LOW PROFILE, IN CASE THEY EVER TRIED TO LOOK FOR HIM.
EVENTUALLY, THE TRIO ATTRACTED LESS AND LESS ATTENTION, SO YOUR FATHER DIDN'T FEEL THE NEED TO VISIT THEM SO OFTEN.
MY CLASSMATES AND I WONDERED WHY DEMETRIOS WENT THROUGH ALL THAT TROUBLE WHEN HE COULD'VE SIMPLY KILLED THEM. I THINK YOUR FATHER WANTED TO ***BELIEVE*** THEY WERE GOOD.
BUT THEN, OF COURSE... THEY KILLED YOUR FATHER. AND MOTHER AND SISTER.
...
BUT WHY YOUR FATHER DIDN'T USE THE SWORD THAT TIME TO DEFEND HIMSELF AND HIS FAMILY, I DON'T UNDERSTAND.
I GET IT NOW.
THAT...THAT NIGHT WAS PROBABLY THE FIRST TIME THEY EVER GOT TO HIM FIRST AND SAW HIM WITHOUT THE SWORD. I THINK HE KNEW THAT IF HE TRIED TO GET TO IT, THEY WOULD'VE KILLED HIM BEFORE HE COULD EVEN TOUCH IT.
HE SACRIFICED HIMSELF AND HIS FAMILY TO HIDE THE SWORD BECAUSE IF THEY EVER GOT IT, NO ONE COULD STOP THEM FROM RULING THE WORLD.
YEAH... I GUESS THAT MAKES SENSE.
JEEZ... I STILL CAN'T BELIEVE ALL OF THIS IS REAL.
WELL, ANYWAY...
...I MIGHT'VE SUMMARIZED AND FORGOTTEN SOME DETAILS, BUT...THAT'S BASICALLY THE END OF THE STORY.
NO.

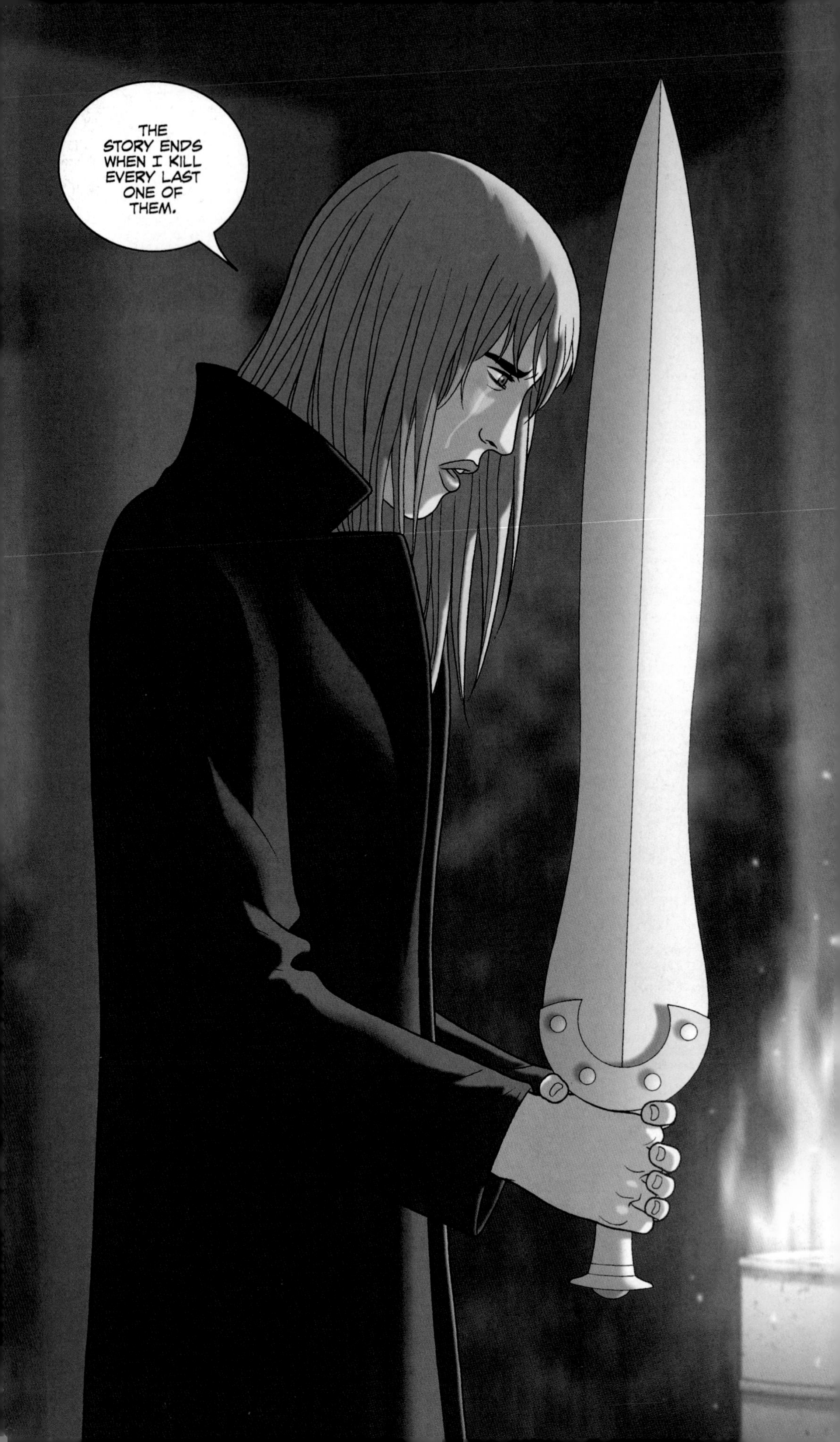
THE STORY ENDS WHEN I KILL EVERY LAST ONE OF THEM.

TO BE CONTINUED...